DEGREES OF AFFINITY

The Tarnished Crown
Book Three

C. F. Dunn

SAPERE
BOOKS

DEGREES OF AFFINITY

Published by Sapere Books.

24 Trafalgar Road, Ilkley, LS29 8HH

saperebooks.com

ISBN: 978-0-85495-715-6

For my pappa

ACKNOWLEDGEMENTS

As ever this is one of the hardest parts of writing a book, especially one written over a decade or more, and I have incurred debts of gratitude to many people. There have been those right from the beginning — my family and close friends — without whose support, enduring patience, and infinite wisdom this series would not have been created. For my husband and friend, Richard, whose depth of historical knowledge is equalled by the breadth, and who readily, joyously, shares his expertise on all things military, architectural, and naval.

Our daughters, Kate and Sophia, who have grown up in the fifteenth century as much as the twenty-first, and who continue to indulge their mother's obsession with great good humour as I write the series. My mother, Mary, who let me watch historical programs on television when still a tot and who bought me the Ladybird *Warwick The Kingmaker* and a library of books. My father, Bill, for taking me to every medieval edifice I could find and who guided me through my first forays in fiction writing. Little did they know where it would all lead. My friend and grammar guru, author Sue (S.L.) Russell, who unstintingly takes the time from her own writing projects to read mine. And Alison King, whose unique skills and specialist knowledge enabled me to see beyond the veil.

I wish to thank those who have offered endorsements — my friend and historical novelist Elizabeth Chadwick, on whose candid opinion I can always rely; and Matthew Lewis, writer, medieval historian and former chair of The Richard III Society, both of whom have so generously given their time. Also, the many authors, historians, friends and readers who have read and reviewed my books.

In addition, I thank my wonderful editor Amy Durant at Sapere Books for her eagle-eyed guidance, and the editors, proof-readers, artists and all those involved in honing and polishing the manuscript. I am indebted to the countless historians, re-enactors, medieval specialists, archivists and museum curators, the enthusiastic attendants at heritage sites and knowledgeable church wardens, all of whom have indulged my quest for knowledge. Nor can I forget the many writers, and academics whose research and analysis — condensed and attainable through their own books and papers — have saved me many years of work. It is impossible to represent the value they have collectively added to unearthing and understanding the complex historical record of the period. You are too numerous to mention here and, even if I did, there would be many more I have unjustly neglected.

When writing *Degrees of Affinity*, I could not help but be reminded of all the souls consumed by the sea over the many millennia Man has traversed it, and how organisations such as the Royal National Lifeboat Institution (RNLI) have given life and hope to those who might otherwise have been lost. For you, no measure of thanks can ever repay your commitment and dedication. Lastly, I cannot end my acknowledgements without thanking my readers for taking time out of their own busy lives to spend it with Isobel. Where would she be without someone rooting for her? And where would I be without my books being read? In my garden like Isobel, no doubt, dreaming up plots. But without readers those plots would remain nothing but a figment of my imagination. It is only when someone picks up a book and turns the first page that stories spring to life and make an author's daydreaming reality.

ENGLAND London

Fowey

Picquigny

Paris

FRANCE

N
W E
S

PORTUGAL

SPAIN

Lisbon

Castelo do Mar

Tangiers Ceuta

Barbary Coast

Barbary Coast

MOROCCO

Fes

Atlas Mountains

Sijilmasa

Agadir

Sahara Desert

LIST OF CHARACTERS

THE FENTON FAMILY:

Sir Geoffrey Fenton (deceased)

Lady Isobella Wray — his wife (deceased)

Isobel Fenton — their daughter (married to Robert Langton)

Andrew (Drew) — her son

Juliana (Liana) — her daughter

Robbie — her son

THE LANGTON FAMILY:

The Old Earl (deceased)

Juliana Langton — his wife

Duarte Langton — their eldest son (deceased)

William Langton, previously the Earl — their second son (deceased)

Robert Langton, current Earl — their youngest son

Felice — wife and countess to William Langton

Duarte — their eldest son (deceased)

Elizabeth (Bess) — their eldest daughter, married to Lord Dalton

Margaret (Meg) — their second daughter (deceased)

Cecily — their youngest daughter

William — their youngest son

LANGTON RETAINERS AND SERVANTS:

Buena — Isobel's servant

Alice — nursery maid

Maud — nursery maid

Lucie — nursery maid

Matilda — maid to Isobel

Nicolas Sawcliffe — Master Secretary to the Langtons

Hyde — steward to the Langtons at Tickhill

Joan — chief nursery maid for Felice Langton

Philip Taylor — sergeant-at-arms

Debden — steward at Langton Place

Baxter — Steward at Langton Place

THE PLANTAGENETS:

Edward IV — Edward Plantagenet, King of England and eldest son of Richard, Duke of York

George Plantagenet — Duke of Clarence and younger brother of the king

Richard Plantagenet — Duke of Gloucester and youngest brother of the king

Edward (of Middleham) — his son

Elizabeth Woodville (formerly Grey) — wife and queen to Edward IV

Henry Plantagenet — Henry VI, King of England (deceased)

Margaret of Anjou — wife and queen to Henry VI

Edward, Prince of Wales — their son (deceased)

The Neville family:

Richard Neville, Earl of Warwick — cousin to Edward IV (deceased)

Isabel Neville, his elder daughter and Duchess of Clarence — wife of George

Anne Neville, his younger daughter and Duchess of Gloucester — wife of Richard Plantagenet (previously wife of Edward, Prince of Wales, son of Henry VI)

John, Marquess of Montagu — Warwick's brother

OTHER CHARACTERS:

Louis XI, King of France

Abu Umar Salim Ahmad (Babu) — self-appointed ruler of Sijilmasa

Dodzi — Rober Langtont's friend

Adil — Robert Langton's 'slave'

Barquerio — Captain of the Langton fleet

Ankarette Twynyho — maid to the Duchess of Clarence

Thomas Grey, Marquess of Dorset — eldest son of Elizabeth Woodville by her first husband, stepson of Edward IV

John de Vere, Earl of Oxford — Lancastrian diehard

Thomas Lacey — previously betrothed to Isobel (deceased)

Henry Lacey — his father (deceased)

Lord Ralph Lacey — Thomas's uncle (deceased)

PART ONE

CHAPTER ONE

January 1472

In the cracks between the rough-hewn stones that made up the courtyard, dried blood lay. Winter rain had washed the flags clean, but nothing except time would remove the stained fissures from Isobel Fenton's memory.

"Never trust a man in armour," she whispered into the furred edge of her cloak. She heard a laugh behind her.

"Is that so?" Robert Langton's breath warmed her ear as he brought his arms around her and held her close to him. "And does that apply to all men, or only those whom you disfavour?"

"It is what my lady mother used to say." Isobel's memories of her late mother were still strong, if tainted now by what she had recently learned.

Robert released her. "Do you believe yourself betrayed?" When she didn't answer, he turned her to face him. "Isobel?"

The dense fog that had crept along the river overnight had frozen, rendering shattered stone and bruised reed white with frost. Isobel's mantle glistened with fine droplets as she wrapped it closer about her in the ruins of her home. She sensed Rob's good humour evaporating and regretted it. "Not by you." She stood on the tips of her toes and kissed him. "Without you — and your armour — rescuing us from the attack," she added with a quick smile, "things might have been quite different."

He grimaced. "Thomas Lacey?"

Isobel thought of the man who had been determined to rip her birthright from her, who had waged war on her home and her lands, the man who was now dead by Robert's orders. "Thomas? Perhaps, but I expected nothing less from him. If a dog is vicious, are we surprised when it bites?"

"My brother, then." He stated it as if he didn't want to hear her answer, his voice dull.

Consumed by memories of the late Earl for a moment, she finally shook her head. "His was a different kind of betrayal. No, I … I think…" she struggled to voice her thoughts, then they came in a rush. "My father, Rob, I feel his treachery more than any other because I trusted him, I *loved* him, and thought he did me, enough at least to tell me the truth." Caught in a swell of emotion, she turned her back on him, saying as if to herself, "He made me promise to be truthful in all things — *all* things — yet was not so with me. He let me believe that his union with my mother was out of choice, but it was not. She was as much a victim of the old Earl's ambition as I was of his son's. We were all victims, Rob, one way or another, but my father benefitted from the old Earl's patronage by gaining a noble wife and these lands. Had your brother and my mother remained married, think how differently things might have turned out. They would have been happy, Felice would have married someone else, and I…" Isobel faltered.

"Might never have been born," Robert said softly, "and then where would we be, but without each other and without our son. Perhaps your father was trying to protect you, Isobel. The truth can be a bitter master."

At the break in his voice, she forgot her own hurt. "As you, too, have found?"

Robert inspected the great ring he wore, his brother's ring, the *Earl's* ring, on his left hand, the ancient intaglio tawny despite the muted light.

Isobel placed her own gloved hand over his. "We each shall live with the past and make of our future what God, in His wisdom, intends." She looked around what once had been the centre of her world, now nothing but stone and mortar and the remains of her previous existence. Without Beaumancote her life could never be the same. And yet she felt nothing, as if the destruction of her home was some remote dream, faded and without purpose. She had been another person then, before she knew what she knew now — before her father's death, before the Earl had taken possession of her. She glanced up at Robert and found him looking at her with a puzzled expression. She squeezed his hand and smiled, and he responded with his own. From where the horses waited she heard the babble of their son, and her heart warmed. "And now, at last, we are free to live our lives."

The following afternoon, Isobel took one look at the Earl's great tower on its prominent motte dominating the town of Tickhill, and her resolve to approach it wavered. A cold sun had dissolved the fog over the course of the day and ashen stone gleamed in the last of the light as she dismounted in the bailey. Isobel's stomach clenched, the twisting knot making her feel sick. She heard a grunt behind her and her maid Buena, carrying Andrew heavily wrapped against the oncoming frost, questioned her with a look. Isobel nodded, gave a weak smile, and Buena pressed her arm in reassurance. It was the first time she had been at the castle since she had fled last August with the wrath of Felice at her heels, and the confession of the dying Earl in her head. A winter had passed, and so much since. Isobel glanced up at the family apartments half expecting to see the countess's face at the window, but it was blank and dark and lifeless.

Robert caught her looking. "She has gone. There are no ghosts there." His eyes followed hers as she raised them to the tower. "And none there, either. These lands are mine now." He stopped as the steward, Hyde, came to greet them and Andrew, waking from sleep, began to cry. Isobel reached to take him from Buena's arms. There was no time to dwell on the past, not yet.

The Duke of Gloucester arrived without ceremony and only a handful of men shortly after dawn, slipping from his horse and handing the reins to a groom before stretching his shoulders and shaking weariness from his bones. He raised a hand in greeting as he spotted Robert crossing the bailey towards him, hastily pulling a gown over his part-clothed body.

"Good morrow, my lord. I would not impose upon you at this hour except to ask your farrier to take a look at my horse. He cast a shoe and I shall not cause him further distress by pressing ahead."

Robert came out of a bow. "You are welcome both to my farrier and what hospitality I might offer, Your Grace." He nodded to Hyde, who had joined them, and issued brief orders to prepare for their royal guest. "If it please you to take your ease and break your fast?" Robert indicated the great hall.

Gloucester seemed to be deliberating. "I would speak privily with you, unless you have other matters to attend?"

Rubbing a hand over his part-shaven face, Robert started to speak, but thought better of it. "As you wish, Your Grace. My chamber will afford greater privacy."

*

The privy chamber had changed little since his brother had use of it. Now he was Earl, Robert avoided sleeping there, preferring instead his old chamber in the family apartments. The air was chill, the fire only now being lit as they entered. It would take time to heat the chimney but longer to thaw the iron in his heart. Robert hesitated at the threshold, and stepped in.

Once settled with warmed ale, he waited for Gloucester to begin.

The younger man drank and set the beaker to one side. He adjusted his position in the lord's chair until finding a more comfortable place for his spare frame. "King Edward was glad to confirm you as the new earl, my lord, although he was not the only one to comment on the... irregularity of your brother's wishes to overlook his own heir in your favour."

Robert heard the question he knew many asked but neglected to supply an answer to appease Gloucester's curiosity. Andrew was believed to be the Earl's bastard son; not many knew the truth. To reveal it would jeopardise not only his own position, but the reputation and memory of his brother and the status of those to whom he had been closest — including Isobel.

Gloucester left a long enough pause to make his interest clear, then continued. "But His Highness is content to ensure the continuity of the Langton line through you, my lord, in the sure knowledge of your absolute loyalty to him."

"And I am as bound to the king as ever I was, and to you, Your Grace, in the surety of our continued affinity."

The men regarded each other for a moment longer, then Gloucester gave a quick nod, which sealed the unspoken understanding between them.

"I travel north in some haste from Westminster where I met with King Edward. Certain matters remain outstanding and these past months have not been easy. John de Vere has proved intractable. He continues to threaten this kingdom and seeks support from any who will give it."

"He is as steadfast in opposition to the king as Your Grace is loyal."

"Has he approached you?" Gloucester asked, a shade sharp.

Robert drank, swallowed, and shook his head. "De Vere knows better than to attempt to sway a Langton. He tried with my brother. He failed."

"You are not your brother, my lord, and the Earl of Oxford is nothing if persuasive."

At the mention of his brother, Robert allowed the stab of tension in his gut to dissipate before speaking. "No, I am not. I am Your Grace's sworn man and I know of no better lord to serve. I respect De Vere's loyalty to his cause, that is all."

"Yet while he has access to funds, he presents a threat to my brother's rule." Gloucester pinched the skin between his eyes, looking older than his nigh on twenty winters. "The De Vere estates were granted to me after he was attainted — the dowager countess's lands as well."

"She still refuses to assign them to you?"

"She finally signed the contract although she fought me at every turn, including through the courts. She would have people believe her to be defenceless, a victim, if you will. And had she been thus, I might have taken pity on the woman. As it is, she is intent on supporting her son, and I believe has been actively doing so and is as much a traitor to His Highness as De Vere himself. She would use her lands to provide the means for him to raise arms against the king; I have no doubt of that and some proof. I *will* have her lands and this seed *will* be struck out before it can take root, else we return to the bitter troubles of the past. The kingdom cannot be at peace until the king's enemies are either won over or laid to rest." Gloucester's colour rose to sharp points. "I hoped to use her to lure De Vere out of hiding, but he has not taken the bait. Now I must keep her beyond his reach. Faith, the woman vexes me. You have met her?"

"I have, briefly, and before she was widowed. She reminded me of my brother's…" Robert hesitated for no more than a breath, "…wife. Once met —"

"— never forgotten." Gloucester nodded. "Ah, yes, the Lady Felice. I see why you might think so. Both claim to have been wronged, both petition the king; but few know the truth that lies behind their guile, nor the extent to which they are prepared to go to exact revenge."

There was a glum pause in which they both contemplated the fire. Gloucester stirred first. "And thus, we are all bound in some way to women from birth to death — from the dam who bore us, to the dame who prepares us for the grave." He gave a slight smile. "I would more were like my noble mother, but I fear few are."

Robert waited to see where this was leading, but Gloucester merely asked, "And what of your lady mother, my lord; she lives yet?"

"By the Grace of God, she does, although she bides in the land of her birth on my estates in Portugal." That still didn't sit easy on his tongue. Silently, he practised it several times until he thought it more under control, then, "She says the sun does her bones good."

Gloucester stretched as if feeling the warmth in his own body. "I can quite see why. Spring seems a long way off."

Again, the momentary silence in which the fire cracked and popped. "Marriage," he said suddenly, "is a blessing, is it not?"

The room echoed as Robert's stool thudded to the floor as he leapt to his feet. He struck his palm to his forehead. "It is a blessing indeed if the marriage is made. For all that is holy, how could I forget!" He looked at Gloucester's startled face. "Your Grace, forgive me; I have a wedding to attend."

"Whose?" Gloucester asked.

"My own!"

This was the marriage Isobel had not dared believe possible, nor the one her father had intended. This was something of girlish dreams, not reality born of bitter experience. Yet here she was, next to the father of her son, the man she would have chosen had she the choice. How many in her position could say the same? Robert turned his head to her, his face alive, eyes bright, as the priest raised the Host, and she had a fleeting memory of Thomas Lacey — the boy she remembered from her youth, the youth she had been betrothed to, the man he became, and the corpse he had made — and considered herself fortunate indeed.

"Amen," she said in response to the prompt, and 'Amen' again and again in her head until all thoughts were cut short as Robert sealed their oath with a kiss. She heard murmured approval from his closest friends, and beside them, saw the Duke of Gloucester break into a grin.

Gloucester returned her curtesy with an embrace. "I would have offered more than my felicitations had I known of your marriage beforehand. As it is, I wish you all joy, my lady, and pray for God's blessing on this match." He sounded so formal, his greeting so sincere, that Isobel felt inclined to laugh.

She resisted, and instead said, "And had I known that Your Grace would be here I would have ensured greater ceremony to greet you. However, we gladly offer what comfort we may, and ask if you will join us?"

"I thank you, but my lord Earl has already given me use of his farrier, his ale, and his time. In so doing, I kept him from his nuptials, something of which I am certain he will remind me from time to time when it suits him." Gloucester quirked an eyebrow in Robert's direction and at that, Isobel broke into laughter.

"Stay a little longer, Your Grace, that we may make amends for our lack of hospitality, and you for distracting my husband." *Husband.* That sat strangely upon her lips, and she warmed at the thought of it, and in thinking it, flushed.

Robert intervened. "And Your Grace was going to tell me something when I interrupted," he reminded Gloucester. "We have but a small feast to mark the occasion, but we will be honoured if you would join us in celebration, will we not, Isobel?"

She nodded with enthusiasm, remembered it was not courtly, and offered a more refined incline of her head instead.

They were joined in the council chamber by the senior members of the household, but no more than that. The chamber had been decked in winter greenery, early sulphur flowers, and a dagged canopy in blue and yellow hung over the lord's dais where they now sat. The magnificent arras Robert's brother had bought from Flanders still hung behind their chairs, a silent reminder — if any were needed — of his recent occupation of the chair, the earldom, and of Isobel herself. It was a thought she stolidly refused to acknowledge.

She welcomed the steady pressure of Robert's hand on hers as if he, too, were crowding unwelcome memories from his mind. Some of those same men that sat before them now had served the Earl and had been witness to the feasts over which she, as his mistress, had unwillingly presided at his side. What were they thinking now? She tried to read their faces, stretched her ears to catch their conversations, but was met with bland smiles and mere nods of heads.

She gave up and turned her attention to the discussion between her husband and the duke. Gloucester was asking why they had chosen to hold the festivities there and not in the great hall, and why so few were invited to such a happy occasion.

Robert's answer was seamless. "It has been less a year since my brother's death." He crossed himself. "It seemed right to honour his memory this way." He did not add that Isobel had insisted on a private celebration whereas Robert had wanted the whole world to know of their marriage. Isobel's memory of Felice's slights, her threats, her condemnation, and the vicious tongues she set waggling in this very castle were still too raw. Many of the servants who served them now had served Felice Langton, and Isobel felt unequal to the past. So, she let Robert's lie become the truth, although from time to time, Isobel caught Gloucester watching them both with an expression she could not interpret, only for him to smile when her eyes met his.

"I did not know," Gloucester said when Robert and Isobel escorted him to his waiting horse, "that such affection could grow between two people in so short a time. It gives me hope." He stepped onto the groom's hands and into the saddle.

"Hope, Your Grace?" Robert asked.

"That, by the grace of God, a good match might not preclude happiness. That one might have both and live to regret neither."

Taking the reins from a groom, Robert handed them to Gloucester. "I am certain of it. I am living proof."

Gloucester looked at Isobel waiting at a respectable distance for his departure. "I believe you are, my lord," he answered, and bowed his head in her direction.

Isobel waited until they were alone in Robert's chamber before asking, "What did he mean, 'a good match might not preclude happiness'? *You* could have made a better match by marrying elsewhere. Perhaps you should have done," she added almost to herself.

Robert kicked the slippers from his feet one by one. "I suspect he was referring to your estates." He came to stand behind her as she warmed herself by the fire and enveloped her in his mantle. "You have fine *estates*, my lady." He drew her heavy hair to one side, revealing the smooth skin of her neck. He kissed it, breathing in her scent, and she leaned back into Him, his oak-brown hair mingling with the honey of her own.

"Did you marry me for my estates?"

His exploring hands came to a halt over her hips. "You know I did not. Your lands are but an addition. A welcome addition, perhaps, but no more than that." His hands took up their paths of discovery once more. "I married you to make you mine," he whispered in a low voice, sending shivers through her; but not before she asked him one more thing. She stayed his hands.

"And Drew," she said. "You married me to make things right by our son, to give him his father's name." She turned to face him when he didn't answer. "Did you not, Rob? To claim him as your own?"

"I claim you — and our son," he said, "and nothing and no one, but God alone, can change that."

Later, when the fire had burned to embers and the sweat cooled on their skin, Isobel found her mind wandering back to the conversation with Gloucester. "Do you think he knows that Drew is your son?"

Robert moved against her, pulling her close. "I have never said."

"I know, but do you think he has guessed?"

"I know not. Go to sleep."

"And what if he finds out about my mother — about the Earl — what then? What if he discovers that my parents were never married and that I am a bastard? I could not look him in the face; I would be so ashamed. Rob?" She tapped his arm, slung heavily about her waist. "Rob?" But his breathing deepened and from his throat came the soft, rumbling sound of contentment.

CHAPTER TWO

"It is expected of us." Robert stood with his hands on his hips, his lips pushed together as he surveyed the chamber, reminding Isobel even more of his brother. As if, standing there in that all-too familiar room, she needed any reminding. She studiously avoided looking at the bed.

"It was expected of Felice, but *she* did not share the chamber with her husband," Isobel said, irritated. "Anyway, you are Earl now, so you can choose where you bide. It is not for other people to dictate."

"That might be so, but we have a duty to be seen as husband and wife, and this is the lord's chamber."

"But the family apartments are more comfortable," Isobel insisted.

"And you have refused to use the rooms set aside for the countess — despite them having been stripped of any trace of the woman," he added with irony. It was true; the memory of Felice Langton's arid scorn was as potent as the scent of jasmine embedded in the very grain of her rooms, which Isobel had ordered scoured the moment she arrived. She still couldn't face entering them without first crossing herself. But was the Earl's privy chamber any better?

"But why can we not continue to use your own room? We can see the gardens from there."

"Because it is not fit for an earl and his countess, Isobel, as I have said before. Several times." He caught her glancing towards the bed and said, softly, "Do not think that I have forgotten. I am reminded of it every time I enter this room." He straightened his shoulders. "But we will make it our own."

"And Drew's," Isobel said quickly. "And then I will be content."

"The nursery is more suited to his needs," Robert countered.

"*Then I will be content*," she repeated, adopting the blank expression which meant that no amount of persuasion — or coercion — would move her on that point.

"And Drew," Robert conceded. "For now." The great painted tree showing his family line had caught his attention, so he didn't see Isobel's quick scowl. Instead, he pointed at the last figures represented, frowning. "This will have to change."

"But you cannot remove him — he was your brother!"

"William? No, not him. That —" he waved a finger in the direction of the countess. Except it wasn't Felice's face that stared back at them in the sombre light, but Isobel's own. She held back a gasp.

"And this —" Robert poked the painted panel, where a little boy's eyes glowed from a cherubic face.

"I… I did not know. I mean, I had not seen," Isobel stuttered. "He must have had these altered just before he died. How could he? Drew was not his son to claim, nor I his wife!"

"Yet he believed so," Robert said, "and better that than he knew the truth. What would have become of you both then?"

What indeed? Isobel quailed at the thought and the room became suddenly cold despite the thick mantle staving off the sharp air. "And you," she said, taking Robert's heavy, broad hand between her own and looking up at him. "What would he have done to you?"

Neither provided an answer because both knew what the Earl did to anyone who betrayed him, and he had died believing in the inviolate loyalty of his younger brother. It would have broken his heart to have been so betrayed. And then he would have killed him.

"So," Robert said, with finality, flicking Isobel's image with a nail, "this will be repainted showing my brother's named ... wife ... and their own son, and this," he said indicating the space beside them, "with the true likeness of us both."

"And Drew," Isobel said. "The new earl, his countess, and their son."

Robert withdrew his hand and rubbed a finger along one brow. "Of course. And Drew."

A week later, as their chamber was rapidly emptied and their belongings were packed for the sojourn at Court, the odour of fresh paint pervaded the room.

"Stop, wait," Isobel said.

"My lady?" The brush wielded by the wispy, thin-cheeked man hovered over the area rubbed clean of the previous images. He hunkered back on his heels and replaced the brush in the narrow pot beside him.

"There — beneath Earl William — paint the images of his daughters Lady Elizabeth, Lady Margaret and Lady Cecily beside his son Lord Duarte and their infant brother."

The man ran his eyes over the tree sprawling across the wall going back generation by generation to the very roots of the family. "There are none other showing noble daughters, only sons, my lady, and the Earl did not specify —"

"He mentioned it to me." Isobel mentally reprimanded herself for her weak lie. "*I* specify it. Now, do as bidden."

He picked the brush from the pot and scratched the side of his nose with the end of it. "And will Lady Margaret be as she were when she, you know?" He crossed himself.

Isobel followed suit. "When she died, yes. And make her gown holly green, with a great furred collar and hem. She was so proud of her wedding gift. She..." Isobel decided against continuing and caught the man looking at her with a mixture of sympathy and curiosity and brought control back into her voice. "Do not bother the Earl, but refer any questions directly to me," she finished, and left the man to his work.

"I miss Cecily." Isobel sat cross-legged on their bed, now devoid of hangings, as Robert surveyed the newly painted figures on the wall before him. "Can we do nothing? Surely Felice has no need of her; she certainly has no love." Isobel encouraged Andrew to stand before her and held him firmly while he bounced on sturdy legs, laughing and waving his arms.

Robert looked at his young niece's sombre face staring back from the wall. "Felice will not hear of letting Cecily live with us. It is less to do with wanting to keep her child and more to do with —"

"Punishing us?" Isobel interjected. "Because we want her, love her, she is withheld, denying both her and us happiness. Felice is cruel."

"Probably, but she is also ambitious. Cecily might make a useful match one day."

"How?" Isobel snorted, startling Andrew out of his game. She kissed his nose and he lit in a smile and resumed bouncing. "What possible match could be made with the bastard child of a dead father with no power and no estate? She would do better with us."

"Granted." Robert came to sit with them on the bed. "But the circumstances of her birth are unknown to any but us."

"Like mine," Isobel said in a dry undertone.

"And Felice is not beyond marrying again."

"Who would want to marry her? *She* has no power or estate!"

"She has her dower lands still, and a modest income. More than that, she has a daughter married to a man close to the

king, and a son in want of a father. And she has her charm —
when she wishes to employ it. She might yet make a contract
with a lord with no son of his own, and then Cecily will have
both a father and a future."

"But no affection," said Isobel again. "No love."

"It is a lack she will have to learn to bear. It will make her
stronger for it and the burdens of life the easier to endure."

"You cannot believe that!" Isobel exclaimed. "How can it
benefit a child to be without the love of a parent!"

"You speak as one who had such affection in childhood. Not
all do; yet still they prosper, stronger, perhaps, because of it."

"As you have done," she asked softly.

He arced a rueful smile. "Does it show?"

She handed Andrew to him and adjusted her position on the
bed to be next to them both. Slipping her arm around her
husband she rested her head against his shoulder. "You do not
speak of your sire and dam; I never thought to ask why."

Smoothing his son's thickening hair, he took a moment to
consider her question. "My father was strong in all ways. He
believed that in order to be a good lord you must show a
certainty of will, dispense justice without favour, and give no
quarter for treachery. He served God with the same iron
mastery and expected us to do the same."

"Rob, you have not answered my question."

"There was no consideration for tenderness, my dove. He
was never intentionally cruel, but he believed his sons would
learn life's lessons best if they were taught with a firm hand.
Duty; honour; strength: those were his watchwords, and he
wanted us to live by them."

"And mercy? Compassion?"

"Delivered with the same..." he struggled to find the right
word.

"Harshness?" Isobel offered.

Robert frowned, considered, then shrugged. "For want of a better word, yes, I suppose he might have been thought harsh."

"And your mother?"

Robert's expression mellowed. "She tempered him — her Venus to his Mars — although none would call her gentle. As children, any tears would be met with rebuke; but they were meant kindly, and we knew that."

It seemed a childhood bereft of kindness, so unlike Isobel's own, and far from what she wished for her own son. "Kindness does not make you weak. The Earl never treated Andrew harshly." She stopped when she sensed Robert tense beneath her cheek and removed her head from his arm. "I mean that for all his sternness he was never unkind to him." That didn't seem to make things better. Robert turned his face from her.

"My brother's mind was softening; he was ailing. His fondness came from his malady, that is all."

Isobel leant forward and removed Andrew from Robert's arms. "I was there. In those last months I knew him best; he loved Drew like his own son."

Robert's mouth curled in a way Isobel had never seen before as he looked at them both. He stood up, jerking his clothes straight. "As you say, *like his own*."

Alarmed by his sudden change, Isobel said. "It could not have been otherwise. He had to believe that, or the consequences would have unthinkable."

He looked over his shoulder at her. "Yes." Then frowning as he saw the disquiet in her face, "There was no other way. You did what you had to, Isobel; I see that. Come," he held out his hand to her. "Drew needs to sleep and we must sup; we have a long journey ahead of us."

Journey, she thought as they ate in their chamber that evening, chatting away as if nothing had passed between them earlier. Did he refer to their travels to Westminster on the morrow, or something else?

Among the men and their painted ladies of the royal Court, Felice Langton felt invisible. As the door to Queen Elizabeth's chamber opened, she resisted being pressed against the wall by the tide of animated women that flowed from it and stood — rock-like and prominent — forcing them to move around her.

"Bess!" Felice's daughter had almost missed her. Was that surprise or dismay she saw reflected in her face when Elizabeth dutifully embraced her mother?

"Ma Mere, what are you doing here? I thought you returned to your manor?"

Felice drew her to one side. "Have you spoken to your husband?" she asked with urgency. "Will he plead my cause with the king?" Her daughter's hesitancy said it all. "Bess, you gave me your oath. I cannot pursue my case without friends at Court. Would you see your brother denied his birthright? Your mother reduced to begging favours from any who might take pity on her?" Bess tittered, an unpleasant sound laced with annoyance. Felice felt her palms itch but resisted the urge to strike her. "Well?" Caught in a draught from the open door, the filmy veil covering Bess's exaggerated headdress blew across Felice's face. She brushed it back with a terse flick of her hand.

Bess tucked the flighty end into her girdle. "Ma Mere, I have been *so* busy. Her Grace wishes me to attend her at all times. I am her favourite." She simpered.

Felice's temper snapped. "Have you forgotten your duty?" she hissed. "Who gave you the position in which you now find yourself? What would your father say? You should be ashamed!"

Bess whitened beneath artificial rose cheeks. "I will ask my husband, Ma Mere, and he will listen. He has cause to be pleased with me." She giggled again, but this time nervously. "I am with child," she whispered, her skin flushing now.

It took a moment to sink in before Felice said, "Then you must press this advantage while you can. In another few months you will become less comely to him, and he not as inclined to pay heed to your desires."

Bess's lips quivered. "You are pleased, are you not, Ma Mere?"

Pleased? That would make her a granddam. She looked at her daughter with fresh eyes, the signs of pregnancy hidden beneath the folds of the rich gown, but flagrant in her plumped skin. Felice felt suddenly old — old and abandoned. A husk. She gathered herself. "Of course. I will have masses said for your safe delivery."

"Perhaps," Bess ventured, "I might have loan of your St Catherine's jewel for my lying-in? The one Papa gave to you?"

"That," Felice said icily, "is no longer mine. Your uncle has it, no doubt for that harlot he has taken as wife should she prove more fertile than the previous unfortunate — your aunt Ann — may she rest in peace." She genuflected without thinking. "Although how she might rest knowing her husband has taken that baseborn whore —"

"*Ma Mere!*"

Felice came to and realised that the people crowding the small room waiting on the queen's pleasure had stopped their conversations. She turned. Standing at the threshold of the chamber, the fair-haired woman of slim form and exquisite dress commanded all before her with a single look. Felice sank to the floor in a curtsey.

Queen Elizabeth snapped her fingers and Felice rose, her gaze suitably subservient. With a cool eye, the queen inspected her, frowned, tapped an elegant finger on her own lip, and raised a carefully shaped brow. In a hurried movement, Felice took a square of linen from the purse around her waist and dabbed at the fleck of foam that still dampened her lip, silently cursing her loss of self-control.

"I did not recognise you," the queen addressed her. "Bess, you did not say that your lady mother paid court today."

"I ... she..." Bess stammered, looking between the queen and her mother.

"No matter." Queen Elizabeth waved an airy hand, cutting Bess short. "How do you do, madam? It has been long since we saw you last at Court." And neither of them had forgotten the reason for her departure. But if the queen held Felice responsible for King Edward's wandering eye, she did not refer to it. As it was, Bess had retained her chastity and was now safely married. Regaining her composure, Felice curtsied again. "I seek redress, Your Grace, for the wrong done to me and to my son."

The queen was already turning away and examining a sample of sky-blue velvet brocade embroidered with rose pink pomegranates held by an attendant. Felice attempted to reengage her attention and shuffled forwards into her line of sight.

"Madam, my son's inheritance has been stolen from him..."

The queen waved the cloth away and bent her head to examine a pair of silk shoes wrought with flowers of pearl. She smiled and nodded, and Felice saw her opportunity slip from her reach because of a pair of dainty slippers. She sank lower and injected a note of dread into her voice.

"Stolen, Your Grace, by one suspected of *treason*."

The queen's hand hovered over the shoes as she looked around at the woman now kneeling on the ground. "Come," she said, and went back into her chamber.

Horrified, Bess grasped her mother's sleeve. "Ma Mere — *treason?*"

"Hush!" Felice whipped, silencing her with a look, and followed the queen.

"I can hear your teeth chattering from here," Robert said as they approached the gates of London from the north.

"I am cold," Isobel complained, attempting to still them despite the movement of the horse beneath her which jolted her bones every step of the way.

"And I am the Archbishop of Canterbury," Robert said wryly. "There is nothing to fear at Court, I will be with you. Most of the time."

"And for the rest? I know no one at Court. What purpose do I serve being here? It would have been better for me to bide at home and oversee our estates."

"That is why we have a steward, to see to my affairs when we are gone. We, Isobel — you and I. Husband and wife. *Together*." He lowered his voice to a gravelly undertone and quirked a brow and she couldn't help but smile. "With Drew," he added, sensing the real thrust of her concern. "God have mercy on any who might wish him ill with Buena guarding him. She would give the Devil short shrift; I fear the woman myself." He glanced behind him where Buena rode with the child bundled against the cold, and crossed himself just in case Satan was listening.

That was indeed a comforting thought, and Isobel was glad she had both Buena and her son by her side where she could protect one and have the abiding friendship of the other in this strange world she now entered.

The road became crowded the closer they drew to the city walls. Carts rumbled and shook over the uneven ground; dappled cattle — with small sturdy dogs nipping at their heels — ambled, and fowl in cages of willow swung from yokes slung across bowed shoulders. It seemed that all the world converged on this point, and Isobel imagined it sucked through the gates and into a city where man and beast would spread out and melt into the myriad streets and alleyways of which she had heard so much, but never seen. At noon they stopped at a shrine by the gate itself, giving thanks for their safe arrival and alms to the children emerging from the cracks like woodlice.

"So many," Isobel said almost to herself, watching bare-legged scraps dart between the cuffs and good-natured curses of her servants as they tried to keep them at bay.

"Too many," she heard Robert say quietly next to her.

The narrow streets inside the patched and ancient walls stank of human and animal waste, the voices around her were strange, the sounds disconcerting. They had arrived in a foreign world, where only the attire of the inhabitants marked them out as English, so unfamiliar were the accents. Isobel held her gloved hand over her nose and concentrated on moving her palfrey forward at a steady pace and hoped the accumulated ordure wasn't being flicked up by the horses' hooves to become embedded in her skirts.

Enveloped by the jettied buildings narrowing the sky above them into a mere sliver of blue, Isobel felt immense relief when they rode into the courtyard fronting Langton Place and saw the familiar robust form and cragged face of Philip Taylor waiting for them alongside a wheaten-haired man she took to be their steward. As unlike Hyde as he could be, the man reminded Isobel of a duck egg — smooth-skinned, round head, sloping shoulders, doughy, although not yet fat. He bowed low. "Debden," Robert addressed him. "How goes it?"

Debden said something in reply. Isobel caught 'lord' and 'earl', thought she heard 'lady', although it sounded more like 'loidee', but the rest was unintelligible, even if delivered with another low bow and a polite smile in her direction. He seemed to expect an answer from her, and she erred on the side of caution and responded with a nod of her own head. Debden looked surprised, then confused. He spoke to Robert, looking worried.

"The countess is quite well, Debden, and our thanks you for your felicitations. We will be all the better for a jug of ale, however."

Debden looked relieved, replied, and bowing yet again, made his leave for the house.

"He is from Kent," Robert said when the man was beyond earshot. "You will become used to his speech. He is a good man — his father was steward to my father."

"I thought he must be from another land," Isobel confessed. "I made out hardly a word he said."

A muffled snort came from nearby. "Taylor," Robert said in greeting to the sergeant-at-arms. He scoured the handsome three-storey brick and timber building, set back from the river, that was their London home, noting the barred and shuttered windows on the ground floor and the heavy sections of wood making up the mullions of the oriel window on the first. "All well?" he asked.

"Aye, all secure, my lord," Philip Taylor confirmed in his clear northern speech, "as commanded; and well fettled up fit

for an earl and his lady, with the privies new-scoured and all."
Isobel swore he winked at her, but he kept a straight face as
Robert addressed him.

"And the munitions?"

"As ordered, my lord. Them rods of iron'll hold all but the
damned out, I'd say." He nodded towards the barred lower
windows. "Or in, if it so please you," he added.

"Are we expecting trouble?" Isobel asked, the anxious coil
that had grown in her stomach the further from Tickhill they
travelled, tightening a notch.

"Hmm? No, not especially," Robert replied.

"But you cannot be too careful." Taylor tapped the side of
his nose and raised his thicket of brows meaningfully.

"What did Philip mean?" Isobel had inspected her new home
and servants with thoroughness, and now rested by the fire in
their solar and warmed her hands around a beaker of ale. The
journey had been long and comforts few. It had grown dark in
the short time they had been there and she was obliged to
examine the large wall-enclosed garden between the house and
river by lantern light. "He did that thing men do — you know,
say nothing and yet say everything in a nod and a wink. What
care do we have to take? And against whom?"

Robert tore the bread he held and handed her a chunk.
"Against any who might wish us harm. This is not Tickhill, nor
Beaumancote, and our many neighbours here might not all be
our friends. It is best to be cautious."

"And prepared?"

He grinned. "Always."

"Rob, did you discuss everything with your first wife ... with
Ann?"

"Everything?"

"Yes, all matters to do with your estates —"

He laughed. "The little we had."

"…and matters *of* estate — yours and the king's," she finished.

His hand hovered above the bowl of meaty broth into which he had been dipping bread. "She was not interested," he said, resuming his meal.

"And had she been, would you have told her?"

He shrugged. "Our own affairs — of course."

"And that of the king and of the country?" she pushed. "Because *I* wish to know, Rob. I do not want to play a game of guessing when all around me are a step ahead. Will you tell me what you know? Discuss it with me, let me help you? *Trust* me? Because I will not sit at home and twiddle my thumbs waiting on your return and for any stray crumb of gossip to enlighten me. I will not do that. I *cannot* do that."

He finished his mouthful and wiped his mouth on the napkin over his shoulder, sitting back and contemplating her as if what she had proposed needed thought. "I believe I will," he said slowly. "I thought you too young, too unaware — perhaps too innocent of such matters to burden you with them." He screwed up his napkin and threw it on the table. "But you are not Ann, you are Isobel, and Isobel — daughter of Geoffrey Fenton — will know these things."

The following afternoon, Isobel's hair pinched where it was drawn tight beneath her high headdress, and her neck ached at carrying the weight of it. She had baulked when she first tried on the framework bearing stuffed and swagged cloth decorated with pearls forming little white roses. The only thing flower-like and delicate about it was the flimsy veil providing a foil to the mass balanced on her head. She puffed out her cheeks.

"How am I to wear this … *thing* all day?"

Fingering his chin and trying not to smile, Robert tilted his head to one side. "Try wearing a helmet then you would know the meaning of *heavy*."

"I have and it felt lighter than this." She waved a hand at her head.

"All day and under a summer sun? You could bake bread in it."

"At least there is purpose to a helmet," she grumbled. "I can see none in this thing."

"You are a countess, my love; you have to look like one." And behave in a similar manner, he might have been thinking, but was chivalrous enough not to say it.

Now here she was, in a chamber with countless other notables, waiting for the king and queen. Everyone else seemed to know each other. Everyone else appeared at ease — including her husband. Even now he raised a hand in greeting to someone across the crowded room surrounded by a clutch of brightly hued cockerels vying for his attention. With hair the colour of mole, the richly dressed figure standing close to the empty dais as if he were about to possess it spotted Robert and beckoned to him. Perhaps it was the air of superiority with which he treated those around him, or something about the hardness in his expression, but he seemed faintly familiar. "Who is that?" Isobel asked.

"The Duke of Clarence," Robert replied shortly, bowing in response to the king's brother. "Stay here; I will return presently."

"Rob!" Isobel protested. "Don't leave me!" But he was already gone, abandoning her, dwarfed among the crowd and conspicuously alone. She pinched the skin between her left thumb and forefinger, squeezing hard until the discomfort of it blotted out the awkwardness of being the solitary scarlet poppy in a field of golden rye, and stood on tiptoe to see what Robert was doing. Heads together, the king's brother seemingly ignored those around him, bringing his full attention to bear on her husband to the exclusion of all others. He said something to Robert, who replied and grinned, and Clarence burst out in laughter. The duke seemed about to say something further when his smile evaporated as a rustle of fine fabrics and a hush from the end of the room announced the arrival of the king and queen.

Resplendent in peacock silk, King Edward towered above his courtiers, his presence occupying the space around him in an invisible, ambergris-scented aura that preceded him. He was accompanied by a slender woman, her expression controlled, her poise absolute. Her eyes grazed individuals as she passed, bestowing a nod and a smile on the favoured, but at no point allowing any one to hold her gaze. Riveted, Isobel watched their progress towards the dais, absorbed by the unrivalled authority commanded by the pair. While she had met King Edward before at Tickhill, here, in this setting, he was in his element. Isobel felt out of place, exposed, an imposter who did not belong amongst so much nobility. They must surely see it in her clumsy movements and stilted speech. She looked for her husband but couldn't spot him among the glittering press of bodies. Isobel felt a sharp nudge from the woman next to her, and realised that the royal couple had halted their progress. Startled, she fumbled a curtsey.

"And who is this?" the queen asked in a light, melodic voice. Then, "Rise, rise," a little impatiently.

Isobel stood, keeping her eyes lowered. "Isobel Fent...Langton, Your Grace."

"Langton?" King Edward put a finger under Isobel's chin and raised it, the billowing silk of his vari-coloured sleeve dazzling, the scent overwhelming. He pursed his lips as he scrutinised her. "Indeed, I recall our meeting," he breathed. "I never forget a fair face, even if this one did steal the heart of one of England's most noble earls. Nay, not one, but two. And I can quite see why," he said softly. "Now, now, look not so alarmed, my lady; I have forgiven your husband even if he did fail to observe my wishes in his choice of wife, for how could he refuse such a delight? I am certain I could not." He gave a playful flick of her chin then looked about him. "Where is that knave you call husband? Ah, there you are, Langton."

Robert materialised at her side. "Your Grace?"

"I would keep an eye on your little wife, my lord, so new to Court. Such a poppet makes a tempting plaything." He chortled again. "Would you not say so, my love?" he asked his wife.

The queen continued to gaze at Isobel with regal impassivity. She turned her head slightly and, raising a hand to shield her mouth, said something low and inaudible to one of her attendants. Then, "As you rightly say, my lord, we must ensure Lady Langton's comfort and safety. We will see that she is well rehearsed in the ways of the Court. We will make it our especial purpose."

"And so you will, my love, and so you will." The king caught sight of his younger brother waiting near the chair of state, and a momentary frown clouded his face. "Now then," he said in an undertone to no one in particular, "what matter is this?" And out loud, "Brother, we are glad of your presence." He moved towards Clarence and the dais, taking the sun with him and leaving Isobel bewildered and confused.

"What did the king mean?" she whispered to Robert. "Why should I need protection?"

Hidden by the folds of cloth of her skirts, Robert took her hand and squeezed it. "Nothing that need concern you. He has marked you out for favour; play the game, Isobel, play the game."

"What game?" Isobel asked when they were finally alone in the privy chamber of their London home. Robert warmed his back against the fire while she exchanged her wet shoes and hose for light, fur-lined slippers that cradled her skin. She wriggled her toes feeling their freedom and set about divesting herself of the weighty headpiece.

"It's all a game, Isobel: who says what to whom; who is granted audience with the king; who is in favour and who is not. Who will rise and who fall. It's all in the look, the nod, the granting of offices, the withheld hand. The king stopped and spoke to you — he bestowed his favour. The queen took an especial interest in you — she showed *her* favour. Now those whom you meet will take care of what they say or do around you, and you can choose on whom you lavish *your* favour."

Struggling with a long pin that had somehow managed to catch itself on the net holding her hair in place and regretting not having her maids wait on her, Isobel said, "And how am I to know who that might be when I am familiar with none here?"

Robert left the warmth of the fire and went to help her. "Well, you listen, you watch, you learn. Above all, keep your counsel until such time as it becomes clear."

"*What* becomes clear?" she said with exasperation, jerking her head away as the pin snagged in his clumsy fingers. "None of this is clear. Everyone wears a mask. I cannot read their thoughts and faces, let alone who might be friend and who foe."

"Stay still! How can I help you if you do not let me?" He rotated the pin and it came loose, her hair falling free and heavy over his hand. Distracted, he had not answered her question.

"Rob — *how* am I to know?"

"Ask yourself, 'How will it benefit us if I talk to this or that person? Whom do they know that might help our cause?'" He lifted strands of her honeyed hair to his nose and breathed in scents of rosemary. He drew it across his lips and Isobel sensed his interest quicken.

"Our cause?" she pressed, feeling any moment that she would lose focus and melt under his now exploring hands.

"Our cause — to retain power over our lands and to increase our influence beyond them. To maintain our position at Court and the favour of the king. To align ourselves with those who share our ambition so that none can assail it and, by mutual interest, uphold the legacy of the family and promote it. That, my sweet, is our cause — yours and mine." He kissed her neck, making her shiver, running his lips in tiny nibbles down to her shoulders until prevented by the edge of her dress from going any further.

"Is that why," she managed to say as he shifted his attention to lifting her skirts and letting the chilly air flow about her calves, "you were talking with the Duke of Clarence?"

He drew back far enough to survey her face, his own flushed with desire. "Clarence understands the game," he said, and in hoisting her skirts further, curtailed the conversation.

CHAPTER THREE

"It is not far from here." Robert waited until Isobel finished weaving the bare stems of the rose into the trellis that circumnavigated the enclosed garden, and he had her full attention. "Isobel, did you hear what I said?"

"Mmm? Yes, of course." In the weak sunshine of the late winter's day, she stood back to view her handiwork, then turned to smile at him. "It will grow strongly now." Sensing his impatience, she relented. "You wish me to accompany you to my lord Clarence's dwelling, where you will, no doubt, talk about things of little interest and drink too much. I am to make myself pleasing to his wife the duchess. Is that all? Ah, no — what else but that I must *listen, watch, and learn*," she intoned with mock solemnity. "And play my part. Though what that *part* might be, I cannot tell."

"Nor can any of us," Robert said, "until it becomes clear." Isobel rolled her eyes and tutted. "Clarence is offering an open hand, Isobel, and I would be a fool not to accept it."

"But you are sworn to the Duke of Gloucester and you called his brother a 'bloated tick' not so long ago!"

"Yes, but circumstances change — people also — and I must do what is best for the family. Meeting with Clarence does not preclude friendship with his brother — nor any other, as long as it is not in conflict with Gloucester's interests."

"And it is not?"

"Not on my part, no."

She bent to retrieve the stick Moth laid at her feet and threw it again for her. The long-limbed hound bounded off to fetch it, no more hampered by her twisted leg than any other dog. "And then we can go home?"

"If the king and Gloucester have no further need of me, and our matters of business are concluded here, yes."

Isobel had seen only brief glimpses of Richard of Gloucester in the ten days they had been at Court. He was as courteous as ever, enquiring of her own health and her son's, but appeared preoccupied, his thoughts turned inwards as if they pressed on his mind. As for business, Robert had been true to his word to include her in all things, and she had escorted her husband to a number of meetings with jowled merchants, whose unctuous civility and sly eyes made her skin crawl.

He took her then to the docks beyond London bridge, where the wind blew sharp and grey up the Thames, and the wrinkled brown and salted skin of the captain they met there reminded her of smoked herring. His strange accent made it hard for her to understand him at first, but she became accustomed to the lilt, and listened with growing fascination to his tales of avoiding the pirates that roamed the coast hoping to catch unwary ships off guard. He had given a spare nod in the direction of the seamen heaving barrels and flagons from the hold in exchange for bales of rank fleeces and hides and said something in a language Isobel did not recognise.

Robert had responded with a frown and a handshake and a string of words in the same tongue. She liked the captain; she liked the way he smelled of the sea and of his honest discourse and plain demeanour. She liked the way he met her gaze with his dark brown eyes and included her in his broken conversation as if she understood the ways of the sea and the trade he made upon it.

"Barquerio's a good man," Robert had said in response to Isobel's question when they left the biting wind behind them, past the cranes standing like wading birds upon the shore, and wove between the smoking braziers and the seamen huddled around them. "Trustworthy and true. I rely on him to oversee our fleet and ensure its safety to and from our estates in Portugal. The coast is ravaged by Barbary pirates and French privateers on the hunt for easy prey; and the Hanse are the worst of the lot." He harrumphed a laugh. "Even Warwick was known to pick off a lone merchant if he came upon it: French, Burgundian, Hanse … all were the same to him."

Isobel had been relishing his use of '*our*' in relation to his ships and land, but said with a degree of indignance, "I hope our ships do no such thing. It is not fitting for us to engage in such behaviour!"

A plume of smoke had changed direction and Robert coughed and drew his kerchief to blow his nose. "What is *fit* for any lord?" he muttered into the fine linen. He cleared his throat and, avoiding Isobel's interrogative stare, pointed towards the waiting horses. "We must away before dusk falls. The streets are not safe even with our escort, and there are things I would rather you not see."

"What things?" Isobel asked, but Robert merely shook his head and declined to answer, leaving it to her own imagination and limited knowledge of the world.

The great house of L'Erber marked it out as the palace of a prince, as it now was since George Plantagenet, Duke of Clarence, had married Isabel Neville, and she had inherited it on the death of her father. Named for its gardens, the stone house lay tucked behind the high walls sheltering it from the ordure of London. It could not, however, escape the many bells of the churches clustered in the streets beyond. Perhaps the inhabitants liked to imagine they rang for them, a sign of

God's favour upon their destiny, as protective a force as the crenellated tower that stood at one end of the complex.

The building loomed over Isobel and Robert, blotting out the sky. Had she not already been intimidated by the thought of the forthcoming visit, Isobel would have quailed at the sight of the London home of the Duke and Duchess of Clarence — if *home* could be applied to so imposing a structure, she thought, feeling both nervous and grumpy and inclined to snap at the merest provocation. "*Look, listen and learn,*" she intoned under her breath as they were led through the cross-passage, past the great hall, to a smaller private chamber beyond. It overlooked gardens and on a summer's day, must have been a pleasant room. She would have lingered at the window, but Robert steered her in the direction of the welcoming fire, where they were invited to warm themselves and served wine in gilded cups.

"Clarence keeps a good cask," Robert commented, savouring the wine, although Isobel could taste nothing but nerves. "He is known to be a generous host."

A young woman of about Isobel's age, wearing fine clothes and an aloof expression regarded them from the doorway. Middling in height, she had pleasant enough features arranged on an oval face, with brown eyes and a high hairline, plucked to perfection. Isobel followed Robert's suit and curtsied as he bowed with courtly elegance. The woman responded with a practised smile of greeting, somewhat tight, Isobel thought or perhaps wary.

If Robert recognised the woman's caution, he ignored it, breaking into his unguarded smile that never failed to warm the coldest temperaments. "It has been many years since last we met at your noble father's house; you wear them kindly, Your Grace." He drew Isobel forward. "If it please you, might I present my wife, Lady Isobel Langton, and offer thanks for your gracious hospitality."

The Duchess of Clarence thawed a little. "You are most welcome, my lord. It has indeed been some years, has it not? My husband begs your indulgence, but he is kept on business and will return as soon as he may. Perhaps Lady Langton will accompany me to my privy chambers; I am eager to hear your news." If she was, she certainly didn't sound it, nor did her face reflect any curiosity; rather she wore the expression of one resigned to pass the time in the company of a stranger. She tweaked the side of her mouth in the semblance of a smile, but her eyes were chilly and observant, and she merely made the motions of cordiality. She held out a jewelled hand and took Isobel's lightly. "You are cold, my lady; come and warm yourself by the fire. I think we might have snow ere long."

Robert gave the slightest jerk of his head and raised his brows in encouragement.

Isobel followed the duchess through several rooms, up narrow wooden stairs and into a low-beamed chamber warmed by a generous fire. Winged and canopied chairs waited with fat cushions by the hearth. Firelight danced off gilded roses and twining stems decorating the rich blue and red plaster panels between each white-painted beam. Pricket sticks, shaped as fantastical beasts, held candles that lit the yellow walls in a soft glow, denying the cold outside a foothold in the welcoming room. Exotic rugs, exuberant hangings, and bowls decorated with bright ochre slip were filled with delicacies and another with the cones of trees, belying the duchess's joyless demeanour. A large earthenware vase of outlandish design sat on a table before the window holding winter stems from which tiny shapes dangled on threads. Isobel peered at the curious foliage and broke into a delighted laugh. She clapped her hand over her mouth and coloured at her uncouth behaviour. Monitoring her carefully, the duchess's brows rose.

"Forgive me, Your Grace, but this is such a pretty chamber and these so wittily fashioned." Isobel touched one of the tiny animals carved in wood and painted in bright colours, setting it swinging gently, and couldn't help but smile again. "My son would dearly love to play with these!" She blushed again because it sounded as if she were asking.

"You have a child?" the duchess asked, her face brightening a little. "Come, sit, and tell me about him."

Supplied with warmed ale and footstools on which to raise their feet from the cold floor, Lady Isabel said with the swiftest smile, "And here we shall hold court," adding, "at least until my husband's return." Her voice drooped a little.

"And shall I play the Fool, Your Grace?" Isobel couldn't help but ask, mentally kicking herself for being just that. Her mind raced to think of something intelligent to say and failed.

Lady Isabel dried her lips and carefully placed the fragile glass beaker on the table by her elbow. "I believe," she said with a straight face, "that I am in need of such a diversion." She looked at Isobel sideways, her eyes hinting at humour and losing some of her lofty reserve. Seeing the chink in the woman's defences, Isobel pressed her advantage.

"When I was a child, my parents would expect me to befriend the children of visiting dignitaries and I would escape to the river and play among the reeds where none could find me. I hated to be told what to do," she added. "The mere expectation of good behaviour had me misbehaving. I must have been a disappointment to my parents."

"Why do parents always believe that children will be friends merely because they are children," the duchess said, "and force upon each the company of the other? I could not abide Nell

Fitzhugh — she would be all smiles while pinching me behind our parents' backs. She used to bait my sister without mercy, poor little Anne." Lady Isabel made pincers of her thumb and forefinger. "I did not like Nell then, I do not now." She hesitated, suddenly cautious again. "Do you know her?"

Isobel shook her head, recalling the nursery maid Joan's spiteful ways. "No, but I know just her sort. I cannot abide such a Janus. There is no relying upon them." She had been going to say something about them being worse than traitors but stopped herself just in time. Any reference to treachery would hardly sit well in a conversation with the Earl of Warwick's daughter.

"I believe we share names," Lady Isabel went on.

"Yes, Your Grace."

"Let us not be so formal; I shall be Isabel and ... how shall we know you apart?"

Isobel thought for a moment, then, "Is-*o*-bel, my lady, but Cecily, my husband's niece, used to call me *Is'bel*."

"*Is'bel*, I like that!" she exclaimed. The door opened in the corner of the room and, turning in her chair, Lady Isabel called out, "Anne! Come greet Is'bel."

Whisper quiet and insignificant, a young woman emerged into the room and into the light from the fire. Huge brown eyes stared from a pale, heart-shaped face, the mouth small and the lips, full. She clasped her small hands in front of her as if they might somehow escape. "Anne, Lady Langton has come to visit as I said she would, remember? And, look, here she is." The duchess drew the young woman forward and put a shielding arm around her shoulders. Anne darted a glance at Isobel. Whatever had been said to her before Isobel's arrival ensured Anne now viewed her with caution. What did they know of her past? Isobel shrank inside herself, avoiding Anne's stare. Did they know she had been the mistress of the Earl? Did she wear her shame so visibly?

"You are welcome, Lady Langton," Anne said, her voice small but with a warm timbre. "My sister has told me about Lord Robert; he was present at our father's court at one time and she remembers him, although … I do not." She frowned, her forehead creasing in soft folds.

"Anne, Is'bel was about to tell me about her son and I think you would like to hear about him, too. Say on Is'bel; we are all ears."

Robert barely had time to accept a second cup of wine when a scattering of claws and a man's voice filled the space outside the door, intruding on the relative peace and forewarning impending interruption. The door banged back on its hinges, letting in cold air and the smell of the river clinging to the man's cloak and the dark expression he carried with him. He threw a curt order over his shoulder and the dogs that accompanied him were called to order. He spotted Robert by the fire.

"Ah, Langton! I am returned from the king; I thought I would never get away. These matters of Court are tedious. I see you are made comfortable enough." He threw his gloves at the attendant, who fumbled the catch. Clarence helped himself to wine. "How like you my house? It is set fair, is it not? Fit for a prince." his mouth skewed. "My wife says we should leave Court and return to our estates. But what does she know of matters of rule?" He drank deeply and flicked the empty cup with a nail. He watched it be refilled. "You have met my wife's sister, Anne, Prince Edward's widow?" Again, that note of agitated sourness.

"Not this day, Your Grace, and not since his father King Henry was alive."

Clarence grunted. "There'll be time enough. She lives here and will for the time being — at least while it pleases me for her to do so." He gave a tight smile. "Let us dine apart. Will you bide a while, Langton, and save me from women's smatter? I would take it as a sign of friendship." He didn't wait for Robert's agreement but continued. "What a prize Anne would make with her father's estates, eh? Young, a widow with an inheritance beyond most men's furthest imaginings. Perhaps you should not have been in such haste to marry, my lord. Anne would have made a fitting wife for so loyal a servant to the king." He probed Robert with hard eyes.

Robert took a small mouthful of wine, eking it out to avoid the numbing effect that would have him stumble into the undergrowth of this man's mind. "I am content with my choice, Your Grace."

"No matter," Clarence dismissed. "You have taken a wife of your own choosing. My brother, the king, could not decide whether to congratulate or chide you on your choice when he heard." He barked a laugh at the memory. "Now, you have secured yourself a swathe of lands along the Humber and Trent no man would have refused, and the offices with it. A good enough choice for some. No title, though, my lord, no title." He ran his tongue over his teeth, staring at nothing. "Still, a pretty face to soften that blow, and titles might be forthcoming from other ... quarters." He neglected to say what quarters those might be. "But, had you chosen merely from the heart..." Clarence flopped into a painted and gilded chair and indicated the plainer chair opposite. Robert sat, curious to know where this strange conversation was going. "Well, the heart plays many tricks, does it not, Langton? As the king knows. To our loss," he muttered, words almost swallowed by the rim of the gilt cup he brought to his lips so Robert didn't know whether he was meant to hear it. "So," he said, sitting up again and setting aside the cup. "To business."

"Business, Your Grace?"

"Ah, there is *always* business — yours, mine ...the king's." He smiled. "And my brother Gloucester's, of course." He pushed his lips into a squeezed 'o', then relaxed them. "He has done well out of these last years of discontent, has he not? He has been well-rewarded for his loyalty."

"He fought bravely at Barnet and Tewksbury, as Your Grace recalls," Robert replied evenly, hearing the changed tone in Clarence's voice and not trusting it.

Clarence must have sensed Robert's caution because he let out a sudden laugh. "He did indeed! I heard he fought like a boar and no man could stop him! My little brother, grown into a man at his first blooding. Well," he shrugged, "so the king thought. He must have been relieved that Gloucester took the opportunity to rid him of Edward of Lancaster. Sweet heaven only knows what we would have done with him if he had lived."

"It was a fair fight."

"He was cornered," Clarence said quickly. "You saw it; you were there."

"I was and I did. Gloucester gave him the option to fight; the alternative would have been execution. What would you have preferred, Your Grace? A public execution or to be counted among the fallen having been given the chance to defend yourself?"

Clarence viewed him with unblinking eyes. He drew his forefinger across his top lip and back again, repeating the movement slowly, methodically. In the moments that followed, Robert wondered whether he had pushed Clarence too far.

"It is a question I have asked myself oft times enough," Clarence said eventually. "As I am sure you have also."

Robert raised his cup in acknowledgement. "I have — more times than I care to remember. So, business. Your Grace has something in mind?"

Clarence had reached for his cup again and was now rotating it between his palms, light from the window and from the fire reflecting alternately grey and amber off the burnished surface. From afar came the sound of women's voices and laughter. "I hear you have been looking to acquire the manors of Bexby and Rushton, but the widow Halton has refused to sell?"

"I offered her a fair price and a pension, but she wished to keep the lands for her grandson."

"And what if I can persuade her to reconsider knowing that she will be well-rewarded and kept comfortable in her infirmity?"

"Her grandson —"

"I will ensure he has adequate compensation — perhaps offer him a position in my household, preferment when he has earned it, even a minor holding of his own. Well?"

"And in return?"

Clarence spread his arms wide in a gesture of accommodation, gilded buttons glinting. "I ask nothing but your friendship. See this as token of my good intent, an opportunity to heal the wounds of the past, hmm? It is within my power to do so; let me honour our future friendship and seal it with this offer of my good lordship."

"And the widow will be willing to accept the proposal?"

Clarence tipped his chair onto its back legs. "Accept? Of course! Her husband was a man loyal to me and it will be an honour for her to do my will in his name. I will even pay for masses to be said for his soul. And hers, when it is her time." He crossed himself and smiled. "So, have we accord?"

Robert had the distinct suspicion he was being played; but what was the game? What, other than friendship, did Clarence think he had to gain from a closer alliance. *Look, listen, and learn*, he had told Isobel before they left home that morning, and so should he.

"There is one other thing," Clarence said on rising to join the women. "There is no need for others to know of our arrangement. I am certain you appreciate that I cannot make such token of friendship to all my acquaintances, and, well, I would not wish to sow discord among them."

Bowing his head, Robert indicated his acceptance of the duke's proviso, and Clarence clapped him on the shoulder, harder, perhaps, than he needed. "That is well, my lord, for I reward such friendship generously, better, indeed than many lords are able — if you understand me?"

Subtlety was not one of Clarence's finer points. Robert understood well enough, and he was not impressed by the duke's attempt to undermine Gloucester's position as his sworn lord. But he forced a smile, noting to himself that, in all the recent conversation, Clarence had not once mentioned what he truly was after.

"So, what *did* he want?" Isobel asked when Robert had outlined the conversation to her when they had the privacy to talk and he the latitude to drink without it compromising his ability to think straight.

"He did not say, so I have to assume he will make it clear when he has a mind to." He offered her a sip from the elegant wine beaker that had once been his brother's.

"Will you tell the Duke of Gloucester?"

"That his brother is wooing me with manors and promises of friendship and advancement if I cleave to him?" Robert inflated his cheeks and released the breath in a slow exhalation as he considered the question. "I'll wait and see," he said finally.

"For what?"

Robert considered the gilt and enamelled images circling the tall, embellished cup, Fortuna with her hand upon the wheel of men's fate, one crowned figure falling while another was raised up. "To see which way the wheel turns," he said.

Robert's answer had not satisfied Isobel, nor did she consider it wise to withhold information from Gloucester. She contemplated going to Gloucester herself, but decided that Robert would probably do so when — or if — there was something worth telling. Anyway, it seemed disloyal to go behind her husband's back. Perhaps Clarence's offer might be taken at face value... Isobel mentally shook her head. What she had heard of the man persuaded her that he did nothing without purpose, so what purpose had he in mind for Robert?

Her fears were no further allayed when she received a message from the Duchess of Clarence a few days later.

"What does she want?" Robert peeled back his shirt to allow Isobel to inspect the surly lesion across his left forearm.

"She did not say." Isobel huffed and frowned at the angry red line that looked suspiciously like the edge of a sword. "Why do you allow yourself to be so injured when you are in the practice yards? One day you will return home without an arm and no amount of healing will restore it to you."

"I promise to keep my arms, for how can I serve you otherwise?" Robert wrapped both limbs around her waist and pulled her tight into him. She made a little squeal of protest and wriggled and tried to pull away, but gave up, laughing. Robert kissed her neck. "And why, pray, do you imagine it was I that was beaten, wife? You should have seen the other man." He grinned as she shook her head in a show of disapproval.

"You enjoy these games of war too much," she grumbled, pulling away and managing to smear a sticky salve over the wound.

"They serve a purpose," he reminded her. "Besides, the duke likes to test his skill against those practised in such arts."

"Clarence?" she said, sharply, ignoring his boast.

"Gloucester," he replied "He is intent on besting me in the yards. And, yes, I admit to enjoying the challenge. He makes a worthy opponent and, unlike his brother Clarence, listens to advice."

She giggled. "The Duke of Gloucester takes advice from *you?*"

It was Robert's turn to frown. "Is that so unlikely?"

Isobel smothered a smile. "No, no, of course not. So," she said, returning to the original topic of conversation, "I will decline Lady Isabel's invitation. I do not wish to be … *wooed*, I think you said."

"Oh, but I think you do, my love." She groaned and he hushed her, his hand gently over her mouth full of protestations. "Go," he said, "I wish it. Be friendly and open with the duchess and perhaps she will reveal more about her husband's plans than he did."

"Spy? You want me to *spy* on the Duke of Clarence!"

"Shhh, no; I wish you to look —"

"— listen, and learn. Yes, I know. I did the other day and learned nothing."

"Then see this as a pleasant way to spend your time and, should you hear or see anything of interest, let me know."

She slapped his hand away and shut the lid of her casket with a thump. "Spy," she said. "Why not use Master Sawcliffe and be done with it?"

"Because I doubt the duchess would find his company as agreeable as yours. Besides," he said, giving her a sidelong look, "he does not possess your considerable ... charms."

Isobel felt less than charming when, on a sleet-grey day, she left her escort to enjoy the company of the servants' hall and joined the Duchess of Clarence and her sister in the privacy of their solar.

"How fares your son?" Lady Isabel asked. "You must bring him with you next time you visit. What age is he now?"

Isobel sent up an urgent prayer that Lady Isabel could not count. "A little over twelve months and two more, Your Grace. He likes to chew everything. I caught him with the dog's bone yesterday." She laughed, but the duchess did not join in.

"Fourteen months?" Lady Isabel asked. "I see," she said quietly, then, "Children are a blessing, are they not? Whatever the circumstance of their birth." She looked to one side. "I still mourn the child born to me and taken too soon. A blessing," she said again, almost to herself. She called to an attendant and ordered warmed milk and ale. "It helps settle my stomach and soothes me when I have sickness. I had it passing bad with my first child." Her voice quavered and she forced a smile. "Yes, I am with child again, and this little one will have a different fate, if it please God." She rubbed her belly, still easily disguised by her thick winter skirts.

Isobel groaned in sympathy. "I sickened most in the mornings but was still force-fed like a duck. I am surprised I did not learn to quack." She flapped her elbows and puffed out her cheeks. Lady Isabel burst into laughter.

Anne's brow curled into a question. "But I thought you recently wed, yet your son is —"

"*Drew* is such a sweet name," Lady Isabel intervened to Isobel's relief. To distract her sister further, the duchess then regaled them with tales of flatulence at Court at which they curled with fits of giggles and, when she took the opportunity to glance at her, Isobel noted that the duchess had let her shoulders relax along with a little of her guard. The door opened behind them and Lady Isabel turned. "We are dropping from thirst here, where have you been…?" she began, then stopped as an older man in clerical clothes bowed to her.

"Madam, the Lady Anne has a visitor."

Anne shot out of her chair, spilling sweetmeats onto the floor which a small dog gobbled noisily. Eyes staring, she took short, sharp breaths, backing behind the chair and towards the door in the corner of the room. "Do not let them take me, Issy. I shall not go!"

"Wait, Anne," Lady Isabel cautioned. "Who is this visitor?" The cleric again bent towards the duchess and lowered his voice. She looked momentarily surprised, glanced at Isobel, then spoke to Anne. "Anne, it is our cousin, Richard. He wishes to see you."

Anne blinked. "He is here to see *me*?" She clutched the high back of the chair as the dog bounced around her skirts yipping. "Tell him I am unwell. Tell him —" but it was too late. Framed in the doorway stood Richard, Duke of Gloucester, drops of water decorating his shoulders, his boots darkened with sleet. He pushed a deep hood from his head and brushed hair from his eyes.

Isobel dropped into a low curtsey as Lady Isabel rose to greet him warmly. When Gloucester spoke, he sounded as if he had hurried and was breathless.

"I ask forgiveness for this intrusion, sister, and beg your indulgence for a little time with my cousin — should it be amenable to you," he appealed to Anne directly.

Anne looked first at her sister, then back to Gloucester. She licked her lips and straightened her back. Even so, she looked more panicked than ever.

"Anne?" Lady Isabel said, when it seemed like she wouldn't answer. "Is'bel and I will wait just yonder in the garden. I need to take the air." She pointed to the corner door. "We will not stray far."

Anne gave a tiny nod and inched around the side of the chair. That was where Isobel and the duchess left her, with Gloucester speaking low and soft before they had even left the room.

Once in the shelter of the high-walled garden and safely beyond earshot, the duchess took Isobel companionably by the arm, each supporting the other on the slippery flagged paths. "That is the third time our cousin has been to visit us when George is away from home, but it is the first time he has been alone with my sister. George hates it when Richard visits without him being present; he always suspects conspiracy." She smiled, making her look younger. "Anne likes it, though, even if she always thinks the king is going to summon her and have her punished."

"Why?"

"Because she likes our cousin — and always has," she added, dimpling this time.

"No, I mean, why does she think the king will arrest her?"

Lady Isabel's face straightened. "Because our father was the Earl of Warwick, who betrayed him, and because Anne's husband was the Prince of Wales and King Edward's enemy. Are you surprised by my saying so? I see that you are; but I shall not muffle the truth to make it easier on the ear. Anne had no part in any of it but feels the weight on her shoulders. She bears the burden of their ... guilt." The smile she gave was tight. "Poor little Anne. She loved our father and saw no fault in him. His death robbed her of all comfort and peace. She has found none here." She cast around the walls of the bare-branched garden as if it were a cell. "But the king has forgiven her all part in the matter; she has nothing to fear from him."

"But you are also your father's daughter, Your Grace, and your husband... Well, he ... I mean..." Isobel stumbled out of words.

"Betrayed his brother?" Lady Isabel said in a matter-of-fact way. "Yes, he did. For a short while it seemed that George's ambition might be realised and my father would make him king instead of Edward." Lady Isabel paused, a small, wistful smile on her lips. "And I would have been queen." She shook her head. "But our father made an alliance with that Anjou woman, and married Anne to Prince Edward, denying George's chance at the throne. Our father would have had a daughter as queen either way — he was so ambitious for our family. Poor Papa. Poor George; he felt robbed of his inheritance, his destiny. He still does. He blames my father; he blames me." In an unconscious movement, she rubbed her shoulder where, for the first time, Isobel noticed a darkening of the skin at the edge of her neckline. Lady Isabel saw her looking and pulled her mantle over the bruise, her face reddening. She became brisk. "It is cold out here; let us go back in."

"What did Gloucester want?" Robert asked.

Isobel gave Andrew a kiss on each plump cheek, eliciting a chuckle, said a few words of blessing while holding her beads to his lips, and handed him back to Buena. She waited until she and Robert were alone in their chamber.

"Lady Anne did not — would not — say in front of me, but she seemed excited and not at all as she had been when he arrived." She paused as a faint wail from Andrew alerted her to the fact that Buena was attempting to put him in his cradle before he thought she should.

"And?" Robert pressed.

"And I was made vow to tell no one that His Grace had been there — except you"

Robert grunted, and Isobel peered at him. "Did you already know of this? You do not seem surprised."

"Gloucester might have mentioned it." He carved a neat crescent from the custard with the side of his spoon. "What else did you talk about?"

"Naught else of interest — except about Drew's teeth and how well he is grown…" At the sound of a little *harrumph* of impatience from the other side of the table where they shared a meal, she smiled. "There is one thing; Lady Isabel had a mark — here, on her shoulder — but she covered it before I could see clearly."

"What of it?"

"It means," Isobel said, labouring each word as if explaining to a slow child, "that the Duchess of Clarence is hiding something she wishes no one to see."

Robert waved his spoon in the air. "So, she has taken injury. It is of no matter."

"When you sliced your thumb and bled all over the table linen, did you attempt to hide your hurt from others?" He looked a little abashed. "No, exactly — you told everyone. If a woman hides such a bruise it is because she is ashamed."

"Of what?"

"Of how it was put there, Rob. The duchess was purposefully harmed; she had no other reason to hide it."

He threw his spoon in the dish with a clatter. "You cannot know that."

"But I do," she said quietly. "When I received such bruises, I hid them from view." She held his gaze as Robert's face clouded. "I was ashamed of what the Earl had done to me."

He sidestepped the memory. "Do you believe Clarence beats her?"

"Perhaps."

"He is within his rights to chastise her."

"Rob!"

"He has a duty and a right to maintain governance over his household, and that includes his wife. You know this."

"Will you chastise me?"

"No, of course not. You never give me reason to."

She felt like giving him a reason right there and then but had nothing to say that wouldn't spill from her mouth in a tumble. Instead, she threw her napkin to the ground and left him sitting open mouthed and alone to contemplate his folly.

CHAPTER FOUR

Queen Elizabeth's words had buttered King Edward's ears all morning when he had other things on his mind and certainly not a widow's entreaty for him to hear her plea. The king pursed his lips as he contemplated Felice Langton's faded charms. He considered the legality of her claim on behalf of her son to the earldom over Robert Langton's. Then whether her claim had any benefit to the rule of the region in question. And lastly, he wondered, if he ceded to his wife's soft words, whether his wife would give him what he yearned for: an hour or two's freedom from other men's problems.

"If it please you," she continued, "might you not direct another to hear her case? Then you will be seen to ensure justice and mercy and yet not have the burden of it yourself." She slipped around him and knelt by his chair and, taking up his large hand, held it to her cheek. "The boy will be forever in your debt if you see fit to return his title."

"The boy, Lizbet, is barely out of his infancy. Should I risk losing a trusted, experienced man whose family has been loyal to mine for the sake of an *infant?*"

Edward withdrew his hand, but she recaptured it and held it to her breast.

"Of course not, that would be madness! Robert Langton is too valuable a friend to us. Perhaps he deserves greater return for his good service than that which he has received?"

Edward narrowed his eyes. "And what *reward* might that be?"

She fixed him with her clear blue, unblinking eyes. "Why, my lord, you said it yourself not a month back — such a debt of loyalty should be richly rewarded. You mentioned something… I only wish I could recall…" She brought a neatly shaped finger to her lips — lips a delicate pink, moistened as she ran the tip of her tongue over them, her brow gently creased in thought. "Ah, yes!" she exclaimed. "You were considering the fate of the traitors' lands in the north and west and how they best be deployed in your service. You spoke of Langton and how you wish to see his estates increased beyond that which he already holds. Such wisdom, Edward! I only restate your words because they are worth the repeating," she finished, leaning forwards until she rested against his knees.

He frowned as he tried to remember any such conversation, but his fingers strayed down the crevice between her breasts and he found his mind wandering from the subject in hand to the promise of greater — if transient — reward. "I will think on it," he murmured, curving his hand and beginning to press his advantage.

Later, in the shelter of the garden wall, Queen Elizabeth sat alone with her thoughts. The wind had eased and the still air and bright sunshine might beguile the unwary into thinking it more clement than it truly was. She was not fooled by the impression of warmth any more than she was by the smile of the courtiers and those that would flatter her. They would have to be subtler than that, and she was already there, planning her own next move.

Elizabeth enjoyed this game. There was art in setting up a situation and seeing it through to its conclusion. Moreover, such games were necessary to ensure the smooth running of the realm and the absolute authority of its king. And not just that of the king, but those on whose support he absolutely depended. She smiled to herself as, in her mind, she drew an imaginary map of the country on which she placed gaming pieces representing members of her family and their affinity and overthrew those that opposed her.

With a flick of her finger, over went Clarence, joining the spill of the already fallen — Warwick, Henry the old king, and his brat of a son — gone, dismembered in her imagination. Dead. She pushed her lips together as she considered next steps: those she would see rise up, those to be cast down. Those who might prove useful in the future and on whose loyalty and discretion she could rely, and those... Well, let's just say that people were either for her or against her. There could be no half measures.

Elizabeth became aware of someone approaching. She tutted. She relished these quiet moments of contemplation and there were few enough at Court. She steeled herself for the interruption and then recognised the tall, thick-set man as her brother, bundled in heavy furs against the cold.

"Anthony." She returned his brief greeting, reminded again of how like their father he was in both manner and looks the older he grew. He sat next to her and adjusted the cloak around himself, taking up the greater length of the bench in the breadth of his shoulders and width of his thighs. He sniffed.

"Cold out here, Lizzy. You'll be shitting ice if you sit here much longer."

A part of her wanted to remind her brother that she was queen and he indebted to her; but she long ago learned that nobody reminded Anthony, Lord Rivers of his place nor of his debt, as he was like to hold both against that person for as long as they breathed. Even her. Even the king.

"You wish to speak to me, brother?"

"Have you seen Clarence and Gloucester this day?"

"No. Why, have you?"

"They are with Edward now, squabbling again over the Neville girl's inheritance." He wore that smug look of one well-pleased. "Eddy looks as if he could split their skulls. Wish he would; save us from doing it."

Despite her dislike of her brother using the king's fond name — her name — she detected he had something else to tell her, so let it pass. "What of it? They have argued over every last manor since Warwick's death. There is nothing new there."

"Except," he said, speaking in an excited undertone, "I have heard that some accord might have been reached between them."

Her interest quickened. "Oh? What and from whom did you learn this?"

He tapped the side of his hooked nose in that infuriating way he had, like an older child in a nursery, baiting the younger with information withheld. "I will tell you when I learn more; but I thought you would want to know in case Eddy said anything to you in passing."

"The king," she said pointedly, "does not always discuss his brothers with me, you know this."

Anthony ran his gloved finger down the length of her arm, making her involuntarily shudder. "I'm certain you have ways of encouraging him to favour you with information, Lizzy; you always have."

She brushed his hand and insinuation aside. "I will learn of it for myself." She rose from the stone bench, her toes inside her furred shoes aching with cold, and a numbness about her buttocks. "Anthony, take a care. You have enemies at Court, remember that."

He stood, casting his shadow over her. "But I have you to protect me, sister. Who would dare harm me when I have you?" He grinned, a wide, toothy grin that some might have found endearing, but she knew better.

Elizabeth heard the raised voices from beyond the weighty door. She waved the guards away and paused, trying to make out the tenor of the argument, although she had already guessed to whom the opinions being vociferously pronounced belonged. And those of the quieter voice, articulating dissent. If this was accord between the brothers then she feared the complexion of conflict. She heard a thud and a third voice boomed out across the others followed by a sudden silence. Then the door hefted open with a crash against the wall and the figure of George, Duke of Clarence, thunder-faced, pushed past her without stopping. Elizabeth stepped into the room as if unaware of the thickened atmosphere that permeated it.

"It is so cold this day I am certain we will have snow," she announced, sweeping her mantle from around her and dropping it on the nearest bench. "How now, my lords?"

Face still clouded, the king muttered something to Gloucester who, giving a swift nod, gave a short bow in her direction and left the room.

"Have I interrupted?" she asked lightly of her husband who now gnawed at his knuckle as if he wished it was his brothers' heads. She came over to him and put a hand on his corrugated brow. "Edward, what is it that vexes you? Do you ail?"

"They will drive me to my grave with their argument," he said roughly. "I shall have no peace until it is settled."

Her fingers still cool from the frost, Elizabeth massaged his forehead. "You must not let them rile you, Eddy; tell your brothers of your decision and let it be done with, otherwise what will people say?"

"What *will* they say?" he growled.

"That your brothers Clarence and Gloucester rule you."

He plucked her hand from his head, his colour rising and contrasting with his dash of fair hair. "Is that what people say? That I am governed by my *brothers*?"

"I am sure it cannot be the case; but the commons remember how ill-served you were when Clarence chose against you; and I am surprised..." She broke off and turned away.

"What?" He took her arm and made her face him again. "Tell me, Elizabeth."

"It is nothing."

"*What* is nothing?"

"It is only that one of my ladies overheard —"

"Women's tattle." He spat, looking almost relieved.

"...that there are those at Court who wonder if you should have punished Clarence more severely as an example to others who might similarly seek to betray you."

"Truly? That is not news."

"And others who say he is seeking to do so again." She let the suggestion hang between them for a moment. "I am certain it is not so, but ... can we be assured of his loyalty?" She clutched his arm, pressing into the deep velvet nap with urgent fingers. "Edward, I am frightened. What if he turns again? None will be safe — not you, nor our sweet babes. All will be lost." She let her voice break, something she rarely did so was all the more effective for it. She controlled herself with effort. "Dearest lord, what must we do to protect ourselves and our family? Your brother Clarence seeks the Neville girl's inheritance to add to that which he already has through her sister. What further influence will he gain if he has the rest?"

"Do you suggest Richard should have his desire and marry Anne?"

"But that would be against your wishes and add fire to Clarence's claim!"

"What, then?"

"Marry the girl to someone you can trust and on whose loyalty you can depend."

"I can think of no other who serves me as loyally as my brother Richard."

She lowered her eyes. "I would hope there might be others on whom you can call. My family —"

"Ah."

"Have they ever given you reason to suspect them? They are your true subjects, my lord. Surely you cannot doubt them?" Again, that quiver of her lip, the falter in her voice. "They have no cause to follow another," she added.

"For which I should reward them, hey? They have had reward aplenty, Lizbet. They have had the choicest of marriages, as Warwick was fond of reminding me. Often. And Clarence even now."

She lifted her chin. "No more than their loyalty deserves."

"Hmm. Perhaps." He thrummed his fingers on the arm of his chair, the patch on his knuckles still raw, and would not meet her eyes. He had grown tired of the conversation and looked for a distraction. She had said her say.

Elizabeth clicked her fingers and from the shadows emerged a groom of the chamber. "His Grace thirsts. Bring sweet wine and delicacies. And *canisiones*," she called as an afterthought. "Your favourite, Eddy," she soothed. "A little marchpane rolled in pastry will set all right."

Gloucester stamped snow off his boots and allowed his water-stained cloak to be taken from his shoulders. "Winter is late in coming, my lord," he remarked, now removing his gloves. "I would it tarry no longer and be gone. Come, Hector," he said to a long-limbed sight hound as slim and quick as its master. It ceased nosing around the stone flagged floor and hastened after Gloucester and Robert as they ascended the stairs to the first floor and the chamber warmed by a lively fire.

Gloucester cut to the matter in hand. "It is decided."

Robert raised his brow. "And the king?"

"Would have it settled one way or the other." Gloucester smiled, but it was tight and the darkened area beneath his eyes spoke of sleepless nights and much debate.

"The lady?"

"Assents. Anne would be gone from my brother's keeping; it has not been … comfortable living there." With an absence of mind, he stroked the dome of Hector's head. "Now I must fulfil my promise to her."

"Have you a notion how it may be accomplished, Your Grace?"

"I do. With your help, should you be good enough to give it." He hesitated, unsure how to proceed and from the lamp table next to him, took up a bowl of walnuts in their skull-like shells.

"Isobel favours them," Robert said. "Might I have some prepared for you?"

Taking two nuts, Gloucester put the bowl down. "My thanks, I prefer to do so myself." He tapped the walnuts against each other, making a hollow *tok*, *tok*, at which the dog looked up before settling back to sleep on the hearth. "Langton, I would ask you to perform an act of … um … distraction." *Tok*. *Tok*, *tok*. "At an appointed time, it would be of benefit to me should you engage my brother George in some discourse or amusement — one that will take him away from home. For a morning, perhaps." *Tok*. Gloucester met Robert's eyes.

Robert reached into the bowl and secured a nut for himself. "An amusement," he said almost to himself and, placing the walnut on the stone hearth, brought the heel of his boot hard on it. The shell disintegrated into fragments. Robert nodded slowly. "I should be able to arrange an entertainment that will keep His Grace busy." He bent to rescue the exposed nut, sweeping the jagged remains of the shell towards the embers before Hector could eat them.

"Good," Gloucester said with evident relief. "There is one other favour I might ask. It involves your wife."

"Oh?"

"Anne is fearful. She has suffered much in the last months and has grown faint-hearted, and living with my brother has only added to that fear." He held up a hand as Robert opened his mouth to ask a question. "I will say no more on that matter; suffice that it is well that she be gone and soon."

Robert chewed a piece of broken walnut and selected another. "So, how might Isobel be of service in this matter?"

"She will be in no danger, be assured of that. On my honour I will let no harm come to the women. I ask only that your wife accompany Anne to a place of safety where she might rest." Forgotten for the moment, the walnuts rested in his hands. A slight breeze from the other side of the room lifted the dark hair over his eyes. He ignored it and through the strands continued to fix Robert with an intensity he found disconcerting.

"Your Grace, I will have to give it my consideration. For my part I am willing to do what you wish, and gladly; but for my wife —"

Hector shred the air with a sharp bark, jumping up and rushing towards the doorway where Isobel stood, snow and cold still clinging to her skirts, Andrew in her arms. Moth pushed past her and bundled into the room in an ungainly gamble of limbs as she greeted Hector with enthusiasm.

"What is it Your Grace desires me do?" Isobel asked. Skin glowing and eyes bright, she handed the child to the girl behind her and, stepping into the room, closed the door. She curtsied. "Your Grace, forgive my intrusion and that I was not present to welcome you, but I had to show Drew the Maids-Of-The-Snow before nightfall. They are so brave pushing up through the snow as if nothing might forestall their coming." She smiled self-consciously. "If there is something that must be done, let me know and I will be of whatever service I might offer."

"Isobel —" Robert began, giving her one of his cautioning looks, but Gloucester was on his feet and crossing the room to take her hands in his.

"I ask that you accompany the Lady Anne from my brother's house to give her good heart and some cheer, that is all. Will you do it? If your husband is in agreement?"

Isobel saw the doubt in Robert's face, and the anticipation in Gloucester's. "I will, Your Grace, and be pleased to do so. Robert, it is so little a thing to ask and I am glad to be of service. Please do not deny me this chance to repay the kindness His Grace showed me at Beaumancote."

Noting the stubborn set in the jaws of both his wife and his duke, Robert shifted his ground and, with obvious reluctance, nodded. Isobel lightly squeezed Gloucester's hands and skipped over to her husband, bestowing a kiss on his head and a laugh at his grumpy expression and stern demeanour. "Then all is well. Perhaps I might take Drew with me; my ladies expressed a desire to meet him."

"No." Robert brought the flat of his hand down on the arm of his chair, making Isobel jump. The dogs stopped their frolicking and Moth whined.

"But —"

"No, Isobel. Go if you must, but the boy stays here. I will not debate it."

Heat rushed to colour her neck and Isobel crushed the desire to argue, hurt by Robert's tone but more that he chose to chastise her in front of Gloucester.

"I thank you for your commitments and accept them gladly, but I have been the cause of dissension for which I ask your forgiveness and shall take my leave." Gloucester gave an awkward bow and edged towards the door.

Robert accompanied him to the courtyard enclosure at the rear of the house beyond which gathered snow lay in grimy piles. Through the gates of the fortified wall, children could be seen sliding with much delighted squealing. Gloucester had been silent since taking his leave of Isobel; once in the open air of the stable yard he spoke.

"If I have caused offence, my lord, I beg your pardon, for it was not my intention. The child will be as safe as his mother, and it might be a comfort to the women to have him present. I guarantee no harm will befall him."

From beyond the walls, the children's laughter became tainted with a sudden wail; crying ensued. One of the men on guard at the gate called out to them.

"I do not fear for his safety, Your Grace, although I would have my sergeant escort my wife. No, it is not that; I do not allow it. That is all."

*

"Why will you not permit Drew to accompany me?" Isobel demanded on Robert's return, her anger fuelled by embarrassment. "What harm could it do?"

"You defied me in front of Gloucester, Isobel. I shall not be told by my wife what she will or will not do when I have resolved on a matter. My decisions are not to be questioned."

"You haven't answered *my* question: why do you prevent Drew from going with me? His Grace said we will be safe; what other assurances do you need?"

"I do not doubt Andrew's safety, nor Gloucester's word he will keep you from harm."

"Then why?"

"Do I have to make it clear to you?"

"Yes!"

He came up close, bent towards her and brought his face to within a finger's length of her own. "His Grace might indulge your whim, but I will not have the Duchess of Clarence and the widow of the Prince of Wales make a mockery of the circumstances in which Andrew was birthed."

"You … you are ashamed of him, of your own *son?*"

"My son? No, but my brother's bastard? For that is what he is, Isobel; in the eyes of the world, he is the natural son of my brother. In the eyes of God, my son or no, we were not wed when he was conceived. Whatever way you see it, Andrew is a bastard."

"And so am I," she whispered, eyes rounded and staring at the stranger standing in front of her. "Is that how you think of me, of Drew — as *bastards?* Are you ashamed of us, Rob? Do you regret *our* existence?"

He blanched, tried to take her hand, "Isobel, no…" But she backed away, fists at her sides and body shaking. "Isobel, please!" He held out his hand, anger evaporating into remorse as she shrank from him. He tried again and she jerked away, furious and hurt, but her heel caught on the edge of the hearth and she stumbled.

Arms flailing at air, she made a grab for the stone hood to stop herself from falling, but failed to grip the smooth surface, yelping as her wrist came into contact with the blistering metal of the fire irons. Robert lunged forwards as she slipped towards the embers, the sleeve of her gown ripping as he hauled her out of the hearth. Burning wool pervaded the air and he beat the cloth of her skirts with his bare hands, defeating flames at the expense of his own searing skin.

Her skirts still smouldering. he threw the contents of the vase at the scorched fabric. Then, holding her to him, neither spoke until they stopped shaking. He sought her wrist, examining the livid stripe and gently kissing the tender skin and murmuring, "My dove, my dove," over and over until he brought the overwhelming emotion under control and was able at last to speak. "Never fear me. Never, *ever* think of me other than as your loving husband, Isobel, and you my sweetest wife."

Still shaken, she could only see the remnants of his anger in her mind's eye, until she saw his blackened hands. She turned the palms upwards in her own. "You're burnt," she said softly.

"Only a little singed." He managed a shaky laugh. "What a pair we make. Buena will have us eat bread and water for a week as penance."

"Oh! Your poor wrist!" Lady Isabel examined the mark despite Isobel's protestations that it was nothing and a mere accident. The duchess gave her an odd look. "I, too, have *accidents*," she said in a low voice.

Isobel was saved from replying as Anne came into the room looking flushed and harried, her maid close behind carrying a small bundle under her arm. "Is he here yet?"

Lady Isabel went to her sister. "Not yet, Scutterbuck, but he will be; you know he will keep his word. Come, see what Is'bel has done. We must scold her so she takes more care."

Anne's wide, brown eyes flashed open at the sight of the red mark. "Does it hurt much? You must have a care not to injure yourself!" She looked beyond Isobel hopefully. "Did you bring your son? You said you would, I so wish to see him."

"Is'bel could not bring him today, Anne. Another time perhaps?" She sent an enquiring glance at Isobel who smiled blandly but didn't reply.

"Oh," Anne's face fell, then brightened as swiftly. "I hear horses. Issy, can you hear them?" She jumped up, hands fluttering to her face as the sound of men's voices could now be distinctly heard echoing up the stone stairwell.

"Quick! Anne, come!" and Lady Isabel, taking her sister by the hand, ushered her towards the door. Anne pulled back.

"It might not be him. What if it isn't him, Isabel? What if George has returned?"

Isobel felt the tremors of alarm coming from Anne in waves. She walked briskly to the door. "I am sure I heard His Grace's voice. He said he would be here, my lady, let us greet him." She swung the door wide hoping fervently she was right.

The Duke of Gloucester lowered the hand about to open the door. He sounded breathless and a sweat of anxiety stood on his brow despite the chill air. "Well met, my lady."

"Your Grace, my lady is ready and eager to leave," Isobel said, placing an encouraging arm around Anne's shoulders. "My lady, the day is fair and the air smells sweeter from the river this morning. Will you come and see?"

"Issy…?" Anne said, looking at her sister and beginning to dither.

Gloucester went up to her, speaking softly but with an unmistakable urgency. "Anne, the horses are waiting. If we are to do this we must not tarry. Rooms are made ready for you and all the comforts you can want. There is even a little dog who awaits his mistress. Will you come with me?"

Anne looked up at him, and a little of the pallor left her face. "A dog?" She nodded, and a wisp of hope filled her eyes. "I will," she said in a small voice. "And Isobel will come too?"

A sudden clatter from outside set Anne in a jitter. Gloucester twitched to be away.

"Of course, my lady." Isobel urged her through the door. "I have seen little outside my own walls and it will be good to venture further afield. I wonder if Maids-Of-The-Snow may be seen in the hedgerows for I have some in my garden here. I have so missed my garden at Tickhill. Do you like flowers, my lady?" Over the top of her head, she caught Gloucester's eye and the slightest gesture of thanks.

Isobel arrived home the following day having seen Anne safely installed in chambers fitted out for her comfort as Gloucester had promised, admired the cinnamon-coloured pup with soft, floppy ears Anne at once named Foxy, and had given her oath to the girl that she would return as soon as she was able. Once home, bursting to share her news, Isobel tip-tapped up the stairs leaving the rank smell of the streets behind and sought out Robert and Andrew.

To her surprise, she found them both asleep — Andrew in his cradle in the room he shared with Buena, and Robert sprawled upon their bed, shirt askew and one boot dangling from his foot. The room stank of stale ale and sweat.

"Rob?" She shook him by the shoulder. He didn't move. "Robert!" she said, louder this time. He grunted, belched in his stupor, but did not wake. Isobel stood with hands on hips contemplating the bedraggled scene in front of her. She turned smartly on her foot, went to the washstand, retrieved the bowl of hand-water ready there and threw the contents over her husband.

"What the...?" he spluttered, half-sitting, shaking water from his eyes which he instantly regretted. He put his hand to his head. "What did you do that for?" he complained, peering at her through one eye part-closed against the sun.

"You stink," Isobel said.

Robert rubbed a hand over his rough chin making the bristles rasp. "What hour is it?"

"What *day* more like — if you can remember."

"How...?" he began, stopped as he turned the colour of tripe, and lurched to the edge of the bed. Isobel thrust a bowl under his face just in time and left him to it.

Robert reappeared sometime later, clean-shaven and contrite. "It was necessary," he explained before Isobel could quiz him. "Gloucester wanted me to keep Clarence occupied and I did."

"By getting yourself into that state?"

"Well, yes. Clarence is a hard man to persuade and he had a mind to return early to L'Erber. I had to do something and I swore to Gloucester I would prevent his brother from intercepting him."

Isobel rolled her eyes. "Ah, of course — you drank yourself into a stupor out of *duty*."

Robert flinched at her acid tone. Or it might have been the ache in his head that threatened to shatter it to splinters. He held up a bandaged hand. "Peace, wife. What is done is done and no harm has come of it." He sensed her ease back a bit, so said, "What of your exploits? Did you succeed in the task set you?"

Appeased, she told him what had happened, adding, "Anne is a mouse of a thing. She seems ready to flee at the slightest provocation. I feel very sorry for her. I wonder…" She paused.

Robert parted the fingers protecting his eyes from the afternoon light sliding at an angle through the windows and peered at her. "What?"

"It is just that she is a little … well, naive in her ways — although very sweet-natured," she appended.

"What matter is that? Not all women can match you in wit and learning." If that was meant to mollify, it failed. He cleared his throat. "Are you saying she is not willing to wed Gloucester?"

"Oh no! No, not at all. Quite the reverse — she is both willing and eager. It is more that she is not someone I see His Grace … well, they are not *sympathia*. Do you see?"

"I see," he said slowly. He let out a cough, that became a grunt and then a laugh.

"Why does that amuse you?" Isobel said, put out.

Robert wiped his eyes with the back of his hand. "Sweetheart, Gloucester has all due regard for the lady, believe me, and for her estates. That is all the *sympathia* he requires. A match between them will give him the lands he desires and the basis of power he lacks."

Isobel frowned. "I thought the king refused the match; has he changed his mind?"

"The king," Robert said, leaning forwards and attempting to pick up the jug of milk and ale warming on the hearth, "would rather see the lady wed to his youngest brother and the lands secured, than either Clarence obtain them or others gain the benefit by marrying her."

Isobel whisked the jug from his hand. "What *others?*"

He pulled a face and reached for the jug.

She held it higher. "You shall have no ale until you tell me. What others would wed Anne?"

"You are a hard woman, Isobel Langton. All right, all right, the queen's kin, or those who serve them. Now, not a word more from your lips about this or any other of the king's business or Gloucester's. Understand? Good. Now give me that jug."

CHAPTER FIVE

One thing Isobel had not foreseen was the repercussion of her involvement in the disappearing of Anne Neville from the charge of the Duke of Clarence. And if her involvement, by default, her husband's as well. She did not see Lady Isabel until sometime later and at a crowded Court heated by late spring sun.

"George was furious," the duchess told Isobel. "He knew not whom to hold to account for Anne leaving, so blamed all."

Isobel noted the tell-tale signs of his fury in the fading yellowing mark the duchess tried to conceal. "I am so sorry," she told her, and meant it.

"It is nothing; I am used to his choler. He does not suspect your husband kept him distracted, nor that you had any part in Anne's abscondment."

"Does he not blame His Grace of Gloucester?" Isobel asked, somewhat surprised.

"I think he chooses not to. It is strange given what has passed between them — especially in recent years — but he is still protective of his younger brother. Sometimes he talks of the time they spent as children in exile. Their mother entrusted Richard's care to him, you see, and he bore the responsibility heavily. George has not said so, but I wonder whether he feels it still."

Isobel imagined a boy — torn from the protection of his family and thrust into an unfamiliar world where strangers spoke in an strange tongue — tasked with his younger brother's safety. Seen in this new light, her opinion of Clarence softened just a little. "It cannot have been easy; he was but a child himself."

"No, it was not," Lady Isabel concurred. "And I have to remind myself of it when he is in one of his rages."

And that cannot be easy for you, Isobel wanted to say; but that would overstep her station and presume too much of their friendship, so instead asked, "If not His Grace of Gloucester, then who?"

Lady Isabel had also been watching her husband, and now came back to the conversation with a little start. "Oh. Yes." She frowned. "He believes his enemies enticed her away. But then George always thinks he is beset by those who would see his downfall, whether it be true or no."

"Enemies?" Isobel asked.

Lady Isabel turned her shoulder to the room and, raising a kerchief to dab her lips, breathed, "*E.W.*", and when Isobel looked puzzled, clarified with a flick of a raised eyebrow, "The queen." She tucked the handkerchief back into the tiny purse at her waist. "*Betty*, he calls her, *Betty Bee*. He suspects she has informants in our household and in that he might be right. You never know whom to trust, do you? At least your husband is an honourable man and would do no such thing."

Isobel detected a question in the statement and, rather than dissemble, chose a noncommittal '*mmm*,' instead, and hoped Lady Isabel would not notice.

Not far from where they chatted in a pool of sunshine, Clarence stood head-to-head with an older man, his shoulders hunched as they discussed something that made the duke's face hard and tight.

"Although he may have an excess of yellow bile and is consumed by it," Lady Isabel continued, "it does not change the outcome, does it? Anne is married to Richard, and George will have to accept it. We all have to accept it," she said thoughtfully. "After all, Richard ceded much of her inheritance to George, so George has little to regret, even if others might."

Isobel's glance slipped to the dais where the king and queen held court: Edward sprawled long-limbed in his chair of state, cup in one hand, the other — big and heavily ringed — gesticulating to a group of young women and exchanging comments with a well-fed man leaning on the chair in which he lounged. Next to him, his queen pointedly ignored her husband's behaviour, choosing to play gracious host to a group of gentlemen Isobel did not recognise. The queen bent towards them in lavish attention, a neat hand flying to her mouth to cover laughter, bestowing smiles and nods at their conversation. They, in turn, warmed at her appreciation, their movements becoming looser as they relaxed in her company. And it seemed to Isobel that the queen wound favours around them, drawing them to her, spinning a web of subtlety into which they willingly wandered. A bee? Perhaps, but she reminded Isobel more of the golden spiders spanning the bushes in her garden awaiting their prey than the banded bees so busily about their labours amongst the flowers for the benefit of Man. The queen looked up and, noticing Isobel watching her, kinked a beckoning finger.

"Lady Langton, how do you fare? I thought to see more of you at Court, but I expect you have been diligent on your husband's behalf as befits a wife." The queen flicked a look in the direction of Lady Isabel. "Wait upon me on the morrow and you shall tell me what you have been up to."

"What *have* I been up to?" Isobel asked Robert that evening as the shutters closed against the night air and the distant sounds of the streets.

Robert picked up another scroll from the pile in front of him on the table. "Mmm?" He broke the seal and began reading.

"When the queen asks, what am I to say?" The contents of the letter were obviously more interesting than her predicament. "Rob," she poked his arm.

"In a moment, sweetheart." The moment came and went.

"Rob!" She plucked the offending paper from his hands.

"Isobel, I was reading that!" He reached for it but she held it beyond his grasp. "It is a matter of great import."

"And my matters are not? Advise me and it shall be returned." She dangled the letter with its shattered ruddy brown seal dangerously close to the fire, and he relented with a grunt.

"I do not see why it causes you so much concern. Tell her of your comings and goings as women do, you know — womanly affairs — and that sort of ... thing."

Exasperated, Isobel squeaked, "And what do I say when she asks me with whom I have visited and why? Shall I tell her, Rob, or merely dissemble?"

"Ah. I see what you mean." He thought, pulling at his top lip as he did so and reminding her sharply of his brother. "Avoid the subject of your visits to L'Erber and talk instead of ... gardens. Yes," he said looking relieved, "tell her about your garden."

"The queen has pleasances enough of her own; I doubt she will be interested in mine. I am of no great estate, have been nowhere, done little; what am I to her? What do I have to amuse her?" Isobel flopped onto the stool, the letter forgotten as she rested her chin on her hand. Robert took it from her loose grip before she dropped it.

"I find if I lack something to say about myself, I ask the other person about themselves. They are only too happy to oblige me with details about their life in which I have little interest, but which nonetheless sometimes proves useful. Ask the queen how the princes and princesses fare. There are enough of them; that should keep you busy."

Bright chatter emanated from behind the painted screens where Queen Elizabeth bathed and dressed. Occasionally, her voice cut through the higher tones of her attendants, a voice moderated by an attractive lilt making it melodic. Scents overlaid one another creating an atmosphere redolent of exotic realms and faraway places of which Isobel had but dreamed: spices and flowers and the undertones of warmed water, damp linen, wet stone. The queen's chambers in the palace were set fair with wall-hung arras of vivid-hued hounds and hunting parties, and decorated hangings with flaming suns in gold thread upon which nestled roses in purest white. There could be no doubt whose queen this was, nor — judging by the interwoven 'E's embroidered on every cushion and on the curtained bed — to whom this queen lay claim. A stamp of authority. A seal. A promise.

In large chests — the lids lying open against the wall — gowns of luscious colours woven with gold or silver and scattered with stones and pearls, lay in soft folds interspersed with sheets of linen and bagged herbs to protect them. Waiting anxiously beyond the circle of intimacy that surrounded the queen, Isobel wondered if this is what great ladies did: boldly make their husbands' marks in thread and paint and, in doing so, their own anchor. She thought back to her mother but couldn't remember her fashioning Geoffrey Fenton's newly acquired arms on anything. Perhaps, she considered ruefully, that wasn't so surprising given the circumstances of their marriage. No, not marriage — bigamy. Isobel swallowed the bile that rose unwanted in her gullet, her throat already tight with nerves. Did the shame of her birth show? Could people tell?

"Lady Langton!"

Jerked from her introspection, Isobel began to make her curtesy only to be stopped by the queen. A sleeveless furred gown covered her nakedness but not her advanced state of pregnancy. "Rise, rise. Come, my lady, and tell me how you do? Bess, fetch a cup and some wine; Lady Langton needs to be fortified, she looks a little pale. Surely you are not so because of me? Why, I see that it is so. Ladies, as I am the cause of Lady Langton's discomfort, let me also be the remedy of it. Come, sup your wine. There, drink a little more; it will give you courage. As you can see," the queen said, indicating the open chests, "we prepare to depart for Winchester for my lying-in. The air from the river is less foul there. Have you been to Winchester, Lady Langton?"

"No, Your Grace."

"It has a fair aspect. Perhaps I will have you wait upon me there. Now, come, tell me about yourself."

Standing in front of the queen, in whose fragrant aura she felt almost trapped, Isobel had not expected this degree of attention, and was unprepared. She accepted the second full cup from the young woman she recognised, with a shock, as Elizabeth Dalton — the late Earl's eldest daughter. Isobel held the cup in both hands lest it spill, and drank as bidden, feeling it progress down her gullet and warm her stomach. "Your Grace honours me." The queen smiled her acknowledgement. "But I fear that there is little about myself that might amuse you."

"Did I ask to be amused?"

"I ...no … well…" Isobel cleared her throat and remembered Robert's counsel of the previous day. "Might I enquire after the health of their Graces, Prince Edward, Princess Elizabeth, Princesses Cecily and Mary? My own son, Andrew, is about the same age as His Highness, Prince Edward." She came to a halt under the queen's gaze and it occurred to her that the woman believed Andrew to be the Earl's bastard son and as such, not worthy of mention in the same breath as the royal offspring. "I … I wish their Graces good health and will pray the Blessed Virgin keep them so."

"Indeed."

"And His Grace the King, also. And Your Grace keeps good health?" Isobel cringed internally as she babbled under the calm eyes of the queen, who kept her gaze fixed on Isobel's face. "Your Grace … is … blessed with health in your *maternité*?"

A little gasp came from one of the nearby ladies, then a titter. A muscle in the queen's cheek twitched.

"Lady Langton, you are too kind in your enquiry; I am certain it is well meant." The queen smiled, or at least, her mouth moved into a tight, upward curve. "However, pray you, tell me about yourself, as instructed."

This wasn't going as planned. Isobel took a sip of her wine, and then another. "I, um, I like to tend my garden, Your Grace…"

Sniggers ran around the room.

"Yes?"

"Yes, and … and … my son is teething. He makes such a fuss!" Isobel laughed but it came out as a nervous bray. She took a hasty gulp of wine.

"And what of your husband?"

"Oh, he fusses too! I mean, I say so only in jest. He is not really teething." She giggled, spilling wine. The room became stiflingly quiet. Someone coughed. Isobel's guts writhed, irritated by the strong wine and muscles tensed and ready to flee. "Your Grace," she said, breathing slowly and sobering enough to say, "what is it you wish to know?"

Queen Elizabeth arched one delicate eyebrow. She raised a hand and waved her ladies away and out of earshot. "I wish, Lady Langton, to enquire after the society you keep. In your position, I consider it important — nay, imperative — to forge attachments with those who reflect well upon your noble husband."

In *her* position? What, as the former mistress to her husband's brother? Or as bastard to a bigamous father? Thankfully, the queen had taken to examining the newly gilded angels acting as corbels to the delicate tracery of the ceiling and did not see the panic Isobel quickly extinguished.

"It is a wife's duty to do all she can to support her husband in his affairs, do you not agree?" the queen continued.

Isobel nodded — a little too vigorously. Wine slopped over her russet gown, staining it bloody. She covered it with her hand.

"So that he, in turn, may serve his liege lord. The king," the queen added in case Isobel hadn't realised. "The king — before all others — as is *his* duty." The queen looked at her directly. "Take a care to consider what acquaintances you make, my lady. Choose well and you will find yourself rewarded. Ill-wise, and … well, let me leave that to your conscience. For it is God's will that we serve the king, who is God's appointed servant in this world, and those that serve the king serve me — for I am the foremost and the least of his subjects." She inclined her head, then sighed, inhaled, and smiled with a radiance that dazzled. She beckoned Isobel closer and briefly — oh, so briefly, like the merest touch of a wing — laid her hand on Isobel's arm. "I know you are my friend in this; let me also be like a mother to you and counsel you. Now, tell me, what friendships have you struck since coming to Court?" She bent her graceful neck so that her pearl earring dangled but a finger's breadth from Isobel's mouth.

"I ... know of no one —"

The queen's head whipped around, a finger to her lips. "Say not another word unless it be nothing but the truth." She placed the palm of her hand upon her breast, her brows furrowed as if in pain. "Oh! But it grieves me so when false words are spoken!"

Alarmed, Isobel stuttered a denial, "Madam ... I —"

"Yes? Ah." The queen sat back, resting her hands on her swollen belly and slowly nodded. "I understand. You need say no more for I doubt not your discretion in matters that concern Lord Robert. Your devotion to your husband does you credit. He bids you keep silent and you must obey."

Heat flared up Isobel's neck. "Your Grace, Robert has done nothing that requires my silence!" But that wasn't strictly true, was it? The flame in her cheeks cooled to a cold film of sweat. Isobel placed the cup to one side before she spilled any more, and clasped her hands in front of her willing her heart to stop the pounding that threatened to deafen her and fill the whole room with her confusion. "That is, my lady, nothing that might be of interest."

"Let me be judge of that." The queen continued to smile, but her eyes had narrowed fractionally and she had become still, as if waiting for some revelation of conspiracy — collusion, *plot*.

"The Duchess of Clarence..."

"Yes?"

"Kindly granted me view of her gardens."

"Go on."

"They are very fine."

"And?"

"And Her Grace indulged me by saying I might have some slips of plants come spring." Isobel took the plunge. "Would Your Grace … I mean, if it please you … might I be permitted to see the gardens here?" Isobel's comment must have confirmed her status of audacious, ill-mannered stupidity, for the queen looked away, lips tightly pressed together. "For there can be none as fair in all the land, Your Grace, and there is much I can learn." That might have gone a little way to ameliorate her in the eyes of the queen. "Although, I cannot hope to recreate such renowned perfection."

"Perfection? Who talks of perfection?"

"Why, Her Grace of Clarence, Madam. She greatly admires the artifice of the fountains."

"And of what else did you speak?"

"Well…" Isobel looked at her hands and mumbled something.

"What's that? Speak up, girl!"

"I was minded to ask her … should it come to pass —"

"*What?*" The queen's composure cracked a fraction.

"If Her Grace thought that I might request … nay, be permitted … to have one scion of the lily from the Papal gardens gifted by His Holiness the Pope to Your Highness?" Isobel rushed all at once, slipping to her knees before the queen had time to respond. "Please forgive my boldness, but the lily will bring such a blessing upon my garden in remembrance of the Virgin and to all who tarry there under her eye. I have a mind to erect a shrine in her reverence; and the lily, should I be granted the honour, will bring such grace to my humble pleasance." Isobel remained on her knees with her head bent, awaiting condemnation but — more terrifying than that — further interrogation. No one spoke in the room. And then a noise — choked off, suppressed.

"A slip of lily! You dare presume to ask the queen of England for a slip of lily?" The queen laughed again, this time with an edge. "I know not whether to censure you for your impudence or be charmed by your innocence! A scion of lily indeed!" She paused, and then said in a low voice, "And this the sum of your conversation while at Court?"

"I like to husband my garden, Your Grace," Isobel whispered to the floor and wishing she were there now, tilling honest soil, while sniggers erupted all around her.

The queen said nothing but held out an arm, still damp from her bath, to be patted dry by one of her ladies. An aromatic paste with hints of sage and mint was massaged into the skin, and the process repeated for the other. From where she still knelt, Isobel inhaled refreshing wormwood: it would block the pores from which headlice would erupt and inhabit the hair. Without thinking, she raised her head to be met with the hard eyes of the queen, quickly veiled and softened with a smile. Isobel blinked, not certain of what she had seen.

"Come, stand, Lady Langton. The wine speaks for itself, does it not? It makes fools of our tongues and incautious our speech."

Better be thought a fool than accused of malice, Isobel thought, although that brought little comfort. Eyes of the queen's attendants shredded her like knives — all no doubt gently born, all the legitimate daughters of noble sires, of marriages consecrated and lawful. She should not be here; she did not belong.

Isobel started to retreat backwards, but bumped up against something soft with edges that moved. Elizabeth Dalton elbowed past her, and Isobel heard *whore* slide from between the young woman's lips. She made a show of rearranging cushions and the queen leant against them, her long fair hair falling over the back of the chair. Then Bess began to run a fine-toothed comb through the strands, scowling at Isobel now and again when she thought the queen couldn't see. She stopped suddenly, using a pinching motion to nip something off the comb and crush it between her nails, before continuing.

"Did you find one?" the queen asked.

"Your Grace's hair is most clean," Bess simpered. "There are no hair worms today."

"That is strange," the queen said, settling her head back again, "for I am certain I felt one before my bath."

"I am sure there are none, Madam." Bess caught Isobel looking askance and scowled at her, giving the comb a tug at the same time.

"Stupid girl!"

Bess coloured. "Madam, forgive me —!"

"Leave it. Give the comb to me." The queen snatched the comb from Bess's hands, and held it out to Isobel. "Lady Langton will do it."

Hands shaking, Isobel took the exquisite ivory and gold comb from the queen, avoiding the glares Bess now openly gave her. Double sided with wide and narrow teeth, the comb bore scenes of lovers under a spreading tree with elaborate EEs growing from the branches entwining the naked couple. The unashamed intimacy made Isobel blush and she covered her embarrassment by setting to the task. The comb caught and snagged on the fine hair. Queen Elizabeth flinched. Isobel tried again but with the same result. "Your Grace, if I might suggest…?"

"Go on."

"My servant prepares an oil for my hair. It makes it easier to comb and prevents hair worms. It is a powerful remedy."

The queen looked over her shoulder. "Can you make it?"

"Yes, Highness."

"Then pray, do so, and let us see if you are more able to number the lice in my hair than Lady Dalton and perhaps, in doing so, might better recall the friendships you have recently forged."

The fog that previously clouded her judgement now beginning to clear, Isobel made a non-committal noise and concentrated on concocting the fragrant oil from the ingredients swiftly assembled before her. Then, carefully, she combed it through the queen's hair, removing lice and their offspring much as she suspected the queen would like to do to those she suspected of infesting the realm.

When at last she was permitted to leave, Isobel passed a small room, the door of which had been left ajar. She caught the sense of movement in the dim light beyond, and an aroma — thick, floral, choking — wafted through the opening. She stopped, her throat constricting and taking her in an instant to the dark days of the Earl and the unmistakable scent of his wife.

Felice Langton had caught snippets of the exchange between Queen Elizabeth and the Fenton girl. She couldn't bring herself to think of her as a countess — *the* countess — but they had their backs to the pallet room where she concealed herself and much detail of their conversation was lost into the high-ceilinged chamber. What had the Fenton whore asked of the queen? What secrets did she share? What lies?

"Bess!" she hissed as her daughter came into the room.

"Ma Mere!" Bess looked up, her eyes still damp. "What are you doing in here?"

Felice reached out and pulled her daughter further into the pallet room and shut the door. "You let that girl make a fool out of you! What did she say? What did she want?"

"Who? Ma Mere, you look very strange —"

"The Fenton wench — what did she say to the queen? Think, Bess, of what did they speak?"

"I … I could not hear all…" She blenched as her mother scoured her with a look she normally reserved for recalcitrant servants, "but I heard mention of the Duchess of Clarence."

"What of her?"

Seeing she had piqued her mother's interest at the expense of her spleen, Bess brightened, forgetting her recent tears. "I think she made a request of Her Grace, a favour…" Her mother's face darkened. "I am not certain…"

"What favour, Bess? Tell me!"

"Ow! Ma Mere, you are pinching me!" Felice released her daughter's arm. "She said something about His Holiness the Pope. Yes, that was it." She smiled hopefully, rubbing her arm.

Nostrils flaring and with eyes stark and wide, Felice took a step back. "You are certain of this?" Bess nodded. "What does it mean? What does it mean?" Felice muttered, breaking away and beginning to pace the length of the small room and shaking her head to and fro as she talked to herself.

"Ma Mere?" Bess ventured. "May I take my leave?"

"Hmm? Yes, yes, you are dismissed." Felice waved a vague hand in Bess's direction without looking up. Had she done so, she would have seen her daughter's face and the concern written upon it.

The Duchess of Clarence? The Pope? A favour from none other than the queen? What did it mean and why was the Fenton girl involved? Did she seek something only His Holiness might grant? An annulment? No! Affirmation. That must be it. Did the girl look for affirmation of her brat's legitimacy? Would she have the boy made *heir*? Her skin became clammy, her breathing halt. If Robert Langton adopted the child might he seek his legitimacy and remove her last hope of her own son becoming earl one day?

Her thoughts were interrupted by voices nearing from the queen's chamber. Pursued by the questions crowding her mind, Felice let herself out of the pallet room through the servants' door and headed for narrow stairs that would lead her to the courtyard and thence from the Palace of Westminster, through knotted streets, to the several mean rooms she was obliged to call home.

CHAPTER SIX

In the innermost sanctum of the palace pleasance, the great urn stood swaddled in sacking secured by thick, hairy twine from which an oily odour arose. Queen Elizabeth did not find it unpleasant; it reminded her of simpler days and of the barns where her boys played as babes when their father still lived, and before she had met her present husband, the sire of the child she now carried. She shivered, but not from the chill air, but the tight, fluttering pleasure that made her loins quiver. She — Elizabeth Grey, widow — had secured the king of England against all opposition and overcome. Warwick; Clarence; Henry the Feeble; Edward, his brat — how the mighty had been brought to their knees before her, a mere woman, the *queen*. She permitted the edge of her lip to rise in satisfaction, the frisson of victory to flood her womb with a swelling pride. The sharp, bright song of a robin broke her thoughts and she crossed herself thrice lest it leave a malevolent spirit to haunt her unborn child. "Be gone!" She threw a loose chipping of stone at the bird and it flew away to a farther branch to scold her. There could be no time for complacency. With one battle won there would always be another to fight, and it was her turn to make the next move.

With care, she parted the folds of cloth covering the urn to reveal strands of silvered straw through which the first green spire thrust its head from the refuge of the soil. Here was proof, if any were needed, of the blessing conferred upon her by His Holiness the Pope. Her plans would prosper; they could not fail. Seeing the lily reminded her of her recent conversation with the Langton girl. She had thought to nurture her, make her useful, for what other purpose could there be than to serve her queen? However, she had found the girl disappointing.

Elizabeth clicked her tongue. No, there was something else. She stroked the side of the new shoot, considering. At first she had believed the girl to be little more than a simpleton, but doubt then prickled. Was her naivety merely a cover for a sharper wit — one that sought to play the fool at her expense? What did the girl want? More importantly, what did she have to offer? Out of context, little that she could discern; but within a wider perspective, perhaps more. Isobel Langton had struck some sort of friendship with the Duchess of Clarence, of that she was certain, and how far it went she had yet to discover. But she would; she had the means to do so. And then? The Langton girl might prove useful after all: a slip — like this lily — in the very heart of the Clarence household.

The queen snapped her fingers and her ladies came running. "Bess, have the Head Gardener fetched." She watched the young woman hurry away as fast as her heavy gowns allowed, her slippered feet sliding a little on the cobbles and wondered at the twists of fate that brought the Langton family across her path.

Robert peered over Isobel's shoulder at the little box on the table. "What is it?"

"It is from the queen."

Robert noted the bored royal messenger waiting nearby scratching his buttock through his parti-coloured hose. "So I see. But *what* is it?"

From its cocoon of white linen and straw in which it had lain, Isobel carefully removed the papery-skinned nodule. "This," she said, holding it with reverence in the palm of her hand, "is a scion of the lily growing in the Papal gardens."

Robert raised a quizzical brow. "It looks like an onion."

"It looks like a *holy* onion," she corrected, laying the small bulb back in its protective wrapping, "and the queen has gifted it to me."

"So, she must have believed you after all," he said under his breath and kissing her earlobe. "I wonder what she wants?"

Wants? That was a good question. As Isobel carefully packed the lily into the box padded with wool scrap, she pondered the gift and what lay behind it, because, if she had learned anything from being at Court these last months, everybody wants something; the issue was, who wants what and what would it cost her?

Felice joined the other women in the queen's antechamber, a score or so varying in age and estates, seeking audience with Queen Elizabeth and preference for themselves and their families. Anyone who had Her Highness's ear hoped it might be a shortcut to the king. Some, Felice knew, had tried a more direct approach. She was astounded that, having tried to catch the king's eye, they had the audacity to approach his queen. Even if he had found her flesh appealing as he might once have done, Felice had more to offer than *that*. She had made subtle enquiry and discovered little except that the Fenton girl spent many hours in the company of the Duchess of Clarence and that, in itself, she believed significant. So, too, was the news that Robert Langton had secured several manors and associated offices in an area not far from her own dower lands. Felice had knowledge of the widow Halton whose land had now passed to the earl. *Earl*. She almost spat the word but restrained the desire in a little grunt instead. The woman waiting next to her gave her a swift glance and Felice made show of a delicate cough to disguise her outburst. Earl — but for how long?

The door to the queen's chamber finally opened and the women outside looked towards it in anticipation, only to be disappointed when a servant walked past without paying them heed. Felice had spoken to the widow — a respectable woman whose late husband had connection with Richard Neville. George Clarence now profited from Warwick's long-standing relationships in the area of influence. Or at least, he tried to. It was notable that Clarence struggled to maintain order among a number of the gentry, whose petty feuds broke out into violence now and then, requiring the intervention of the king to bring peace where his brother failed. Perhaps that was why Clarence had secured the widow's manors for Robert Langton, to extend his influence — or maintain it — hoping to benefit from the strength of Langton associations to bolster his own, failing bonds. William never had that problem among his affinity.

Jasmine — the last she had been able to afford and now faintly stale — wafted from the folds of her light linen headdress as she jerked her head. Almost immediately she stilled the movement into her habitual impassivity, but the woman next to her shuffled a step away and turned her shoulder. Felice sought justice for herself and for her son, who had been robbed of his rightful inheritance by his father's bigamy. If bigamy it indeed had been, for who now was alive to swear to his marriage to the whore's dam?

Felice's feet ached, her back cramped, and sweat gathered beneath her arms. She should be shown greater respect than this — waiting in an ante-chamber with women fallen from favour or yet seeking to rise. If her husband were alive... But he was neither alive nor her husband. He carried his secret to his grave, but who else knew? William's harlot, of course; Robert Langton — almost certainly. Master Secretary, Nicolas Sawcliffe? Hmm, perhaps. She had told no one and was certain Robert and the Fenton strumpet would not, for it made the girl a bastard as well as a whore.

A hopeful hush fell on the ante-chamber interrupting her thoughts. Head bowed before the queen, her calves aching from the depth of the curtsey she felt obliged to make, Felice waited to be given permission to rise. The queen continued chatting to one of her ladies and Felice wondered whether she even realised she was there. She made the slightest noise in her throat.

"Madam," the queen said at last. "Rise."

The queen gave a small *hurrumph* of annoyance. "This is thrice now you have petitioned me on the same matter, madam, and thrice have I made the same answer: His Grace has given due consideration to your plea and will not hear your case again. If you have nothing more to say, I bid you good day." She turned her face and beckoned to an attendant. The next woman was already curtseying and beginning to make her plea when Felice pushed her out of the way resulting in a squawk of protest.

"I have information, Your Highness."

"You promised me that before and gave me nothing of substance."

"This time, Your Highness, there is something I am certain will be of interest, and," she added in an undertone, "I have a *confidant* close to the source who will supply more."

"Close? How close?"

"An intimate, Your Grace." If this stretched the truth it was only by a little. "One who sees and hears all. Pardon my

102

presumption and allow me to supply you with such evidence as serves the King's Highness."

The queen beckoned her closer and, levelling her eyes and her voice, captured Felice in the web of her stare. "Make certain of it and I will not forget this service. Falsify your intelligence to obtain my favour, and you will know the depth of my wrath."

Weeks later, drops of shining water hung for a moment on each blade as the oars of the boat carrying Isobel to the palace rose and dipped into the river. Fresh leaves burst the confines of their buds and the banks hummed with bees and hoverflies amid the frothy white heads of angelica and celery and tall-stemmed grasses where cattle grazed near the water's edge. The air was colder by degrees here on the water and the current was with them taking Isobel ever closer towards Westminster. How she wished she was back in her own domain surrounded by familiar faces and recognisable landscape. She drowned under the squeezed sky and sullen smoked houses of the narrow streets where she fought for air. Here, on the water, was an altogether different aspect and, if she did not relish the prospect of talking with the queen, she could at least escape the suffocating atmosphere of London. Surrounded by the sounds of water and distanced from the all-pervading streets. Isobel rehearsed what she believed the queen wanted to hear.

Crowding the riverbank, the palace walls stamped their authority. The oars were withdrawn and the boat slid neatly into dock where a beet-faced man wearing the livery of the royal house and a scowl, stooped to help Isobel and her servant onto dark, slippery planks warped with age and use.

She was still mentally preparing her report when she arrived at the queen's apartments, hearing the now familiar hum of female attendants and the more distant drone of men. Among the hubbub she picked out another voice. Isobel stopped dead in her tracks, her servant almost running into her.

"My lady…?"

"Shhh," Isobel said sharply, stretching her ears to catch the faintest sound. There it was again — closer than before. Her heart compressed, squeezing up her throat and nearly choking her. "Move!" she said, beginning to pivot towards the way they had come. Around the corner, words whipping some unfortunate as yet unseen, came Felice Langton. Isobel froze. Stay, and there would be no avoiding the woman. Leave, and it would look like retreat, and Isobel would do anything to avoid *that*. Still directing vitriol at someone behind her, Felice hadn't seen Isobel standing like the stump of a tree in her path. She looked around and her expression changed from ire to surprise and then to venom in swift succession. She came to an abrupt halt. Neither woman moved.

"Give way," Felice snapped. Isobel stood her ground, and Felice moved forwards. "Get out of my way!"

Isobel said nothing, planting her feet and squaring her shoulders.

The woman's lips writhed wordlessly. Then, in a slow exhalation, "*Whore*."

A small hand grasped Felice's gown. "Ma Mere!" and a girl appeared from behind the woman.

Isobel rocked on her feet. "Cecily!" The girl looked around, eyes widening in recognition. "Cecily, it is me — Is'bel." She shook herself free of the anchoring ground, taking a step towards the child. Cecily remained rooted, dark eyes sunken and staring, the area beneath puffy. Only her oak brown hair — like her uncle's — seemed the same but pulled tight and confined beneath a stiff hennin. Not the Cecily Isobel had known; not the little girl she once was, but older — too old. "Cecily?" Isobel said, holding out her hand and hesitant, almost fearful now.

Drawing her daughter behind her, Felice looked at Isobel with contempt and, pushing roughly past, continued down the hallway and out of sight, leaving Isobel shaken and bereft.

"Ah, Lady Langton, there you are! It is some time since last we conversed — before my lying-in with Margaret, was it not? Now, I wish you to supply me with the unguent you used upon my hair. His Grace remarked upon it and I would fain see it shine as it did." The queen held out a length of wispy fair hair and viewed it with scorn. "Faith, but it is dry as grass."

Dull-voiced, Isobel answered, "It will be my honour to do so. Your Grace is to be congratulated on the birth; how fares the princess?"

Queen Elizabeth appraised Isobel with sharp eyes. "You look out of humour; do you ail?"

Isobel sat where indicated without meeting the queen's gaze. "I am quite well, Highness."

"Come, I know what my eyes tell me. Speak, say your say."

The power of thought and speech eluded her. All Isobel could see were Cecily's eyes staring from an ashen face, becoming bigger, burning orbs of accusation and hurt. The queen waited. Isobel began to form words, faltered, tried again. She was aware of the queen saying something, of the murmured queries from her ladies; but the room had become faint, the perfumed air thick and heavy, and a thrumming drummed her ears, getting louder and more distinct until it became a voice that cried over out and over again, '*Is'bel*.'

Feeling suddenly nauseous, Isobel leapt from her stool sending the cushion tumbling. "Forgive me," she said and rushed from the room with her hand over her mouth.

Master Secretary Nicholas Sawcliffe raised a neatly trimmed brow in a manner Isobel always found irritating.

"Do I make my instruction clear?" she asked him. "I want information on Felice Langton. Where she resides, her movements, anything that might be of interest."

Clutching both manicured hands close to his chest, Sawcliffe now opened them in a way meant to placate. "My lady, as you command. However —"

She tapped one foot. "What is it?"

"I require ready coin. You understand that such information will take a certain amount of *delicate* ... persuasion?"

Isobel dropped a small, heavy bag into his hands. "That much?"

Bowing his dark head, he tucked the bag into the purse at his waist without looking at it. "I will report as soon as I have intelligence, my lady."

He left the room leaving the heavy scent of clove and a distinct feeling of unease in his wake. She didn't like setting him to find information, but then that was what the Earl had used him for and now her husband, also. It was expected. The unseen world of secrets and spies, smoke and shadows and footsteps in the dark. She shuddered and sought out her garden to cleanse her mind and spirit.

Sawcliffe returned sooner than anticipated. "The lady," he said, careful to avoid using Felice's former title, "lodges with her son and daughter and two servants." He waited for Isobel's response. When she didn't, he offered, "My lady might wish to know the quality of her abode?"

"Mmm? Oh, yes. Tell me."

"The lady about whom you enquire takes two rooms on the middle floor. She and her son sleep in one; the girl and the servants in the other. The lower floor is taken by a widow and her cat. It is from the widow that the lady rents the rooms for a small sum. The rooms on the top floor are occupied by the wife of a ship's master and their six children." He paused. "I say *their* children, but I believe that at least one has a different sire. It is of no import." He smiled. "After dining, the lady leaves her rooms and travels to church where she makes confession —"

"What, *every* day?"

Sawcliffe inclined his head. "The lady has a most regular habit; it makes things easier for me."

Isobel made a mental note to vary her routine.

"After confession, the lady repairs to Westminster where she waits for audience with Her Grace, the queen."

"*Every* day?" Isobel repeated. "What do the children do when she is gone?"

"If the lady does not take her son with her — which she does each Friday — she leaves both children in the care of the servants."

"And they stay in their lodgings?"

"If the weather is set fair, they will venture out. The servants like to visit on market days. It is my understanding that one has made an attachment to an apprentice — a weaver from Flanders, I believe. Not a suitable match for a lady's servant, but then the girl is of low birth and the lady of humble means."

Isobel couldn't care less if the servant formed an attachment with a donkey. "How close are the children watched?"

"My lady?"

"I believe you know my meaning well enough, Master Sawcliffe. Is there opportunity to remove a child from the watch of the servants or not?"

The secretary's normally impassive air cracked a little. "My lady, I would counsel against taking such action."

"I do not ask for your counsel, master, I request an answer to my question."

"The children — child — might be acquired with some little care; but, my lady, Lord Langton —"

"— is not to be told any of this, do you understand? What he does not know cannot be laid at his door." *And he cannot prevent it*, she might as well have added. "Very well. I will require a man I can trust."

"My lady, more than one will be needed."

"I intend to do this myself. I will also take one of my ladies with me, but I need a man to watch for us, that is all."

"Madam, I must protest! Such an action is foolhardy, nay, illegal."

"I am aware of the legality of the action, master, and as for *foolhardy*, am prepared to accept the consequences should any arise. But the child cannot be allowed to remain with the lady any longer. I cannot allow her to suffer. I *will* not."

Sawcliffe no longer smiled but looked quizzical, almost speculative, as if this was a side of Isobel he had not seen before. He bowed, his head inclined longer than was customary, before straightening and removing himself from Isobel's presence.

This was something about which she had thought long and hard: she owed it to Cecily; she owed it to herself.

The market teemed as the early summer sun drew people from their dwellings and into the narrow streets. Even dressed modestly, Isobel felt conspicuous in this quarter dominated by Flemish weavers and tradesmen with their strange accents that could almost be English, and their stranger clothes that definitely were not. She kept her hood over her head and wandered among the wives and maids milling about the stalls and shop fronts, while keeping ear and eye primed for two servant women and a little girl.

Waterfowl pined in wicker coops, and onions, leeks and green leaves wilted in baskets of willow. Dogs snuffled around the open-fronted shops, dried spiced sausages hung in long ropes or in loops, swinging like nooses in the light wind that made sunless cheeks glow. She caught glimpses of another world beyond the open workshop fronts and in the deep, dim interiors where apprentices laboured under their master's eye. Some took their ease seated on three-legged stools or leaning in open doorways, their restless eyes following the skirts of the women that passed.

"Keep close," Isobel warned Maud as she dawdled. The girl had been recommended to her as someone who had grown up within the walls of London and knew it well. Nonetheless, Isobel was thankful for Philip Taylor's stout presence just a few paces behind them. He had made his views on the matter clear but knew Isobel well enough not to try to dissuade her. She could hear him muttering to himself between the odd sniff; but that wouldn't detract from the effectiveness of his broad shoulders, nor the deterrent of the sword he carried. It was he who spotted Cecily first.

He touched Isobel's elbow and nodded in the direction of a striped awning and the small group beneath. A youth in weld-coloured hose whispered into a young servant woman's ear making her giggle, while the other — her back towards them — fingered bales of bright cloth and pretended not to notice.

Squinting in the strip of sunlight slanting at an angle, Cecily stood a little apart, watching pigeons on the rooftops high above their heads take flight into the blue. The second servant turned and Isobel muted an oath. It was Joan, and judging by the cast of her lip, she was saying something characteristically waspish to Cecily.

Heart pumping, Isobel said, "Follow me," and using the stalls as cover, started to make her way towards Cecily. Philip broke away, circling the marketplace but keeping Isobel and the maid in sight at all times. Marking the points of exit, Isobel came within calling distance of Cecily.

"Be ready," she whispered, looking over her shoulder only to find Maud hanging back. Isobel beckoned to the girl, but she did not move. Tutting to herself, Isobel looked for Cecily, thankful to see the child facing her, eyes towards the sky again. "Cecily!" she called as loudly as she dared. "Cecily!"

The little girl looked about for the source of her name and saw Isobel beside a stall of broken-necked fowl. Isobel beckoned urgently. "Come. Cecily, come!"

Cecily showed no signs of moving. Isobel took a swift look around her, then dashed to where the child stood, taking her by the hand and pulling her away. She looked for Maud to help, but stalls blocked her view. Philip, on the other hand, was heading determinedly in her direction when his head swivelled at the sound of a shout, and his hand went to his sword. Alarmed, Isobel followed his line of sight. A small group of armed men made their way towards her. With effort, Isobel picked up Cecily and turned to run.

A figure blocked her way. "An' where do you think you goin'?" A rough hand secured her arm with iron fingers. "I'll take the lass." The man removed Cecily, tucking her under one arm and hauling Isobel after him with the other.

"Let go!" Isobel said, trying to extricate herself from his grasp. "Do you know who I am?"

"Aye, I do — the wench who'd take someone else's lass. 'Ere, Sergeant!" he called as they neared a trio of watchmen. "This'll be the one, I'll warrant," and he threw Isobel stumbling towards the sergeant and set Cecily on her feet.

"This one yours?" the narrow-shouldered sergeant asked Isobel, surveying without emotion the bloodied faces of his men and the broken nose of another and, restrained between them, a barely subdued Philip Taylor.

"He is under my orders, yes," Isobel said, chin jutting. "Do him no harm and I will not report this assault."

The sergeant fingered his stubble. "You'll not, eh? Well, *my lady*, I have it under writ that you intend to abduct this girl and that, by my reckoning and the law's, is an act against the king's justice, and you know what that means, don't you?" He leaned close in, his breath reeking of ale and onions. "You'll be up before the King's Bench to answer to your crime."

"You will do no such thing! This child is my niece and has my protection."

"Is that right?" He knelt on one knee and spoke, not unkindly, to Cecily. "This lady your aunt, then, lassy? Do you know her?"

Cecily continued to stare at the straw-strewn cobbles.

"Cecily, tell the sergeant who I am," Isobel said.

A crowd had gathered to watch and Joan now pushed through them with noisy protestations and accusations of child-abduction. Up close, the skin of her round face appeared webbed by fine red threads, but her eyes spat spite much as they had always done. She grasped Cecily to her ample chest. "My poor chick!" she wailed. "Taken right from under my nose! What will her lady dam say? What will she say?"

"That ye weren't doing your job o' watchin'," the sergeant said caustically. "This lady says the girl's her kin. What would she be about making such claims if there's no truth to it, eh?"

"It's true enough," Philip interjected. "If you ask me —"

"I'm not. Keep yer peace or it'll be kept for thee. Now then," the sergeant continued, turning back to Isobel, "what call do you have on the lass if the girl has her dam, eh? Tell me that."

Isobel managed to pull her wits into some order. "Cecily used to live with me; she was my…" she couldn't think of any better way of putting it, "….ward, but I… er, I … lost her."

"That's mighty careless of ye," he said dryly, raising laughter from the gaggle of faces pressing close about them to catch the drama.

"She's lying!" Joan said, shrilly, wagging her finger in Isobel's face close enough that Isobel was tempted to bite it. "Lady Felice said so. She said the whore'd say as much and not to believe her!".

"Now, watch yer jangling tongue, girl," the sergeant said, "or ye'll find yerself facing charges an' all." Placing his hands on his skinny hips, he looked first at Cecily and then at Isobel. "I don't know what this is about, but I don't like havin' me ropes plucked nor the Courts have their time wasted. We'll have this out with thy mistress," he said to Joan. "Take us to her."

The manner of dress of the woman in front of them belied the shabby room in which they now stood. Felice held a fair-haired child, little more than Andrew's age, awkwardly in her arms and viewed the sergeant with disdain. "Am I to understand that this … *abductress* has yet to be arrested? Do your duty and see to it."

"That I would, mistress … my lady," he amended rapidly as her eyes flared, "but she claims wardship of the lass, and —"

"She has no such claim," Felice retorted. "The strumpet lies; she should be brought before the magistrates and whipped. She would have removed my daughter from her mother's care." Felice placed a hand on Cecily's head, but the girl ducked away from her touch. "See how she cowers! What did the woman do?" A snort of incredulity escaped Isobel, and Felice pointed at her. "Look how she makes mockery of the law. I shall bring this to the attention of the queen's Grace when next I am at Court."

The mention of the queen had the sergeant visibly start, giving Isobel the chance to say, "Why *are* you not at Court, Felice? Is Friday not the day when you visit?" She marked the flash of surprise cross Felice's face, quickly followed by suspicion. She must have wondered how Isobel had come across such information. And then something else occurred to Isobel, something that made the last hour insignificant by comparison: if Felice had suspected — if she had *anticipated* — Isobel's attempt to take Cecily that day, who, in Heaven's name, had told her? She felt her face pale and her hands become clammy and was sure Felice noted it too.

"Sergeant, this is a dispute between the lady and myself; let us dispatch it privily for it has bearing only upon ourselves. No crime has been committed. Let the matter rest, I pray you."

"You think to avoid prosecution?" Felice addressed her directly for the first time, the child in her arms forgotten. "I will see you punished; I will see you humbled and returned to the state from whence you came." She moved closer, her features magnified, eyes pools of bitterness, lips drawn into a thin, hard line as she hissed, "I will ensure that you and your dam are remembered for the base-born harlots you were — you *are*." The boy began to cry and squirm and Felice thrust him at the younger servant. "Leave us, and take Cecily with you."

Free of the encumbrance of the child, Felice aimed a sharp finger at Isobel's chest. "Your infamy will follow you wherever you go; you will have nowhere left to hide." She gave a particularly vicious prod, enough to send Isobel stumbling backwards.

"Hey, that is enough now!" Crossing the room, the sergeant placed a restraining hand on Felice's arm. She spun around.

"Take your hog hand from me, you lazard!" And then back to face Isobel. "The queen will know who you *really* are."

Regaining her footing and mustering her resolve, Isobel planted herself squarely in front of Felice. She was not that girl — new to the castle — quaking with fear at the countess's feet. She was not her subordinate and she was *not* going to be bullied.

"In which case *all* things will become clear. All. Things," she emphasised. "For I will have nothing to lose, Felice, and you — *everything*." Moments passed in which Isobel's heart pumped fury through her veins and Felice's colour flared and waned.

Isobel saw her meaning had hit home. "I believe, sergeant, that we have the basis for accord." She waited for Felice's reluctant nod of agreement.

The sergeant grunted and shook his head and left the two women alone in the wretched room. Letting her temper cool and buying time in which to think, Isobel went to the narrow horn-glazed window through which hazy light smouldered. She held her palm to the muted luminosity, seeing her skin glow.

"What do you want?" Felice said to her back.

Isobel turned her hand over and the light caught the blue stone in the ring Robert had given her in token of their marriage.

"Do not presume to play games with me, girl! What do you want?"

Isobel thought of all the times she had been in awe of this woman ... no, not awe, fear. Fear and dread — of who she was, what she could do, and the power she represented. Now that she saw her here, in this room, she realised just how diminished she had become, not just in her estate, but in herself — shrunken and shrivelled and withered inside.

"I want Cecily to live with us. I want her to have everything she should have had —"

"*You* took that away from her when my husband's brother stole my son's inheritance!"

"— the approval, the recognition, the *affection* she should have and which she lacks. She will be as a daughter to us and a sister to our children. That is what I want, Felice, nothing more."

"I can break you; I can take everything from you as you have taken from me — my title, my estates, my *name*. With a single word I can bring you down and crush you ... crush you." She ground her heel into the worn surface of the floor.

"Then why haven't you?" Isobel saw a wariness replace Felice's scorn. "Madam, you can bring me to ruin; you can condemn me in the eyes of the world; but I vow that my fall will bring about your own doom because, whether you wish it or no, our fates are entwined."

"My son should be Earl—"

"Robert is Earl and he will continue to be so, and our son after him. I did not look for this; I did not wish to be Countess, but Fortune has made it so and I will not see Robert, or our son or Cecily harmed. If you speak out, so will I, and what hope have you in securing any future for your son then?"

"Do you think I believe you would risk all to discredit *me*?"

"If you give me no choice. But there is another way: let Cecily bide with us. Let her be happy and have a future. Think on it, Felice — Robert will find a good match for her and provide a generous dowry."

"Since I cannot?" Her features soured. "No, you shall not have her."

Isobel could see it written all over the woman's face. She would deny her because she could. It was her little triumph, her mean victory. Cold despondency doused the slight hope Isobel had maintained that, somehow, Felice would listen to reason and seek a better future for her daughter.

There was nothing more to say. Isobel pulled the hood back over her head and her cloak around her and prepared to leave. At the door to the room, she stopped. "How much, Felice?" She turned around. "What will it take to persuade you to let Cecily go?" On seeing the calculation in the woman's eyes, Isobel said quickly, "A manor; I will give you a manor for Cecily. If you agree — now — I will have the contract drawn up and the lands released to you immediately."

Felice observed Isobel through shrewd eyes. "Which one?"

Isobel grasped the name from thin air. "Hamden," she said. "I will give you the manor of Hamden in exchange for Cecily."

"Hamden," Felice said slowly. Then, with a decisive flick of her hand. "Have the papers made up and brought before witness forthwith, and you shall have the girl."

"No, I shall take her now."

Felice hesitated and then gave a small shift of her shoulders. "Very well. The girl is nothing but vexation. Take her, if you so wish; she is nothing to me." Holding out her hand, Felice examined her nails with a slight frown. Then seeing Isobel still in the doorway, said, "You may go," and turned her back.

*

"You did *what?*"

Isobel began to explain once again what she had done but was stopped by her husband, incandescent, holding his hands over his ears. "Hamden. What did you think you were doing? *Hamden!* Do you know what it took to secure that manor? Why did you not come to me first? No, no, do not answer me. Why would you come to your lord and husband — the one you trust and to whom you owe natural allegiance? Mmm? Answer me *that!*" Placing his hands behind his head and looking at the ceiling as he strode in angry circles around the chamber, he swore again. He ceased striding and instead aimed a kick at the table leg making the silver cup jump and the vase fall, spilling stems and flowers in a flood over the surface and onto the floor. "This will make me the fool of Court!"

"I did not know you cared so much about what others think of you."

"Care? It is not that I care but I have our family name to uphold — part of whose estates you have discarded with little thought and no authority."

She pushed at an unopened flower bud with the toe of her shoe, fighting guilt. "Exchanged. For Cecily. I thought you would approve."

"No, Isobel, you did not *think*; you merely acted without thought of the consequence. And stop sulking; it does not become your station."

"And now you are quick to judge me! Am I so reduced in your eyes that you must refer to my *station?* What is that, Robert — what is *my station?*"

"Do not be so childish. You have transgressed, now take the rebuke."

"I did it for Cecily —"

A brief knock preceded the door swinging open and one of the grooms of the chamber appeared bearing a cloth covered jug. "Get out!" Robert barked, and the man bobbed out again, but not before Isobel caught the briefest glimpse of Cecily and Maud waiting white-faced beyond. "For Cecily? Did you? Really? You did it for yourself. I know how long you have harboured regret at leaving her behind when William died. The guilt is graven on your soul every time you mention her name."

Isobel's eyes jerked wide and she gulped air, resisting tears of resentment and denial. "I ... I did not do this for me. Robert, look at me. I did not do this because of my guilt. I did not want to leave her behind, but I had no other choice. I want her to be as happy as she was when she lived when ... when..."

"William was still alive?"

"Yes," she said softly. "When he lived." She raised her head. "But he does not now. Cecily does, and we can be like the sire and dam she needs. You want her happiness, do you not? You shall not send her away?"

Resting his knuckles on the table, he released a long sigh. "No, I would not send her back to that harpy she calls dam, nor to any other." He stood up straight. "Cecily is kin and I would see her content. But at what price, Isobel — of all our manors, Hamden!"

"It was the first name that came into my head," she confessed a little sheepishly. "If I had known it was of such import to you, I would have —"

"— offered Beaumancote instead? I think not." He came around the side of the table and sat down in the chair beside her and she saw that the worst of the storm was over. "Hamden, Isobel, is of greater importance than its yearly income, or its produce and tenants. It lies to the south-west of our main holdings and places us in an area of influence where we would otherwise have none. It provides the means to motivate gentlemen of some standing to act on our behalf — not easy in a region so bridled by the queen's kin. And Hastings, it would seem," he adjoined. "Increasingly." He rubbed his forehead with the heel of his hand. "It is a grave loss and I can only hope we will not live to rue it."

Isobel slumped further into her chair. "*Nolo contendere*," she whispered.

He grunted. "You might *not wish to contend*, but it is too late for that. In admitting no guilt but offering yourself for judgement, do you hope to appease me? Or merely appeal to the gentleness of my heart in respect of my niece?"

Still marshalling broken flowers and pushing spent water down the cracks between planks, Isobel could not find it in herself to regret bringing Cecily back home with her. But she was sorry to have been the cause of such discord, and even more so for inadvertently relinquishing such a jewel as the dull manor of Hamden now appeared to be. One of Moth's favourite branches lay close by and Isobel took to rolling it back and forth beneath her foot in a disconsolate manner, shedding bits of bark and moss. "What can we do?" she asked eventually.

"Do? There is nothing to be done. Felice knows as well as I do the value of that manor; she will not surrender the land now that she has the gift of it." Pressing his hands on his thighs he rose from the stool on which he had perched. "There is nothing for it but have the contracts drawn up. Ho, there!" he called, and a manservant materialised. "Have Master Sawcliffe wait on me." The door closed. "At least we will have this done properly. Felice will get the manor, but we will acquire a ward."

"Ward?" Isobel said, dully.

"With the king's authority Cecily will be made our ward. At least that will offer more protection than the —"

"— agreement between women?"

"Would *you* trust Felice's word?"

He had a point. "She knew." Isobel said. "Felice knew that I would be there in the market and what I would be trying to do."

"And that is something else we must discuss," Robert muttered. "I wish to talk to Master Taylor anon."

"Do not lay the blame at Pip's door; he was acting under my command. But that is unimportant. How did Felice know? Who told her?"

Isobel was interrupted by the door groaning open and Sawcliffe entered. She watched the secretary move smoothly towards them, humble in manner and knowing in looks. She nudged Robert, frowning at Sawcliffe's sleek head as he concentrated on laying out his writing instruments on the wooden board he carried. Robert's brow furrowed in silent query, then his eyes widened as he understood. "Right then." He cleared his throat. "To business."

As soon as the contract had been drawn up, signed and sealed and Sawcliffe had left the room, Robert turned to Isobel. "I cannot believe Sawcliffe would betray us. He has no reason to."

"He served your brother for many years and Felice made use of him. And I am certain he does not like me." Isobel remembered with dread the long hours spent locked in the basement rooms of the tower at the behest of Felice, waiting for Sawcliffe's interrogation to commence, the threat of punishment and even death.

"It is neither his place nor concern to like or dislike you; you are his countess. He will obey you. And he knows what I'll do to him if he doesn't," Robert added grimly.

"I can never tell what he thinks and I doubt I would like it if I did. Sawcliffe had knowledge of my enquiries into Cecily's whereabouts. He knew of my plan. Who else could it be but him? I do not trust him, Rob. He knows things about us we would not wish revealed. He is a dangerous man."

Shortly after, they made the return journey to Tickhill, taking with them the scion of lily and the child who had not been there since her father's sudden death.

Barely had they arrived than Isobel took Cecily to the wilderness garden in the last of the day's sun. A chill accompanied them but buds had broken on the Lady Snake tree, and blossom braved the steel wind from the east. Isobel fingered the trunk where the carved coils of Eve the Temptress pinched the expanding bark. At some point in the future, either the Lady Snake would have to be cut from the trunk or it would strangle the tree.

She patted the rough surface. "This was always your favourite place, do you remember?" she asked Cecily who as yet had not spoken. Isobel assumed she must be a little shy after so long spent apart, and filled in the silence with comfortable chatter until Cecily felt able to answer. "We used to come here and sit under the branches and I would tell you stories while you played with Nan, and Moth would roll in the grass. Sometimes you would join her and you would roll together." Isobel laughed at the memory. "Where is Nan, Cecily? You could never be parted from your poppet."

She walked on down the path that led back to the family apartments, Cecily a few steps behind. "I cannot tell you how glad we are to have you here with us. It has been too long and we have missed you." Isobel stopped and let Cecily catch up. She held out her hand to the child, but she did not take it, nor did she meet Isobel's gaze.

Isobel knelt on the stone setts, careless of the damp that seeped through the fabric, and brushed the sable curls that had fallen over Cecily's eyes. "I expect this is all rather strange. It will take you time to become accustomed to your new circumstance. You will have your old chambers and new playthings. Lucie and Maud will take care of you, and Buena will always be there to watch over you as before."

As they approached the stair to the family apartments Cecily's expression changed. She held back. "Come, sweetheart, Drew is having his bath. Will you not say your devotions with him before he sleeps?" Isobel reached for her hand but Cecily snatched it away and, spinning around, fled the way they had come.

"I do not know what to do," Isobel acknowledged to Buena once Cecily had been located and brought back to the nursery kicking and thrashing. She refused to cooperate with the nursery maids and had sunk into a remorseless ill-humour from which no amount of cajoling could shift her. "I thought she would be pleased to be back here with us and away from her dam."

Buena canted her head and observed Cecily for a moment. Then she began to speak with her hands, her brows rising and falling as she emphasised words.

"It will take time, I understand that, but surely this is better than the life she had with a mother who did not want her?"

Buena waggled her head and placed her hands together, resting the side of her face against them in imitation of sleep.

"Yes, we will let her rest and then, in the morning, perhaps she will feel better."

Isobel first went to the crib in which Andrew lay asleep and gave him his nightly blessing, then over to the little girl in the bed, eyes wide and emotionless, staring at the decorated tester above her head. "Good night, Cecily, may your dreams be blessed." She leaned forwards and placed a kiss on her brow. From the corner of her eye as she turned to leave, she saw Cecily raise her hand and quickly wipe the embrace from her skin.

PART TWO

CHAPTER SEVEN

Spring 1475

"Ama!"

Isobel found the presence of Nicolas Sawcliffe disconcerting and the child dancing around her skirts did nothing to help her sense of composure. "Not now, poppet; I will play with you shortly. I must listen to what your fader has to say."

The little girl took hold of her mother's hand in both of hers and began to shake it. Isobel frowned. "Juliana, you must be patient. I will not be long." Isobel looked over her shoulder but the nursery maid had vanished from the chamber. "Shh! Go, find Cecily and Drew," she urged, but her daughter continued to bounce and plead.

Robert put the sheaf of papers on the table with a thump. "Juliana, sit down and be quiet. *Now!*" The child stopped, put her thumb in her mouth, and slumped next to Isobel's feet looking sulky. Isobel wished she had the same command of her daughter as Robert seemed to enjoy, but her heart softened, as it always did, and she placed her hand on Juliana's chestnut head. The girl nuzzled into it.

"As I was saying before the interruption," Robert said, winking at his daughter's scowling face, "I know not how long I will be in France — as long as it takes to bring King Louis to heel, I suspect — but it will be some months. Isobel, you have my seal, and the reeve will continue to report to you on our lands as he has done before. Hyde will serve you well in keeping the household to account, and the constable has his instructions on maintaining security while I am gone. Who knows what spoils might come of this campaign." He bent down and scooped Juliana into his arms. "Perhaps I will find a fine French poppet for my little maid to dance a jig around her maman. But take a care not to tire her," he whispered audibly into the girl's ear, "for she carries a treasure of our own." He leant forward to kiss Isobel fully on the mouth, careless of his secretary's presence and the expressionless smile he always wore.

And who will take care of you? Isobel thought as she watched Robert ride from the bailey with his retinue amid the joyful explosion of impending war that had filled the castle for months now. She saw in Robert's bearing and in the brightness of his eyes his eager anticipation. There was nothing she could have said or done that could have persuaded him from this venture. "It is for the honour of our house and of our king," he had said when she voiced her anxiety. "This has been long in the making and Edward has called all of England's nobility to his great enterprise; would you have me sit at home to the discredit of my name and my family?"

"Men die in war, Rob. Would you make me a widow and our children orphans? Is *that* honourable?"

"Isobel, my dove," he said, adopting the annoyingly patient tone of one explaining the obvious to a slow-witted child, "I could die in my bed or fall from a horse just as readily. Life is a risk we all must share —"

"But you are courting death!"

"And I will do whatever I can to preserve my life for you and our babes. Look, we have an army greater than any yet assembled — fully 13,000 men — and ordnance that will carry away our enemy if Louis dare face us on the field. And I hope to God he will, for has meddled too long in our affairs, and France owes this family my brother's life. Be of good heart, my love, together with Charles of Burgundy's army and the support of Francis of Brittany, we will crush France and honour will be ours. *Ours!*" he had said, hardly containing his excitement. "Just think, all those sovereigns — France, Scotland, Danmark — that made mockery of us, will not presume to provoke us for fear of our just rebuke. This will be the making of our realm for we are promised great riches from this opportunity…" He had gone on to list the benefits of the campaign to the country. From the artificers kept busy night and day making arms and weapons, to the victuallers supplying them, every trade engaged in war, and the ale houses and churches, the Court and the solars buzzed with it as if the whole country had set aside its petty squabbles and was united in this common cause.

As for their own family, supplying men, weapons and horses had cost them dear, but not as much as the eye-watering *benevolences* King Edward had managed to squeeze from his nobles over the previous few years to fund the expedition. If men grumbled and their wives whined, they had little choice other than to accept it and hope that their contribution was negligible compared with the rewards they were promised on the king's triumphant return. Robert had put a brave face on it, but Isobel knew the demands on their finances had forced him to take risks further abroad where his vessels sought new markets in dangerous waters. Evidently, from the way he had listed the lords who would accompany the king to France as if they were merely participants at a joust, the thought of testing his mettle in the trials of combat far outweighed any previous doubts and inconveniences.

Now, as she returned to the solitude of their privy chamber, Isobel resigned herself to lonely months without her husband as she awaited his return.

*

Restless horses sent a choir of tiny metallic voices from the decorated harnesses they wore, the shiny emblems of their masters winking in the light from the noon-day sun. Clarence squinted as he assessed the lines of French noblemen, their colours mockingly dancing in the light breeze. They watched King Louis advance in state towards the equally splendid figure of King Edward waiting on the purpose-made bridge that was to be their place of treaty.

"This was not how it was supposed to be," Clarence muttered. "We could have vanquished the French and made our fists felt. It is defeat by any other name and brings dishonour to the realm. This treaty is none of my making, Langton; I would not have been bought so easily. No good will come of it," he finished, glowering in the direction of his older brother.

Robert felt inclined to agree, but for different reasons. "Your brother the king has made plain his will in this and has his own motives for the truce, no doubt; but for mine own, I would that we had the chance to put right some of the wrongs done to us." His hand felt the gilt pommel of his sword, untried in battle, idle. "My blade aches to douse those tinsel heads and remind them of the cost of war." His voice dropped so it became his own. "For it cost us dear."

Clarence threw him a look. "Oh?"

"My brother Duarte fell under a French blade in the long war. His death has yet to be avenged."

"And you would be the one to do it?"

"There is no one else left."

"With God's blessing you will have a son; let him carry your name. Perhaps he will have greater opportunity to avenge family honour."

"A son, yes." Robert looked away to the west as if seeking his home, but saw instead striped pavilions and the smoke from many English campfires and, beyond them, tousled heads of trees under a Picquigny sun. Home was a long way off. Momentarily, he wondered whether he might have another child by now. And then, with a cold twist of his gut, if Isobel yet lived. No word had come from Tickhill, and with each passing week, his dread grew.

Beneath a canopy of gold and separated by a cautious barrier, Louis and Edward met to calls and clapping and the clarion of trumpets. Clarence twitched his reins and his mount shimmied and settled. "I will be dead and buried ere this amusement is done," he muttered. "It flatters my brother to think he has won without a blow made." He leant to one side and spat into the cloven ground. "What games our cousin France plays; Edward is made a fool and all will laugh. What say you, my lord? Will you uphold your head when we return to England with nought but gilded promises and empty coffers to show for all … this? How can we press our vantage when all mock us? There are riches here beyond gold. Land, alliances…" He nudged his horse closer to Robert's, his face flushed. "My brother is content to take this *bribe* —"

"It is the king's will, Your Grace. Without the aid of Duke Charles and his Burgundian army, the outcome was less certain than it might have been. King Edward saw wisdom in a known conclusion rather than take an unmeasured risk."

"It is a *corruption*. Think, instead, of what a well-wrought plan might have made of this opportunity. Edward has his prize and no further ambition. We … *we*," and he stubbed a finger on his own chest, "have greater foresight than *that*." He looked about him as if expecting to be overheard. "Even my brother, Gloucester, would have nothing to do with the negotiations."

"But Your Grace did," Robert pointed out.

Clarence shrugged. "It is better to shape Fate than be at its mercy. I offered what counsel I saw fit. But why should I do all the work when another benefits from it?"

He didn't expect an answer and Robert didn't supply one. He had become used to the duke's carping on his brother's rule and would rather not be subject to it. It could lead nowhere but discontent even if he did sympathise with some aspects. Clarence was not always as circumspect in his views as he might have been, and sometimes less than discreet. It was as if he courted trouble — pushing his luck to see just how far he could go. And, so far, the king had let him play his games as long as they were within the York fold.

Robert was relieved to see an imminent interruption in the form of Philip Taylor, whose squat body ploughed through the watching throng towards them. And then he saw what he clutched in his paw.

"From Tickhill?" Robert said, reaching for the oiled square of cloth protecting the paper within and feeling sweat gathering at his neck as he saw the seal of his steward.

"Aye, my lord, post haste."

Then it must be good news, or did good news travel fast but bad news faster? He broke the seal and tore the cloth from the letter and saw, in a flood of relief, Isobel's own matrix. She had been alive to seal this letter a week before. He scanned the few lines and then read them again, this time, with care. The faces around him spun. He breathed out, letting the hand holding the letter drop to his side, conscious that both Clarence and Taylor watched him closely.

"It is a boy," Robert said. "I have a son."

*

"A son?" Gloucester pressed his hand to Robert's. "You have an heir; that is glad tidings indeed. And Lady Isobel, she fares well?"

Robert accepted a cup of wine and took his ease by his duke. "Well enough to write in her own hand. Her trials were long — longer than with our little maid — but she recovers well, thanks be to God."

Gloucester crossed himself and raised his cup in salute. "Amen to that. What name does the boy take?"

"We considered Duarte, after my oldest brother, but Isobel would not use the name of the dead, nor that of Geoffrey, her father..." He hesitated, wondering if that were the real reason. "Isobel would have us use a name from my own family."

"William, then, after the late Earl?"

"No," Robert said bleakly. "Not him."

"Forgive me; I forgot the circumstances. But you have an heir, and that is to be celebrated whatever name he takes. A man with an heir is a man with a future. He should take his father's name."

"Robert. Rob — Robin — Robbie?" He raised his cup. "He will be Robert, then, and I thank you for the suggestion, Your Grace."

"Now I have done you a service, I would that you do the same for me."

"You are in need of a child's name?"

Gloucester smiled. "I would that being in want of a name was the sum of my concerns. No, I speak of this current matter of the king's."

"Ah."

"Indeed. You know I did not favour this negotiation; it is not the honour I would have sought for England and it makes us look weak. Still, it is as it is and I will abide by my brother's decision. The treaty has bought us peace, a marriage settlement between the dauphin and my niece, Princess Elizabeth, and a mutual assurance of military support should we need it — that is more than Charles of Burgundy gave us, which is why we have this settlement in the first place. The pity of it is that had we pressed ahead with the campaign we would be crowning my brother King of France now instead of supping at Louis's table as his guests."

"But His Highness takes home a fortune. Seventy-five thousand marks in exchange for peace and a promise of an annual pension of fifty thousand more? This peace has cost France dearly," Robert pointed out, "and that for the king's Grace alone. We are all beneficiaries of this treaty — some more than others," he added wryly.

"Louis must have emptied his treasury to have bought so many English lords so handsomely. Hastings, though, would not sign a receipt. Did you hear? Said he would not have it evidenced that he accepted largesse of the king of France lest he be thought a pawn in his game." Gloucester chuckled into the depths of his cup, drank, then held it before him thoughtfully. Wrought with gilt and enamelled panels from Limoges it was set with gems from countries with strange names and stranger tales. "I am to visit Louis," he stated suddenly. "On the morrow and with George."

"King Edward, also?"

Gloucester tapped the rim, making a tinging sound in the near-empty vessel. "No, just he and I. Neither of us sought this treaty — a rare agreement between the two of us — and Louis is aware of it. No doubt he looks to court our favour. I know of no other reason why he would seek us out so especially." He frowned, looking up. "I am minded to refuse, but the king would have me go."

Robert detected an unspoken question. "Given the Duke of Clarence's previous association with King Louis, perhaps His Highness considers it prudent for *both* his Royal brothers to attend?"

"To ensure no misunderstanding befalls either party?" Gloucester's face cleared. "I believe, my lord, you might be right."

Watchfulness in every sinew of his lean frame, Gloucester was uncertain what he had anticipated, but if the shoddy-clothed individual with a prominent nose was the king of France, he certainly didn't look like it. A merchant of middling rank, perhaps, but not a king. Gloucester had been warned not to be taken in by Louis's appearance, nor was he as the king embraced each brother in the manner of the French. Gloucester responded with a stiff bow, but Clarence executed an elaborate, if shallow, obeisance.

King Louis looked momentarily amused. "*Mon cousins*, you do me great 'onour in your presence. Cousin Clarence, we 'ave met before. Negotiating with one so proficient in the art of politics teaches even this old dog new artifice. One so skilled is most surely a trusted advisor to his royal brother." Louis was turning towards Gloucester, so didn't catch Clarence's gratified expression dissolve. "Ah, now, my lord of Gloucester, you and I 'ave not yet become acquainted. It is my loss. Your Grace was not present when the treaty was signed." Louis moved his finger side to side. "I was disappointed not to see you, but per'aps you had more important duties to attend, eh?"

The king held Gloucester in a probing stare, then released him with a morose smile. Behind Louis' archly affable guise Gloucester detected a ferret.

"No matter. Come, come, let us speak together like brothers…" Louis hesitated. His choice of analogy might be ill-chosen given the history between the York brethren. "Like friends," he amended. Checking over his shoulder and not wishing to be overheard, Louis leaned in closer, his head bunching into his squat neck as he trained a long-nailed finger at Gloucester and Clarence. "I must make confession to you, my princes: this treaty is one written in the stars and ordained by Almighty God. Do you know how this might be? Non? I tell you the truth — I had a portent. I 'eard a great thunder on the feast of St. Sylvestre. Oui, it is as I say, a storm of snow on the very last day of Décembre. Can you believe that? Snow and thunder! I knew then that there would be no war but a great accord such as we 'ave now concluded with your most royal brother." He straightened, looking pleased. "What say you to that?"

"Amen," Clarence said in a caustic undertone.

"And you, Your Grace?" Louis asked Gloucester.

Gloucester felt the weight of the French king's interest fall on him, thought that anything he said might be deliberately misinterpreted in Louis' perpetual campaign against England. But nor would he leave Louis in any doubt that the treaty solved the underlying issues of trust that had brought them to the brink of war. "If the treaty is by God's design it cannot fail, Majesty, and any that breaks it denies His will and shall reap such consequences that, by God's resolve, he shall surely be crushed." He met Louis's gaze. "That is what I say."

For an instant Louis's pretence slipped — long enough for Gloucester to gain his measure and to see the man beneath; but no sooner seen than the veneer was back in place.

"You perhaps wonder to yourself why I ask you to dine with me?" Louis continued, picking up a heavy gold ewer standing next to equally extravagant goblets, whose embellishments betrayed their Italian origins. He poured tawny wine and handed Clarence the first goblet. Gloucester accepted the second while Louis took the third for himself. The king perched on the edge of his own great chair, a flash of red winking through a ragged moth hole in his dust-fringed houppelande. He made a show of sampling the wine, nodding his satisfaction.

He held the goblet aloft. "To our alliance and mutual accord." He drank deeply, watching over the rim to see if the dukes followed suit. Clarence sniffed the wine then took a mouthful, savouring it. Gloucester placed the goblet to one side, untouched.

"You will forgive my lack of English, but I will be to the point. There 'as been much discord between our countries, 'as there not, *mes amis*? But it 'as not always been so, and it is time to put such enmity behind us. There is much to celebrate, *non*? And much to gain. As such, we must rejoice, and in my country we give gifts to mark the ... ah, *occasion*."

Beside him, Gloucester sensed his older brother's interest quicken. Louis had seen it, too. He addressed Clarence. "You like the goblet, eh? I see that you do. It was gift from Pietro Mocenigo. The Doge of Venice — the very finest workmanship. It is yours — the ewer also." Wine slopping, he thrust the heavy jug into Clarence's hands. "Yes, yes, 'ow can you have the one without the other? Pour me more wine, my prince. And you, gracious lord," he said, turning to Gloucester, "cannot be, er, *les mains vides*."

"Empty-handed," Gloucester translated.

Louis devised a smile. "Oui, yes, I thank Your Grace. Empty-'anded. What largesse can I make to you?"

"I have no desire for gifts, Majesty," Gloucester said, but Louis went over to a table on which sat a gilt centrepiece in the form of a ship with billowing silver sails.

"Come, my prince, what do you say of this?" He waited for Gloucester to join him, to take in the intricate detail of rigging in silver wire, barrels banded in hoops of gold, pennants from the masts in enamels that reflected the light from the window. "A fine *sal*, is it not? You will not find better in all Christendom."

Before Gloucester could refuse, Louis picked it up. "'Ere," he said, placing the weighty salt in Gloucester's arms, "it is yours. Even King Edward, with all his riches, will envy this gift." Gloucester stiffened, and Louis backtracked. "But of course, your royal brother will be glad you 'ave accepted this gift, this little show of friendship between us. *Bateau d'amis*, eh? A Ship of Friends." Louis laughed at his own joke, an uncomfortable sound as if he were unaccustomed to mirth.

Clarence joined them, his eyes gleaming as he took in the *sal*.

"I see you admire it also, *mon cousin*. Alas, I have no other to give you, but I do have this..." Still speaking, he navigated Clarence in the direction of an array of plate. "My noble princes appreciate horses, do you not? We will visit my stables once we have dined, ah, and my ordnance. I know Your Grace of Gloucester to 'ave much knowledge of cannon. Perhaps you will grant me your opinion on my latest acquisition?"

Wine and gifts had worked their magic on Clarence, overcoming his initial distrust and opening his mind to potential opportunities. He had even begun insinuating ideas of his own, Gloucester noted, which Louis had been quick to steer. But Gloucester remained guarded, water to Louis' oil, and the gifts and flattery did nothing to diminish his initial impression of the French king. It was mutual, he thought later, Louis having sent them on their way with gilded promises and riches piled into wagons escorted by his own guard. Louis had spotted cracks in Clarence's armour; but of Gloucester he was unsure. He could not blame Louis, for to trust would show a remarkable act of acceptance and security on the part of the French king that Gloucester himself did not share. Louis remained wary of this son of York, and so he might, Gloucester concluded. So he should.

CHAPTER EIGHT

Isobel touched the tip of her finger to the tiny nose. "Good morrow, sweet one," she whispered so as not to wake Juliana and Andrew still sleeping soundly next to her. She shifted to ease the discomfort of the recent birth and detected the first stirring of dawn in the blackbird's song. Light from the lantern on the nightstand reflected in her son's open eyes. She kissed his fluffy hair and raised him to her breast. He latched on immediately. She relished the closeness this brought them, an intimacy that was theirs alone. Countess or no, she would not share him with a nursemaid, and she reflected how different the circumstances of this child's birth were to Drew's, and then how much had changed since those dark days of fear, ignominy, and loneliness.

She sensed movement outside the bed hangings, a softly cleared throat, then a tentative hand parted the curtains and the head of her young maid appeared, sleepy-eyed. "My lady?"

"He needs changing, Matilde, then take more sleep if you can."

Isobel lay awake for a while longer then decided the bed wasn't big enough for all of them, slipped from beneath the covers, and soft-footed to the stairs leading to the room above her chambers and the roof access outside.

From the tower parapet she watched the sun breach the distant hills and heard birds break into full-throated welcome. Rising from the kennels below, the dogs set up their barking, soon silenced as the kennel boys fed them. Smoke from the kitchens scented the cool air and, beyond the river, the town stirred. It was hers — all hers and Robert's together. The days when she had watched the world fettered as a mistress were long past, but the memory of it left its stain.

She ducked through the low frame and pushed open the door into the ordnance chamber she had once occupied. Her belongings had gone and the fireplace lay empty and cold, but the barrels of quarrels and heavy bows on their hooks still imbued the room with grease and iron and the scent of war. There had been a sense of peace here, too, away from the world and part of her missed it. She had had no responsibility except for her own, no children to guide, no household to oversee. Even her manors had been taken from her leaving her penniless — until the Earl had returned with King Edward and life had resumed a different sort of normality. She let drift a sigh, allowing her shoulders to drop and release the tension the remembrance had brought, and made her way back to her chamber to resume the duties of her present life.

The children were awake and leading the nursery maids a merry dance. They didn't see Isobel enter the room and she caught each one under her arms and spun the squealing pair in a circle of laughter. She put them down in a wriggling heap on the floor. "Drew, go to and bide by Kath's instruction. Wash first, eat later. Juliana," she said, retrieving her daughter from under the bed, "go with Matilde and have your hair combed or mice will nest in it." She squiggled her fingers through the child's tangled hair, and her daughter made little squeaking noises and ran to the maid.

Isobel looked around for Cecily. The girl sat in the window overlooking the wild garden, seemingly oblivious to the antics in the room. She was already washed and dressed, and her unruly curls combed into submission and neatly arrayed. At nearly nine winters there was little of the boisterous child left in her, and for that, Isobel mourned. Even after the last three years living with them, Cecily remained placid, compliant, a shell. Trying to communicate with her was like pushing water. Sometimes Isobel caught herself wondering whether she had done the right thing, or if she had misjudged the situation and should have left Cecily with her mother. This was one of those moments.

She didn't have time to ponder further because Hyde appeared out of nowhere with an air of expectation. "Earl Robert is returned, my lady! By the Grace of God, he is here!"

"Why did you not let me know you were coming!" Isobel exclaimed once Robert had put her back on her feet. "I would have made myself fit to greet you."

"I am my own messenger. I rode through the night and none could have outridden me." He kissed her again, stubble grazing her skin, the night air still in the folds of his riding cloak, and horse sweat staining his boots. She inhaled his smell, laughing and rubbing her cheek.

"I could raise the nap on leather with your bristles." She beckoned to the boy waiting by the door to their chamber. "Have hot water fetched for my lord." And turning back to her husband and running her finger along his chin, "I would have these removed before they inflict grievous injury."

He slipped his arm around her and inched her back towards the bed with the intense look he adopted when he meant business. "And I would make up for my absence ere another hour passes."

Pushing him away, she lowered her voice so none might hear but the two of them. "And I might remind you that I am but lately birthed and have yet to be churched. Your ardour, my lord, will have to wait."

"I forget," he grumbled, but trying not to smile. "Now, where is my son? I have a name for him."

If he saw her face fall in a flash of disappointment, he didn't mention it, but was already on his way to the nursery where the children spent their day in play or at lessons. Puffing a little from the long flight of steps to the bailey and the effects of the recent birth, Isobel caught up. Robert was in the nursery on bended knee, Juliana balanced on the other with her arms tight around her father's neck. "You will throttle me!" he was saying, and then made her laugh by rasping his chin over her soft hair, the threads catching on the dark bristles. "Now, Juliana, take me to my son." She bounced to her feet and took his big hand in hers.

"He here, Fader," she lisped, dragging him towards the window where Andrew sat at his little desk next to Cecily, perched on the edge of his stool with his face lit in anticipation. But Robert had seen the cradle where the sleeping baby lay. Leaving go his daughter's hand, he gazed at the child. "Here he is." He bent low, carefully picking up the swaddled bundle. "My son," he murmured, kissing the tiny head. "My own sweet boy." He cradled him as If he were the most precious object he had ever held.

Andrew watched his father sombrely. He saw Isobel, slipped off his stool and ran to her. "Rob," she said, her arm around Andrew. "Robert." At her sharp tone, he looked around. "Your *son* and niece await to greet you."

Robert tore his eyes from the baby, kissed him again, and handed him to Matilde. "Andrew, Cecily," he said, holding out his hands to them. Neither moved. "Come, I will not bite!"

"Go to," Isobel said, giving Andrew a gentle push.

"Drew," Robert said, bending to greet the boy. "How fare you? I see you have grown. Have you been obedient of your maman, and attentive in your lessons? Cecily," he spoke over Andrew's head, "have you been helping to look after the baby?"

"They have missed you, Rob; you have been away for a long time." Isobel made a hugging motion with her arms and gave him a fierce look. He looked blank for a moment, then catching on, crouched down to his son's level, encircling him in his arms. "It *has* been a long time," he said. "How I have longed for you all." He looked over Andrew's head at Isobel. "You are my life."

"I wonder if the king will stand as godfather?" Robert said later, lying on his back, arms behind his head, staring at nothing in particular. He shifted onto his side, making the bed frame squeak. "What say you; shall I ask?"

"If you wish."

"What an honour that would confer upon our family," he mused, turning onto his back again. "Robbie, godson of the king. Think on it, Isobel, what it might do for his prospects."

"Mmm."

"You do not believe it likely?"

"Why not? You are high in His Grace's favour." On the wall opposite the bed, the Langton earls traced their lineage up the branches and into the dark of the ceiling.

"What is it? You do not seem yourself. Do you ail?"

"I do not."

"Ah, it is women's trouble. They say it takes time for the womb to find its natural place again. And birth stirs ill humours, of course." He appeared content with this received wisdom. "Do not be troubled; rest and it will pass."

Isobel tutted and rolled over with her back to him.

Robert patted her shoulder. "You must not concern yourself; I do not take affront. I will bide until you are ready."

Staring at the aumbry on the other side of the room, the memory of Robert's brother returned as a sharp pain, and Isobel's mood sank further. "Why," she said, turning now to face him, "do men believe that women's humours are so very different to theirs? And that all ill-humour in women is because their womb floats high or low, or their courses flow, or do not. And why," she said, her voice rising, "in Heaven's name, do you think that I might have offended you in any way that I should care?"

"Do not be vexed, my love, I understand," he soothed, putting a placating hand on her own.

She shook her hand free of his. "No, Robert, you do *not* understand, for if you did you would not be talking of *Robbie's* godfather, and his prospects, as if … as if…" she swallowed hard, "as if Drew does not exist. *He* has no godfather to further his prospects at Court. You talk … nay, behave, as if he is not your flesh and blood, not *your* son!" There, she had said it, and once out of her mouth the simmering discontent she had been nurturing for too long overwhelmed the banks of her composure and flowed in a flood of resentment.

He looked at her, started to speak, then shook his head and, climbing from their bed, grabbed his gown. Flinging it about his shoulders, he left her biting her tongue and fuming as Chou and Moth whimpered by the fire.

It didn't take long before her temper waned leaving Isobel regretting her outburst. But there was truth behind her words and the image of Drew standing alone while his father cradled the baby was enough to make anger swarm again. She could not leave it there. Shoving her feet into slippers, Isobel donned her own gown, took up the chamber lantern, and went to find her husband.

She found him on the battlements silhouetted against the summer moon. He must have heard the door bang shut behind her, but he didn't turn around.

"Rob?" she ventured. "We must talk…"

He hunched his shoulders into his robe, shortening his neck. "There is nothing to discuss."

"There must be or you would not be up here." She took a step towards him, mindful of the unseen hazards of the slippery lead roof. "There are things left unsaid —"

"I think you have said enough. I know your mind; you made it perfectly clear."

"You do not, and I have not. You are dishonest with yourself and with me if you believe that."

"What do you want of me, Isobel? What, exactly, is it you think I have done that so offends you?"

She took a deep breath, clearing her mind and focusing her thoughts. "It is not so much what you do, but what you do not." And, seeing his expression change, amplified, "I see it when you speak to Drew; I saw it most clearly when you met Robbie. Drew is your firstborn, yet you treat him almost like a … a…" she struggled to find the right word. "Changeling," she finished.

He grunted. "I was not aware I treat him in any such way."

"Yet you do. Why? He is as much our child as Robbie and Liana. Did you see his face today? Did you not see how he needed you to greet him?"

"I saw no such thing."

"Exactly. You didn't notice him at all."

"He is old enough to wait his turn; he must learn to govern himself."

"He needs his father to guide him, Rob."

"His father, yes." He turned to look at her directly, moonlight reflecting off his hair giving him an eerie halo. "Am I?"

Had she heard him correctly? "*What?*"

"Am I his father?"

"How can you say that? You know you are!"

"I wonder sometimes; he is not unlike my brother. The older he gets, the more I see it. And you, Isobel."

"What about me?"

"Do you not question it also? I think you do; you mention him oft enough."

"I do not!"

"Yes, you do. I think, sometimes, that you wish William were here rather than me; that Drew call him 'father'; that he had never died."

Aghast, she choked out, "How can you even *think* it?"

He leant close, his head tilted to one side, his eyes enquiring slits in which moonlight gleamed. "*Do* you wish he were here instead of me?"

She stood her ground, feet planted to prevent her knees from shaking. "No. *No!* I love *you*. I have always loved you and none other. But William treated Drew like his … his…"

"Son? Perhaps he was right to do so."

"Drew is not his child, Rob, and I did not love your brother. But I did pity him."

"You felt *sorry* for William? After what he did to you, even when you learned the truth about him and your mother?"

She sought in the depths of herself the memory of his ravishment, of the betrayal of trust after she had been placed in his care, the melancholia which draped itself around him like a shroud — and found, deep, deep inside her, compassion. "Yes," she said simply. "He lost far more than he gained."

"And I have not?" Robert said.

"You married for love; he did not."

"My wife *died*. Our babes *died*."

Isobel looked up at the wounded boy seeking reassurance, heard his pain, felt it deeply, but could not allow it to deflect from the issue that placed their own happiness at risk. "I referred to me, to our marriage, Rob, to *us*. We live, our children thrive. Your brother's heart was empty. If he gained a little happiness in the belief Drew was his son, what harm could that do? How could it make you any less our child's father? You must trust me, as I have to trust you."

He faced her sharply. "What do you mean by that?"

"I do not ask what you did in France."

"I have told you."

"You have told me what you want me to know, that is not the same. I have not enquired whom you saw, nor the details of how you might have ... entertained yourself."

"I do not have to explain myself," he said indignantly. "You should trust me —"

"Yes, Rob, exactly. We have to trust one another. You cannot know my mind as I do not know yours, but you can trust that I have — and always will — remained loyal to you in *all* ways, and that includes telling you the truth." She let that sink in before saying briskly, "Now, we need to sleep or before long our children will be waking and they will want to see their ama and fader, and Drew will wish to show you how he can write his name." She did not need to add 'and you will not disappoint me in this' because her meaning was perfectly clear.

*

146

"Juliana, this is for you."

A little gasp escaped the child's lips. She took the proffered doll in both hands, holding it to her chest, bright eyes peeping over the top of its head.

"What do you say to your fader?" Isobel prompted.

"She need say nothing for the gift of her smile says it all." Robert ruffled her hair. "That, my sweet, is a poppet fit for a French princess. When King Louis learned I had a girl-child, he insisted he make a present of this. There, what do you say to that!"

"It's mine," she said, "mine own," and she hugged it hard.

Robert laughed, "It is indeed and I would not try to take it from you lest you bite me." He made chopping noises with his teeth. "Now," he said, delving into a large coffer within which lay parcels of varying shapes and sizes, some wrapped in wool, others carefully bound and nestled in straw, "what do I have here?"

Drew had crept closer and closer towards the coffer and now peered over the edge into its depths. He looked at his sister, then at Robert and finally at Isobel. She gave him a smile of reassurance.

Robert found a small package. "This is not for you, Juliana, unless you are in need of something on which to cool your gums, but you may open it if you wish." The little girl eagerly unwrapped the gift, frowned and pouted. Robert took the coral and ivory teething ring with little silver bells from her and gave it to Isobel to see. "For Robbie — when he has the teeth to chew it."

"Another gift from King Louis?" she asked.

"No, this one I found myself to welcome our infant son."

She nodded without looking at him and handed the teether to Buena.

"Where is my niece?" He saw Cecily in her usual place by the window and beckoned to her to join them by the open chest. "Ah, now, I thought this would become my Cecily. She is too well-grown for a poppet, and a young lady." With great solemnity, he proffered a flat, red leather case tooled in gilded vines. She took it and returned to her seat where the gift lay untouched beside her. "Will you not open it?" Robert asked. Obediently, she picked it up and unfastened the case. She removed the contents and stared at the carved ivory hand glass without evident emotion. Isobel joined her.

"Oh! It is beautiful. Such workmanship. Hold it up, Cecily; let us see your reflection."

The girl did as requested and her unsmiling countenance stared back from the silvered surface. Isobel bent down next to her and they looked into the mirror together. "You are grown so pretty," Isobel remarked, brushing a curl back from Cecily's forehead. Their eyes met in the polished plane and Cecily looked away. Isobel straightened. "I am certain the gift is well met. Your uncle chose fittingly." She placed a hand fleetingly on the girl's shoulder and Cecily cast her eyes downward, and Isobel could not tell if the gift was well-received or somehow had caused offence. But that is how it was between them and had been since Cecily joined the family.

Andrew was also retreating towards the fireplace where Moth rolled and yawned next to Chou. He sat down by her and placed his head on her warm flanks. Her pink tongue licked his hair and he wrapped his arms around her neck.

"I must have something for your maman," Robert was saying, hunting again in the coffer. At this point, with Cecily in her own world and Drew lost in his, Isobel was beyond caring whether she had a gift or not. "But what can this be?" He lifted a long, flattish object and held it up.

"Ama, for Ama!" Juliana jumped up and tugged at Isobel's hand.

Robert shook his head. "No, not for your maman. For Buena, perhaps? No." He paused, looking over to the fireplace. "Moth?" The dog opened her eyes at her name, yawned, and went back to sleep. "Or perhaps it is for ... Drew." Robert rose and took the object over to the boy. "Andrew," he said, holding it out. "Take it."

Drew sat up, hesitated, then took the object from his father. The folds of protecting cloth fell from the item. Andrew's eyes rounded and Isobel gave a small gasp. Robert's lowered voice lent gravity to the gift. "This is indeed from the king of France — a noble gift for my first-born son. I will instruct you on its use and with it you will learn to protect your family and serve the king as the son of an earl should, with honour and with loyalty."

"Thank you, fader," Drew managed, unable to take his gaze from the weapon.

"Hold it," Robert said. "Feel its weight, know its quality. You must earn the right to wield it, Andrew, for a knight is not born but is made through valour and purity of heart and with the blessing of Almighty God."

Andrew nodded gravely and, carefully bearing the heavy sword — as long as he was tall — went back to his table to examine it in the daylight. Watching him, Isobel swelled with gratitude.

"But what about Ama?" Juliana insisted

"Do not be concerned for your maman; I have something for her later."

"Well?" Robert asked, a little anxiously when he and Isobel were alone, "do you like it?"

Isobel let the kingfisher-blue silk — shot with gold and as smooth as water — slip through her hands. She had never seen anything like it, nor the glossy black jewel with a circle of white like an eye he told her was onyx. Set in a square of gold and surrounded by pearls, it felt too sophisticated for her, as if it were meant for someone else entirely. "The silk is beautiful."

"From Florence." He nodded with enthusiasm. "And this jewel," he said, taking it from her and holding it to the cleft of her breasts, "has the power to protect the wearer from all harm and especially poison."

She wondered whether he considered her at risk from poison but decided not to spoil the moment by mentioning it. "It is very fine." She looked at the gold vessel, the silvered hand glass in its case of ivory; the little Book of Hours with exquisite miniatures in brilliant blue and vermillion with tiny strawberries and pied birds decorating the borders. "It is all very fine."

"But…?"

"But at what price?"

"Price? None that we paid. Louis bought peace for his country and saved us the cost of battle."

"*Nothing costs as much as war*," she murmured, remembering her father's words. "But some peace is bought at the expense of honour."

"You sound like Gloucester. He worries the amity will be short-lived without a battle to ram the message home. Clarence, on the other hand, sees opportunity in it."

"And do you?" Isobel asked, laying the silk to one side.

Using the tip of a new and fabulously jewelled eating knife, Robert scratched his neck. "Do I?" He paused, thinking. "Such an accord brings greater opportunity for trade, the promise of further treaties — even potential matches between our children."

"And buys King Louis more time in which to build an army with which he can defeat us."

"Perhaps, but accepting such gifts does *us* no harm, Isobel."

"And thus was Troy lost to the Greeks," she intoned in a suitably portentous manner.

"Gloucester agrees with you, but Clarence says such caution wins no favour. Nothing is gained without risk."

"So," she said slowly, "are you a Greek or a Trojan?"

"I … am inclined towards Clarence's way of thinking. In this," he said rapidly, as she made to protest. "You must remember that my family has land in Portugal and we have had commerce with France throughout the troubled years when England was at war with it."

"But your brother was killed in France; how could you forget *that*!"

"I do not forget it, Isobel, how could I? And had we come to blows I would have struck such a severe one that France would never have forgotten it. But would you have others profit from the opportunities that might otherwise benefit us and our children? Clarence would not; he is looking to the future and what can be made of it. He looks to France to further his ambition, and I am inclined to agree, whatever Gloucester's reservations might be."

"I did not think loyalties could be so easily set aside."

"Are you thinking now of Clarence — or of me?"

"Clarence makes me uneasy. He proved himself … changeable when he cleaved to Warwick's cause, and what I have seen of him since makes me believe that little has changed."

"And what you have seen is nothing. Let me be judge of what is best for our family. You have not the experience to have a say in these matters. You must not —"

"Meddle?" she offered, with an edge.

"That is not a word I would choose, but if you like, yes. You must not interfere in concerns that you do not understand and cannot influence. I will act in the way I see fit. If I desire to be on terms with Clarence, then you must trust me to do so to our greater advantage."

"*A man cannot serve two masters*," she reminded him, taking the quote out of context; yet it served the purpose just as well.

"And I have said before that my loyalty to Gloucester is not in question."

"Muck sticks."

"Isobel — enough!" He closed his eyes and counted silently until his temper cooled enough to open them. "As my wife I expect you to support my decisions as is your place to do so."

"As your wife, it *is* my duty to support you, Robert. But what good to you is a wife who says 'yay' or 'nay' at your bidding and does not test the strength of your conviction against the wisdom bestowed upon her by God? Who else can you rely upon without fear or favour and who will *always* tell you the truth whether you wish it or no? If you wanted a wife who will simper and defer then you should have married someone else, for I am not she."

"No, that you are most certainly not," he muttered. "Nor did I wish to marry a harpy who nags my ears about all and nothing."

"Harpy?" Isobel inflated her cheeks not sure whether to laugh or scold, pursue the argument or relent for the sake of peace. "You, Robert Langton, instructed me to *look*, *listen*, and *learn*, and I have — dutifully. I am not your little poppet or an empty mouthpiece. I have thoughts of my own and I will use them."

He looked at her — hands bunched, lips tight, eyes wide and challenging — weighing up the situation as the air, thick with unspent rage and desire, vibrated with tension. He stood, slowly, until he arched over her slight body, the breadth of his muscled shoulders throwing her into the shadow he cast. Refusing to be intimidated by his greater strength, she met him eye to eye. Gradually, he released the breath he had been holding in a low, slow exhalation through clenched teeth. His head cocked to one side, his eyes glinting as he assessed her, a strange sound emanated from deep in his chest — a rumble, rising up his throat and exploding in a thunder that became laughter, until he shook with it, making the frame of the bed rattle as he clutched it to steady himself.

"How," he said when able to speak, "could any man withstand you? You are not a harpy, you are an Amazon!" and before she could recover her senses, he secured her in both arms, crushing her to him, gathering a handful of honey hair as he kissed her long and hard and deep.

CHAPTER NINE

Middleham. To Richard, Duke of Gloucester this was home. He had warred against the memories embedded in the walls and shed the ghosts of its previous occupants, mastering all. It hadn't been easy; Warwick's presence had dogged his thoughts and there were times when Gloucester considered his cousin to have never been slain at all. He imagined resentment oozing from the pores of the stone. He, Richard Plantagenet — the boy who had grown up within these walls under hawk-eyed Warwick, survived the jibes of his peers, overcome the limitations of his own body — had secured the youngest daughter and the northern kingdom of the Nevilles, which he now governed. At nearly twenty-four he at last felt he had come of age.

He sent his retinue ahead into the castle and dismounted outside the walls, preferring to feel the earth beneath his feet before they touched the stone of the bailey. He imagined the strength of the soil absorbed through the soles, running like roots through his legs, lending strength and certainty to his being and anchoring him to the very bones of this land. He inhaled the sun-warmed wind blowing from the fells towards him bringing scents of fresh growth and the distant song of birds. If he closed his eyes, he could visualise the glint of water spilling around the rocks of the nearby river Cover, just over the rise past the old castle and down the slope. He longed to bathe his feet and feel the cooling currents joggle and josh as it flowed across the stony bed and eventually to the sea. But first, there was duty.

He entered beneath the gatehouse, emerging briefly into a shaft of sun before being enveloped into the deep shadows thrown by the high, strong walls. Anne came running across the bailey, almost tripping over the small, ginger-hued dog he had given her before their marriage in her haste to greet him.

"Noble husband!" she exclaimed, puffing a little. "You did not send word you were coming!" She scooped the dog up and tucked a string of dark hair back under her headdress, her large brown eyes both hopeful and anxious to please. "I would have made preparations for your arrival and had Edward ready to see his sire. I will send for him forthwith and for further provisions and have the hall made ready. We must celebrate your safe return."

"There is no need."

"You must be fatigued from your journey." She clicked her fingers and their steward approached from the respectful distance at which he hovered. "Have sustenance brought to our chambers. Quick, quick! And bathing water heated." She turned back to Gloucester. "Do you wish to bathe now? I know how it eases you," she added in an undertone. "I have secured precious oils which you will like, I am certain of it, all the way from... I forget, but I had some sent to the king. I know it would please you to have me do so." Her brow puckered. "Should I have made a gift of some to His Grace of Canterbury?"

Her words crowded and cluttered his thoughts. "Peace, Anne. Let me step inside awhile. It is hot out here."

Her hand shot to her mouth. "Forgive me, dearest lord!" Adjusting her hold on the dog, she took Gloucester's hand. Sensing freedom, the dog wriggled. She kissed the silky fur and put it down, whereupon it bounced around Gloucester's heels, yipping. "There, look how Foxy has missed you!"

Once inside their privy chambers, Gloucester allowed her to fuss around him, ordering servants to do this or that, pouring water into the great silver basin into which she added drops of precious oils which perfumed the air with giddy scents of remote lands. Her words ebbed and flowed, asking questions of him and not waiting for answers, recounting gossip, telling tales, filling in every little detail of their son's growth, her butterfly mind flitting from one subject to another until all merged.

There was a certainty here — not peace, exactly — but a comfort in knowing that in his wife he found absolute acceptance. With weary eyes he watched her bustle about with the assurance of someone in their element. She reminded him of a brook — rarely still and full of bubbles, but somehow lacking in flavour. Yet she understood what comforted him, made a home to which he could retreat, a haven in which to rest, and for that he was grateful. Later, when they were alone, she would ask him about Court and he would tell her of the politics and the people, and the hopes and disappointments with which he had met — and she would frown and nod in equal measure at the nuanced interplay he described. He kept from her that which she might let slip in innocent, idle conversation, and to himself his darkest doubts and fears. And, in the empty hours before dawn, he would wonder whether all the lands and manors and comfort he had gained were worth the marriage he had made.

"Isobel, we will be late and Gloucester expects us before nightfall," Robert admonished when she appeared more interested in the flowers lining the wayside at her feet than his plea.

"But I have not seen any like this before. Do you know what they might be?" She knelt in the coarse scrub and parted stems around one plant, isolating it. "It is the colour of Peter's Pence," she mused.

"I neither know nor care. For the love of ... *Isobel*."

"I am coming." She carefully nipped a section of leaf and flower, wrapped it in her kerchief, and took one last look at the sheltered dip in the high moor through which they passed. "All else is heather," she said to no one in particular, stepping onto the hand of the servant and into the saddle once again. "Perhaps it is the aspect that lets it grow here. Or the soil?" She left the thoughts behind, much as she had done the children, although their absence proved the harder to bear each mile that passed. The sooner they reached the castle the quicker they would be away again. "Are we nearly there?" she called to Robert's back.

"Nearer than when you last asked," he threw over his shoulder and, pressing his knees into his horse's flanks, urged it on.

Anne, Duchess of Gloucester peered at the lifeless strip of plant and its bruised flowers when Isobel presented it to her. "It grows commonly enough here, but I have not paid heed to it and do not know its name. It is an ugly little thing."

"Only because I stole its beauty, Your Grace." Isobel saw Robert frown, and added, "I mean, it looked beautiful when first I spied it. It is spoiled because of me." She felt a dash of disappointment at her own flagrant disregard for this plant's life.

Gloucester put out his hand. "Let me see if I can name it." He took the kerchief with the plant lying limp in the folds, examining it closely. "We call it felwyrt, but you might know it as bitterwort."

"Ah! I know of bitterwort, Your Grace. It is marvellous well at settling the stomach when appetite fails; but I have never seen it growing at Tickhill, nor Beaumancote. I wonder what makes it prefer this land?"

"It grows in abundance where the sward is thin or the ground strewn with stone; the land favours the plant there," Gloucester said.

"Might Your Grace grant me a root that I might try to grow it?"

"Isobel!" Robert said, exasperated. "His Grace has greater matters to occupy his time than the acquisition of plants for your garden."

"It is of little inconvenience, my lord," Gloucester said. "I believe I saw a swathe growing not far from here. We can take the hawks while Lady Isobel hunts flowers, and discuss *great matters* as well from horseback as around a table."

"I thank Your Grace for indulging my wife's caprice," Robert said, observing the land before them from horseback.

At the top of the world skylarks decorated the morning air with their trilling song. Ahead of Gloucester and Robert, Isobel — on a palfrey prettily bedecked in trappings of grass green and amber — appeared mindful of their conversation while Lady Anne chatted away beside her.

"There is no hardship on a day like this."

"Isobel can be … impetuous when it comes to flowers." Robert saw her shoulders twitch and smiled to himself.

Gloucester laughed. "So I have observed."

"Once she even asked the queen for a slip of lily from the palace garden. And was granted it." Robert shook his head. "It flourishes still."

"Your wife was kind enough to gift a scion to Anne. They spent much of yester eve discussing great urns in which to keep it. There is no harm in it and my wife has enjoyed the company as well as learning of her sister's present disposition."

"Even so."

"And some good may come of a benign fancy if it allows concourse where there might have been none, for who would suspect one so fair in nature as well as countenance? Such as she might go where others may not and have the wit to make honest observances."

Robert made a sidewise look at his duke and noticed the slight lift to his mouth, indicating humour.

"Of course," Gloucester went on, "such tasks are only undertaken at the discretion of the husband."

"Of course," Robert said drily, remembering the last time he had tried to stop Isobel doing what she wished. Something else was on Gloucester's mind, but Robert was now used to the duke's oblique approaches, and let time take its course.

"This forthcoming occasion of my father and brother's reburial — you are familiar with the itinerary and your role?"

"I am, Your Grace, and the great responsibility placed upon me. I will endeavour to uphold the trust the king has seen fit to bestow upon my family in honouring your own, and pray God I do so."

"As do I in the charge I have been given. I cannot say that it is something I look forward to and the grief it will stir up for my lady mother, my brothers and sisters, for me — although the memory of my late father and brother Rutland is not as sharp as it is for my kin. The moment is long in the making, and in this the sons of York are as one; it is important that we are seen to be. Do you understand?"

"I do, Your Grace."

They rode on, snatches of Lady Anne's chatter floating towards them, and Isobel's briefer replies.

"My wife is concerned for her sister, the Duchess of Clarence,' Gloucester continued. "She has not been herself and Anne worries for her. She would visit her, but as matters are, such things cannot be." He paused as his horse negotiated a dip in the ground. "Lady Langton has formed an attachment with my sister-in-law, I understand. And you are close to my brother, are you not? You spent much time in his company when we were in France a year past."

Gloucester's directness caught Robert off guard and he found himself trapped in the young man's stringent gaze. "I would not say *close*, Your Grace."

"But enough to be in his confidence?"

"Not even that. We share common interests." Gloucester said nothing but continued to look at Robert until he felt obliged to amplify his last statement. "Alliances that benefit foreign trade and matters that impede it. Piracy, mostly." He felt irritated at himself for being drawn on matters he regarded as confidential to his own estate.

It must have shown because Gloucester broke his gaze, instead bringing his horse to a halt, and shading his eyes against the sun as he made out the landscape revealed before them. "Pirates are indeed a vexation," he concurred. "This is the place." He motioned to an attendant to catch up with the women and watched as the man relayed the message. Without taking his eyes from the small colourful group ahead of them, he said, "Forgive my enquiry, Langton, your business is your own; but when the security of my brother's realm is at stake, I will be direct."

A trickle of ice ran down Robert's shoulders and spread to his fingers, making him flex them to dispel the discomfort. "Your Grace, there can be no question of my loyalty."

"And I believe it, otherwise we would not be having this conversation. But not all are of the same mind and this peace is dependent on the continued goodwill of those sworn to it. For some, an oath of loyalty is like a breath of wind: sincere until it fails. My brother Clarence is ambitious; he is also discontented," he stated without clarification. "At some point the wind will fail, and then who knows which way it might blow?"

Throwing reins to a groom, Gloucester slid to the ground somewhat stiffly, leaving Robert to ponder as the duke went to join his wife, striding in the long riding boots he favoured through coarse heather and sending butterflies and bees skywards in a drowsy dance.

Lady Anne was busily directing the servants in their tasks — something she did with confidence and enthusiasm — while Isobel had spotted a group of flowers some way off and was picking her way across uneven ground, scattering grasshoppers and holding her skirts above the rough vegetation that threatened to snag them. She stopped and bent down. Robert went over to her.

"What is the matter?" she asked without looking up and he wondered, not for the first time, how she could read his mood so easily.

He glanced over to where Gloucester was now talking to his Master of Mews, then crouched beside her. "Gloucester suspects Clarence is brewing treason again. He wants to know where I stand." He plucked a stem of longer grass and began to peel it down its length.

"And did you tell him?" When he didn't answer, she ceased her rootling through the base of the felwyrt and looked at him. "Rob, you assured His Grace of your loyalty, didn't you?"

"I did." He chucked the stem away and selected another.

"So?"

Robert placed the fresh green of the stem between his teeth and drew from it the sweetness hiding there. "So, he wants it substantiated."

"I cannot blame him after everything that has happened, can you?"

"No, not really. But…" he hesitated. "Isobel, it would help satisfy his doubts if you were to spend more time with the Duchess of Clarence."

Sitting back on her heels like a street child, she squinted up at him in the strong light. "Why? And why did he not ask me himself?"

"I am your husband; of course, he must consult with me first."

"No," she said slowly. "He spoke with you so you would know of his doubts." She threw her head back suddenly and laughed. "It is a double test of your loyalty: first, to ask you directly, and second, to see if you will allow your wife to go forth into the nest of vipers. Hmm," she angled her head and watched Gloucester over the grassy bumps between them. "I must know His Grace's thoughts." She dropped her gloves and trowel.

"Isobel, no!" but she skipped out of his reach and marched determinedly towards Gloucester. He was to one side with the mewsman, fitting a long hawking glove.

"Your Grace?" she interrupted. He looked up and, seeing her expression, waved the man away. "If I serve as you wish, will it be proof enough of loyalty to you?"

"I have never doubted your loyalty, my lady."

"And my husband's?"

"Would you tell me if he were not?"

She thought about it for a moment. "My father once said to me that I must be the mirror of my husband in all that he says and does, but that my conscience is my own."

"Then, lady, do you speak for yourself or for your husband?"

The glove remained loose about his wrist, capturing her attention. She reached for the buckle, aware of the intent with which he examined her and proceeded to tie it for him. She pulled the strap tight, then looked at him, her blue-green eyes to his steady observation. "I am Your Grace's loyal servant."

He held her stare, examining the depth of her sincerity. Then, covering her hand with his own, said quietly, "Thank you," and released her from his scrutiny.

CHAPTER TEN

Squeals of laughter rose up the walls around the castle's pleasance and filtered into the chamber in which George, Duke of Clarence sat alone and brooding. The sound of his daughter and wife enjoying the late afternoon sun roused him from his reverie and drew him to the window. Their images flickered across the uneven surface of the small glass panes, becoming distorted and unnatural. Clarence opened the casement. The movement caught the eye of his young daughter and she broke into cries of 'Papa, Papa!', jumping up and down as she was wont to do when excited. The nursery maid had his son upon her knee and played a game involving letting the infant fall so far only to be raised up high to his evident delight. She saw Clarence frowning and ceased the game. Turning away, Clarence went to the table from which he had risen and the documents that lay upon it.

Since his return from France the previous year, Clarence had taken stock of his position. Promises of greater wealth and opportunity had failed to materialise and the maps, manorial accounts and offices scattered in front of him were the sum of his holdings, but not of his ambition. Early suggestion of the highest office of all had been curtailed by Warwick's fall from power, and even before that when the earl had married his youngest daughter to the Prince of Wales. Such a hurdle might have been overcome, but the birth of a son and heir to King Edward and his ultimate overthrow of the remnant of the old king's line, put paid to any hope that he, George, Duke of Clarence, might one day become king.

Looking back, Warwick's ambition had been ill-advised, his moves to control the crown based upon shifting sands and mercurial motivation. Most of all, Warwick had made the mistake of relying upon his own English affinity to secure the kingdom. This was a short-sighted plan, Clarence now understood. While Warwick had managed to persuade the witch, Margaret of Anjou to wed her son to his youngest daughter and, in one fell step, disinherit Clarence, it couldn't have lasted. He saw that now as clearly as if the veil of his mind had lifted and all was revealed by Divine sight. For what Warwick ultimately had lacked was a broad basis of power, unhindered by the squabbling families locked into conflict by over two decades of bickering.

England needed clear leadership from one who could cut a swathe through the rubble that was once the country's nobility — a country strong enough to take possession of lands across the seas and hold them. Their failure in France was evidence that Edward couldn't do that; he lacked the will to govern his unruly country, to drive home the advantage abroad. Gloucester had said as much, Clarence gave his younger brother credit for that. Edward made himself look weak; he had been blown off course and bought off, and any foreign power wishing to take advantage would press it. Edward, the once unstoppable, implacable, son of York, had lost the right to rule in his willingness to accept what amounted to a *bribe*.

Clarence writhed his lip in scorn. Yes, he recognised that he, also, had taken advantage of what had been offered by Louis – who wouldn't? But his acceptance wasn't blind; it had led to other advantages, and ones which he now pursued with single-minded determination. Warwick had relied on an English-based affinity; he would not. Warwick had been brought to heel by Anjou and become dependent on her — and France's

— goodwill; he, on the other hand, had taken steps to ensure this was one mistake he would never make. If he was to secure his rightful place in England, he would first look to the lands beyond. Only then, with alliances made with foreign princes who had no vested interest in the politics of this realm, would he be in a position to make his claim. Edward needed him, of course he did, but was he too blinded by those around him to see it?

Outside, he heard his wife call to Margaret as drops of water hit the stone sill. He rose, began to close the casement, but watched instead as his children were gathered by their mother and hurried from the pursuing rain. He lifted his head and breathed in the scents of moist soil. He sensed change in the air, a movement away from the life he had known. Planets were in revolution, shifting, and so would he. It was time to put in motion the plans that had been breeding in his mind like mice, gnawing away until he felt compelled to act.

Below, his wife saw him and raised a hesitant hand in greeting. Without responding, he turned away. He must take steps to pursue his rightful place at his brother's side for none else could be relied upon to provide it. All must change. From beside the documents on the table he took a quill and the ink pot in the shape of a great tower, a pennant bearing his arms flying in stiff undulations from the silver parapet.

'Right trusty and well beloved,' he wrote, 'we greet thee well.'

His conversation with Gloucester on that summer morning had left Robert questioning his own motives. More importantly, perhaps, the wisdom — or otherwise — of the decisions he might subsequently make. So, when the handwritten letter arrived bearing the Duke of Clarence's personal seal in the week following Rob's return from the magnificent, sombre reinterment, he felt the anxious knot in the depths of his stomach twist just that little bit more. To all intents the message was an open invitation for him and Isobel to join Clarence and his family at L'Erber; but Robert knew the duke well enough to know that he never did anything without motive.

Understanding what drove the man had kept Robert, if not one step ahead of the game, at least on a level footing. Now, he began to wonder whether friendship with Clarence was too high a price to pay for dubious advantage abroad and the odd manor thrown in to keep him sweet. With Gloucester, he knew where he stood; could he honestly say the same of his brother? He was still considering the invitation when Isobel came into the chamber with their youngest child under her arm and a small scrap of paper in her other hand. They were followed by a servant struggling with a bulky roll of cloth.

"Look what I have been sent!" Isobel plonked Robbie down on his father's knee and indicated for the fabric to be released across the table in a river of ruby and gold. "It is a gift."

Robert adjusted the baby so he sat more comfortably. "From whom?"

"I know not." She waved the note and shook her head. "I do not like it."

"It seems very fine to me."

She tutted. "I mean it disquiets me that I do not know from whence it came. There is always a reason for a gift. Who sends a thing of such value without naming the giver? It is unnatural."

"Does the message not say?"

Isobel waved the paper in front of him. "It has but a single letter upon it."

He took it from her. It was indeed blank on one side, with a florid *G* scrawled on the other, and no seal to designate the sender. Robbie made a grab for the fabric, nearly unseating himself in the process. Robert caught him just in time. "Perhaps you have a secret lover?" he suggested, largely in jest.

"You must mean the one I keep for idle moments between bearing children, running the household, and keeping your bed warm. That one?" Isobel slapped her head in mock surprise. "No, of course, it is from the king, how could I forget!" She paused, scowling. "Or mayhap the stable boy has been saving his pennies — or the Constable. Or it might be —"

Robert held up his hand. "I hear you, I hear you. I made but a jest, Isobel; I meant nothing by it."

"It is only a jest if the other person finds it so," she pointed out. "And I do not. I ask again, who would send such a gift and *why?*"

He leaned forward and ran the fine fabric through his fingers in little juddering motions as it snagged on his sword-calloused skin. "Why?" he asked as if to himself, turning his thoughts inwards as he ran through options. "Who? Could G be Gloucester?"

Isobel inspected the letter with her head on one side, recalling a note she had received in Gloucester's own hand that had accompanied a brightly hued ball he had sent Cecily to replace that shredded by Hector. "It is not his script and I do not think he would be so … secretive."

Robert had all but forgotten Robbie who had discovered the dangly bits terminating in little gilt bells decorating his father's doublet and was busily stuffing one in his mouth. Isobel retrieved him, dislodging something that fell to the floor. She bent down and picked up the letter, recognising the seal at once.

"The Duke of Clarence has written to you?"

"To us. It is an invitation." Simultaneously, they looked at the fabric, then at each other. He shrugged. "It is possible. The only way to find out is to accept. Shall we accept, Bel? Shall we go?" He noted her hesitation, her doubt.

Finally, she nodded. "It is some time since last we met; I suppose we must."

"Because I say so, or because Gloucester wishes it?"

She smiled in the way that could mean one thing or the other, her eyes creasing and her mouth tipping upwards in a most appealing way. When she did that, she became the girl he once knew before all … this, and he wanted to reach out and take her, wrap his arms around her and shield her from the world and its cruel vicissitudes. But she was not that girl; not his dove, but a woman who knew her mind and voiced it and that, for all the frustration it might cause him at times, made her Isobel, his countess, his wife.

Isobel felt uneasy as they approached the walls of L'Erber by river. She had argued that there was simply no need for them to stay with the Clarences given their own dwelling lay within a short distance. Nor had she wanted to take the children. But on that point, Lady Isabel had made her mind very clear: Juliana would be good company for Lady Margaret, and perhaps the infants might play together. And would Andrew not like to see the pleasance and the marvels that lay within the estate?

"I am so pleased you brought the children," Lady Isabel exclaimed when the family arrived. Robert had been whisked away by Clarence immediately, leaving the women and their offspring to make their own entertainment. "Margaret, look who is here to be your friend." The fair-haired girl, with a chin that gave definition to her otherwise rounded features and dressed in clothes that matched the splendid gown of her mother, surveyed them without smiling. "Margaret, greet your friends," Lady Isabel insisted with an edge.

Margaret extended her hand to Cecily and to Juliana said, "Come," as if she were a puppy.

Juliana looked up at her mother. "Ama, do I *have* to go?"

"Of course. Off you go and play. Lucie will go with you and make sure you behave." It was the only reason Isobel had been persuaded to bring the children. Lucie — a plump, kindly girl, who could adopt a voice of iron when necessary — would accompany the Langton children when they were not with their mother. If the duchess understood Isobel's reticence, she only demonstrated it in the slight sadness with which she watched them disappear from sight.

"Now," Lady Isabel said, brightening, "let us keep company and you can tell me what you have been about since we last met — apart from breeding heirs," she added, this time with more of the humour she had once displayed freely, patting her own extended belly as she did so.

As she led the way to her chambers, Lady Isabel stopped in the doorway. "I had hoped to have seen more of you recently, but we have not been so often at Court. George does not feel welcome now that there are so many new faces." There was disappointment in her voice, but something else. Doubt? No, wariness. "Still, you are here now and we shall make our own entertainment."

A forgotten poppet lay in a small cradle by the cold fireplace; but it was a tiny, exquisitely decorated casket in bright enamels sitting on its own stand that caught Isobel's eye.

"Gifts from King Louis. He was most generous to my husband." Lady Isabel's mouth skewed before she realised. She rearranged it. "I hear Lord Langton similarly prospered from the great *victory* over the French."

"He did — as did all the lords who accompanied the king," Isobel replied with care.

"Except my husband's brother. I understand he refused gifts?"

Isobel was about to say that Gloucester had eventually accepted the gifts of the French king, but possibly only because he had been ordered to do so by King Edward to ease the process of negotiation, but she thought better of it and instead went to examine the casket at closer quarters. "It is so very pretty, Your Grace."

Lady Isabel joined her, opening the lid to reveal a jewel in the shape of a cross, a lustrous sapphire in the centre surrounded by a quartet of rubies and four pearls. She picked it from its bed of silk. "Yes. So beautiful." She turned it over. Behind the rock crystal cover in the middle of the back lay trapped a dull splinter of wood. Incised images of the Passion — sponge, whip, and lance — decorated the smooth gold around it. "A fragment of the true cross," Lady Isabel said in awe, holding it to her lips, eyes shut in momentary prayer.

Isobel crossed herself. When the duchess opened her eyes again, they glistened around the lashes, and Isobel felt a rush of compassion. "Your Grace, you are not yourself; what ails you?"

Lady Isabel rubbed a hand across her eyes. "Nothing that safe delivery of this babe will not cure — and my sister's company. I pray to the Virgin for the one, but the other… I sometimes wonder if I will ever see my Scutterbuck again."

"Might a visit not be arranged?" Isobel asked gently. Lady Isabel raked her lip and gave a scant shake of her head. "Not even once you are delivered and churched?"

"George fears for my protection should I travel alone, and he will not accompany me to see his brother."

"Protection?" Isobel queried. "His Grace of Gloucester would ensure your safety. He is a most diligent host and you are kin, after all."

"It is not my *person* George wishes to protect, but the information I carry." Lady Isabel spoke so quietly that Isobel had to stretch her ears to hear. "Rest assured, I have tried to persuade him oft times."

"Surely he trusts his own wife!" Isobel exclaimed, regretting her outburst as the duchess shot a glance towards the closed door.

Raising her voice and injecting a levity not reflected in her face, Lady Isabel said, "I suspect I have been in London for too long. There seems less light here, somehow, it is all so closed about. And the stench! I swear I could walk from here to Westminster on the ordure and never touch the ground." She forced a laugh and wrinkled her nose. "And George is so contentious when he is here and apt to scold. Still," she said, "that is of no matter and all will be well now you are here. The men will keep to themselves and we shall have our own company. What could be better?"

Isobel thought that the complete absence of Clarence might make things considerably better for his duchess, but reprimanded herself for entertaining such an idea. "Perhaps we might see the children before long?" she suggested.

"Is it the children you wish to see or the pleasance in which they play?" Lady Isabel asked, raising one brow.

Isobel put a hand to her breast and inclined her head, "*Mea culpa*, you know me too well."

"I hope to know you a great deal better." Smiling now, Lady Isabel fanned herself with her hand. "Perhaps it is cooler outside in the garden." *And where there are fewer ears*, she might have said.

Linking arms, they left the chamber.

"In return for granting your wish, Is'bel, tell me about my sister and how she fares. You are so fortunate to be able to travel freely and to be made welcome by my husband's brother. Richard is a generous lord, is he not? He was always thus, as I remember. Still, Lord Robert is a favourite with so many." They left the stuffy gloom of the interior and emerged into the scalding light of the summer afternoon. "It seems an age since I saw Anne last and now she has a son. My brother Gloucester must be relieved to have an heir to secure his name. Does the child thrive? Are they content? I know that Anne finds comfort in Middleham; she feels closer to our father there. I think, of all his possessions, we were happiest in the north."

There, that touch of genuine wistfulness; but also something else, held back, suppressed, rising like bubbles in the myriad questions she asked, but never quite breaching the surface. Isobel itched to ask what Lady Isabel really wanted to know, but the rush of small feet along the paths distracted them, and the moment passed.

"Ma'mere, ma'mere!" Margaret shouted, running full tilt into her mother. "Papa says we go in a boat."

"A boat?" Lady Isabel repeated with a puzzled frown as Andrew came to a halt beside his mother, pointing back the way they had come, his face animated.

"Ama, His Grace says we can go on the river and Fader says we can, too. Can we go, Ama? Please?"

Isobel followed his pointing finger and saw the men by a great urn set on a low stone plinth in the centre of the inner pleasance. The brick paths all led towards the intersection as if this urn — beyond all else — was the focus of the garden. Clarence, resplendent as always in vivid silks that competed with the flowers and complemented his form, was busy expounding something to Robert and had not noticed the women making their slow progress towards them.

"Ah, the lily," Lady Isabel said as if that explained everything. "The queen made a gift of it. She knew George to be most desirous of a piece." Isobel secretly wondered what the queen wanted in return but kept that thought to herself. "You have a scion, do you not, Isobel?"

"We do. It has spawned several itself. We gave one to the Abbot at Roche and another to the hospital of St Leonards — do you know of it, Your Grace? It tends to our sick and the lepers amongst the people of Tickhill. They have placed it in their physic garden as a blessing to the halt-footed and feeble-minded, so that on a fine day the sick might sit before it and pray. It brings great comfort." Isobel recalled the royal, resplendent lily with a smile. "I also made gift of one to their Graces of Gloucester."

Lady Isabel murmured under her breath, "George *will* be pleased to hear that he shares a scion with his brother and with lepers."

The two women regarded each other and Isobel's lips began to quiver. A smile broke on the duchess's face, and a laugh escaped. "Will you be the one to tell His Grace, or shall I?" Isobel said.

"I believe," Lady Isabel said, taking a kerchief from her purse and wiping her eyes, "that there are some things best kept to ourselves. Ooo." She put her hand to her stomach. "This one does writhe so."

Clarence turned on his heel at the sound of his wife's voice and his eyes became probing as he saw Isobel with her. Then he broke into a wide, inviting grin. "Mesdames, we will venture out on the river on the morrow and make merry while this weather holds, and show our honoured guests what pleasures there are to be had in our company. Lady Langton," he said, giving an overly deep bow and scooping up Isobel's hand. Holding it to his lips, he looked up at her through thick, fair lashes.

"Your Grace, may it please you," she responded, withdrawing her hand.

He dismissed her with a practised smile and turned away. "Langton, let us repair to my privy chamber."

"I wonder what it is they discuss?" Lady Isabel said, watching the men's retreating backs as, heads close together, they conversed in earnest, and gave Isobel an enquiring look.

Isobel surreptitiously wiped the back of her hand on her skirts. "I doubt it is the lily's finer points," she said lightly, but she, too, ached to know.

Accompanied by the resonant drone of bees and melodic whine of hoverflies, Isobel and Lady Isabel walked in dappled light by the bank of the river. Absorbing the lush greens and the stippled colours of bark and flower, Isobel allowed herself to be beguiled by the warmth, becoming lax and careless in her movements, her thoughts less guarded. They returned to the airy pavilion erected for the day out by the river away from the noise of the turgid town. Carpets spread across the sward, cushions awaited, and their husbands lounged in lively debate fuelled, no doubt, by copious amounts of alcohol. No other guests had been invited, and Clarence wooed Robert with his full attention.

Isobel helped the duchess sit in welcome shade and popped a plump cushion behind her back upon which she could rest.

Accepting the wine offered to her, Lady Isabel said in a low voice, "George insists I drink red wine only. He wishes to ensure a son."

"The late Earl said the same," Isobel whispered. "He gave *many* instructions on what I must and must not do when with child." She rolled her eyes and Lady Isabel smiled.

"Of what do you speak?" Clarence called. Then, "Ladies, you must settle this argument: I hold that mead is the noblest of drinks and Langton, here, that wine is to be preferred. What say you?"

"That too much of either softens the head, Your Grace," Isobel laughed, going over to Robert and tapping her finger on his forehead. He caught it and kissed the tip and pulled her down onto his legs, offering her sips from his cup, his arm snug around her. From the corner of her eye, she saw Clarence watching them, a drop of mead on his lip, his interest intense. He wiped his mouth, slowly.

Growing self-conscious, Isobel slipped off Robert's legs and sat beside him, pulling her light gown higher over her breasts. Clarence raised an eyebrow, looked away, and drank again.

"I prefer perry," Lady Isabel called. "I tried it first when in France — do you recall, George?"

"Perry is a woman's drink," Clarence said. Cloud, soft as bulrush seed and as white climbed into the heavens above them eclipsing the sun. The air cooled.

"I like fruit syrup," Isobel said to fill the awkward silence, "if not too sweet."

"Syrup is for children," Clarence muttered.

"Bramble murrey, too," Isobel mused, refusing to be crushed. "And rhubarb distillate — my lady mother used to make it. Mmm," she said, closing her eyes and remembering, "it was most wondrous on a summer's morn —"

"And no doubt gave you the shits," Clarence said into his drink, ignoring the looks his wife shot him. "Mead," he saluted the sun as it emerged from the cloud, "is the drink of princes."

"I'll take a good ale over mead or wine — fresh-brewed and plenty of it," Robert observed. "But not beer." He shook his head, pulling a face. "It makes dough of a belly —"

"And makes you fart," Clarence added.

Lady Isabel clapped her hands and called for food to be served before he could say anything else. Willow baskets stuffed with straw held smaller ones containing linen-wrapped breads, hard yellow cheeses, pies and patties, candied fruits and dainties — simple fare for the Clarence's, but a feast nonetheless.

Clarence helped himself and lay back, one arm behind his head the other clasping a goblet as it balanced on his chest. A wavy-edged pikelet collapsed in Isobel's fingers and a piece lodged in the cleft of her breasts. Robert retrieved it, popping it into his mouth with a wink and a grin and feeding her a piece of his own. She became conscious of Clarence watching, seemingly absorbed by the movement of her hand to her mouth, until she could not bear such attention anymore, and ceased eating altogether.

Away from the adults the children played or slept under the watchful eye of the maids. Lady Isabel dozed and Isobel's focus drifted in and out of the men's conversation as thrushes foraged under the willows. A bold robin bounced nearby. She threw crumbs for it, enticing it closer. Robert stood up, stretching his arms above his head and excusing himself. The robin bobbed, its black-bead eye watchful. Clarence rolled over onto his side next to her and chucked the remains of a crust towards the bird. It flashed away to a branch only to return moments later to peck at the crumbs. "It shows too little caution," he commented to no one in particular.

"I like how brave he is," Isobel said, smiling at the bird's courage as it came within arm's length of them again.

Clarence shifted, searching with his spare hand under his hip to move the clasp of his belt that had become lodged there. He regarded Isobel with a slight smile, reminding her of a fox basking in dappled sunshine while watching its prey. His hand, resting near hers, played with the gold end of his belt, flicking it back and forth. "Did you like the gift I sent you?"

"Gift, Your Grace?"

"I hoped I would see you wearing it. Pomegranates are such a strange fruit and not one to my taste, yet they spill their seed so freely." He let go of the belt and caught her hand, pressing his lips to her skin. She felt the tip of his tongue and tried not to flinch, but he released her and took up the belt again. "The cloth would make much of your *forme la plus succulente*." The cloth. G for George. Of course. *Never something for nothing,* her head warned, her pulse quickening and an uncomfortable lump in her throat.

"Earl Langton," he said, "instructed me in the use of arms when I was a boy; did you know that?"

Isobel shook her head, her thoughts jumbled by his sudden change of subject. It was possible, of course, although Robert would have been but a youth himself. "He has made no mention of it, Your Grace." Willing his return, she craned her head to see if she could spot him.

"Did he not?" *Flick, flick.* "I expect," he said, "that he also instructed *you* in many things." He ceased playing with the belt and his finger stretched to stroke the side of her thigh through her skirts. Surprised, she jerked away. "An ant," he said in way of explanation. His expression had not changed and she wondered whether she was mistaken in her suspicion. "So, did he *instruct* you?"

"In arms?" she said, nonplussed. "Why would he do that...?" And then it dawned on her. "Your Grace surely means the earl, my *husband?*"

"Who did you think I meant?" He adjusted himself into a sitting position, his head now level with hers, his eyes hazel-flecked in the strong slanting light of the sun and no longer fierce, but intent. Checking his wife still slept, he inclined towards Isobel, his well-formed mouth inviting.

Alarmed, she leaned back until she felt the strain in her spine. "Your Grace, it is not meet!"

"Meet?" he said, his voice thickening. "Who is to say what is *meet* if they do not see it?" She began to protest, but he stopped her. "*Shhh*. It is but a moment and no one shall know." He placed a finger on her lips and then attempted to trade it with his own while his other hand sought her breast through her gown and squeezed.

Isobel yelped and, placing both hands against his chest, shoved hard, sending him backwards against a painted stool. She scrambled to her feet as Lady Isabel stirred.

"What hour is it? Have I slept long?"

"Not long." Isobel welcomed the excuse to help her sit up. "But it must surely be time to return so that you might take your ease in comfort?"

"Yes, it is time," the duchess agreed and then, "Lord Robert, where have you been?"

"Just yonder," Robert said, ambling up and pointing along the river where a bend made a perfect curve. "It is a good place to spot fish."

"Did you see any?" Isobel asked, tidying her hair and her skirts.

"Yes. Some." Robert looked at her flushed face, frowned; glanced at Clarence who had ceased rubbing the back of his head and now, pinch-mouthed, glared into the distance. "Fine, fat trout. Perhaps you would like to see them?" Surprised by her enthusiasm, he let her grab his hand as she started to pull him back the way he had come.

Clarence by now had climbed to his feet. "We leave. Now," he said sourly.

"Surely there is time enough for Isobel to see the fish?" Lady Isabel began, but Clarence stamped over to the pavilion and was shouting at the servants to hurry up.

"What was that all about?" Robert asked Isobel when they had a moment together out of earshot as the ducal barge moved steadily along the river towards L'Erber. "He has barely said a word to you. Have you offended him somehow?"

"Nothing," she said. "It was nothing." And she hoped, for their sakes, it wasn't.

Clarence shrugged his gown from his shoulders to be caught by his groom of the chamber before it touched the floor. The man bowed and backed from the room leaving the duke and his wife alone for the first time that day. From where she sat up in bed against bolsters, Lady Isabel waited, watched, until she detected the nature of his humour and dared to speak. She didn't need to; he spoke first.

"Well?"

"It was a most pleasant day."

From beside the empty fireplace, he looked at her. "Was it?" he said, his words laden with irony. "I am glad you thought so."

"I only meant... I believed you found it entertaining —"

"What did you learn?" he interrupted, "other than the medicinal value of *herbs*. Langton's married a gardener; did you see her hands? No better than a yeoman's wife raking shit among the pigs. And as for taking an oar, she'd be better suited as a river wife than married to an earl of Langton's degree."

"George!"

"What of it? You know it to be true."

"Isobel is gently born and you have said before how you find her company spirited. You do her great disservice. And as for rowing, I believe it says no more about her than she does not let her station limit her. She grew up by the Humber and the Trent after all; why should she not be able to take up an oar? I like her," Lady Isabel added. "She is honest and is a good friend to me and asks for nothing but my friendship in return."

He thumbed the carved and painted shields decorating the fireplace lintel. "I might have found her company interesting once, but her wit palls on knowing her better. As for you *liking* her — that is as well, but what did you *learn* from her?"

Isabel examined her hands clutched together on the bed cover protecting her enlarged stomach. "They have but recently returned from your brother Gloucester in the north —
"

"I know *that*," he sneered. "It is no secret. Tell me something of value."

"I do not think —"

He swung away from the fire and approached the bed in three long strides. He lent towards her, his knuckles sinking into the covers. She smelled fresh mead on his breath, saw the ribbons of veins on his temple. "I did not tell you to *think*. I told you to get the woman to talk. *I* think, and you give me the information I want. Is that clear?" He put a knee on the bed, bringing him closer. "Is. That. Clear?"

Isabel flinched away. "Yes."

"Good." He climbed onto the bed beside her and put his arm around her shoulders in a companionable way, except his fingers pinched the soft skin of her arm. "Now, what did she tell you — word by word?" He pulled her closer to him, his fingers biting a little bit deeper as he mouthed into her hair, "I want to know *all*."

Robert cleaned his mouth with a cloth dipped in minted ash, taking care to rub each tooth to its gum, rinsing the residue and the dregs of wine that clung to his teeth, and spitting the contents into a bowl left for the purpose. He walked, a little unsteadily, to the bed, climbed in, and drew the covers over them. He tucked the folds around his wife to keep out the draughts. "So, what did you learn?"

Isobel snuggled into his chest, feeling the smooth rise and fall and hearing his heart beat beneath her ear. It was the first time since they had arrived at L'Erber that she had felt safe. The house had a presence she found difficult to define, and she did not like its welcome. The atmosphere hung heavy here. Perhaps, after today's episode with Clarence, she understood why.

"Not much. The duchess kept things close, but she is frightened of her husband, that I do know. Also, she asked a lot of questions."

"About?"

"Where you have been, to whom you have spoken. About His Grace of Gloucester, also. But she was not easy in the asking; she did not do so out of curiosity, but as if she had been charged to do so."

"By Clarence?"

"Probably."

They lay in comfortable silence as they each thought about their day. Then, Isobel asked, "Did you learn anything from His Grace other than the generosity of his cups?"

Robert grunted. "Only what he wanted me to hear. Small talk about trade, his horses. But," he added, "he is brewing something."

"What? Apart from ale." She giggled and he humoured her by laughing.

"That, I believe, I will learn shortly. He wants to talk again tomorrow; he said it is important."

"And then we will see?" she asked.

"And then we will see," he confirmed.

CHAPTER ELEVEN

Clarence looked around when Robert entered the room sometime before noon the following day. "Good morrow, my lord. Good of you to join us."

Us? It took a moment for Robert to realise that more than one man occupied the low-ceilinged room in which Clarence sat, his head resting against the high-backed chair, cup in hand. Robert gathered what wine-soaked wits were about him. "Your Grace, my lords, masters, I beg pardon for the lateness of my arrival. I did not realise a company had assembled and I admit to overstaying abed. Your Grace's cellar is wondrous good to keep a man asleep, but the fault is mine. I will make a point of being woken earlier."

"By your wife, eh, Langton? Should she not have bidden you rise before times?" Thomas Grey, Marquess of Dorset emerged from the deep-set oriel window overlooking the river and crossed the room to help himself to the contents of the silver ewer sitting on the board. He moved more easily than his height and breadth suggested, the richness of his garb exaggerated by the fall of light from the widow reflecting off the silk. His heavily ringed fingers made a chinking sound as he picked up the ewer. "Or perhaps, having *risen*, you found it necessary to *chastise* the lady for her negligence, eh?" Amber wine stained Dorset's full lips. He smiled, an easy lift of his mouth that made it insincere, and raised his cup in salute. "A little censure to add spice to the marriage bed. I'll drink to that."

A rumble of laughter reverberated around the chamber from the handful of older men, but both Dorset and Clarence remained watchful of Robert's reaction.

Robert's temper prickled. With effort he quelled it, and poured himself a cup of wine to chase the dog that sat in his head, foul-mouthed and growling. "After, what, two years of marriage and two sons already under your belt you ask us to believe your bed needs ginger, my lord? With such appetite I wonder you find the strength to rise at all. Pray, tell us your secret." He lifted his cup to the younger man in return, drowning his annoyance in the following swig he took.

Dorset's light blue, unblinking eyes appraised him. In the esquires' yard as a youth, Robert imagined him to be one of those lads standing on the side-lines of a fight, slipping comments between the combatants and watching the effect of his veiled barbs. With all the weight of his mother, Queen Elizabeth, and his heiress wife behind him, Dorset no longer felt the need to watch; he liked to be in there stabbing, needling and seeing how far he could go before he gained a reaction. Robert recognised his type and refused to fall victim to it. The one thing that did surprise him, however, was his presence here in the first place. Clarence's antipathy towards the queen's family was hardly a secret, so that either meant he had something to gain from the association, or he didn't care. Whatever the case, what did Thomas Dorset have to offer, and what did he seek in return?

The scattering of other men included ones Robert remembered from previous meetings — lesser nobility, gentlemen, merchants of some means — mostly from London, several from Essex, one from Kent. The rest were strangers to him. Clarence indicated the two men standing together, subservient and waiting. "Langton, you know Ashby and Dennison?"

He recognised Dennison for his round face and red complexion topped by a shock of clashing tawny hair; but the smaller, fair-haired Ashby with skin recently browned was unknown to him. He nodded his head to them and received lower bows in response.

Clarence continued. "Ashby is my agent in matters concerning business in foreign lands. He has but this very morning returned from Burgundy and, before that, Portugal. He has intelligence that you might find interesting."

Robert raised a questioning eyebrow and Clarence made a flicking motion with his hand permitting Ashby to talk.

"My lord, there is word concerning the safety of your ships."

"Oh? And what is the nature of the threat?" Robert asked.

"Pirates, my lord — Barbary infidel."

Robert grunted. "That is not news. They are as a swarm of locusts that come and go with the season. My ships are well defended against the Barbary pirates. We kill more men than we lose. The Hanse ... well, that is another matter; their ships are slower but the damage they do is far greater." He lifted his shoulders briefly. "But they are less of a problem than they were since the treaty."

A merchant by the name of Adams — an older man, well-dressed in robe and manner — furrowed his brow and raised a fat finger. "My lord Earl, they do not profit from your fleet alone. They have attacked my ships also and threaten —"

"None is alone in this, Adams," Clarence intervened. "We sink or sail together. In numbers we have a greater chance to strike a swift blow and make ourselves felt. That is why we are gathered here. Together we have strength. We cannot rely on aid from any other..." his lip curled, "...quarter."

Some seemed to approve of Clarence's statement, others were clearly at odds with it. Adams appeared to be speaking on behalf of the merchants and lesser men, who lacked the wealth and status of the older man. "Is the king aware of these latest incursions, Your Grace? Should he be told?"

Clarence shrugged. "He knows. I have made my complaint clear. Again." Behind him, Dorset smirked into his cup.

"But His Highness has made it his policy to counteract piracy," Adams pursued in bass tones no doubt deepened by a rich diet. "The treaty His Highness signed with the Hanse —"

Clarence tutted. "What? To run together and come to each other's aid in case of attack? That is all very well, but what ship's master will put his vessel in danger for the sake of a stranger? They have orders to protect their own; they will flee if they can. That is why we have an agreement between us, is it not?" He addressed the company but kept his eyes on Robert. "That aside, words are cheap but action says all. Since my royal brother made treaty with the Hanse, he has been less than willing to press our cause against those that continue to harry our ships. He has other matters to attend and we are left to defend our own vessels. We must make our mark against these pirates, my lords and gentlemen, and make it well." There was a general murmur of accord. "But you know this; your own ships suffer grievous loss as do ours." He leaned towards Robert. "And that is not all, Langton," he said, then speaking up, "My lords, gentlemen, masters, I thank you for your observance this day and for the agreement we have reached. I have business with the Earl and so must bid you all good day."

When all had left apart from Ashby and Dennison, Clarence took on a more urgent tone. "Langton, it is not without purpose that I requested your presence for the threat is immediate and very real." He directed his agent to continue.

Innocuous, bland, Robert could imagine Ashby slipping unnoticed from port to town, market place to inn, gathering seeds of information as he went.

"My lord Earl, my sources report these pirates do not act for themselves alone."

"Oh?"

"It is said that a certain foreign gentleman pays well for each ship taken by pirates, and that a blind eye is turned against any privateer who might venture to profit from English and Portugean vessels."

"And do your sources say who it is that sponsors this piracy?" Robert helped himself to a hot meat chewit from a newly replenished dish.

Ashby cast a look at Clarence, licked his thin lips, and lowered his voice still further. "Don Arenado."

Robert ceased eating, his eyes suddenly hard.

"You know this man?" Clarence asked.

"I know of him," Robert said through his teeth. "He has long since opposed us in Portugal."

"But yet more, my lord," Ashby quickly said. "He does not act alone but is said to be in alliance with Chefchaouen and its lord —"

"Infidel?" Robert interrupted, the chewit discarded.

"You know of this place?" Clarence said again, watching Robert's reactions closely.

Robert didn't answer immediately, instead rubbing his forefinger repeatedly across his top lip as he absorbed the news. "Chefchaouen, Your Grace, is a new-made town set to deprive my mother's people of their lands on the Barbary coast. Ports, like that at Tangier, were taken, in part, to prevent safe haven for pirates and to provide one for the Portuguese and Holy Church; but keeping them has proved a trial, and some have since been abandoned. Chefchaouen is as strong as its lord is determined to be rid of Christians." He glanced at Ashby. "You say Don Arenado has accord with the Infidel who rules over it?"

"So God is my witness, my lord."

"Then he is traitor to both God and King Afonso as well as all Christendom."

"Now, Langton, you see what we are against," Clarence said. "Our king fails to act against infidel pirates so we must do what we can to protect what is rightfully ours. Do his dirty work — as ever. Your noble mother lives close to the coast, does she not?" Robert nodded, registering that Clarence seemed to know more about his mother's circumstances than he remembered telling him. "Then this last piece of intelligence will be of the utmost concern to you." This time, Clarence bent a finger in Dennison's direction, who had, until now, made no move to comment. "Dennison, state your business and the nature of your intelligence."

"Eh, Your Grace?"

Clarence raised his voice. "Tell Lord Langton what you learned."

"Oh, aye." Fumbling the hat he clutched in front of him, the burly man cleared his throat and faced Robert. "Me lord," he said with a thick accent, "I were out o' Bristol by five days with wool and hides when a gret wind blew and we were blow'd off course and only made safe harbour by the Grace of God Almighty, the Lady Mary and all the blessed saints." He raised his eyes heavenwards and crossed himself.

"Get on with it, man," Clarence said.

Dennison flushed horribly. "Aye, pardon Yer Grace. Anyway, we were blown off course and fetched up in port a day's fair sailing south from Faro, me lord. Huelva," he said when it looked as if Robert was about to ask. "We supped in the 'arbour there, and there were some that were talkin' in their cups, as it were. Rough looking, an' all..."

A sharp *thesk* issued from Clarence as he drew the tip of his tongue against the side of his teeth in a hard, impatient sound that needed no words to express his frustration at the man's slow speech.

Dennison shot a harried glance at Clarence. "There were some forrin-lookin' men and a gentleman — that's what caught me ear, like. Rich-looking an' all, not like to find such as he in a place such as that. He were talking as if he didn't want to be heard, soft like."

"And you *heard* what he said?" Robert said with a degree of scepticism.

"Eh? Oh, aye, my lord, I heard everything and I sees more."

"What tongue did they speak?"

"If yer thinkin' I mistook their speech, my lord, *Eu entendo bem.*" *I understand well.* He grinned broadly, showing missing teeth in all their gappy glory.

Robert sat back. "*Bom,*" he replied in Portuguese, "so, you know the language, but might you have *misheard* the words said?"

Dennison tapped his right ear. "Not been hearing since bombard 'sploded next to me as a lad." He turned his head enough for Robert to make out the thick scars and lack of earlobe beneath ragged red-ochre hair flecked grey. "I been seeing words since then." He placed a finger to his eye and then to his lips and then pointed directly at Robert. "I see words," he said again, "and this gentleman, he were clear in what he said on account of them he was talking to were not of his kind, if you see what I mean."

"What *do* you mean?" Robert asked, this time noticing that the man stared at his mouth as he asked the question.

"Well, I reckon they were Barbary folk, their clothes being alien like."

"Did you understand their speech?"

"Didn't need to, me lord, they waved their pingies and nodded their heads like there was no stopping 'em. They made themselfs clear enough. And the purse he gave 'em said more'n words could. But," he added, "it were the mention of the name that made me say to myself, 'Aye-up and there's mischief afoot right enough'."

"Name? What name?"

The man cleared his throat. "Senhora Juliana. The gentleman made sp'ific mention of *Senhora Juliana* —the lady of the English lord. They was to raid the castelo and sack the estate. *Inferno*, he said." He sat back, looking pleased with himself while Robert's head rocked.

Ashby ventured, "Who is this lady, my lords? What is she to our ships and the matter in hand?"

Clarence answered. "Lady Juliana is Lord Langton's noble mother."

"When?" Robert squeezed out.

"Eh? Oh, aye. Next moon, m'lord."

Robert looked towards the window as if he might judge the phase of the moon despite the bright light of the day. "The moon is waxing now. They will want high water at full moon to make their attack. My ships will be in harbour then, and my mother…" His knuckles bleached as he curled his hands into fists against his thighs. "My mother will not abandon the land of her fathers so easily, nor her people. Sweet Jesu, this is news that must not wait, but my fleet is already under sail and I cannot warn their captain nor my dam." Grim-faced, he stood.

"I will take my leave, Your Grace. Come what may, I must find a vessel willing to sail without delay."

"Wait, my lord." Clarence said, rising to join him. "I have ships ready to leave and men I can make at your disposal. Between friends we look after our own, and one day I might have need of *your* aid." He thumped Robert's back as if to seal the pact. "Have no fear, Langton; from what I have heard your lady mother reminds me of my own." A dry smile lifted his mouth. "I pity any man who tries to cross either lady — dead or alive."

Robert threw his travelling cloak onto the bed, paused with his eyes closed and thumb against his brow as he thought, then opened them suddenly with an "Ah!" and walked swiftly to the other side of the room where the coffer sat. He opened the lid with a clunk. "I will take coin with me but leave you with ready means until more can be sent from our treasury. I've instructed Hyde on estate matters so you do not need to do so. Now, where did I put the pouch?" He rummaged about and Isobel, watching from the window, went to help him.

"You have never told me much about your mother. Why does she not bide in this country? Surely she wishes to see her grandchildren?" She found the pouch tucked away beneath Andrew's caul and took them both out. "Do you not miss her?"

Robert pursed his mouth in consideration. "I suppose I do. She was always a steady presence and intensely loyal and devout. She is also fearsome and pragmatic. Nobody crosses her or questions her judgement for fear she will flay them alive. She chooses to live in the land of her birth, not because she shuns us, but to serve the family." He slipped coins into the pouch, counting silently, then drew the string tight and weighed the bulging bag in his hand. "She manages the estates there, ensures continuity of trade, seeks out new markets, negotiates with merchants — protects our interests in Portugal and further abroad. And she makes representation to the king of Portugal on our behalf. I suspect that is why we have come under attack."

"Someone wants what she has? Or is she pursuing interests that clash with another?"

Robert looked at her appreciatively. "I expect a little of both. Whatever the case, I must go to our estates and assess the situation."

"When do we leave?" she said with little hope.

"No, my dove, you must stay here and run our estates while I am gone."

"But —" she began to protest, and he placed his finger on her lips.

"I need to know things are being overseen here. Besides," he added, "I do not know what dangers there might be, and I will not expose you and the children to them needlessly." Seeing her face fall, he replaced his finger with his lips. "I will return, never fear, may it please God."

She proffered the linen cloth that contained Andrew's baby caul. "Then you must take this to keep you safe at sea. Drew has no need of it whilst on land and I will rest more easily knowing you have the benefit of it." She put it carefully into his hands, but he handed it back.

"This is Drew's and I would not deprive him of it. I have this to preserve me from harm, and keep it with me always." From inside his doublet, wrapped in a scrap of cloth, he unwound a brittle brown stem sprigged with dried blue flowers.

"The rosemary!" Isobel exclaimed, recognising the bundle she had gifted him before they were married. "I did not know you kept it."

"Of course. What is more precious than this token of our love? This will keep me afloat." He tapped her on the tip of her nose with it. "Now, I must to the ship; the tide will not wait. In the meantime, Lady Isabel has bid you stay with her in her confinement. You will have the friendship of the duchess and I will rest easy knowing you have the protection of the duke."

Aghast, it took her a moment to find her voice. "Rob! How could you agree such a thing? I do not wish to stay here with them!"

"It is all approved. The children will benefit from the company of the Clarence children, and you and the duchess are on good terms, are you not?" She nodded, bleakly. "There, that is settled then. Besides, His Grace insisted." And something in the way he said it made her take note. "I am indebted to him, Isobel; I could not refuse."

Robert left on the evening tide, Philip Taylor by his side, taking ship in one of Clarence's vessels and accompanied by the duke's men and what arms-bearing soldiers of their own they kept at Langton Place. Isobel watched the old but seaworthy cog as it was eased by the smaller picard into the current down river of London Bridge, and the square sail fill and catch the steady breeze that would accompany it to the mouth of the Thames and out to sea.

Reluctant to return to L'Erber, she spent a little time in the streets that fed people and animals, baggage and carts over the great bridge that spanned the river, then slipped into a nearby church to find space and peace to think. Folding her skirts under her knees to cushion them against the red and white tiles that patterned the floor, she stayed a while, listening to the voices beyond the rood screen and adding her own prayers until the voices ceased and the priest appeared. She left him with coins for masses to be said for Robert's safe passage and for her family's protection. But protection from what she did not know, only that dread settled beneath her breastbone and would not shift.

Children's voices filled the great pleasance, cutting the overheated summer air with a clarity that seemed at odds with the atmosphere that so often clung to L'Erber. Isobel found Drew chasing Margaret down the paths that intersected the neatly planted borders, applauded by Lady Isabel. They ran to where the Papal lily bloomed in its urn at the centre of the garden and away again, taking their game with them, while Juliana did her best to catch speckled butterflies.

"Take a care not to catch bees!" Lucie called out to her, laughing. Not wishing to curtail their sport, Isobel remained hidden from view and let their unbridled joy fill her emptiness. Juliana skipped around the corner in pursuit of a butterfly. Engrossed she didn't see her mother until, "Buzz, buzz, buzzzzzzzz," Isobel caught her under her arms, swinging her into the air and making a *zzzz* sound against her ear. Juliana squealed in delight, rubbing her ear and kicking her legs.

"Again, Ama! Again!"

"What, does my little bee want to fly again?" Isobel laughed.

"Yes, yes, yes!" Juliana flapped her arms setting her hair bouncing. "I'm a bee, I'm a bee. Look, Drew, I'm a buzzy bee!"

Margaret observed for a moment then ran to her mother and raised her arms; but Lady Isabel bent to kiss her instead. "I cannot lift you, my love; you are too heavy for me."

Andrew bowed, dark hair flopping over his eyes. "Let me lift Lady Margaret, Your Grace, I am very strong!" and to prove it he flexed his skinny arms.

Lady Isabel's smile broadened and she swept a shallow curtsey, placing her hand upon her heart. "Gentle knight, you are most courteous. I must accept," she said, stepping aside.

Andrew carefully put his arms around Margaret and, bracing his legs, swung her about twice and put her down.

"More, more, Drew!" she cried, lifting her arms and turning her back to him.

Hoisting her again until she dangled like a poppet, he began to rotate. Around and around, her legs flying out, the pair of them spun in widening circles encouraged by Margaret's delighted giggles. "Be careful!" Isobel exhorted but he continued to spin wildly to Margaret's shrieks of laughter.

"What is this rabble!"

Startled by Clarence's fierce voice, Drew staggered. He managed to drop Margaret safely to her feet, but with his arms flailing like a falling sycamore seed, his mouth open and eyes wide, he lost his balance, toppling backwards against the urn. In no more than a breath, Drew and the urn teetered together, wobbled, and fell. He landed with a thump as the urn crashed to the ground shattering stone and sending the lily into the air. In the deathly silence that followed, child and lily lay in the remains of soil and shards.

"Are you hurt?" Isobel said, running over to him and putting her hands around his ashen face, feeling the bones in his skull, then his arms.

A shadow fell across them. "Idiot boy!" Clarence roared. "Do you know what you have done?"

"He knows well enough, Your Grace; can you not see he is hurt?" Isobel said over her shoulder, controlling her temper but only just as she helped Drew to sit up.

"The child meant no harm; they were merely playing," Lady Isabel pleaded, putting her hand on his velvet arm. "Look, the flower will bloom again." She held out the decapitated remains of the lily in her trembling palm.

Clarence threw her off and the bulb was crushed beneath his foot as he moved to lower over Isobel. "Stand aside, madam; the boy will take his punishment and learn from it."

"Your Grace, *I* will reprimand my son!"

But he reached around her, grabbed Andrew by his thin wrist, and jerked him to his feet. Drew yelped.

Furious, Isobel tried to pull Clarence's arm away, then attempted to lever his fingers from her son's wrist. She located his thumb. "Do not touch my child!" she blazed, giving it a sharp yank.

He let go, but puce-faced, raised his open palm to strike.

"Don't hurt my Ama!" Drew yelled, taking hold of the first thing that came within his reach and sinking his teeth into the man's flesh. Clarence's bellow of pain turned into malice. Sucking his bleeding wrist and pivoting on his heel, he snarled, "Get that bastard from my sight!"

"He is gone from home awhile; the children can play again," Lady Isabel said when Isobel escaped alone into the garden the following day to assess the damage to the lily. Bleakly, Isobel nodded. "I am sorry for it, Is'bel; it was not Drew's fault." She dismissed the sun-worn gardener and came around into the light and Isobel was shocked to see the reddened skin around the woman's cheekbone and the darkening colour about her eye. "It is nothing," Lady Isabel said. "It is no more than I deserve."

"How can you say that!" Isobel said, horrified. "You were not to blame."

"Oh, but I was. I am — always." Her smile turned down. "I did nothing to placate my husband's anger, to turn his rage from you and Drew." Her fingers touched the developing bruise. "I have been made mute by his blows, Is'bel. He is so easily displeased, more so now than ever before." She sat on the stone seat and patted the space next to her.

The crushed lily in her hand forgotten, Isobel sat down. "You cannot be the source of such displeasure; you try to please him at all times."

Lady Isabel gave a short laugh. "George believes the world is against him and if he cannot set it to rights, he ensures that I, at least, will be mastered." Her resigned smile became bitter. "Even my little Margaret believes her maman must be in error."

"My husband has *never* hit me," Isobel said in a whisper. "How can you suffer such treatment? Can you not appeal to the king?"

"And say what? George is within his rights to chastise me. If the king were to mention anything, my husband would only beat me the greater for betraying him. I must endure. I have little choice; it is a test of my forbearance and duty as a wife to try to satisfy him. Yet, if I keep quiet and avoid him, he seeks me out and beats me. If I say *yay* and *nay* thinking to appease him, he beats me. It is not me he beats, Is'bel, but the world."

"And the children?" Isobel asked, remembering the venom on Clarence's face as he reached for Drew.

"No, they at least are spared his wrath, for which I thank God daily. For now. Margaret knows better than to cross her father and for that he loves her. When we were first married, I made the mistake of voicing my thoughts in the belief he might wish to hear them." She smiled at Isobel's raised brows. "Well, I was younger then and ignorant of my husband's choler. I soon learned that I should have no voice of my own even if I did sometimes speak out when I could not hold back, and always rued it after. Now I need only look at him and it causes offence." Looking down at her burgeoning stomach she said, "I am grateful he spared the child from the beating; he would not wish to harm his heir."

"Yet he was prepared to strike my son and *his* father's heir." It popped out of Isobel's mouth before she could stop it, and she coloured. "Forgive me, Your Grace, I spoke out of a mother's desire to protect her child."

"You speak only the truth, Is'bel. Drew defied my husband and George will not forgive such a slight — even from a child defending his dam — and more so because of the boy's bastardy..." On seeing Isobel blanche she stopped. "Now *I* have caused offence. My dearest Is'bel, please, I beg you, do not be offended. Earl William was a great man —"

"William," Isobel said with a harsh edge, "was *not* Drew's fader..." She clapped her hand to her mouth as Lady Isabel's eyes widened, and she shut her own eyes, steadying her mind. "I mean that Andrew is as much Robert's son as Robbie is, or as Juliana is his daughter." She opened them again. "He is beloved by us both."

"Of course he is!" Lady Isabel exclaimed. "He is a dear boy, brave and courteous; and Earl Robert shows such a gentle nature to take his brother's child as his own. A truly noble act of great charity." The duchess offered a small smile of appeasement. "Let us not quarrel, Is'bel. I do not think I could bear to lose your friendship." She looked on the verge of tears, her Neville pride subdued, and the determination Isobel had mustered to leave the place softened.

"You must know I do not wish to remain here, not after what happened, but Robert made me agree to it. I will stay only because he would have me do so, and because…" Isobel didn't want to presume; this was, after all, the sister-in-law of the *king*.

"We are friends?" Lady Isabel ventured, almost uncertainly.

Isobel nodded and then smiled — a warm smile and genuine, and the duchess threw her arms around Isobel's neck, the first truly spontaneous act of this normally reserved young woman.

PART THREE

CHAPTER TWELVE

From this angle the small boats looked like any trading vessels that frequented these waters. Standing among the scalding rocks and brash scrub on the Portuguese cliff edge, Robert screwed his eyes against the sun and counted one — two — five lateen-rigged boats rounding the low headland protecting the bay and the entrance to the river Mira where his own ships lay at anchor. Small and swift, they cut the inky foam-capped waters, riding too high to be heavily laden with cargo. He couldn't make out how many men each boat carried, nor whence they came, but the determined way in which they made for the narrow opening to the river had the hairs on the back of his neck tingle, and he always took note of his hackles.

From the pouch at his waist, Robert took a small looking glass and, catching the sun in its surface, sent a series of flashes. Moments later, winks of sharp light returned from Philip Taylor across the bay. Turning, he repeated the action, waiting until he saw the response from the defensive walls of Castelo do Mar from where he knew his mother watched. Pungent, bruised herbs scented his path as he slid and ran down the slopes towards the river anchorage, sending small stones rattling into the coarse brush.

"*Cinco*," he called to the closest moored ship when near enough to be heard over the steady wind blowing from the sea. "Five." He pointed towards the mouth of the river and held up spread fingers.

From the forecastle of *The Dove*, Captain Barquerio shook his head and presented both hands. "*Não, meu senhor, sete* — seven."

Robert followed the direction of Barquerio's extended arm. Chalk-coloured sails fattened by the wind made elongated triangles the length of each vessel and marked the course of the galleys. Seven of them — too many to be traders or opportunistic Barbary pirates; this was something else — and they had knowledge of the treacherous shoals, which they approached at speed. Robert swore in Portuguese. Whoever they were, these raiders came well prepared.

The warning given, the men from the boatyard retreated from the foreshore, leaving the skeletal remains of their trade in slings of wood to whistle alone in the strengthening wind. Women and children from the clustering houses at the harbour side withdrew into the surrounding landscape, melting like ghosts between the laden vines and behind low stone walls until merely the flapping washing strung between houses or draped over walls marked their previous occupation. The bells in the church tower remained silent. No birds sang. Only the persistent rasp of invisible crickets sawed the air. Crouched behind nets, Robert could make out the galley boats more clearly and his chest tightened. Each vessel was crammed with men and light reflected off drawn weapons. There could be no mistaking their intention now.

His own ships strained at their anchors against the tide filling the deep channel of the river where they were moored. They appeared empty except for the bales stacked on the decks ready to be offloaded, and the barrels of sweet wine and boxes of pomegranates waiting to be placed in the holds. The quayside built by his grandfather was piled high with sacks, crates, kegs — the rewards of a good harvest and brisk trade. Easy targets. Rich pickings.

The first of the raider galleys passed the mouth of the river, the second close behind. Men in strange clothing with unfamiliar weapons crowded the gunnels with barely a breath between them. He could hear them, smell them, feel their anticipation as they headed past him along the narrow channel between shore and sand bank, and towards the village. Three more vessels broached the river entrance making directly for the moored ships as Taylor thundered to join him.

Calls in foreign tongues had men scrambling, letting fly the ropes that bound the sails and releasing the wind. The galleys slowed. Long poles with hooked ends reached out towards the raised gunnels of Robert's own ships and latched on. The men on the enemy galleys raised their weapons, bent legs tautened and made ready to spring. Placing finger and thumb to his lips, Robert gave a long, low whistle.

Instantly, men erupted from his ships' holds, emerging from behind barrels, leaping off the high forecastles and trapping the raiders between gunnels and sea. From small boats bobbing mid-stream, crossbowmen threw off canvas covers to fire into the backs of the pirates hunching behind each other. The stricken rag-tag scrambled over the bodies of the dead and dying to find refuge in the water or risk the ropes dangling over the sides of the English vessels where they made easy targets. Several made it to shore where they were picked off to lie beached and bleeding in the sand.

"My lord!"

Robert swung around and followed the direction of Taylor's finger. The two Barbary ships making upriver had passed the pinch point where tide and river met. "Now!" Robert yelled and, on each side, teams of men took hold of giant loops of rope lying buried in the sand, and heaved.

From the water, a heavy snake of metal reared, creating rainbows of falling drops as it was lifted free of the surface, preventing any further movement of galleys up or down the river. But the two pirate vessels had reached the village, sliding into the shore where near three-score men poured over the bulwarks into the shallows, and spread out like fire between the low buildings. Slavers. Finding the women and children gone they would push into the surrounding fields to flush them out. They would kill the old and infirm and harvest the women and tender seedlings that were the future of this land.

Robert could hear the progress of the raiders in the smashing of pots and overturned tables, the guttural sounds of their course voices amplified by close-set walls. Then there was another noise — metal on metal, broken cries of alarm, and a slow grin spread on Robert's face. Raiders appeared from between buildings, spilling haphazardly onto the sand and, behind them, Englishmen and Portuguese were running them down, pinning them like needlework. The raiders were already raising sail, picking their men out of the water from ropes trailing behind the retreating ships, but making no attempt to retrieve the wounded who had only made it as far as the river's edge.

The tide was running fast and taking the galleys with them. With a sickening crack, the foremost vessel shuddered, slewed and began to list sharply, caught as a fish in a net against the metal boom slung across the river. Shouts came from the second galley as men braced themselves with poles in an attempt to break the impact as the second ship collided with the first.

"*Meu senhor, o castelo!*"

Robert smelt it before he saw it: a thin plume of smoke rising from the castle. Men, like beetles, crawled up the defending walls, others teemed over the tumbled ground on which the castle sat on its raised promontory. Small dots moved around the wall heads and something glinted briefly in the sun. There was a faint cry and a figure plummeted, scattering the men below before breaking upon the rocks. Gathering saliva in his mouth, the taste of battle as sharp as lemons, Robert drew sword and rondel and, calling to his own men, sprinted towards the castle.

Within the hour, blood and pitch was baking under the sun. The rocks beneath the castle walls were smeared with it. The air reeked. This land had seen many such deaths. Time and rain would wash it clean and ash would scour blackened stone. Robert picked his way through the bodies lying contorted on the broken ground. How easy it was to kill a faceless enemy. And to be killed. The pile of dead grew on the sand of the outgoing tide.

Amid the frenzy, Robert had itched to fight, to kill, to wreak vengeance on those who had brought war to his lands. Yet, stripped of their clothes, the foe lost their identity; they were no longer the enemy, nor infidel, just men. They had wives and children, mothers and sisters waiting for their return. He despised what they did, but that did not equate to hating them. If anything, he felt nothing. Was that worse? He should feel something — pity, remorse, even loathing would be better than this void.

A low moan issued from a body nearby, a foot twitched. Trapped under a headless corpse, eyes unfocused, skin bleached, breath uneven, the man's life ebbed to mingle in the dust. Robert shoved the decapitated body with his boot revealing the man below and with a single, swift thrust of his sword, ended his life. With the man's blood dripping from the tip of the blade, Robert stood looking down at the carcass. Nothing — no regret, no shame, no guilt. Numb. How many would he have to kill to feel something?

*

"Roberto."

Robert bent his knee and his head and received his mother's blessing in the touch of her hand once he had entered the castle's courtyard. Careful not to anoint her skin with blood, he kissed her ring and held it briefly to his forehead. He rose to be met by her unwavering blue-grey eyes that reduced him to a child again.

"You are wounded?" The dowager countess scrutinised the laceration on his arm.

"It is nothing, *senhora minha mãe*. The threat is over; they are vanquished."

"So I see," Dowager Countess Juliana said in her accented English as if she had not spoken the language in a very long time, running her eyes over his blood-spattered face. "Are all the infidel dead?"

"All but one. We took the captain of a vessel alive. He will tell us what we need to know." He didn't amplify his statement nor did his mother enquire how he might elicit such information.

"And those other men — are they of our affinity?"

Robert looked at the soldiers sheltering in the shade of the castle walls, taking turns to drink from the cup dipped into the bucket of cool well water as Taylor went among them checking names. "Mostly, but some serve the Duke of Clarence. We would not have secured such a victory without his assistance." He hesitated as she raised a brow. "I would not have *known* of the threat to you without his warning."

"Then we owe him a debt that cannot be lightly repaid," she said without emotion. "Meanwhile, we have much to discuss. Come inside; there are too many ears in these walls."

He welcomed the marble floors of the rooms darkened by shutters against the heat of the day. Only a faint aroma of burning wood remained to remind them of the recent incursions, for all else in the dimly lit interior looked precisely as it had done when he was last here over a decade before. They climbed stone stairs to her private apartments where great windows gathered the cooling breeze from the sea.

The sun had not yet reached this face of the tower and Robert allowed the wind to bathe his flaming skin. From here the chopped waves of the ocean were no more than ruffles upon the water, and he felt the draw of it, the urge to plunge into its depths and expunge the death clinging to his flesh. As if reading his mind, his mother snapped her fingers, sending servants scurrying to prepare a bath for him, but with her own hands, helped him remove his blood-soaked gambeson. He sat in the chair — with its x-frame and worn leather seat embossed with the ancient arms of his mother's family — that had not moved from its position overlooking the ocean in all the years he had known it. The walls of the single chamber were freshly painted in white and red checkers, the mats new-made, the hangings billowing in the sea breeze, clean; but the simplicity belied his mother's status. He had noted the stiffness of her knees as she had climbed the tower stairs.

"Why do you choose to live in the tower, *senhora minha mãe*, when the house Grandfather built still stands? Would it not provide greater comfort and be more fitting to your needs?"

"Perhaps, *meu filho*," she said, "but the castle was built for defence and I sleep the sounder for it. I am content here. Alone."

Robert pushed himself out of the chair, opening the laceration on his arm again. He watched a ribbon of blood track its way down his arm through matted hair, gather at his fingertip, and fall in a carmine drop on the white marble floor. *Blood will out*, he thought. He turned back to his mother. "*Como vades*? How fare you, madam, do you keep good health?"

She clapped her hands for clear water and linen to dress the wound on his arm. "Your Portuguese is lacking, Roberto; you must practise more. I am as you find me and as your brother last left me. I had hoped to see you before now; your presence might have acted as a deterrent to those with ambitions towards our lands." There was no reprimand in her tone only a statement of fact. She applied a salve to a wad of linen and pressed it against his arm. He flinched.

"I meant to visit before now —"

"Intention is not enough. I believe Don Arenado to be behind this attack, and only steel will dissuade him from launching another assault. I will bring this incident to the attention of King Afonso and hopefully turn it to our advantage. Afonso has neglected to purge the Barbary pirates from our waters and it has taken my son and his English duke to do so. The king will not wish to be shown wanting; he will acquiesce to my demands."

"Clarence is not my duke," Robert said, more sharply than he intended as she bound the wound.

"If he is not your lord then he must truly be a good friend. Why else would he offer such assistance?" She dropped the soiled linen into a bowl.

"We have mutual interests, that is all. This piracy is one. Why did you not tell me of this latest threat?"

"While your brother was alive, Don Arenado kept his distance, but he always coveted our lands. He knew what would happen if he breached the treaty between us, but now Guilherme is dead, so is the accord. Don Arenado thought at first to flatter me with talk of an alliance between us, he even proposed marriage." A derisory laugh escaped her lips. "It could not have been for my youth and beauty nor any hope of bearing him sons. When I refused, he sought to outbid me in the markets and put pressure on those I would call allies." She tapped her finger on the arm of her chair. "I did not concede one grain of our land, nor give way in any market in which we hold sway." Her mouth tightened, her iron-bone jaw defiant. "And now it has come to this! If your brother was alive…" She looked out over the ocean as if willing him back from the dead.

"But William is not here," Robert said sharply. "Why have you not told me any of this before?"

"Would you have come if I did? You were too busy with your own affairs — your wives, your king. This is my land; these are my people. I promised your father I would uphold family honour, defend the land, trade for the benefit of his sons and the Langton *dinastia*, and this I have done. Guilherme understood what it meant to maintain the stronghold here, to protect our lands —"

"*I* understand, *senhora minha mãe*. I am here defending you and *our* people, *our* lands. When William was earl, he took it upon himself to maintain his lordship here as well as in England, and brooked no meddling in his commerce nor his governance from me or any other. It was not for lack of interest on my part."

"Five years, Roberto. He has been dead five years."

Robert leaned his burning head against the stone of the window. Five years. Had it been that long? He felt the faintest touch on his shoulder.

"I do not remind you because of my own need to see you, my son, but because your attendance is necessary to maintain your presence. Don Arenado is not the only one who would take advantage of your absence. This is not the first test of our defences."

Robert wasn't sure whether it was her subtle admonishment that stung more or the fact that she voiced no desire to see *him*. But she had a point. "You are right; I have been away too long. I thought the estates too well maintained to need my mediation. I stand corrected." He bowed his head to her. The sincerity of his admission must have mollified her to some extent because she gave a short nod of acknowledgement.

"Come, Roberto, you have seen to the needs of your men; now you must see to your own. Bathe and dine, and then we will discuss the future."

The wound on Robert's arm itched. He picked at the edge of the new scab and earned a sharp tap from his mother; he had to make do with scratching around the wound instead. He had surveyed the estates, met the reeve and the *alcaide-menor*, Senhor Alves — their steward of many years — and tenant farmers. He and his mother discussed opportunities for trade, new markets, diversification of crops. They bemoaned the piracy that plagued the coast, considered options and concluded that, without the intervention of the crown, direct conflict was inevitable and, in some cases, desirable. Which had brought them back to the subject of Clarence.

Clarence's ship had sailed once the threat was deemed over, taking with it messages to the duke and letters to Isobel. That left Robert's own vessels to patrol the section of coast and his men to scout the surrounding country for any word of retaliation. To Don Arenado, his mother devised an additional communication in case the first had not rammed home.

An elaborate box lay open and empty on the table in front of them. "It is a fine casket," Robert observed. "Too good for a man like him."

"Yet it will serve its purpose well enough. Anything less will raise suspicion. He will see it as his due, and so it is. He is *cocksure* as your father would say, *Senhor Arrogante*." She averted her head and spat into a fine linen kerchief. Folding the fabric into neat quarters, she placed it in the bottom of the box. Seeing her son's expression, she raised a rare smile. "The *filho da puta* deserves no less. He wanted me; now he has a part of me. You think your mother acts like a *pescadora*? Maybe so, but the fishwives here are more noble in spirit than he will ever be." Another box — this time of iron — was brought forward for her inspection. Inside, tightly wedged with straw was a smaller box of dull lead.

Robert reached out to open it. "Do not touch!" his mother said with a warning finger to her lips, and, donning a leather glove, she opened the box herself. Inside, surrounded in a coffin of ice, a lumpen heart lay, blood greyed by crystals, frozen, inanimate. "There are other ways of sending a message. This is one."

Robert swallowed and took a step back. "And the other?"

She didn't answer but had the smaller box placed in the larger, and the larger into the fine casket, and the whole crammed with yet more straw. Then, taking a small glass vial, she carefully removed the top and sprinkled a fine powder over the contents. Holding her breath, she agitated the straw until the powder became less visible. Equally carefully, she closed the lid and nodded to the waiting messenger. "Take this to Don Arenado as the spoils of war. Let him believe the attack was successful and this the first of much plunder."

"You will *poison* the man?" Robert asked, incredulous.

"Poison? *Não*! Unless his heart is weak."

"And is it?"

She pursed her lips, her stone-blue eyes gazing out somewhere across the tops of the citrus groves. "It might be," she said, and went to her chair.

"Whose heart was it?"

"You think I carved it from a living man's chest?" She laughed. "I see that you believe me capable, my son. Guilherme would have seen the truth of it; he knew me better." She rested her head against the chair back and draped her hands over the arms taking in the sea breeze after another long, hot day. She looked weary now, age etched in fine lines around her eyes and mouth, but still handsome for all that. "It is the heart of a swine, no more. The meaning is clear enough."

"It is. Both of them."

"You do not approve?"

He patted the pommel of his dagger. "I prefer a direct approach."

"You always did like to settle a score with your blade. When barely old enough to scribe your name, you could be found rolling in the dust, fighting with the boys from the village even if they were winters older than you. Guilherme would have to pull you out of trouble and break a few bones to remind them of their place. You would stamp and shout at him for his interference."

"I remember. I wanted to settle my own fights and William would never let me."

"He wanted to protect you, his younger brother." Her face softened. "He adored you, Roberto. Many times he took the punishment meant for you."

Robert stretched his memory back to those dim days. "I did not know."

"He would not say."

"He was proud," Robert agreed.

"He was *loyal*. You do not recall him as he was then. You were too young to remember."

"And you did not know him in later years," Robert retorted.

"No, that is a loss I bear," she said quietly. "And now I shall have to bide my time until I see him again." She took the beads hanging around her neck and kissed the large cross of antique form suspended there. He had forgotten the knack she had of making him feel five again and insignificant compared with his older brothers. Thinking about it, he could not recall her dangling him at her knee, only her stern rebuke at his many failures. He looked away, struggling to control the desire to confront her.

"Roberto, you must not let your temper hold sway over you. It was always your weakness; do not allow it to be your doom. Guilherme —"

"Ah, William the Golden, always the dutiful son, as you oft reminded me. Well, William is dead; but I am still here. *I* am Earl and *I* make decisions for this family. I have children — your grandchildren — a dutiful wife, an affinity greater than any before, and all you have talked about is William, and what William achieved. If you only knew the truth, what he has done…" He stopped himself just in time, biting down hard on the black anger coiling inside.

"What did he do?" his mother asked calmly.

"If he did not tell you then I will not; but let it be known that he failed the family, *senhora minha mãe*, and be not so fierce, but look more kindly upon me, for I have had to right the wrongs he did."

"By taking the earldom from his heir?"

214

Robert gave her a swift, hard glance. "Is that what you believe?" He grunted and said almost to himself, "But why should you not, for you know no better."

"Then tell me, my son. Tell me what Guilherme did."

Distant sounds of men working in the shipyard carried up the stone walls of the tower and, out in the bay, seabirds called. Robert squeezed his eyes shut against the temptation to let it all spill out of him. "I... It no longer matters."

"But as you say, it cannot harm him now," his mother pressed, like winkling a sea-snail from its shell.

"No," he relinquished with a sigh, "but it might harm another and that I will not allow — not for you, not for anyone."

His mother nodded slowly. "You, too, were always loyal. I remember Duarte had defied his father and slipped off to the village to bed the shipwright's daughter. You were only a boy, but you refused to say where he was, despite the beating it earned you. My sons — my courageous, loyal, foolhardy sons. So like your father; you throw caution to the winds yet stand like oaks when others would seek to fell you. I cannot begin to understand what happened between you and Guilherme... Wait," she held up her finger to prevent his interruption, "but you are Earl now and you have a son to follow you and a wife that has proved more fertile than your last. The earldom is in your hands, so defend it, but choose wisely whom you follow, my son; be not beguiled by false promises of friendship."

He looked at her and frowned.

"Do not think that because I live in my tower I do not hear of the world beyond these walls. Remember, *meu filho*, I once attended the English Court when the old king sat on his throne, and I know its ways as surely as you do. This duke you speak of, Clarence, he betrayed his brother, did he not?"

Robert gave a quick nod of confirmation. "He might serve your needs, yes, and you may benefit from the association, but do not be deceived; once a snake, always a snake, and a man who professes to be something else is sure to betray your trust. Heed my warning, Roberto."

The last heat of the day carried the scent from the orange groves in a perfumed caress that drew Robert outside to trace its path. He knew it well enough and let his feet find their way down from the rocky promontory on which the castle sat, through the walled gardens where small green lizards bathed in the last of the sun, and out to the orchards and stands of trees on the fertile slopes of his land. It had a timelessness about it. For centuries his family had nurtured this land and, before that, it had been kept by the infidel they helped defeat. Yet even the infidel were but fleeting custodians, for Romans had lived here once. Perhaps it was they who had brought the vines that covered the gentle undulations and left a scattering of pottery and coins to mark their occupation. Now the soil produced the wine that graced the tables of kings and filled Langton coffers.

Twisted trunks of olive trees and their elongated silvery leaves offered shade for women shepherding goats. They averted their curious eyes and bowed their heads as Robert passed. He greeted them even though he didn't know their names and supposed them to be of the same families who had herded animals for his forefathers.

Passing the walls of the great fortified house his grandfather had built, he followed the line of olive trees marking the edge of the vineyards, where workers trimmed back leaves to expose the fruit to the sun. He broached the crest of the rise and stood looking down on the heads of vast groves of dusty pomegranate trees and glossy-leaved citrus. He inhaled, dislodging the clinging odour of death that still drenched the soil of the castle, replacing it with a fragrance that took him back to earlier years.

At his feet a thirsty sapling, the height of his calf boot, struggled in the late summer heat. The rains would fall come winter, but the nascent tree would die before then, and all that promise of abundance with it. It seemed such a waste, so futile. He hunted about him, locating a shard of stone with which he began to scrape at the earth. He loosened it enough to free the shallow roots and ease the young tree from the ground.

Binding soil and roots in his kerchief, Robert secured it under his belt. He felt a sense of achievement, as if in rescuing this one plant somehow made up for the lives he had taken. William had planned to bring Isobel here, to escape the turmoil of his life and his unhappy marriage to Felice, and find some semblance of peace among the fruiting groves. He imagined him now, a happier man in a white shirt open to the sea breeze, sword exchanged for a walking staff, looking back and smiling and holding out his hand as if to say *follow me*. In his mind's eye, Isobel stepped lightly towards his brother and took his outstretched hand.

Isobel would like this place. She might have been happy here. With William. An ugly sensation rose unbidden to lodge in his gullet. Robert recognised it for what it was, resented its intrusion, and swallowed his jealousy. He had been away from home too long.

The sapling stood in its pot of red clay upon the wharf next to his bundled belongings. It had drooped for the first few days but now stretched its head towards the sky as if relishing the sun upon its face and the fresh, moist soil around its roots. In seeing it, it reminded him of his own little saplings, and then of their dam. His small wound had healed, the scab falling away to reveal new pink skin in a bright line against his sun-bronzed arm. Isobel would fuss and tut when she saw it and he would smother her admonishments with embraces. He ached for her.

"William wanted to return here, *senhora minha mãe*; it was his dearest wish."

"Alone?" his mother asked, ever perceptive.

He hesitated. "No, not alone." He bent to pick up the plant.

Robert watched his mother from the deck as *The Dove* gathered wind in its sail and made towards the river mouth to the bay. She was a solitary figure, despite those moving about the shore, distinguishable by her stillness and the composure with which she conducted herself. And then the pilot negotiated the sand bars, and the calm waters of the river gave way to the chapped surface of the open sea, and she was lost to sight.

CHAPTER THIRTEEN

"Ama?" Pushing the letter Isobel had been reading out of her way, Juliana crawled onto her mother's knee where she sat in the window to catch the light.

"Yes, poppet?" Isobel cradled her sleepy daughter with one arm while continuing to read.

"When is Fader coming? Can we go home?"

Not as soon as Isobel had hoped. She read the last few lines and Robert's distinct signature, and put the letter to one side, feeling glum. They would perforce remain in the household of the Duchess of Clarence, carefully avoiding the duke. "Your fader will be home as soon as his business is concluded in Portugal. You know where that is, don't you? I showed you this morning."

Juliana shook her head.

"I do, Ama. L-let me show her!"

Isobel watched Andrew fetch the map from the table where she had been studying it earlier that morning. He looked happy enough, here, with his family and out of sight of Clarence; but his new hesitancy of speech worried her. The map flapped stiffly as he returned and held it up for his sister to see.

"There," he said, "Fader w-went here," he pointed at the inked outline. "He went t-to see our granddam and our estates." His little chest puffed with pride, his thick oak-dark hair making him look just like his father. Isobel momentarily conjured an image of Robert as a child, and then how Andrew might look in ten — twenty — years' time. "You are named for our granddam, Liana," he went on.

Juliana swivelled on Isobel's knee with a quizzical look.

"That is correct," Isobel confirmed. "Your granddam is Dowager Countess Juliana. She is a very great lady in Portugal and you are our first-born daughter, so are named for her."

Juliana popped her glistening thumb from her mouth. "I am a great Port lady!" she declared, jiggling about and wrinkling her nose.

The map forgotten, Andrew leaned against his mother. "Who am I named for, Ama?" he asked. "Why am I not *Robert* like Fader, b-but Robbie is?"

Isobel put her spare arm about his slight body, kissing his hair. "You, my sweet son, are named for St Andrew, on whose hallowed day you were born. There can be no greater honour in all this world than to be named for a blessed saint who served Our Lord Christ so faithfully."

"But St Andrew was…" he sought the word, frowning, "…cru-cruic … killed, like this," he said, giving up and crossing his arms in an 'x'. "Must I die like that if I work for Jesus?"

A lump formed in Isobel's throat. "No, my love," she whispered. "We do His bidding, but our paths are different according to His will."

"What is my path, then?"

She looked at her son, whose tendency to serious conversation made him seem older than his nearly six years and loved him until her heart cracked. "I do not know, Drew. Sometimes we only know our path when we are on it and, even then, the way is not always clear. You will know in time." She kissed his frown and smiled. "Now, it is time for the Order of the Bath." She put her protesting daughter on her feet and stood up. "Your poppet needs to bathe, my little bee, she smells like Moth when she has rolled in the stable yard. And, Drew, will you sail your boat as you bathe?"

Andrew made a wave motion with his hand. "I will sail my b-boat over the sea and fetch Fader home!" he declared.

"Can I come, Drew?" Juliana asked in a small voice.

"And me," Isobel said, hugging her children to her. "Shall we all go and find your fader?"

"Can we, Ama?" Andrew asked, serious again.

"I fear we must wait; but let us put ink on paper and say how much we miss him and our words will bring us closer to him. Then we will seal our words with kisses and send them on wings of doves across the sea to find him." She made her hands into wings and flew them around Juliana's head.

From her solitary stool apart from the family, Cecily tutted. Andrew went over to her. "Cecily, do you not wish to see Fader?" he asked solemnly.

"Lord Langton is not my father," she said stiffly, sounding too like Felice for Isobel's comfort and, yet again, Isobel wondered whether she had done more harm than good in taking the girl from her mother. And then she recalled the last time they had met and the ease with which Felice had let her daughter go — all for the price of a manor.

"My lady?" An older woman, kind-faced and garbed as a widow, stood at a respectful distance by the door. Isobel recognised the Duchess of Clarence's attendant.

"Mistress Twynyho! How fare you this day? Pray, do not stand there but come in and join us by the fire."

Ankarette Twynyho gave a shallow curtesy. "I thank you, my lady, but if it please you, Her Grace requests your presence. She says that His Grace is from home, and she is in sore need of your physic."

"Her Grace did not send a message?"

"I am the message, my lady. Her Grace said that you would understand if she did not write one herself."

Isobel did indeed.

Lady Isabel almost disappeared against the bleached linen of her bed. She held out her hand. "Bide with me a while, Is'bel. This child punishes my womb and he is relentless in his thrashing. I cannot sleep night or day." She did indeed look tired, the dark area around her eyes making the pallor of her skin all the greater.

Isobel settled next to the duchess and took her hand in her own. "It will not be long now. Ere soon you will be celebrating his marriage and bouncing your grandchild upon your knee. You will have jowls and silver hair and your children will refer *their* children to you for counsel and wisdom."

Lady Isabel burst into laughter swiftly censured by discomfort. She rubbed her enormous stomach with a rueful smile. "Ow! Do not make me laugh so! You will make a grave for me with your jesting. I cannot see tomorrow let alone a score years hence." She hugged Isobel's arm, laying her cheek against the cool, smooth silk. "You bring such light with you, Is'bel, I am gladdened by your wit. Never stop, will you? Always be yourself. Seek joy where you can and do not let it elude you. This world is so full of cares I sometimes forget what it is to be free of them. I cannot remember what it is to be happy." She sank back against the pillows, dampness filming her skin.

That cut Isobel to the core. "I would that I could magic some for you, but all I can do is pray to Our Lady that she lessens your suffering and beseech Christ Jesu that he grant you joy." She took her chaplet from her purse and kissed the jet cross suspended there.

"Amen," Lady Isabel murmured, then brightening said, "There, pay no heed, it is but a melancholia. I seem to be afflicted at this time of the year when the leaves fall and winter beckons." She pulled the covers to her chin. "It always seems colder by the river in Warwick, but George says the child must be birthed there, although," she added, "this one writhes so much he seems eager to be born afore time." She rolled her eyes and smiled. "Whether he be born sooner or later I will be right again by spring." She cocked her head. "They are pretty beads; how came you by them?"

Still draped over her hand like fat beetles, Isobel viewed the chaplet of jet and coral, adorned by the cross and the crudely fashioned acorn she treasured. "They were my mother's," she said, hoping that would satisfy Lady Isabel's curiosity and not be drawn into a conversation about her dam.

"I, too, have beads from my mother; rather, they were gifted to me by her but they were our father's — and his before him. They are the loveliest green, do you recall them? They are so finely striped and soft to touch. I think," she said, gazing at nothing but perhaps some image in her mind, "that my Scutterbuck would be glad of them. Yes," she said softly, "I will make a gift of them." She inhaled sharply as the child moved. "I will never sleep for his wriggling!"

"I have something that will help," Isobel said, and called to Mistress Twynyho. "Fetch the waters I prepared earlier — there, by my casket — and the cloths, I pray you."

When Mistress Twynyho returned, Isobel dipped a folded square of soft linen into the scented waters and bathed the duchess's face and neck, seeing the premature lines on her young brow smooth, and the tightness of her mouth loosen.

"Mm, that smells so good I could eat it; what is it?"

"Camomile, rosemary, lavender and mint."

"Is that all?"

"Yes, that is all, Your Grace. Herbs to quieten the mind and cool the skin, bound by a prayer to lift the spirits."

"So simple," Lady Isabel murmured, her eyelids drooping. "Not magic at all."

Meanwhile, across the ocean, sails billowed and belched and *The Dove* slewed in an uneasy sea. Sullen clouds gathered to the south-west but as yet no rain fell. The air felt heavy against Robert's skin and the uncertain movement of his ship made his guts churn. Taylor had already given his all to the waves and now crouched miserably with his short mantle over his head. Robert leant against the bulwark, debating whether to make himself throw up or try to suppress it. It could go either way. On the forecastle, Captain Barquerio glanced repeatedly at the oncoming storm, exchanging comments with a sea-worn sailor. To the east, the coast still lay under bright sun, while close to shore, the sails of smaller vessels showed white against the dark swelling water. Only the larger carracks and smaller, sea-worthy caravels, such as Robert's own, ventured further from the coast, using their bulk and greater area of sail to outpace the Barbary pirates that ravaged this shore. So far, praise God, the small fleet that accompanied *The Dove* sailed alone.

"*Meu Senhor.*" Captain Barquerio appeared at Robert's side. "That," he nodded towards the ominous pewter clouds, "ees a problem."

Wind cuffed the oily surface of the ocean and the ship trolled. Robert grabbed the mast shrouds, sweat pumping to the surface of his skin as his stomach rebelled. The captain waited until Robert was able to focus on more than his mutineer guts.

"What do you counsel?" Robert managed after a moment.

"We can not outrun thees storm," Barquerio said in his thickly accented English. "If we stay our course, we might, as you say, be over-whelm'ed. Keep to the shore and we risk to be driven on the rocks —"

"Or run against pirates."

"*Sim, meu Senhor*. But they wish to avoid the storm, also. There is safe harbour, but we must make haste to get there."

Robert searched for the other ships from his fleet that had sailed with them and saw that they, too, were struggling to make headway. "How far?"

The captain raised his shoulders in the way men of his nation did, in a slow elevation that expressed everything and nothing. "Some leagues. But maybe more. Or less. It ees difficult to tell; there are no marks on the land." He pointed out the terrain which had become an indistinct blur since Robert last looked. A gust of wind filled the sails briefly and then dropped and the canvas sagged again. Barquerio shook his dishevelled head. "No wind, then much wind — too much. *Meu Senhor*, we make for the harbour, *sim*?"

Robert looked at the expanse of ocean between him and home and considered what it might be like to end up sinking through the depths further and further from Isobel into oblivion. "*Sim*," he said, decisively. "Yes, make for the harbour."

The wind caught up with them two leagues or so from safe anchorage, the sails cracking as they filled, the timbers protesting at the sudden surge. Robert felt the exhilaration of speed, all sickness evaporating as the ship dug into the water and found its course, riding the rising waves with a new-found surety. He clung to the ropes, intermittent spray washing him free of sweat, salt burning his lips. He closed his eyes and, raising his face to the sky, laughed in the sheer liberation that was to be had unbound as he was by clumsy land.

His elation was short-lived. Shouting broke out around him and he followed the direction of the gesticulating crew. Searing from the south through cresting waves, three lateen-rigged xebecs made directly for them.

"*O corsário! Piratas!*"

"Taylor, on your feet! Ready the men for action." Using the bulwark to steady himself, Robert went hand over hand along the slippery deck towards the sterncastle and Barquerio. "Will they risk an attack in a storm?" Robert shouted over the gathering wind, screwing his eyes against the spray.

As they watched, the first of the pirate vessels was nearly upon the last of his fleet as it lagged behind, heavily laden with the bounty of his lands.

"We must go to their aid!"

"*Não, meu Senhor,*" the captain shouted back. "We cannot; the wind, it is too great." He turned and yelled orders, sending sure-footed sailors to the masts to reduce the canvas before the wind shredded it.

Robert looked on helplessly as the xebec caught up with his ship; but, instead of trying to board, it sailed past at speed. He frowned, trying to make out its bearing. Then he understood. Cupping a hand around his mouth he yelled to Barquerio, "They're trying to cut us off!", simultaneously making chopping signs with his other hand and pointing towards the harbour. "Prepare the guns!"

Barquerio nodded vigorously, shouting orders to his men and taking the helm himself. In the waist of the ship, either side of the hold hatches, armed sailors removed oiled covers to reveal two serpentines lashed, preloaded and tompioned, and with the vents protected from sea spray with sheepskin stalls.

Taylor stumped from one to the other, checking alignment over the bulwarks and ensuring the powder was kept dry, the lantern lit and muttering threats to keep it so. He sought out Robert watching from the sterncastle and lifted his thumbs.

A squall brought the first rain and the wind picked up. Through the spray, Robert made out the xebecs converging to create a moving blockade between his caravel and the safety of the harbour, with every passing moment bringing them closer and closer. His own ships were lost to sight and he murmured an *Ave* for their safety, adding one for his own. He slid his way to the quarterdeck where the captain and coxswain wrestled with the great tiller keeping the ship on course against wind and sea.

"*Muito rápido*! Too fast!" Barquerio translated in case Robert hadn't understood.

Robert didn't need to. Even if they avoided the raiders, at the speed at which they approached the coast they would sink within sight of the harbour on the ragged islets crowned in foam that protected it. They could not turn and head seaward in time and the wind was driving them forwards. Drop sail, and they would quickly founder and be consumed by the sea leaving his other ships to the mercy of the pirates. But they might get a shot in. Just one.

Measuring the angle and distance between *The Dove* and the xebecs, Robert shouted, "Barquerio, bring her bow around!" and pointed to the gun against the bulwark.

Barquerio craned his head, judging the fullness of the sails then with the coxswain, locked his legs and took the weight of the sea. Within moments, the ship's relative position had shifted enough to bring the xebecs within range.

"Taylor!" Robert bellowed, and brought his hand down.

Nothing.

The men at the starboard gun gesticulated frantically: the slow match must have gone out. Robert swore. He started towards the waist and would have seen to it himself but Taylor pushed the men aside and, taking up the lantern, bent over the gun. Robert held his breath.

The thunderous explosion ripped through the squall, sending black smoke billowing and the crew cheering wildly. Robert watched for the impact. The stone had been well-aimed but it fell between xebecs causing nothing but a ripple of alarm among its crew.

"Again!" Robert yelled, but Taylor shouted, "Powder's wet, my lord!", holding up a fistful in disgust. Robert's oath was lost to the wind as he saw the opportunity slip and the men's morale with it. The xebecs had regained their position and were closing in on the caravel.

"Ram them!"

"*Meu Senhor?*"

"*Forçá-los.* Ram. Them." He jammed his fist into his hand. "Do it!"

Orders to prepare for impact ran the length of the ship. "I hope you're right, my lord," Taylor muttered beside him, taking his wooden beads and kissing the cross. "Or else my lady will hold me to account and have summet to say about it."

The pomegranate sapling he had brought for Isobel sat forlorn in its pot lashed to kegs. There was nothing in this world Robert wished more at this moment than to give her that plant. "I hope so, too, Sergeant."

They were close enough to see the individual faces of the men in the xebecs, close enough to see them change from eager anticipation to confused alarm as they realised the caravel was bearing down on them. Faintly through the storm Robert picked out cries of panic as pirates flung themselves at the lateen sails in a desperate attempt to alter course.

"Ram them to Hell!" Robert shouted through the wind and rain, wrapping his arm through a shroud and tightening his legs. Momentarily, he lost sight of the xebec as his own ship rolled and then a tremendous *crack* and a shudder ran through the decks and up his spine, wrenching the ropes free of his grip and throwing him against the bulwark.

Everything stopped. He lay, winded, time suspended, becoming aware of shouts, cries, and the weight of something lying across him heavy and suffocating. Canvas. He fumbled for his dagger fighting to free himself, and canvas gave way to his blade. Gulping air, he emerged.

A hand reached down and hauled him to his feet and Taylor's broad face appeared. "Rigging's gone, my lord."

Robert squinted up through the rain to where the main mast's yardarm should have been, then around him at the confusion as men ran like rats over the broken rigging cutting away tangled lines and torn canvas. The ship had taken on a strange list and the yardarm lay broken across the deck. The mainsail draped over the side of the vessel, a bloated cadaver filling with sea and dragging the ship at an angle.

Robert was faintly aware of Captain Barquerio clinging to the tiller and giving commands to take the remaining sails down before they were dragged under, but his ears rang with a high-pitched whine. He shook his head to clear it, felt the sting of salt spray, and put his hand to his scalp. It came away bloody. He heard Taylor say something, saw him point at another xebec materialising through the storm and his hand reach for his short sword.

Taylor took the first pirate as he clambered over the side of the ship using his grappling iron, slitting him from shoulder to stomach and shoving him over the side. More followed, reckless, indifferent to the raging sea and the waves now breaching the deck and washing them clean of blood.

Dead in the water, the sail acting as a sea anchor, the caravel wallowed, unable to ride the waves. Closest to the ropes, Robert dodged a pirate blade, swiftly turning and cutting the man's leg tendons with his sword. He left the man writhing on the sloping deck, and began hacking at the lines to release the sail. Catching movement behind him, Robert ducked, receiving a glancing blow to his shoulder. He stumbled against the ship's side, swinging his sword in an arc and taking the raider's arm off at the elbow. He finished him with a second strike and, slipping on blood, returned to the ropes as the ship began listing dangerously.

"My lord!" Taylor, red-faced and puffing tried to pull Robert away. "We must leave. The ship's gone."

"We can save it!"

"Captain says not, my lord." He pulled Robert with him to the side where men had already jumped clear of the drowning ship. "Time I learned to swim anyways."

Robert caught sight of the potted tree and broke from Taylor's grasp, lurching towards it, but then saw one of the crew clinging to the shattered mast, his ear severed and dangling, immobilised by shock. Forgetting the tree and grabbing the man by his arms, Robert half dragged, half carried him to the ship's side. "You keep with me, understand? You, too, Taylor," and together they plunged into the water.

Ink smooth, the churning sea swallowed Robert into its silent depths. For a moment the quietness enveloped him, and then his lungs began to burn and he kicked his way towards the light. His head breached the surface to be immediately engulfed by waves and shrieking timber. Fragments of ship knocked against him as he struggled to stay afloat. He managed to lose his waterlogged cloak and found a timber big enough to bear his weight. The remains of the first xebec dotted the water around him. He searched the tormented surface for any sign of Taylor and instead saw the wounded crew man not far from him clinging to a half-submerged bale.

"My sergeant?" he called out to the man only to receive a shake of the head.

The wind lessened and the rain became heavier now, flattening the waves into oily undulations. He became aware of new sounds and saw the sails of his remaining fleet making for them. Robert abandoned the wood swimming strongly towards more of his men. Taylor was not among the crew. He sensed their despair, their fear. He helped a struggling man onto a smashed spar and instructed another to hold him there. "Our ships are nearly upon us; take heart," he said pointing towards the now clearly visible carracks. "You will soon be safely aboard."

He left them, and continued seeking Taylor among the wreckage. Bodies now joined the flotsam — his men, theirs — bumping into him. In death they all looked alike. He swam further, ignoring the beginnings of cramp in his legs, mindful of his draining strength.

Floating alone some way off, rising and falling with the heavy swell, he saw someone with untidy hair concealing his face. "Taylor!" he called and the man responded with a weary wave of a hand. Robert was within yards of the man when the dark complexion marked him out as a pirate. He floundered in the water, kicking feebly, each new wave overwhelming him a little bit more.

Robert trod water. He was about to turn back when the man saw him, his eyes widening in hope. In reaching out, he dropped beneath the water, reappeared, mouth open, gasping, terrified. He tried to swim, failed. Then he saw Robert's hesitation, and understanding, then acceptance, crossed the man's face, and he stopped trying. The next wave consumed him, and when it passed, the man had sunk out of sight.

In that look of resignation, Robert recognised their shared humanity. In that instance, he saw not his enemy, but a drowning man. He could not abandon him. Robert lashed out at the water, expending the last of his reserves to duck down and haul the man to the surface.

Engorged clouds absorbed what light was left of the day. The slack sails of the carracks stood out like a beacon, but Robert had swum further than he realised. He could just make out activity at the bulwarks and men being pulled from the water. He summoned strength. "Here!" he yelled, waving while trying to keep the semi-conscious man above water, but his voice came out as a broken caw and was lost in the rain. "Swim," he urged the man. "*Nadar!*" he tried in Portuguese, but the man could do no more than kick weakly. If Robert had any chance of reaching the ships, he would have to leave the man to his fate because his own was in the balance.

They rode another wave. The carracks looked further away now and he could see no sign of the xebecs. There was little point in fighting the waves and he ceased swimming and let the currents take them.

The rain began to ease and the wind dropped entirely. He was so tired. Water caressed his legs, kneaded his shoulders; he no longer felt cold and the water enveloped him, comforting as a pillow. Strength seeped from his limbs and he needed to close his salt-sore eyes just for a moment. Lulled, he would rest his head next to Isobel's and together they would ride the ocean...

He jerked awake, coughing sea water. The surface lay quiet about them and he was unsure if the man whose head he supported was alive or dead. Did it matter? Out here in the beyond, he and this stranger were as insignificant as the stars emerging from the clearing sky. Only God would mark their passing. God — and Isobel.

He had made a vow to return. He could not leave her alone, not like this. Robert searched the sea for signs of his ships, but saw nothing but the points of light that marked the distant shore. He accepted then that the night would take him, that the sea would swallow them both. He had betrayed his promise to Isobel, and from the depths of his memory, saw her ocean eyes mourn.

"Forgive me, my dove," he whispered. *"Dómine, convértere, et éripe ánimam meam.* Lord, convert, and rescue my soul. Amen." And in roughly making the sign of the cross with numb fingers, surrendered himself to the sea.

CHAPTER FOURTEEN

"Your Grace, you have a son." Mistress Twnyeho spoke softly, cradling the naked, wrinkled child in one arm and holding him out for the Duchess of Clarence to see in his entirety. "There, madam, see? Almighty God and Holy Mary be praised, he is whole and well."

Lady Isabel raised her head from the pillow to see her infant son and nodded weakly. She indicated her satisfaction and let her hand flop. She felt a mess. Sweat and blood soaked her smock, and the sheets — swiftly changed — were already stained again. She did not dare move but allowed her women to mop and bathe and dab, fighting tears of discomfort as they sought to mend the damage her son had caused as he tore his way out of her to life.

She had done well, she knew that, and George could have no reason to deny it. Another son. He had every cause to be satisfied, even if the child could not wait until they reached Warwick to be birthed. She was pleased, though. She liked this simple room at the abbey, and the abbot of Tewkesbury — a kind and sincere man who served God as faithfully as he knew how — had ensured her comfort in all things spiritual and temporal. His prayers had been answered for she had survived, her son bellowed for milk as fierce in his new-born hunger as his father was in life, and the rain had stopped long enough for the sun to cast across the room and adorn the plain cross in gilded light.

At peace, Isabel, Duchess of Clarence, slept.

*

"A boy, Your Grace, hale and sound of limb, may it please God."

Clarence felt a brief swell of pride. Another heir to secure the future of his dynasty. He had already decided on a name — Richard, after his father, a man whose dim memory had grown sharper and brighter in his mind the more years that passed. He remembered him now as much maligned, his memory abused, the nature of his murder so horrific that Clarence felt the death blow himself. Even now he sensed the blood drain from his face and a sickness surround his heart where, but moments before, pride held sway. He heard a small cough behind him.

"Your Grace, may God be praised, the duchess is also safely delivered— "

His back to the man, Clarence had forgotten he was still there. Overly pious and tedious in the extreme, the man irked him. "I did not ask about Her Grace. You may go." Another York grandson. His father would be proud of him. Edward had two; Richard only the one — his bastard son didn't count — and Clarence allowed himself a small smirk of satisfaction. He had done well.

"Your Grace." Another voice intruded and irritation snapping, Clarence spun around to find a breathless messenger hovering behind him.

"What is it now?"

"A message, Your Grace."

"I can see that, dotard. What is it?"

"The *Bridgit* is returned to port…" Sweating heavily, the man wavered.

"What of it?"

"The captain reports attacks on ships out of Portugal. Not the *Mary*, Your Grace, for it came on another tide, but Lord

Langton's vessels. Infidel ships confronted his fleet. Most were spared, but *The Dove* was stricken. It's Lord Langton, Your Grace." He mopped sweat from his neck. "He's missing."

"Drowned?" Isobel forced her lips to move to release the words wedged in her throat. "Where?" Did it matter? a part of her asked herself, but it seemed it did because she heard herself asking again, "Where? How?"

Clarence repeated what he had already told her once quite clearly: the ship; the storm; the Barbary pirates. The other ships in Robert's fleet had watched, helpless, as his had foundered. The survivors pulled from the water once the pirates had been beaten off or killed, reported seeing Robert in the water and then … nothing.

"Drowned," she whispered to herself, trying to make it mean something, make her feel anything other than this numbness filling her. Clarence was talking, but she couldn't hear him. She should have insisted Robert take Andrew's caul; he should never have left without it. It might have protected him, saved him from… An image of him sinking below the water, lost, alone, caught her unawares and skewered her heart. She gasped, clutching the fabric of her gown over her breast.

Clarence stopped. He looked at her cautiously. "You ail, madam?"

She? *Ail?* How ridiculous! Her husband dead and all Clarence could ask was whether she *ailed*. An involuntary laugh broke from her. Clarence stared. At the look on his face another laugh escaped and then she found she couldn't stop. Her eyes became wet, gathered drops turning into tears that coursed freely, laughter becoming sobs that made her chest hurt and her throat sting.

Hand on his dagger, Clarence took a step back. He snapped his fingers. "Call Lady Langton's attendant. Now!"

Buena entered Clarence's chamber, took one look at Isobel and, without stopping to make due obeisance, pushed past him to gather Isobel in her arms.

"He's dead," was all Isobel could say, bewildered, over and over again as Buena led her from the room. "Bayna, he's dead."

"I am so, *so* sorry, Is'bel." Lady Isabel looked earnestly into Isobel's downturned face. "George told me what happened to Lord Robert. Sweet Jesu have mercy upon his soul!" She crossed herself and waited for Isobel to do the same.

Isobel turned her face from the duchess's pity and kept her hands compressed by her sides. What did God have to do with it? If He had been there in the sea with her husband, would any of this have happened? Where was God when he drowned? Again, she saw Robert alone in the vast wilderness of ocean she had never seen and could only imagine, and earned a swift stab of red hot pain in what had once been her heart. "What will we do?" she said, her voice breaking. "What will my babes do without their fader?" She felt as lost as her husband, adrift and without rudder or star by which to navigate the rest of her life. It stretched out ahead of her, featureless and devoid of colour, of hope. Her hope had drowned with him.

"You must stay here," Lady Isabel was saying, taking Isobel's cold hands in hers and squeezing them lightly. "You and the children. Until you are right in yourself."

"My duties, my people… I cannot leave them. I must return, I must ensure masses are said fo-for his soul." His soul. His poor soul. He had not been shriven. He could not confess.

How long must he suffer the agonies of Purgatory before gaining the kingdom of Heaven? She felt her skin bleach and the iron hand that gripped her throat tighten until her breath came in short, sharp pants that made her head swim and her stomach sicken. She covered her mouth and fought the nausea, repeating silently the names of the herbs growing in her gardens: lovage, marjoram, thyme and hyssop, lavender, rue and rosemary. Rosemary. For remembrance. She dug her nails into her palms until the skin broke, but the pain dulled the agony inside and cleared her head enough to hear Lady Isabel.

"Instruct your stewards," Lady Isabel was saying, "and they will inform your reeves of their duties and maintain your household, and make certain that masses are said for the earl in each of your manors."

"I must tell the king," Isobel murmured.

"George has already notified him."

Isobel looked up sharply and Lady Isabel swiftly added, "He felt it his duty, Is'bel, and did not want you inconvenienced in your grief."

How considerate, a small corner of Isobel's mind piped up like a wren in a bush, shrill and insistent despite the miasma clouding her thoughts.

"I am mindful of your circumstance, let me help in any way I can." Lady Isabel hesitated. "Would it not be wise to let George manage your estates? He has much influence and no one would dare cross him." She smiled, hopefully. "Say you will stay and let us help you. Your children will be tutored with mine and you and I can spend many hours together and watch the baby grow."

Isobel looked at the sleeping infant in his gilded crib hung about with blue velvet embroidered with the emblems of the Royal house and crosses — the very embodiment of Clarence's ambition for the here and now and the hereafter. She thought of her own children growing up without their father's guidance and protection, without his love. Then she considered Clarence. She withdrew her hand. "I thank you for your kindness, but I must return to my people."

Lady Isabel smiled her concern. "I understand, but do not hasten to leave. Stay a while longer and let me nurse your grief. The children can play together and it will help ease their sorrow."

"I will think on it," Isobel said, although she had already made her decision.

Later, kneeling below the suspended image of Christ, Isobel tried to focus on prayer, but each time she rotated a bead of her chaplet, her mind drifted away into the beamed ceiling where the fragrant incense lingered. She raised her head and followed her thoughts and the smoke only to meet the eyes of God gazing in perpetual beneficence upon her. She felt a spike of anger at His desertion, then guilt as she looked at her own bloodied palm and remembered His sacrifice, and anger again at her husband for being so foolhardy to think he could best the sea and leave his children orphans and she a widow.

A servant of Clarence's household intercepted her as she left the Lady Chapel. "His Grace wishes to speak with you," he informed her in a manner that told her she had little choice in the matter.

Standing before the oriel window in an aura of sunlight, his former caution seemingly forgotten, Clarence opened his arms in magnanimity. "Lady Langton, I trust you have found comfort in the offices of my personal chaplain?"

Isobel came out of her curtsey, avoiding his eyes. "I thank Your Grace."

He waited, seemingly expectant, and when she failed to offer further flattery continued. "I have seen fit to instruct my man to bear messages to your steward — Hyde, is it not? — informing him of his duty."

Isobel bristled at the insinuation that their — her — steward might need instruction from anyone other than his countess, but remained staring at the tiled floor where knights and fleur-de-lis vied.

"I have also notified him that you will be staying at my pleasure for the foreseeable future."

At that her head jerked up. "Your Grace?"

"You have no need to thank me," he said, waving a jewelled hand airily, "although someone in your position might wish to do so. Arrangements will be made for your necessities to be brought from … wherever. In the meantime, you and your children will lodge with the duchess's household, where you will continue to attend her."

"Your Grace —!"

"You will not concern yourself with the detail," he continued, brushing her protest aside. "And as for means, I will forward to you the monies by which you will pay for your board until such time as your quarterly rents become due, when your steward will make recompense for my loss." He smiled at his largesse, calculating.

Isobel gripped her hands and clamped her mouth shut. Such indignity heaped upon her by this man, no more than two years her senior, but who claimed lordship where he had none. None.

"Your Grace," she said, using measured tones to prevent her anger spilling. "If it please you, I will take my leave on the morrow and return to my manors and my people in time for Michaelmas. I have made no arrangement for their supervision and, in the absence of their lord, must stand in his stead." That hurt. She felt it in her gut — a wrenching, twisting sensation as if, by saying it out loud, she acknowledged his loss, and by acknowledging it, made it real. Isobel steadied her thoughts and brought herself back to the moment.

Clarence was looking at her, narrow-eyed and tight-mouthed. "Am I to understand," he said slowly, "that you have already made ready for your departure?"

"I have, Your Grace. On the morrow." What matter was it to him when and whither she went? Lady Isabel was safely delivered and had no need of her now.

"Yet you assured the duchess you were content to remain and attend her. Was she incorrect in that assumption? Has she *erred*?" He breathed out the final word, cutting off the 'd' like a thud.

Isobel heard the threat, saw the glint in his eyes, and realised that, new-birthed though she might be, Lady Isabel would bear the brunt of his wrath. "I…" she said, searching for the words to make it right.

He tapped the pommel of his dagger with an impatient finger. "Yes?"

"I do not wish to inconvenience Your Grace —"

"Did I say you were an inconvenience?"

"But my presence must surely vex you?"

"Why so?" he asked.

She hadn't forgotten the incident by the river and neither had he judging by the way he flogged her with his eyes every time he looked at her. "I … merely wish to … to…" *get away from here, from you*, she wanted to yell, *go back home*, where she and her children might grieve surrounded by all that was familiar and safe. "Do my duty," she finished lamely.

"As indeed you shall by biding here. And I, in return, shall be your good lord and offer my protection."

Isobel bent her head, both angry and flummoxed at being manoeuvred into a position of his choosing. She mumbled at her feet.

"What is that you say?"

"Your Grace, my husband is … was sworn to His Grace of Gloucester, and I should bide by his choosing. On behalf of our children, I can accept no other as lord."

A muscle in his cheek twitched, all pretence at pleasantry forgotten, his neck thickening as he hunched his shoulders and glared at her as bull-like as his device. "Do you refuse *my* hospitality, my lady? Do you deny *my* lordship?"

She stepped back, catching her ankle on the chair leg. "I mean no offence, only —"

"Then we are in agreement." And at that, he dismissed her.

Isobel all but ran back to the small chamber she shared with the children and her servants. Buena and Maud looked up as Isobel tumbled into the room, bending double to catch her breath. "He will not let us go," she panted. "He intends to keep us from leaving."

Buena raised her brows in a question.

"Why? I do not know; he makes it clear he does not like our company. He says it is so he can be my *good lord* and I can attend the duchess, but neither can be true. What are we to do? We cannot stay here." She sat with a thump on the pallet next to Buena and lifted Robbie into her arms. He was cutting a tooth and fretted against her, gnawing his little fist and dribbling. "What shall we do, my babe?" she said again, speaking into his soft hair as she considered their options. She came to and looked around the room. "Where are the children?"

Buena made her hands do the speaking.

"I do not want them to leave our sight henceforward, do you understand? Even if it is with Lucie. Buena, I entrust this to you; at no time are they to be left alone without you. Maud, go and fetch them. If anyone asks, I want them with me." Isobel waited for the girl to exit the room then turned to Buena. "Listen," she said urgently, "we must leave here while we can and before Clarence departs for Warwick. We cannot stay, it is not safe. No, I know not why, except … except he frightens me. He does not speak what he thinks, and what he thinks makes me *uneasy*. You see it, do you not?"

Buena nodded her agreement.

"Say nothing to the children or the maids, but pack what we need quickly and I will make arrangements for the horses to be brought to us. It does not matter *how*, Bayna, I have means." She patted the purse hidden by her skirts.

Isobel rose to go but Buena touched her arm and grunted. Isobel stopped and her face fell. "I cannot say farewell to the duchess, she … she is under duress and it might make her all the more so. I will send her a message when we get home." *Home.* What a strange word to describe a place without him. Briefly, she considered fleeing to Beaumancote, to the walls that once defined her sanctuary, but then dismissed the notion. She had seen first-hand how illusory such security could be.

CHAPTER FIFTEEN

The spell of dry weather was short-lived. Rain fell steadily, dripping from eaves and spewing from the gargoyles of the abbey church, gathering in pools and making rivulets of the paths. Stone smelled dank, the air hissing with the sound of it like spitting fat on a griddle. But it kept folk inside and spying eyes by the fire, even if Isobel's feet were soaked by the time she crossed the short distance between the infirmary and the church. Buena bore Robbie swaddled against the cold, while Isobel carried Juliana to save her feet from the sodden ground. Andrew trotted beside them holding Cecily's hand and, huddled under hoods, the maids followed close behind.

Eyes adjusting to the diminished light of the vaulted interior, Isobel spotted the young monk waiting for them by the Despenser tomb, and followed him to the Lady chapel at the far east end of the ambulatory, where she knelt, ensuring the children and servants followed suit. Drawing her veil over her head, she steepled her hands in prayer, and let the slow course of tears for her husband gather and fall.

At one point, she became aware of movement beyond the chapel doors, a shadow cast upon the floor where tile and door did not quite meet. From the corner of her eye through the filmy veil, she watched, waited. There, again — distinct and purposeful — not the meanderings of a monk, but someone close enough to press their ear and eye to the open crack. Prayers neglected, distracted Isobel listened, every fibre alert; but whoever had been there had gone. She could not risk waiting any longer. Isobel rose swiftly, silently urging her maids to do the same. Placing a finger against Juliana's lips and bidding Andrew to follow, Isobel opened the door, then slipped from the chapel leaving the drone of prayer behind.

"Quick!" she said in a whisper. "The boy is close by with the horses. We must be beyond the river before they know us gone."

"Ama —" Juliana piped up in her arms.

"Shhh, not now, my sweet. We must be as mice, like this," she made her fingers scuttle up the little girl's arm, "and as quiet. Can you do that?" Juliana nodded gravely and Isobel kissed her head. "Good girl. Now, let us be away."

Keeping close to the walls as cover, they crossed to where the stable boy waited with the horses in the narrow shelter between two buildings. Isobel clarified the direction they must take then pressed a coin into his hand. He nodded his thanks and was away before she could add hers.

They led the horses through the passageway to the open streets, and mounted at the nearest block. Water spilled from the overwhelmed roofs, splashing Robbie awake. He began to cry. Isobel looked about in alarm, but Buena took him and swaddled him in her cloak, crooning softly until he quietened.

The streets were empty of people and even the stray cats kept from the rain. Within minutes, they saw the river ahead as an opaque brown line, swollen and testing the banks with tan tongues. It reminded Isobel of the Humber in flood and she knew what would happen next. "We must hasten!" She urged her horse towards the bridge but realised the stone starlings were already below the surface and the river breached the bank where the low walls met land. Mats of lank grass wavered in the currents like drowned hair. Should she risk the crossing?

She looked back over her shoulder towards the town where the abbey rose above the roofs through the rain towards Heaven. It would be dry there; they could always try and make good their escape when the waters went down in a few days' time. Would a few days matter? She knew in her gut they would.

As she stared through the rain, she thought she made out darker shapes moving towards them. She squinted, wiping gathered drops from her lashes. Men — on foot — making straight for them. She kicked her mount forwards towards the bridge, but in those few moments the water had risen, submerging what remained of the stone span.

"Move!" she exhorted, but the animal shied from the water sending whinnies of alarm through the other horses. The men were nearly upon them, intent clear in the way they moved and the arms they bore. In one last attempt, Isobel called to the other women, "Follow me!", nudging her horse and dragging its head to face down river where she hoped they could outrun the pursuing men.

"Ama!" Juliana cried, wriggling to escape the confines of the high pommel pinning her as Isobel leant forwards and pressed the horse into a run. A scream behind her had her turning to see Maud and Cecily intercepted by a man who had managed to grab the bridle and bring their horse to a standstill. Another two backed Lucie and Andrew's horse against the flood waters and, as she watched, their horse stumbled, throwing maid and boy from the saddle. Isobel wheeled her animal around and galloped back towards them.

A burly man bearing Clarence's livery plucked Andrew from the swelling waters like a drowned puppy, and waded to higher ground. Lucie had been hauled to her feet and now stood cradling her left arm. Another man began pulling her after him and she squealed in pain.

"Let her go. Now!" Isobel yelled, passing Juliana to Alice and sliding from her horse. "You — do not touch her!" She checked Andrew and Cecily for injury then went to Lucie. The girl's wrist had developed a reddened line and she shivered from shock and cold. "Do not be afeared," Isobel said in a low voice, taking her own kerchief and binding the girl's arm to prevent further movement. "They will not harm you." Then to the man who appeared to have some authority, "What do you mean by frightening my children and injuring my servant? Do you know who I am? Let us pass and I shall not take up this matter with His Grace."

The man stared down at her from his considerable height. "I know who you are, *my lady*, and I know my orders because *His Grace* gave them to me himself. You are to come with us — all of ye."

Before long, they were sitting in a miserable huddle in the room from which they had fled. The neglected fire had become ash and attempts to reignite it fruitless, and the wet wood scrounged by Alice smoked and died. Isobel did her best to make Lucie more comfortable. The break to her wrist seemed clean enough, and once splintered and bound, the bindings gave her some relief. She accepted the dwale Buena conjured from herbs supplied by the abbey infirmary, and now drowsily rested her head against Maud's shoulder. At least the children were in dry clothes and played their games as if nothing had happened, while the adults watched pensive and subdued. They must have been seen leaving the abbey; that, or the stable lad had played a double game and told Clarence of their plans. What did it matter now? They were back right where they started.

Isobel jumped as the door flew open. There was little point in refusing to comply with the liveried man's request to accompany him.

Clarence made no attempt at pleasantries. He paced back and forth, thumbs hooked into his lavish belt, his demeanour clouded. "I believe I made myself clear the other day, yet you insult me by removing yourself without my leave."

"Your Grace, I did not think I needed permission. Why have I been fetched back here forcibly?"

"Why did you make a show of attending mass for your husband when it was nothing but a means to escape?"

"Escape? Am I a prisoner then? Does Your Grace intend holding me against my will?"

He stopped pacing, looking at her with his head tilted slightly and a shrewd glint to his eyes. "You look a little wan, my lady; do you sicken?"

That took her by surprise. "Ail? No ... I am quite well."

"Yet you shake and you are confused."

"I am but cold —"

"You there!" he called over his shoulder to a groom. "Fetch my physician and the priest forthwith." He turned back to her. "Did I not say I will be your good lord in all things?" he reminded her with the hint of a dark smile.

The men must have been waiting to be summoned because they appeared within moments, the physician black-robed and narrow, and the young monk who had conducted mass, visibly nervous and twitching. It was the monk Clarence addressed first. "Repeat what you told me."

"Y-Your Grace?"

"Come, Father, you were free enough with your talk not an hour since."

The young man darted a glance at Isobel, licked his skinny lips. "Well, I ... er ... that is, my lady ordered Mass to be said."

"Yes. And?"

"And my lady seemed … ah, inconstant in her attention and left before I had finished. Sh-she left in a hurry."

Clarence made a show of crossing himself. "Let us be clear: the lady did not make proper observance?"

"I … um … she did not, Your Grace. My lady seemed all a bustle and could not settle to it."

"You say she did not attend to her devotions as she should? Lady Langton showed inconsistency of mind? More so than even might be expected of a woman?"

The monk nodded vigorously making the wooden beads at his waist rattle, and Clarence tutted, shaking his head. "I fear the death of the earl has caused Lady Langton malady in both mind and soul."

Hands clasped in front of him, the physician stepped forwards. "If Your Grace will indulge me, might I make examination of the lady?"

Isobel drew away from him. "You may not!"

Clarence waved the man forwards. "Do so."

Trapped between the fire and the table, Isobel couldn't move as the physician bent towards her and peered with rheumy eyes into her own. "Hmm." He pushed his blue-tinged lips forwards into a tight shape and breathed nosily through his nose as he inspected her. "Is there prolonged melancholia, a loss of appetite?" he enquired. "And sleep is fitful, waking often and beforetimes?"

Isobel scowled. "I am but lately grieved and my babe is teething —"

"The countess is irritable and her temperament argumentative. Look how she plucks at her hands," Clarence cut in.

"So I can see, Your Grace; the lady is agitated." The physician hummed and hawed, finally placing the tips of his fingers together and then tapping them once or twice before declaring, "It is my opinion that the lady suffers from an excess of black bile."

"Oh?" Clarence said, joining the physician in surveying Isobel.

Alarmed, she crushed herself against the wall feeling her shoulder blades bruise. "I am wet through!"

"Observe the colour, Your Grace, to the temples and the cheeks. A certain sign of congestion in the brain giving rise to unnatural feelings."

"And I am *cold*," she stated.

"As can be witnessed by her confused state." He uncoiled to his full height. "I am grieved to report that this lady is sorely afflicted and must be given every care to prevent further injury to herself. She cannot be left without close oversight. Has she suffered loss recently?"

"You know I have!" Isobel interjected.

"The sudden death of her husband and my good friend," Clarence said, as if she were invisible.

"Ah, well, that explains much. The noble lady must be entrusted to the care of a male relative for her own safety."

Clarence pulled at his chin looking thoughtful. "There is none."

"Might Your Grace be not persuaded to stand in the stead of such a relative, indeed, to show such compassion as Christ our Lord would applaud?"

"I have offered my protection, but the lady rejected it."

"This," the physician said sorrowfully, "is to be expected in one suffering from a melancholia, and no account must be taken of her desires, for they are —"

"*Unnatural*," Isobel finished, glaring at him.

"Quite," Clarence said. "On which count — and for your own comfort — you will continue to reside under my protection until you are deemed fit to leave."

"Hah! So, a prisoner after all. What is my ransom to be?"

"Ransom? My dear Lady Langton, there can be no ransom for you are merely a prisoner of your own mind."

"Then I might leave when I wish," she challenged, raising her jaw and feeling obdurate.

"Sadly, no."

The physician gave a little cough. "On that note, I believe the air here by the river is tainted, Your Grace, and should it please you to remove yourself and Her Grace, greater efficacy might be found ... elsewhere."

"My thoughts exactly," Clarence declared. "Somewhere," he smiled, "secure."

"Where?" Lucie asked, eyes wide and frightened.

"He did not say, but I suspect it will be Warwick as it's his own domain where he can keep me *safe*," Isobel said bitterly.

"Can we seek sanctuary, my lady? Surely the abbot will give us protection."

Isobel cast a short, harsh laugh. "Do you not recall what happened in this very place when the Duke of Somerset sought sanctuary in the abbey after the battle nearby? He was dragged from this holy place and tried and executed as a traitor. The abbot could not offer him protection and he certainly will not grant us refuge now. The abbey church is not a *sanctuary*," she clarified. "We cannot use it as such."

"But we are not traitors!" Maud said, her face scarlet.

"No, nor will we be executed," Isobel assured her, aware that Cecily was listening. She reduced her voice to a whisper. "I might send a message if I get the chance."

"To who?" Lucie asked, all goggle-eyed.

"Not so much *to* whom, but *by* whom?" Isobel said. "But how am I to get a message out when I am so close watched?"

"I am so pleased you decided to stay!" Lady Isabel declared from her chair, holding out her arms to Isobel and embracing her warmly. "George said he managed to persuade you." She moved gingerly on the deep cushion so didn't see Isobel's disbelieving grimace. "You are the only one who can make such a salve as to stop this itching. And if it doesn't itch, it burns. Oh! If only our children knew what pains we suffer in the bearing of them!" She laughed, but she looked more drawn than before. "Look how the babe sleeps; he knows nothing but comfort, sleep and his nurse's milk." She gazed at the contentedly sleeping baby. "I hope he sleeps as well when we travel tomorrow. I know I want to. I feel so tired yet cannot sleep enough to shift it."

"Tomorrow?"

"Yes, and you, too, Is'bel. We will not leave you to grieve alone." She held Isobel's hand lightly. "Did George not say? He has so much weighing on his mind of late he must have forgot. We leave for Warwick on the morrow."

"Warwick," Isobel said glumly. "Packed up like baggage and sent hither and thither." She kicked Juliana's brightly coloured ball back to her, remembering in that instant the time when she and Cecily played catch with a similar ball. It was then that she had first met the Duke of Gloucester. It seemed a past life — one of greater innocence — not hers at all. But it gave her an idea. "Find me quill and ink," she said, drawing a scrap of paper from her casket. "Be quick!"

She wrote to Gloucester, speed making her less guarded than she otherwise might have been, imploring him to intervene and restore her liberty. She rolled the paper, squashed it flat and, taking her father's matrix from the purse at her belt, sealed it.

"Liana, please lend me your ball," Isobel said, holding out her hand. Juliana skipped over and plomped the leather ball into Isobel's palm. She turned it over and over until she found a loose thread and began to pick at it.

"Ama! My ball!"

Isobel opened up a thin slit in a seam. "Your ball is going on a very important journey, my poppet." She eased the sliver of paper into the centre of the ball. "It will help us get home. You want to go home and see Moth, don't you?"

"I do, Ama," Andrew said, "And s-so does Liana, don't you?"

She nodded, adding, "I want my ball."

"And you shall have it when we get home," Isobel assured her, folding the tiny seam and handing it to Alice to sew in place. "Now, let us bind it up and send it on its way."

Wrapped in a square of wool and tied with ribbon, the ball bore an additional message, one clear for all to read but that only Gloucester would understand "Now," she said, "we must find a messenger."

Amid the bustle the tall, austere man stood as a tree around which the other household servants flowed. He looked down on Isobel's upturned face, his own expressionless. "I would ask another," she said, "but with so little time and so much to do…" she waved a hand at the general busyness around them. She placed the round package into his hand. "And I know Her Grace trusts you above all others, master," she added.

With minimal movement, the man tucked the ball under his cloak, gave a slight bow, and left without saying anything, leaving Isobel feeling as if she had somehow missed something. Heady and out of sorts she went back to her own chamber where their belongings had been packed and made ready to be loaded on wagons. The children were helping while the maids busied and flapped. And still it rained. The journey to unknown places and unfamiliar people would prove to be a damp and uncomfortable one.

She took herself to the far corner of the room, leaning against the window to watch the rain create rivulets down the uneven glass. Caught up in the excitement of the last few days Isobel had had little time to examine their current situation other than try to escape it. Now, waiting for the off, she was as much adrift as when all but a captive of Earl William. Even as a widow — widow, *wi-dow* — it seemed so alien a term to use — she appeared less able to determine her own fate and that of her children as she had there in the ordinance room at the top of the tower of Tickhill, waiting for the Earl to summon her to his chamber. For all his faults, she had felt secure in at least knowing where she stood with him. Or perhaps it was because no one depended on her except herself. Now she had responsibilities to her children, her servants, the household and those working her manorial fields. So many, so much to do and no autonomy with which to do it. Was it her lack that led to her husband's death? Or did he act recklessly because she was not enough for him to value his life to come back to her? She shook her head free of the thought, irritated by how easily she slipped into doubt. How could he have left her in this situation? Clarence would never have moved against her if he had still been alive.

Alive. He had been alive and now ... was not. He was gone. Dead.

The hollow part of her which he once occupied with light and warmth and love had remained vacant since learning of his death. Now it began to fill. Oozing, thick and black the darkness crept into the hole until it rose up her throat and threatened to choke her.

The nagging nausea persisted as did a growing suspicion. By the time she had endured the swaying and jolting of the covered carriage heading north, Isobel concluded that she must be correct. By the end of the second day, having recoiled at the scent of hot horse and excrement, the stench of wet wool and sweat, the piss and mauled mud in a ditch, there could be no doubt.

"How long until your lying-in?" Drawn, Lady Isabel looked as Isobel felt. The inn at which they stayed overnight might not have the splendour of the ducal residences, but at least the chambers were warm and dry, and the uneven floors remained still as Isobel walked unsteadily across them leaving wet footprints. Now dry-shod, she sat next to the duchess as the baby nearby suckled greedily at his nurse's breast.

"I do not recall." Remembering the last time she and Robert had lain together brought unlooked for pain; she welcomed the interruption as Mistress Twynyho entered the room carrying a small phial. "It is time for your physic, madam," she said, bobbing and bustling and handing the murky liquid, now mixed with almond milk and honey in a gilt cup, to the duchess.

Lady Isabel pulled a face. "I need no further physic; I am well-enough healed."

Lifting the sleepy baby from the nurse, Mistress Twynyho smiled and kissed his fluffy hair, before handing him to his mother. "The physician insists, Your Grace. You wish to be strong again for Yuletide, yes? *A remedy a day keeps the —*"

"*— physician at bay,*" Lady Isabel intoned, screwing her face as she swallowed the draught, and flapping her hand in disgust. She swiftly followed the liquid with clary warmed with honey and cinnamon to disguise the taste. "Ugh, even the wine tastes bitter. Is'bel, can you not make something else that will mask it? Stir up some magic for me, I beg you."

Mistress Twynyho tutted and wagged her finger in her good-natured, motherly way. "My lady must not make it *too* pleasant or the efficacy of the remedy will be lost."

Lady Isabel whispered loudly behind her hand, "Nay, Is'bel, switch the physic for your own and I will be well and the physician none the wiser."

"Tsk, madam, you will be the undoing of me. What would His Grace say if he heard such a thing!"

"How dare you speak to me in such manner!" Lady Isabel flared, catching both Isobel and Mistress Twynyho by surprise at her sudden ferocity. "Be gone and take your blethering tongue with you!"

"Mistress Twynyho meant no harm," Isobel said once Ankarette had curtsied awkwardly and left. She smoothed the fur coverlet over Lady Isabel's legs and tucked the ends in. "She spoke merely in jest."

"It is not for her to jape; I have a fool for that," Lady Isabel snapped. Then, seeing Isobel's mouth straighten. "Forgive me my choler, it is not for you. The woman should know her place and keep it."

The duchess sounded more like her husband and Isobel suspected it was the mention of him that sparked her sudden wrath. "She meant nothing by it," Isobel said again.

"Do *you* now seek to reprimand me?" And, when Isobel reddened and shook her head, Lady Isabel's rage dissolved as quickly as it had emerged. "I am out of sorts. I cannot shift this weariness; it settles on my limbs. Do you have physic for *that*, Is'bel?"

"You are but lately birthed. Give yourself time and all will be well. Time is the best remedy for what ails you."

Leaning forwards, Lady Isabel peered into her eyes. "And you, Is'bel — will time heal your heart?"

"Time and my liberty. Only then will I find freedom from what afflicts me."

A deep furrow formed across Lady Isabel's brow. "Your liberty? How so?"

Had the duchess accepted her husband's lie so blindly that she did not question it? Or did she choose to believe it? Either way, Isobel thought it cruel to disabuse her, for what could Lady Isabel do in her present state? Quite frankly, she thought, what could her friend have done even without the burden of childbirth, for it seemed to Isobel that, as the years had passed, the duchess's freedom — which had always been wafer thin — had become nothing more than an illusion.

"Think nothing of it, Your Grace; I speak out of my grief. It will pass — all things pass."

Warwick castle reared out of the dissolving mist, the soaring towers of the barbican painted gold by the morning sun. Everything gleamed. The rain had cleared from the east leaving a sharp edge to the air, and the drops on the remaining leaves were clear gems through which the burnished colours of autumn shone.

"It is … beautiful," Isobel said out loud, surprising herself.

Lady Isabel leaned forwards so she could see. "Yes," she said, viewing it with dull eyes, "it is fine." They had travelled since before dawn regardless of the duchess's recent birthing. She looked increasingly like the mist that had enveloped them for most of the last leg of the journey — drawn, thin, almost translucent — despite the insistence of the physician that the physic would remedy all.

"Are you not glad to be back?"

"No." Lady Isabel let the fabric fall across the window, cutting the castle from view. "I cannot breathe here. This place … it sucks the life from me." The carriage hit a stone and gave a violent shiver. The duchess winced and shut her eyes. "I thank God you are with me, Is'bel; I can better face this place knowing you are here."

Isobel scanned the towers, the walls stretching between them, the dots of pigeons huddling on crenels — and imagined the castle anew through the duchess's eyes, less a home and more a place of keeping.

The carriage and accompanying household had drawn to a halt in the bailey and Lady Isabel taken to her apartments. Fighting nausea, Isobel hung back with her children. Handsome the castle might be, but a presence clung about its walls and lay upon her chest. She remembered seeing the Earl of Warwick riding with Clarence by his side — a notable figure with a sense of purpose and dignity derived, perhaps, from his noble exploits. Was that what lingered here? He had been so alive, so vigorous, but despite that, had been cut down and was now nothing more than bones and memory. As was her husband. As would she be one day. So little stood between life and death — just a breath and then … nothing.

"Ama?" Andrew wrapped his arms about her waist and she looked down on his upturned face.

"What is it, my sweet?"

"When are we g-going home? I don't like it here and Liana wants to know; she wants to play with Moth. And will Fader be there waiting for us? I think Robbie misses him."

"Do you miss your fader, Drew?" Isobel asked softly. He screwed the toe of his boot into the moist earth and nodded without looking at her. Searching the silken blue skies in which the cold sun hung, she breathed out, "So do I, my love, so do I."

CHAPTER SIXTEEN

Dawn spread over the low-lying hills of Warwickshire, illuminating the brazen treetops and deepening the shadows in the vales. Dogs barked in the distance and slow smoke rose from new fires into the still heavens, scenting the morning. Isobel drew lungsful of steely air, breathing away the fug of her sleepless night. Her children slept soundly; only Robbie stretched and stirred as he made little sucking noises.

Lady Isabel had moued her disappointment when Isobel said she wished her children to remain with her rather than joining the Clarence siblings in the nursery; it was the one thing she had insisted upon and the only thing she had managed to achieve since arriving at the castle. Yet, looking out of the open casement and witnessing the tranquillity that lay upon the land, it was hard to imagine anything more benign. She watched birds taking flight as one, rising and swirling in a rush of wings out over the rooftops and away towards the rising sun. Before, she would have found peace in the sunrise and welcomed the new day and all the possibilities it might offer. But where was her peace now and what promises did this dawn bring? Unease lay upon this place, a place of waiting and watching.

Her disquiet grew when she entered Lady Isabel's chamber. The shutters remained closed against the light and candles infused the hangings around the bed with their thick, waxy scent. A sombre air prevailed.

"I sicken this morning," Lady Isabel said, patting the bed beside her for Isobel to sit. "I rose to dress but my head hurts and my legs feel so heavy, so I have returned to rest in the hope that it will pass."

Isobel laid the back of her hand against Lady Isabel's forehead. It felt hot and dry, but not with fever. "Are your waters clear?"

"Yes, yes. I truly believe it to be nothing more than the journey here. What else could it be?" She gave a thin smile more to convince herself than her ladies. From a discreet distance on the other side of the bed, Mistress Twynyho caught Isobel's eye.

"I am sure you are right, Your Grace. Let us open the windows and chase the night away. I will make your favourite posset to strengthen you and add my secret ingredients."

"Laughter and a prayer?" Lady Isabel said, beginning to smile.

"Of course. What else could incite better healing than joy and God's blessing? It certainly tastes better than Master Physician's foul remedy."

"Do not let him hear you say so," Lady Isabel warned. "He thinks women should leave healing to men. '*Eve pollutes all she touches*,' he said the other day. '*It is in her nature to deceive and we must be vigilant against her deceit.*' I do not believe he thinks of me as a woman," she added, looking thoughtful. "I do not believe he thinks of me at all. He offers remedies because George says so, but I might as well be a horse. He would not be surprised if I ate hay." Her expression was so comical that Isobel could not help but laugh. "There, you do me good just by being here. Thank you, my friend."

"I will do you more good if I make that posset for you." Isobel rose, then hesitated. "There is one thing: His Grace requires me to attend him; do you know why?" She looked sideways at Lady Isabel and was met by a blank expression.

"My husband does not discuss such matters with me, Is'bel, you know that."

"Matters?"

"Matters of … business," she said vaguely. "I am weary now; let me rest."

"My lady! Lady Langton!"

Isobel had been thinking about the forthcoming meeting with Clarence when she heard her name. She stopped and paused for Mistress Twynyho to catch up. The older woman panted, fanning her face with her hand and breathing heavily.

"My lady, pray you, a word." She peered back over her shoulder then around the courtyard, watchfully. "Privily, if it please you." She took Isobel by the elbow and drew her to a sheltered place where they might not be seen or overheard. Isobel thought the caution somewhat overplayed but was equally curious to know what might be so urgent.

"Has Her Grace sent you?" Isobel asked.

"Nay, my lady, but it is about Her Grace I would speak." She drew closer until Isobel could smell mint and sage on her breath and see the fine lines on her softly downed cheeks. "How find you Her Grace?"

"As you saw yourself. Why?"

"Did my lady not think her weakened?"

Isobel thought back to the morning's visit and then recalled previous days. "A little, perhaps. But she has endured a long journey and is but recently risen from a difficult childbed."

Mistress Twynyho nodded. "Yes, my lady, and so I thought. But Her Grace is well-healed from the birth, is she not? And she had regained her strength most wonderfully. Both she and the little one were doing so well."

"What are you saying?"

Mistress Twynyho cocked her head, shrewd-eyed and not at all the woman Isobel was used to seeing flitting and fussing about Lady Isabel's chamber in her matronly way. "Nothing, my lady, that you have not considered yourself."

"Have you spoken to His Grace or any other about this?"

"Nay! And nor will I. It would be like stirring a boiling pot and putting my own hand in it. I trust no one. No. One," she emphasised, with a meaningful glance towards the tower Clarence frequented.

"Yet you entrust me with your notions?"

"My lady, I trust you because you are not of this household and you have been a fair friend to my duchess."

"Then tell me, why do you impart your concerns to me? What do you wish me to do with this information, for you have shared it for a purpose, have you not? What would you have me do?"

Mistress Twynyho looked confused. "Do? Nothing can be *done*, my lady. I pray daily for Her Grace knowing she is in the hands of our Lord. It is not what I want you to do, it is what I want you to know in case … in case something happens."

"To Her Grace?"

"To Her Grace…" her voice wavered, "or to me."

"I have been giving consideration to your affairs." Clarence stood with his back to Isobel, his hands clasped behind him. "And have concluded that, while in your period of mourning, I shall oversee the running of your estates." He turned on one booted heel to face her. "These are not times in which to leave a widow undefended. You must be conscious that there are parties who would use any means to secure the Langton inheritance for themselves."

Other than Felice? That came as a surprise. "I was not, Your Grace."

"Be assured it is so." He smiled and as quickly dropped it. "You need be aware that I have petitioned the king to allow me to provide protection for yourself and your family."

Isobel bridled. "I have no need of protection, Your Grace, nor do my children. We are sufficiently defended by my husband's retinue and retained men, which are numerous and well-armed." Her threat did not go unnoticed. Clarence's mouth sharpened. "However," she continued before he had a chance to respond, "I am certain the king will not allow any harm to come to either myself or my children — from *any* quarter."

"He will not, which is why he will afford me the honour and responsibility of your security." Clarence burrowed down into her eyes, challenging her to deny him the right to do as he pleased, and Isobel stared back, anger bubbling below the surface and only just contained.

"Then I will ask His Highness to reconsider on the grounds that my husband's sworn lord is His Grace of Gloucester and our natural protector."

"As I have reminded you before, lady," he said, his voice low as if he struggled to control it, "your lands abut my own; it is a question of practicality as well of rights of lordship —"

"You have no rights of lordship over me!"

"On the contrary, your late husband placed you in my trust, as this bears witness." From the table by which he stood, Clarence took a small parchment, recently unfurled. He gave it to her, waiting just long enough for her take in the signature and the tenor of the letter. "I believe you will agree that this is your husband's mark and seal?" Words jumped and swam like fish upon the surface, and Isobel struggled to pin them down long enough to read them through again. Clarence held out his hand. "Perhaps you have difficulty with letters?"

She snatched it from his reach as if his touching it somehow allowed him mastery over her husband's memory. "I can read perfectly well." She turned away to catch the light from the window, aware he watched her. As she read, carefully this time, the despondency that darkened her mood, deepened. She let the parchment drop to the floor. Clarence picked it up and tucked it in his belt from which its pallid face taunted her.

"As you see, in the event he did not return, your husband placed his family in my control."

"Care. He used the word *care*," she said, dully. "'*If it pleaseth God to take me from this life, I, Robert Langton, earl, charge Your Grace with the* care *of my Lady wife and children, that they may not be burdened overmuch in their time of grief*.'" She looked up at him. "That is what he said, Your Grace. '*In their time of grief*.' That time is now past."

"I think not. Moreover, your consideration should be for the welfare of your children —"

"They are my first and *only* consideration," Isobel retorted.

"— and, as such, their wardship."

"*I* am their mother. Rob … Robert would wish me to oversee their education and welfare, none other." It was the first time she had spoken his name out loud since she had learned of his death and it stung. She felt the beginnings of angry tears and brushed them away with a swipe of her hand in case Clarence thought she weakened.

"The education of the new earl is not a matter for a woman," Clarence stated bluntly. "He will enter my household and begin his training when of an age to do so. I will personally oversee his education as I do my own son." He obviously considered it to be an honour, but to Isobel's mind, she could envisage nothing worse.

"Drew will not leave me nor enter anyone's household."

"Andrew? I do not speak of your bastard son, but the new earl — Robert."

Her mouth opened. She shut it again. Swallowed. With as much dignity as she could muster, she curtsied low, swung around, and made to leave the room.

"And I believe Lord Robert's niece — Lady Cecily, is it not? — is coming of an age where consideration must be given to her marriage."

Isobel stopped with her back to him. She thought about answering, but could not trust herself to refrain from lashing out with fist and tongue, and who knew where that might lead? Instead, straightening her shoulders and holding her head high, she said nothing and left.

She continued step by step until she met the outer wall of the bailey. Damp and covered with mounds of moss, tiny drops of last night's dew still speckled the surface. She pressed her face against the cool cushions breathing in earthy odours, its honesty, until she regained some semblance of calm and could think straight. Gloucester had not responded to her message. If he couldn't — or wouldn't — help, she would appeal to another woman — someone whom no one, not even the king's brother, would dare cross. She would entreat the queen for help.

"Take this." Isobel slipped the purse into Maud's hand. "No one will stop you. You are on an errand to buy more spices to ward off the chill of winter: cinnamon; ginger; saffron. Make sure you are not followed. When you get to the inn, wait until the end of the day, find a woman who is willing for you to accompany her, and leave as soon as you can."

"My lady, what if I find no one who will take me?" Maud asked in a tremulous voice.

"It is market day, Maud, there will be a great thirst upon the people and where do folk go when they thirst? The inn — that is so. Take the road east and go as far as you can from this place. Tell no one who you are, where you are from and whence you are going. When you reach Tickhill, relay your message to my lord steward alone and ensure he knows the urgency of it. Give him the purse. He will know what to do. There now, ready yourself. And be warned: do not take up with any man unless he is with a woman and, even then, take a care not to be alone with him. Do you understand?" Maud nodded, looking more and more like a scared coney. "Good, now when you reach Tickhill, you can stay there."

"You do not wish me to return, my lady?"

"No, you will have done your duty. You may remain in safety until such time as we join you."

"Thank you, my lady," Maud said, looking relieved. She squeezed the little purse and gave it a shake. It rattled and something crackled inside.

"Goodness, girl!" Isobel exclaimed. "Keep the purse out of sight and no one will give a mind to it. And do not squeeze it so. How many purses do you recall sounding like that!" Maud looked sheepish and Isobel softened her voice. "Go to. Accomplish this task and you will have the contents of the purse and a safe bed in which to lie."

From a hidden vantage point Isobel watched Maud cross to the gatehouse, speak briefly when challenged by the guard, and pass out of sight beneath its arch. If Maud managed to get to Tickhill without incident and relay the message sewn in the lining of the purse, she knew Hyde would do everything in his power to petition the queen to intervene on Isobel's behalf. If the girl failed... Isobel closed her eyes, pressing her lips tightly. Failure could not be imagined because the consequences of doing so, could.

Her travelling cloak dusted with whitelime, Maud cowered against the wall, shaking.

"Did you believe I would not find out you had gone behind my back?" Clarence raged, pointing towards the frightened girl. "What aid did you think the queen might offer, hey? Do you really believe the woman has any regard for you? What can you give her in return? You have nothing she wants."

"But you do?" Isobel countered, stepping between the duke and the girl. "Your Grace is mightily concerned with my affairs and that of my estates. Maud, return to the children."

"I did not give her leave to go."

"No, but I have and she is *my* servant and a member of *my* household and this does not concern her. Go, Maud — *now.*" She let the girl scuttle out of the room before turning back to Clarence. "I petitioned the queen because I and my children are held here falsely and against my will. I have been prevented from returning to my husband's estates and making proper provision for his memory. My son cannot enter into his rightful inheritance nor be prepared for the duties and responsibilities he will face as Earl. In short, I believe this to be an act contrary to the law of this land and, as such, is —"

He thrust his face close to hers, his darkened eyes staring, words hissing. "What? What do you believe it to be, my lady? Treason, is that what you were about to say? Were you going to accuse me — brother to the king of England — of *treason?*"

Yes! She wanted to scream. *What else is it?* Instead, she kept her silence and her dignity.

He stood back to his full height, looking down his straight nose at her with a slight sneer. "I am not required to justify myself to *you*."

"We are all bound by the law."

"*What* did you say?"

"Your Grace," she said with effort, avoiding looking at him in case she lost the strength of her conviction and her courage failed, "none is above the law, no matter his degree."

"And what makes you believe you know more about the law than the king's brother?"

"My father, Sir Geoffrey Fenton, had me study the law. I do not say that I know more than Your Grace; I merely say that on this matter, as it pertains to me, I understand it."

She risked a glance at him only to see him examining the edge of his perfectly groomed nails. But it was an act, his nonchalance a cover for the disdain he evidently felt towards her. If she had been his wife, no doubt she would have felt his fists by now.

"You may wish, Lady Langton, to consider your own position. I believe it customary for women in your situation to seek the solitude and solace of the veil. I suggest you give the thought your full attention."

Instead, Isobel sought the solitude of the castle pleasance. Here, among the growing things that cared nothing for station and preferment, where she could come and go as she pleased without fear of judgement, this was a sort of freedom in which she could think. The sun's fire had gone from the trees, and the garden slept in its bed of earth, tender shoots protected from frost with coverlets of sacking and pillows of straw. She wished she could sleep like the plants. The weeks of uncertainty and mourning had worn her into a shadow of her former life; she could hardly recall how it had been with

Robert and the children. He was there — the memory a ghost of itself. The certitude she had shown in front of Clarence now wavered, her ability to think in straight lines as her father had taught her, diminished. Perhaps Clarence had a point: what could she, a widow, offer her children in terms of education and marriages compared with a royal duke?

Bastard. Isobel recalled Clarence's scorn in that single bitter word, bringing her back to the situation on the point of a blade. Robbie's succession as Earl would be at his brother's loss, and denial of Andrew's birth right was something she would not — could not — accept. She must not retire from the world; it would be an abrogation of responsibility. More than ever, Andrew needed protection from those who would deny him his rights, and who else would fight for him as fiercely but his mother? And what of the child she carried? She felt his weight in her womb, the flexing of his limbs. A child without a father had little future in this world. So, she would not enter the life of a nun, and she and her children were vulnerable if she remained a widow.

There was no other choice: she must abandon widowhood; she would have to remarry.

PART FOUR

CHAPTER SEVENTEEN

Dawn brought Robert little relief, and through the single barred window set in the mud brick wall, he smelled dust and air swollen by unremitting heat. Urine stained the sandy earth outside and mounds of animal matter, baked dry in the sun, were so pungent he could taste them. Occasionally, light-robed men in course baggy cloth passed by the window onto the narrow passageway between buildings, leading beasts laden with panniers or dragging litters of wood. Trapped in the airless room, he tried to recall the chill of winter on his skin, or a spear of ice pendent from low-hung eves. He closed his eyes, striving to visualize a landscape made white with frost or transformed by snow with his breath suspended in frozen air. But all he could hear was the harsh rasp of insects from dry stems and the dull drone of flies attempting to settle on his skin swathed in sweat.

He swatted them away, more out of habit than hope and shifted his position, feeling his bruised bones protest. His shirt cracked with dried salt, his lips split and stinging, his wife would have a hard time identifying him from the others. Isobel. At the thought of her his gut convulsed.

He leant back against the wall, having brought up nothing but bile that burned his gullet. He was thirsty. There was nothing he wouldn't do for ale — even water would suffice. The wooden pail by the rough door had long since been emptied by the men sharing the squat room with him. A dozen or so — Portuguese from his own ship, a few Englishmen taken from a vessel bound for Bristol, and a tall foreigner in strange clothing with a long, matted beard. He kept apart from the others, repeatedly rocking and muttering as he picked lice from lesions on his skin. How long he had been there nobody seemed to know.

Thirst expanded and grew until it dominated Robert's consciousness. He licked his lips, regretting it as the cracks stung. He tried to think about escape plans but couldn't focus his thoughts long enough to make any sense of them. It was evident they must still be near the sea — he could hear rigging *thwack*, *thwack* against masts and could sometimes smell stranded seaweed and stale fish. The call of seabirds confirmed it — but where, he could not be certain, for the voices jabbering as they passed spoke a language he did not recognise.

He had been there for three nights, but what had passed between him being dragged half-drowned from the sea and being deposited in this room by a one-eared brigand he couldn't recall. If they knew his identity they didn't say, nor would he reveal it until he knew the purpose of his being kept there, and by whom. Was Isobel aware he was missing? Did she think him dead? Sweet Christ protect her and his babes! Robert reached for his paternoster at his waist, but his belt and purse were missing and their absence made his captivity fact. *Captive.* He would die here and she would know nothing of it.

The sun shone directly overhead, illuminating the narrow strip between buildings, and the men fell silent as the oppressive heat of noon bore down on the cramped, low-ceilinged chamber. Even the incessant flies were subdued by it. Robert cradled his aching head lest the slightest movement bring on the hammers that threatened to crack his skull inside out. His skin smarted, dry and brittle, and he had nothing left to sweat.

He jerked awake at the sound of voices outside the plank door and his hand went to his waist where his dagger once hung. Darkened men with heads bound in cloth and bearing short, curved swords entered the chamber and began prodding the captives to their feet and driving them through the door. Robert staggered into the sunlight, shielding his eyes from the glare, and was shuffled into a rough line with the other men.

"*Meu Senhor*," one of the Portuguese sailors whispered to him, "what we do?"

"Watch and bide," Robert murmured back. "Wait until I give the signal."

Small boys with brown skin dusted in sand gathered to watch as an older man dressed in long, loose robes proceeded to walk down the raggedy line of prisoners. He pointed with a horse switch and two of the men — broken-toothed and past their prime — were ushered towards the shore where a boat waited.

The inspection continued, mimicked by the tallest boy. At the bearded individual, the overseer stopped. The man rocked back and forth on his feet, muttering continuously, his hands balling and stretching and balling again. The overseer prodded his chest, but the beard kept nodding and jerking. Pulling grotesque faces, the boy copied him. The overseer barked a command and the man, arms pinned behind his back, was dragged to an open spot and forced to kneel. Standing behind him, the one-eared guard took a handful of long hair, yanked the man's head back, and slid a blade across his throat.

For a moment, the bearded man's eyes widened, then glazed, and he fell forward into the dust. The boys crowed and danced. One of the English merchants whinnied, his eyes rolling as he broke from the line. A sharp blow brought him down and the boys jigged around his cowering, prostrate form until one-ear beat them back with sharp words and fists. The other merchants moved uneasily.

"Stay still," Robert warned them in an undertone. "Make no move until I say."

The overseer looked around at Robert's voice. He came to stand in front of him, staring with yellow eyes. Eagle's eyes. Robert held them with his own steady gaze. The man spoke.

"I do not know your tongue," Robert said, his voice hoarse. "Speak mine that I may answer you."

The overseer blasted a stream of words ending with a sharp poke against Robert's chest with the end of the whip. Robert looked at the salt-stiff linen of his own shirt, and then at the man. His mouth tightened. The man's eye's sharpened and a sly smile revealed worn teeth. He raised the whip and repeatedly stabbed Robert with it.

"Do not vex me, I pray you," Robert said, a muscle working in his jaw.

The overseer looked over his shoulder at the men behind him, speaking rapidly and evidently enjoying the game. "Eh, eh?" he said, giving a particularly sharp jab.

Robert's hand flashed out, seizing the whip and bringing the length of it against the man's throat until he began to choke. "Now!" he said before the startled Moor could recover.

The men from his own fleet sprang forwards, but the English merchants stood gaping.

"Move!" he shouted at them. "Attack, or we are lost!"

The older Englishman came to, striking out at the captor closest to him; but, panic-stricken, the younger men scattered like sparrows, leaving Robert and his men outflanked. Robert caught a flash of movement from the corner of his eye and a clout to the side of his head floored him.

He came to, disorientated. The dead man's eyes gazed blankly at him, his lank, fair hair matted with drying blood. Flies supped at the open wound on his throat and crawled among the threads of beard. Robert tried to move but his hands and feet had been bound behind him, and he lay face downwards on the gritty surface. He spat blood and sand and attempted to roll over onto his back, but a foot thrust against his shoulders, pinning him down. A pole was threaded under his arms and legs and he hung suspended like a deer from a hunt, his dripping blood leaving a trail as he was swung about by two grunting brigands, and they moved off.

Robert became conscious of a rocking motion and the sound of slapping against his ear and a repetitive wooden squeak, followed by a *whoosh* and *clunk*, *squeak*, *whoosh*, *clunk*. Heat seared his face. He could neither open his eyes nor move. He must be dead and this was Hell. But he didn't remember dying nor facing the Judgement he knew he deserved. *Kýrie, eléison, Christe, eléison, kýrie, eléison.* He formed the words in his head, unable to articulate them through swollen lips, and found comfort in their repetition. *Glória in excélsis Deo. Benedícimus te. Have mercy on me, O God, according to Thy great mercy.* His eyes wrenched open to be blinded by light. "For I deserve none," he said out loud.

"Shh," a voice cautioned next to him. "Do not give them a reason to beat you."

Men lay or sat in the stern of a low-slung vessel, hands tied, legs bound at the ankle to the man next to him. Seated on thwarts, row upon row of semi-naked men of many nations sweated in pairs at long oars, and it was from their labour that the *squeak*, *whoosh*, *clunk* emanated as the oars dipped and ground in the sea. The clunk came from the leg irons that bound each man and ran through shackles the length of the galley. If the boat foundered, all would drown.

The vessel was making speed, the sea striking the sides and reverberating against his ear. Robert moved his head and it hurt worse than he had ever known it. Gingerly feeling his face, he felt numerous cuts and, when he pressed his cheekbone, a deep welt still seeping blood.

"Aye, that's a mark and some," the man Robert recognised as Phipps, one of the English merchants, remarked. Robert raised his head and scanned the rest of the faces. "We're all here — your men, too. Not that strange one, of course. Reckon he was a Rus. Bit touched in the head, he was." He lifted his bound hands and tapped his forehead. "There was nowt they could do with him. Perhaps better mad and dead than going where we're headed."

"Where is that?" Robert croaked.

"To Hell or the slave pens and they be much the same thing, or so Holy Church would have us believe." He made a tiny genuflection. "It makes no odds. We'll all end the same way — at beck and call of some hairy-arsed Infidel. As long as we're worth more alive than dead, that is." He crossed himself again, then surveyed Robert with a questioning eye. "Unless you can pay a ransom."

"Water. Is there water?" Robert dodged.

"Aye, and plenty of it." Phipps nodded over the thwarts at the sea. "Of the drinking kind, up there." He jerked his head towards the bows where a keg sat lashed in place. "But you'd better not be asking or One-Ear'll be at yer. Best lay low."

The crossing was short and rough. Even hardened by years at sea, pirate and captive alike emptied the contents of their stomachs seaward. Seagulls followed, snatching the mackerel that fed in the churning wake of the ship. Robert had nothing to offer. Baked by the sun and blinded by its glare, he slipped in and out of sleep to the sound of gulls and men and the incessant slop of water against the hull.

They made landfall as the sky grew dark and the first stars appeared. A scurry of activity saw the sails lowered and oars thrust over the side and, a short while later, the vessel slid smoothly against a wooden jetty that blocked out the evening sky.

Standing with the rest of the men, Robert attempted to gain some sense of their location. The air smelled alien. The wind had dropped with the sun, and smoke from numerous fires bore heady scents of cooking meat and spices; but without the benefit of light, and before he could guess their position, they were herded away from the shore to an open space encircled by a rough fence of staves. Amber eyes observed them as cloven-hooved goats with wispy beards reluctantly gave way as the prisoners were shoved into the enclosure and the gate secured.

"*Meu Senhor!*"

Robert looked around as Captain Barquerio pushed past the animals, his own few men in tow trying not to trip over the binding ropes in the near dark.

"You are hurt, *meu Senhor?*"

"You live!" Robert rasped. "Thanks be to God, for I believed you drowned. How long have you been here?"

"A day past, *meu Senhor.* But, you are hurt?"

"My thanks, it is nothing," Robert said, touching his fingers to his bloodied scalp. "Do you know this place?"

"*Não, meu Senhor.* It is one of many such. These Barbary pirates are like the *praga de gafanhotos.*"

"Plague of locusts," Robert translated in a murmur.

"*Sim* — plague. They come to the villages along the coast to take men, women, children. These people — these families — they do not return. Only men of nobility might be *resgatado*."

"Ransomed?" Robert considered this piece of information. "Where are they taken?"

Barquerio lifted his shoulders and waved vaguely inland. "Many places — *terra dos egípcios* — Egypt. And to the south where there is but sand and the skin of the men is black. The sand, it eats men. Christian men who go to these lands never return. They must never return," he amended.

"Why not if they make their escape?"

Barquerio shook his head slowly. "These men, they are *contaminado*." To make his point clear he spat into the dust and crossed himself. His men followed suit. "It is better to die a good Christian in these lands than return to our families *contaminado*. That is worse than death itself."

"But if a man returns uncontaminated?"

"His family, the people of his village, *think* he is *contaminado*, that he is foul, that he is turned Moor and lost his soul." His mouth turned into a sharp downward bow and as one, the men crossed themselves, muttering Aves.

Robert had heard of such men in distant childhood tales whispered between adults when they thought he wasn't listening. He had paid scant attention then, but now those exchanged looks and disapproving brows began to make sense. "Then it is incumbent on us to ensure we do not suffer the same fate," he said grimly. "We must escape as I, for one, will not lose my soul in this place nor any other."

Robert awoke to a nasal wailing some way off and a tickling sensation and warm breath upon his face. He opened one eye to find two blank ones observing him. Nostrils flexed and flared with a whooshing sound, and Robert suspected he smelled worse than the offended goat. He rolled over and sat up, displacing the indignant animal. Barquerio had formed a rough guard around him with his men, and they still slept. Robert became aware of his aching shoulder, a head like Hades, and a throat dryer than the dust surrounding them. He pushed all aside and searched for the source of the strange singing.

Flat-roofed mud houses bordered the open space on three sides in which the animal enclosure sat. On the fourth, as far as he could make out between the dusty flanks of the goats, he glimpsed the sea. Except for birds taking flight, he detected no other life, and the rising and falling notes from the thin tower rising above the huts filled the dawn with an eerie solitude that crawled under his skin. Despite the building heat, he shivered.

He leaned over and shook Barquerio awake. "Ready your men. I see no guard and there is nothing to this fence. We can break through and make for the boats. I will not stay here waiting for my fate to be decided by others..." He stopped. "Why do you look at me like that?" He felt his scalp and his hair encrusted with grains of dried blood. "Ah, it must look worse than it is. Come, before the guards return; I cannot abide that noise any longer. If we move as one these bindings will not hold us. Ho, you, there!" he called softly to the other man to whom he was bound. "Rouse yourself and make ready."

The man rolled over and sat up. His mouth dropped open as he stared at Robert.

"I do not need my looks to flee," Robert said dryly before the man could. He knelt on one knee, found his legs to be stronger than he had feared and pulled his companion up with him. Barquerio followed his lead. "Wait!" Robert held up his hand. He peered towards the far side of the enclosure. "Get down!" he hissed. There, kneeling with his head bent and his back to the enclosure, one of the pirates seemed to be eating dry earth.

Barquerio spoke into Robert's ear. "He prays towards the Kaba — in Macca. When the muezzin ceases the call to prayer, the guard will rise." He pointed to the prostrate man. "We go — now."

"We must first alert the others."

"*Não, meu Senhor!* We cannot help them."

"We can take the guard before he raises the alarm."

"It is too far. We go now or we do not go at all." Still Robert wavered. "*Meu Senhor*, they have no need of you like this." He indicated Robert's head and sliced his own throat with his forefinger. "The other men — they have value. They not harmed."

Robert gave a terse nod. "We go."

Shuffling at an ungainly run and keeping low, they made it to the jetty when the call to prayer ended. Barquerio directed the boat cast off and prepared to scramble into the nearest vessel, using the ropes left hanging for the purpose. He halted suddenly and Robert, leg already over the edge and about to jump, looked down.

Grinning up at them, armed and ready, a dozen pirates waited in the boat below.

CHAPTER EIGHTEEN

Felice lowered her lids and looked up through her eyelashes in what she intended to be an alluring manner. "My lord," she murmured, "you do me great honour."

Anthony Newton regarded the slope of her forehead, her finely cut mouth, the cleft of her breasts just visible beneath the filmy linen making them decent, and thought he could do worse. She was unlikely to bear him any sons, but she brought one ready-made to the marriage and at least it dealt away with the urgency of bedding her once the formalities of the consummation were over. He could always find his pleasures elsewhere; meanwhile, she knew exactly what was expected of her and came with impeccable lineage. And if she chose to flatter him with *my lord*, so be it; it was where he headed and this would butter the way and plant the idea where it mattered — in the mind of the queen and, therefore, the king. It was true she brought little in the way of lands to the match. He wondered whether he could do better, then thought that, given she had the ear of the queen, probably not. Some things were worth more than land in the short term and he was in it for the long game. He was on his way up and, while he was not unaware of her reputation as a beauty, her allure came mainly from her marriage to the former earl, and William Langton's repute counted for more.

She remained still and demure until he had completed his examination. Then he said, "Lady, the honour is mine."

She looked him in the eye. "Do we have an agreement, Anthony?"

He smiled back. "We do," he said.

*

A sharp wind channelled through the passage between the jettied buildings bringing the turgid scent of ale and privies that always seemed to accompany the men that drank at the nearby alehouse. It might be an incongruous place to meet, but drunk men had no ears to hear and no eyes to see, and Felice preferred it that way.

"But he's only a *gentleman*, ma mère. He has no rank, no nobility. How can you agree to wed with … with *that*!"

"Hold your tongue, Elizabeth!" Felice bit back. "And show some respect. He is young and ambitious and he will be your father whether you agree to it or no."

"Papa would be sorely grieved to have his widow sink so low —" Bess gasped as her mother's palm caught the side of her face.

Felice grabbed her by the arm. "Your most *noble sire* left me to shift for myself. If matters had been otherwise, your brother would be Earl and I in a position to pick and choose my match. As it is, your father is dead and Anthony Newton has a name to make for himself and I will help him make it. You have your marriage and child and I will have mine." She let go of her daughter's arm and Bess rubbed it looking sulky.

"What will the queen say when she discovers you have agreed to marry a common man, ma mère? Will she allow you to serve her still?"

"Who do you think proposed the match? You do not believe I would make a marriage without the queen's knowledge and consent, do you? I might have fallen low, but I have not yet lost my wits. Anthony's father was only a gentleman, it is true, but Anthony was knighted by the king and has an eye for preferment, and only last St Andrew's feast he was granted further offices." She paused at the sound of light footsteps running towards them. She turned to face them. "I have told you not to run like a cotter's brat, William. Next you will be rolling about like swine in mud. Come, here is your sister."

The small boy with brown hair and a heart-shaped face and ears too big for his head raced up to them, tripped over an uneven flagstone, and went flying headlong at his mother's feet. He lay there, beginning to wail.

"Get up," Felice snapped. "You will be taken for a fool."

William clambered to his feet, his nose dribbling. "Bess, greet your brother, the earl."

"Ma mère," Bess whispered, "William is not the earl and it is not right to address him as such."

"With your uncle Robert dead and his son yet an infant, your brother will come into his rightful inheritance with none to oppose him."

"What about … *her*." Bess did not dare shape Isobel Langton's name. "She will not stand by while her son is put aside."

"As I was obliged to do?" Felice gave a chilly smile, revealing the gap where one of her tiny teeth had been recently pulled. She remembered and adjusted her lips to cover the loss. "I have it from a credible source that the Fenton harlot will not pose a problem. William! Stop fretting and stand still."

Her son ceased pulling on her sleeve and sat down on the damp ground with a scowl and a thump.

"You need not know the source," she added before Bess could ask. "And say nothing — not even to your husband, do you understand?"

Eyes round with curiosity, Bess nodded.

"Now, how is my grandchild, Elizabeth; does she thrive?"

"Yes, ma mère, wonderfully well. She is making stitches on her own and has such a pretty way about her. She can even dance…"

But her mother had ceased to listen and was instead making a protesting William stand up and have his clothes straightened and brushed free of earth and dog fur from the hounds that frequented these passages. "And Bess."

"Yes, ma mère?"

"You must curb your appetite lest your husband is obliged to find himself a mistress. You are no longer young and few men desire a woman run to fat." Felice tapped her cheek. "You may kiss me."

Marriage to young Anthony Newton, Queen Elizabeth mused, might appear to some at Court as an unreconcilable reduction in status for the dowager countess, but then members of the Court did not always see the bigger picture and that, she thought, was the one thing she did rather well. And Felice Langton was not in a position to pick and choose. She would give him credibility and a son, and he would give her three manors and a house in London. Not much by her standards — or anybody with any standing — but he was rising fast, had a keen eye for a chance, and his queen's patronage.

Newton had also proved his loyalty, not least in agreeing to marry the aging widow. Yes, she thought to herself, this match solved two problems at once: what do with Felice Langton, whose carping about her son's inheritance had worn thin the ears she battered, and how to reward Newton for his services. Edward had been glad to grant Newton valuable offices if it rid him of the woman's nuisance. As for Elizabeth, it bound the young man with gratitude without her having to reach into her own purse.

Meanwhile, there were other matters to address. The unexpected death of Robert Langton left a void that needed filling, a void that represented an opportunity and one which — if her source was to be believed — Clarence had already seized. Another widow; another heir. She had been in the same position as Isobel Langton once and look where it had led. Not one for introspection, the queen nonetheless found herself fingering the ring Edward had given her, thinking back to the early days of widowhood.

She shook herself free and galvanised her thoughts. If this potentially volatile situation were to be resolved satisfactorily, she would have to tread with care and caution, for as widow and Dowager Countess to the infant earl, Isobel Langton was in a stronger position than she probably realised. She was also fair game.

"I am so tired, Is'bel, yet I cannot sleep. Will you make me one of your potions?"

Looking insignificant in the light of the flames, Lady Isabel sat by her solar fire, wrapped in a fur-lined gown and with her feet propped on a stool. Isobel tucked another mantle around her, checked no draughts could find their way in, and took the chair beside her. Her gentlewomen had retired for the night and only Isobel and the duchess remained awake to talk away the hours.

"There are days when I feel closer to Our Saviour and wonder if soon I shall be." Lady Isabel laid her head back against the chair and contemplated the ceiling. "Do you think about your death, Is'bel? I do. If I should be taken from this life … no, no, wait dear friend, let me finish." She moistened dry lips. "If I die before my time, I wish you to do something.

Will you take a letter for me? It has been playing on my mind and I trust none other."

Isobel recalled the tall, austere man who resembled a saint and was called so behind his back. "I thought your Master Secretary is to be depended upon?"

"I thought so too, but this is something I wish only to entrust to you."

"Of course, if it please you."

"Over there, in my jewel casket. Bring it to me."

Isobel did as asked, bringing the casket with its bright enamels she remembered first seeing at L'Erber long ago. Or so it seemed. Lady Isabel opened its lid, removing the contents piece by piece, and retrieving several folded letters each sealed with ribbon and her personal cipher.

"This is for my lady mother. I have seen little of her since my father's death, but I know she mourns him still." She gave a wistful little smile. "Anne and I always knew he came first in her affections. We were welcome heirs, of course, but she loved him above all others and even us. Is that strange, do you think, Is'bel, to be jealous of your husband's affection for your daughters?"

The duchess contemplated the flames. "Well, so it was," she said, coming back to the moment. "She lives with her loss and we could give her no comfort, not even in her grandchildren. Perhaps my mother might have been more gently inclined towards us if George and Richard had not been granted her lands. Oh, do not look surprised at my mentioning it! All of Court knew there would be no peace until the lands had been settled upon them. George did squawk about it so! He insisted he was unfairly treated but, then," she frowned, "he always thinks so. My poor mother — declared dead even though she lives, and all for the price of her estates."

Another pause while Lady Isabel mustered her reserves. She held out the second letter, its translucence warmed by the light of the fire. "This is for my sister Anne. We were close before I married, even if we did fight over who was our father's favourite. When we asked him, he would say that I was his preferred oldest daughter and Anne his favourite youngest. It took Anne a long time to work that out. She was always rather fuddle-headed about such things." Lady Isabel smiled fondly. "Take this to her, when you can, and the beads of green stone from my jewel casket, there."

Isobel looked at the casket on the side table and the letters she now held. They placed a burden on her she could not explain. Perhaps it was because these letters signified more than familial responsibilities, but proof of death as well, because that is what it felt like: that these represented the final words of a dying woman. "I will do what I can, but I do not know when that may be."

"Poor Is'bel, you do so want to go home. Do not worry; it will not be long now."

Isobel's heart jumped. "Has His Grace said I might return?"

"Hmm? George? No, he has said nothing about you leaving. But when I die, there will be nothing left for you here and I do not think you will wish to remain." She had closed her eyes so did not see Isobel's face drain of hope. "Will you miss me, Is'bel?"

Isobel thought that, of all the people she had met over the years, she counted the duchess as one of the few she considered a friend. "I cannot miss someone who is not gone, can I?" she said stoutly. "You are still here and will remain so — and so will I," she added.

"Until the end?"

"This talk of death makes me shiver," Isobel said, using the excuse to throw more wood on the fire to cast off the chill that had entered the room. "You will bring the ghosts of our forefathers to haunt us."

"Do you believe that?"

"I ... have never given it much consideration."

"You must miss him," Lady Isabel said softly.

Isobel rose suddenly and went over to the small table where she had earlier brought her own casket and began concocting the duchess's favourite sedative.

"Is'bel, why do you not speak his name?" she pressed.

How could Isobel begin to explain that the very shape of it in her mouth was dust and ashes, that its mere articulation made the reality of his absence so sharp, so intense that the core of her blistered. *Rob!* She cried in her mind. *Rob!* In silence she screamed his name and felt the child inside her move to the rhythm of her anguish.

"Come, sit, you look faint. Perhaps you should take a little of my strengthening physic?"

Isobel mustered a jest. "You say that only so you need not take it all." She distorted her face into a mask of disgust and Lady Isabel smiled. Becoming serious again, Isobel said, "The physician was quite clear: you are to take *all* of your physic."

"I will not tell if you do not. A little less will do me no harm and might do you some good. Mix it as you do for me and it will not taste so foul."

"Well, I might..."

"Nay, you *will*. I would see you smile again. Mistress Twynyho puts it in the aumbry out of little Edward's reach. You know how he delves into every nook and cranny." The doubt must have showed on Isobel's face because Lady Isabel adopted the insistent look she used when she was adamant.

"The physic must be doing me good because I feel *so* much better than I did."

Isobel had to admit that the duchess did have a little more colour and her voice was stronger than before, so she acquiesced. If nothing more it might appease her. With a candle on its stand, she went to the aumbry, unlocked the door, and peered in. Items personal to Lady Isabel lay inside: a tiny shoe, a broken comb, a small box which rattled when she lifted it and, on closer inspection, revealed baby teeth. Another shelf held papers, some with broken seals, others closed with ribbon and Lady Isabel's own matrix. The highest shelf contained more practical items relating to health and cleanliness: a gold and ivory toothpick, a seeing lens hidden away in case it was discovered her sight was weak. And, at the far back and concealed, twists of paper leaning one against the other like little pasty soldiers.

"Have you found it?" Lady Isabel called.

It? *Them*. Frowning, Isobel took one, sniffed it, and unrolled the paper to reveal a finely ground powder.

"That's it," Lady Isabel said. "Mix it with ale and your herbs and all will be well with you."

"What about your measure, Your Grace?"

"Mine will wait on the morrow. No doubt Master Physician will bring me another." She pulled a face.

Isobel glanced at the phalanx of papers and rearranged the contents so they were hidden once again. "We can share this; you must not miss your dose." She made up the warmed ale and herb potion as usual except this time it was she who added the powder and stirred it in until the grains dispersed. She held it out to Lady Isabel. "If it please you?"

"It does not," the duchess answered, taking it and sipping from the cup anyway. She handed it back to Isobel. "It is your turn; I have left plenty for you."

"You are most kind," Isobel replied dryly. Holding her breath, she drank. "Ugh! How can you stomach this!"

"'*The worse the potion the better the cure*'," Lady Isabel quoted.

"Then you should be up and dancing." Isobel wiped her lips with the back of her hand. The bitter liquid dried her mouth and curled her tongue. She looked around and saw the dish of delicacies always kept nearby, grabbed an exotic-looking item, and stuffed it into her mouth. "That," she said between chewing, "is more foul than it was before. Master Physician is intent on making you well so that you no longer have to suffer his physic. By my oath, it is so … so…"

Lady Isabel sat up, alarmed. "Is'bel, what is it?"

Isobel shook her head, tried to swallow, couldn't and seizing the nearest receptacle, retched. Dazed, she flopped back in her chair as Lady Isabel called out for help.

One of the maids came in first, quickly followed by Mistress Twynyho looking just wakened and anxious. She summed up the situation in a glance. Sending the maid to fetch Buena and another to clear away the bowl, she made Isobel more comfortable as the sickness subsided.

"Madam, are you quite well?" Mistress Twynyho addressed the duchess, who was looking bewildered, and when Lady Isabel nodded, said, "Did my lady Langton complain of sickness before?"

"No, not at all. We were talking and then Lady Langton sickened. Perhaps it is the child within?"

Isobel managed to shake her head without throwing up again, but she broke out in a thin, clammy sweat instead. "It is not the child. I ate a delicacy from the dish." The women looked where she pointed, shakily. "It did not taste tainted ... but anything tastes better than that physic."

"My lady took Her Grace's physic?" Mistress Twynyho said with an uncustomary sharpness.

"Yes, from the aumbry; there is plenty to be had."

"Plenty?" Lady Isabel commented. "I thought it as scarce as nepenthe."

Mistress Twynyho turned away with a set expression, removing the dish of delicacies. "These must be spoiled, madam," she remarked, taking them to the fire and throwing the prettily coloured contents into the flames. "Away with them and a message took to the kitchens that all food be tasted before Her Grace receives it."

Even in her woozy state, Isobel read Mistress Twynyhos jerky movements. She caught her eye, and the woman set her mouth into a single line. She couldn't follow with a question because Buena ran into the room, pushing past the ladies and servants who had gathered there in various states off readiness, and up to Isobel. She felt Isobel's brow, looked at each eye in turn, and laid her hand upon Isobel's stomach.

Isobel removed her hand. "It is nothing, Bayna, just a little sickness, and it has now passed."

The following morning, Isobel rose from her bed feeling as if she had spent the night in her cups. Head swimming, she moved with weighted legs from bed to stool and sat, leaning her aching head on her arms against the table. The smell of damp, newly cleansed wood and ash and lye was too much for her parlous state and she sat up again.

Buena grunted her concern and, for the sixth time that morning, tested her hand against her mistress's temple. She shook her head, imitated eating and the food's violent expulsion, and ended with a query.

"It must have been the delicacy, Bayna. Except," Isobel paused, thinking back to the previous night now her head was clearing a little. "Has Mistress Twynyho said aught to you?"

Buena's eyes slid sideways to the maids playing with the children and the door beyond which Lady Isabel's apartments lay. She held out her hand and made it flutter uncertainly and then raised a finger in caution.

Isobel lowered her voice. "Well, has she?"

Buena wobbled her head as if unsure, pointed to Isobel and then to the door. Then, slowly and deliberately, she mimed grinding, pouring, and finally the mixing of a liquid. She held out an imaginary cup and quirked a brow in question.

Isobel felt a chill run through her. "In the duchess's aumbry I found powders of physic. I mixed one for Her Grace and she insisted I drank some, too." She looked up at Buena. "Mistress Twynyho suspects something. She made mention of it before, but I thought it fanciful. Unless … unless it is she who…" She gave a firm shake of her head. "No, I have seen her enough times to know she is devoted to Her Grace. She is an honest woman and bears no ill-will towards any. So, who does?"

She stood, shakily, the gravity of what she was swiftly coming to conclude making itself known. The physician supplied the physic, Clarence retained him; but who would wish injury to Lady Isabel — not her husband, surely? Might another, pursuing retribution against Clarence, seek to harm the mother of his children? Or was it something else entirely? What drove people to such actions and who — on God's good earth — had the most to gain?

CHAPTER NINETEEN

Not even at the height of summer when the lands of his mother lay parched under a relentless sun had Robert seen anything like this. From the ridge of rock from which they now surveyed the terrain, undulating swathes of tawny sand stretched as far as his raw eyes could see. Behind them, deeply fissured slopes ascended in naked regiments from the bed of a river beside which they had travelled for days. Beyond that, snow-topped mountains rose from foothills where patches of green marked the water courses and their tributaries.

Bound at the ankle, the straggling line of captives extended fore and aft flanked by guards. At the front, the swaying rumps of the strange, humped creatures Robert had only seen in the bestiaries of his youth indicated the caravan was on the move again. The ranks of the captured had been swollen by the addition of men, women and children at a crowded slave market in a bustling town to the north of the mountain range from which the caravan had emerged. The misery of his situation was made worse as Barquerio and his remaining crew were hustled away leaving the small group of Englishmen and a few Portuguese crammed into a slave pen underground to await their fate.

When Robert tried to find out where Barquerio had been taken, he was answered with the cosh. "East, I reckon," the merchant Phipps had said. "To the Gyptians, much good it'll do 'em."

The foetid conditions and lack of food and clean water had taken one of the Englishmen with a bloody flux within a week. Most suffered from one gut problem or another. Then, after what must have been at least a fortnight without seeing the sky, they had been taken out into the searing sun and the small party of English sent separate ways, leaving Robert alone.

The caravan moved at a steady pace, irrespective of age or infirmity. If he craned around the lean back of the man in front of him, Robert could just make out the slighter figures of women and the insignificant frames of children. They no longer cried and had fallen mute some days before, stumbling in their efforts to keep up the pace set by the men behind them. Robert ached at the sight and the thought of his own wife and children, but pushed their memory to one side lest it undermine him further.

The animals seemed to know where they headed, although nothing but sifting sand and scattered rock marked their way. At the height of the sun, the caravan stopped in the shade of an outcrop. The animals buckled their legs and settled with snorts and grunts onto the sand, while the guards, pulling cloth over their heads, formed huddles and chatted amongst themselves. Robert listened to the melody of their distant conversations. So normal, so every day, that if he leaned back against the hot dune and closed his eyes, he could almost imagine the other squires in his youth and the hubbub they made as they bathed in the river, he on the cool grass, his skin drying in the mild sun with little but the thought of wenches to occupy his mind. But this was not England, and the voices he heard spoke an alien tongue. He had nothing to look forward to but a life enslaved and that, he had been assured, would be short.

He sat up again. A guard supervised the distribution of water from bellied skins, the thin stream issuing into gaping mouths and dribbling down dust-covered chins. Waiting his turn, Robert wiped the back of his hand against his parched lips in anticipation. There was no distinction of rank here, no observance of manners, no pedigree — all were made equal by servitude.

Robert opened his mouth, relishing the warm, stale water shared with people from lands he had never heard of, their customs so foreign to him, yet they were united by their humanity. He had learned that the dark-skinned man in front of him was a trader and had been captured with his brother, who had since been sold on, and that the short, swarthy man behind came from the kingdom of Sicily. Others, like Robert, left behind wife and children. All mourned the loss of freedom and clung to the only identity they retained — their names. These they kept to themselves as if sacred and secret.

None spoke of lordship or chattels: those seemed as irrelevant as the future currently appeared. What mattered was here among the flies and dust. Robert thrust his hand into the sand, lifting a fistful and letting it drop in a steady fall to merge with the countless other grains. Numberless fragments, like the people that must have passed along this route over the centuries to die in a foreign land nameless and forgotten, their bones turning to dust to mingle with the sand and oblivion.

Where was he in all this? What did it matter who sat on the throne, who rose and who fell in the land beyond the sea? Where was Lady Fortune now, where was God in a land of many gods and none? He reached to his waist in a movement so habitual that he had done it before he remembered the pouch with his beads wasn't there. Did the emptiness inside his chest reflect an absence of God? Yet desert fathers had found divinity in such places as this and, if he looked deep inside, he knew the lack lay in himself. But he still mourned the loss of certainty that had accompanied him since his youth.

A sliver of stone protruded from the sand by his foot. Robert tried to remove it and, finding it embedded, began to excavate the rock. Lifting it free it looked such a curious thing, like a sand-coloured rose petrified in the act of shedding its petals. Curiosity overcoming the present, he held it in awe, wishing Isobel might share this moment of wonder. She would marvel at its flower shape and together they would discuss what miracle drew it forth from the earth.

Holding up the rock in the cradle of his palm, he saw beyond the petals the scraps of people chained together in knots of living flesh, some sleeping, others absorbed in their own memories. Robert looked at them, his heart went out to them, and in them, he saw God. He took the rock rose — his miracle of the desert — and, wrapping it in a piece of linen torn from his shirt, secured it from sight.

The lean, muscular trader stumbled, crashing to the ground and pulling Robert with him as he fell. Winded, the man began to rise, but a guard ran towards him and brought the stub end of his whip down on his back. The man staggered under the blow and Robert, seeing the guard readying to strike again, twisted around on his knees and grabbed his arm, his teeth grating on grit as he resisted the downward momentum.

The guard turned his attention to Robert instead, beating him with the flat of his hands and knocking him sideways where he continued to berate him, waving his arms and yelling like something possessed. Robert grabbed a handful of sand and was about to throw it in the guard's eyes when, "*Não!*" the trader said in a hiss.

Robert stopped. Had he heard correctly? Did the trader speak to him in Portuguese? Still on his knees, the trader was speaking rapidly, all the while bowing and pleading to the guard.

A sudden shout went up from the line ahead and, distracted, the guard moved away.

Robert climbed to his feet and stared into the vastness before them but could see nothing but the blurring of the horizon in the heat of the afternoon. The horizon shifted, becoming black dots, the dots men on horseback that kept pace with the caravan at a distance. *Nómades*, the word travelled in a whisper of fear from mouth to mouth, and the caravan shuffled forwards again but this time with a greater urgency.

"Dodzi," the ebony figure said over his shoulder.

Robert quickened his step to close the gap. "I do not understand."

"Dodzi," he said again, this time placing a hand over his own chest. "Dodzi."

Robert grinned. "Robert," he said, tapping his own chest.

"Obet," Dodzi tried.

"Robert."

Dodzi nodded. "O'bert."

"O'bert, that is near enough. You speak Portuguese — *você fala português?*"

"*Não*," Dodzi said. "Leetle Engleesh, leetle Port'gees."

Robert indicated ahead. "Where?"

Dodzi said something unintelligible, then, more slowly, "Si-jil-masa," directing his gaze to the skyline and making an eating motion with his fingers, then resting his head on his arm as if asleep. "We go Sijilmasa."

The first indication of life other than their own and the great wheeling shapes of birds high above them was a blur of dark green that slowly became trees as they neared, and an animated babble coursed through the enslaved. Arching, serrated leaves cast welcome pools of shade beneath which they made shambolic progress along a foot-hardened way. Clusters of flat-roofed, daubed constructions — some fort-like and clearly defended — marked a settlement from which children darted to stare at the strangers. Women worked around fires or at woven baskets into which they laid alternate layers of leaves and small, dark objects.

Dodzi nodded towards the baskets and rubbed his stomach.

The sporadic trees became groves where men laboured. Open channels ran with clear water from which others drew to tend young plants, and camels — loaded with baskets — swayed their way south and west. All about them became green, the air cooled and savoured with moist earth and the constant whine and drone of insects and the chatter of birds. Sensing water, the camels picked up their feet to be led away towards the thickest stands of trees leaving the caravan to struggle on without them.

Exhausted, one by one the younger children began to drop. Without ceremony a boy not much older than Andrew was deposited in Robert's arms. He and the child, strangers except in circumstance, surveyed each other; then Robert swung him up and onto his shoulders, and secured him by the ankles. After a moment's hesitation the child wrapped his arms around Robert's neck and silently began to cry. Robert ached for the boy's loss and his own, torn as they were from all that they knew and loved, and wept silently inside for them both.

Thick lines of trees marked the course of the river, broadening into wide lush groves. Here, as the day cooled, activity intensified until long-legged camels and robed men became as numerous as trees, and beasts laden with baskets through which leaves poked, made lines of swaying commerce along dusty paths. No one paid attention to the tawny-coloured caravan emerging from the swollen sands and Robert realised that theirs was just another in what must be a frequent spectacle. How many stolen souls have passed this way and for how many years? Too many to count, like dust, like sand.

They halted as the sun melted into the evening sky and the first stars appeared. Herded towards a clearing, Robert caught the scent of damp ground and saw, running in stone channels, clear water reflecting silver as it crossed one side of an open space fringed with trees. Released from their bonds, women, men, and children vied for space along the channel, kneeling haphazardly in the dust and thrusting faces and hands into the water and drinking greedily.

Dodzi pulled Robert towards the higher end where the water welled untainted by man or beast. Relieving his shoulders of the additional weight, Robert lowered the child to the ground. The boy immediately lunged towards the water, while Robert cupped his own palms and scooped handful after handful into his mouth, splashing it over his head and feeling it run down his open-necked shirt, making the fabric cling to his chest.

Satiated for the time being, he sat next to Dodzi and the boy. The sea had deprived him of his fine leather boots and, sunburned, his feet were a mess of cuts and abrasions. The chains around his ankles rubbed the skin, leaving it snarled with blood and sand to form a crust at which small flies nipped. He brushed them away with a weary hand then dropped water over the cuts, flinching as they stung.

Excited voices came from further down the line of bedraggled bodies as captives held up their hands to slaves who deposited small objects into them. A leaf-wrapped parcel dropped into the sand and following Dodzi's example, Robert picked it up and opened it. Elongated, soft, plump brown fruits lay partially squashed in his palm.

Dodzi made eating motions and began to consume the fruits with relish. Robert contemplated them without interest and Dodzi put his hand beneath his and urged him to eat. Robert tried a corner. A date, but not the mean, wrinkled, mouth-searing confection he had eaten before, but flesh melting with a fibrous sweetness that left his mouth clean and his awareness sharpened. Dodzi nodded and grinned, making the short, scored marks on his cheek merge with the lines of laughter at the corners of his eyes.

Robert made the sign of the cross, closed his eyes, and murmured words of thanks. When he opened them, he saw the boy watching, and Robert winked and began to eat with a grunt of pleasure. Having already finished his own, the boy watched hungrily like a malnourished puppy. Robert looked at his remaining dates, sighed, and gave the rest to the child.

Dodzi finished eating and lay back against the water channel with a contented belch. "Dodzi say O'bert friend. O'bert help Dodzi."

"That was a shrewd move you made yourself back there," Robert countered, and when Dodzi appeared not to understand, tried, "*Dodzi* help *Robert*," and imitated a fist full of sand.

Dodzi grinned. "O'bert need sleep; O'bert go *raaaaaa*." Dodzi made claws of his hands. "He make guard..." He screwed his face as he sought a word.

"Angry?" Robert suggested.

"An-gry. Not good make guard an-gry. Guard kill O'bert."

Robert considered for a moment. "In my land we say *rash men make mistakes*. This is true; I acted before giving due consideration to the situation and I thank you for your timely intervention." He bowed his head. Dodzi looked blank. "I think," Robert said, considering the other man, "that Dodzi and O'bert are friends." And at that, Dodzi broke into a wide grin.

For several days they were kept unbound but in close confinement in the clearing while their wounds healed and they rested in the shade of the trees, feeding on dates and flat bread cooked on fire-baked stone by women covered to the eyes in cloth. They were being fattened for market like geese, Robert speculated, allowed to rest and feed before being led to slaughter.

Early on the fourth day, they were taken in small groups to an expanse of water in which they were made to strip and wash — men and women together — the water becoming filmy with their accumulated sweat and grime. Then they were told to clean whatever clothes they had worn since being captured. Nonplussed, Robert held the remains of his fine linen shirt — now stained and torn — in the water and waved it about a bit. Lifting it out, dripping, it looked as dirty as when it went in only wet.

A guard shouted something incomprehensible from the bank. Robert was at a loss. The guard shouted again.

"You do it if it is of such import," Robert muttered, thrashing the shirt in the water and surreptitiously watching a young woman with hair the colour of wheat to see how it should be done. She saw him looking and covered her reddened nakedness with her wet clothes, and Robert cursed the situation in which they found themselves that she should be so exposed to the eyes of a stranger.

Averting his gaze, he flapped his shirt and lifted his shoulders in a question. She spoke softly, with a lilting cadence, at the same time taking her skirts in both hands and rubbing them vigorously together. He bent his head in thanks, a gesture so artlessly courteous that she responded with a smile that lifted the corner of her blue eyes. In that moment, and in any other circumstance, they might have been a man and a woman potently conscious of their sexuality. Here, they were stripped of their identity, without gender, nation, and name. This young woman has a story, he thought, but in the desert land it would remain untold, as would his.

At sunrise the following day, thin shadows of trees kept them company dipping and wavering as they were driven south alongside a wide canal. '*Midrariya*', Dodzi called it.

"Have you been here before?" Robert signed, to which Dodzi nodded, forming a story with his hands and a jumble of words telling of long journeys and trade and riches worn as necklaces and bangles, and earrings. "Gold?" Robert asked, and again,

Dodzi bobbed his head. Much, much gold from far away to the south. It had been on one of his many journeys that he and his brother had been captured by slavers.

"Where is he now?" Robert asked, only to have Dodzi spit out a word into the sand with bitter lips.

Shapes of buildings began to appear among the trees, some were abandoned and their roofs open to the sky; but others gathered in small groups around a square defended by something akin to a squat tower reminding Robert of a fortified manor. But defended from what? The buildings became increasingly bigger until, bloated with importance and gilded by the new sun, walls founded of stone and topped by russet mud brick rose above them, blotting out the sky.

"Sijilmasa," Dodzi said, and there was reverence in his voice.

Tall gates made of bronze, fashioned with such ornamentation that they looked out of place in the desert land, barred their way. Gathered at the entrance waiting for the gates to open, people took the opportunity to cast insults at the captives and to hawk at their feet. Ahead, a stone flew from nowhere catching the scalp of a woman, the free-flowing blood staining her face and neck. Her scream attracted the attention of a guard who chased off the onlookers and then turned to beat the injured woman into silence. Bewildered, the other captives looked on, mute and numb, as if their compassion had leached from their bones into the desert sands.

After a heated negotiation, the gates swung open and the caravan made its slow progress into the city. They emerged into sharp light and an onslaught of sound and colour and scents. Robert wanted to cover his ears and retreat into the darkness, but the curly-headed child pulled him along, chattering in his high-pitched voice. Unbound, he could have escaped into the crowds and disappeared, but the boy clung to Robert, babbling and pointing, his dark eyes dancing with excitement as if he had forgotten why they were there.

Men and women tended multi-coloured cloths spread over the ground on which they displayed wares in woven baskets or in heaps and stacks: pungent spices, redolent of Yule, dried herbs, and fruits the like of which Robert had never before seen. Skinny chickens, in gappy coops or tied by the foot, flapped and squawked and pecked. Songbirds swinging in airy cages from poles startled into a flutter whenever someone came too close. All were captive, all bound to someone else's whim.

The child jumped up and down, gesticulating towards a brazier on which finger-long objects griddled producing an acrid smoke. Robert tried to make them out. The child pointed to his own mouth and gabbled and rubbed his stomach, then at a close-sided box from which harsh rasping noises came. The blackened shapes suddenly made sense.

"Grasshoppers? You eat *grasshoppers*, child?" Robert asked, at once equally nauseated and fascinated.

Seeing the look on Robert's face, the boy laughed out loud, an exuberant sound so at odds with their situation. So much was new, so many strange customs.

A thought suddenly struck him. "Dodzi." Robert called. The man turned and Robert made a chopping motion on his forearm, then pretended to eat it, before raising his eyebrows in the way he was now used to communicating a question.

Dodzi looked at Robert's arm, then at his querying face, and burst into deep, rumbling laughter.

"I did but ask," Robert grumbled. "Who knows what men might eat in these lands? I have seen stranger sights before now."

The caravan burrowed through narrow streets of cloth stalls selling silks, through alleys dedicated to silver, ringing to the sound of hammers. They passed stacks of copper and bronze vessels embellished and burnished like the setting sun. Others sold the hollowed shells of what Dodzi explained were hardened fruits for carrying water. And one displayed implements of iron — tools for fashioning wood and stone and things to bore and chisel — and knives, with blades gleaming like an overcast sky, laid on a trestle tantalizingly close.

Robert checked the guards weren't looking and lurched against a laden table scattering pots in a metallic clatter. Bent as a bough and tiny, an old woman with skin creased into myriad folds like water-worn channels let loose a volley of invectives and blows, her small fists hard against Robert's arms and chest as she battered him, spraying spittle through broken teeth. One of the caravan guards pushed aside the gathering crowd and she turned her attention on him, standing on the tips of her toes to screech in his face. Unseen, Robert backed towards the adjacent stall, felt with blind fingers, and tucked a small knife into his sleeve.

As the alleys broadened, the buildings lining them became fairer and taller. Plain, rusty mud-daubed walls formed the outside, but open doorways revealed another world. Courtyards — cooled by orange trees — sang with the chatter of women and small birds. Paving made of squares of coloured stone and vivid tiles were softened by glowing carpets and, above them, carved and pierced balconies hung with vibrant cloths undulating in the wind. But it was just a brief glance of a bright normality all too soon passed merely to linger in memory.

Narrow streets now gave way to a wide, open place, where wind stirred swirls of dust into little eddies, reducing criss-crossing footprints and cloven marks to no more than impressions. It had a stench all of its own, which Robert recognised with a lurch, as fear. Men leaned on elbows under canopies or squatted in the shadows to watch the strangers pass. Towards the centre, stout poles the height of a man stood sentinel and the caravan at last came to a halt where awnings flapped over a dozen large wooden cages. Robert found himself shoved into one with other men, and the chains binding their legs were exchanged for rope fed through metal rings in the frame. Kicking and writhing the boy was dragged from Robert's side and taken to where the women and children were being similarly incarcerated. Robert had never thought to ask his name.

As morning grew so the heat swelled and the captives, shuffling on their knees, followed the course of the awning's shade. Jammed into a corner and partially shielded from view by Dodzi's back, Robert eased the knife from his sleeve and began to saw at the rope. The first strands broke, springing under tension and revealing the unbroken threads beneath. He redoubled his efforts.

"*Tsssst*," Dodzi warned and Robert saw slaves bearing buckets approach. Hiding the knife under his leg, he pressed his wrists together concealing the frayed ends of rope and accepted the brackish water gratefully. Then, watching until the slaves moved away, he fished the knife from the dust and began to hack at the rope until the strands gave way and the ends sprang apart. Releasing his ankles, Robert rubbed feeling back into them. He nudged Dodzi and passed the knife to him. "Make haste," he urged, "they might return at any moment."

Dodzi's bonds fell free. He scraped dust in a pile over the ends and together he and Robert surveyed the area beyond the cage noting the alleyways branching off the square, the number of guards watching them, and then the cage itself. Rough it might look, but the structure was sound.

"The longer we stay here, the weaker we will become," Robert said. "We must strike and strike fast." Dodzi nodded agreement. Robert raised a forefinger as if flicking at a fly. "That alley — where does it lead?" Dodzi shook his head. "And that?" Robert asked.

Dodzi exhaled through pursed lips, thinking. A quick nod, then he ran his fingers along his leg, made them jump down next to it, and ran again.

"A wall? How high?" Dodzi wobbled his head. "Not so high, then." Robert sat back, watching the guards scratch and yawn. Soon the sun would beat its way along that alley blinding any in pursuit of them. *If* they could get to it in the first place, that is, and then only if they could escape their coop. The other cockerels with whom they shared the space were looking decidedly crestfallen. Even if he managed to release all from their bonds, few seemed to have enough spirit to help him overcome the guards and flee. It was too much to ask of broken men; but if he stayed, he feared he would eventually lose the will to fight. Robert saw no choice but to try. Dodzi seemed as set on escaping as he, but the slight man was not built for battle; Robert would have to fight for them both.

Each guard carried a sword of curved form and a shorter blade at their side. He had seen them use these weapons against defeated men and weary women, but not in a fight with one equally armed. The guard nearest to them had his back turned and his head bumped against his chest as he fought heat-induced sleep. But what good was a dozing guard or a sword if they were out there and he stuck in a cage? He hissed his frustration, earning him a scouring look from a thin-faced man nearby.

"Save your spleen for your captors, you will need it," Robert growled. Shuffling noises of shackled humans and the shouts of slave drivers diverted his attention to the pitiful sight of more captives entering the square. Darker, like Dodzi, they bore similar patterns of lines scoured into their skin; others had embellishments of bone and coloured beads in tightly woven hair and in the remnants of their clothing. They walked in silence, looking neither left or right but at the ground in front of them. Dodzi said something softly and looked away.

Time was slipping. Robert felt it as clearly as his own pulse and a welter of desperation rose in his throat. He had to get out. He concentrated, summoning from inside himself years of iron-hard focus, willing his blood to rally and burn his veins, saliva gathering in his mouth and whetting his appetite for battle.

More captives were led into the square. He recognised several from the market at Fez; they must have been only days behind his own caravan, and he searched the bedraggled men for any signs of his own. He caught sight of a tousled head, balding and burnished.

"Barquerio!" he yelled through the bars and several of the men looked around at his voice. Whip raised, a guard came storming towards him. "*Barquerio!*" Robert called again.

The man twisted about but, to Robert's sharp disappointment, became another unknown face among the many. Through the splintered bars of the cage the guard shouted in Robert's face, venomous eyes as black as his chaotic teeth. Robert turned his back, but a blow struck him on the side of his jaw sending him spinning against the nearest captives. Dazed, he spat his mouth free of blood and struggled upright to see the guard opening the cage door and picking his way between the prisoners, firing a barrage of curses as he went. He raised his arm to strike again.

Robert ducked sideways, brought his head low and rammed into the man sending him tumbling backwards. He relieved him of his sword before he could react and with a single slash opened the man's throat. Dodzi took the dagger from his hand and joined Robert at the threshold of the cage.

Guards were running towards them with swords drawn. The unfamiliar weapon felt clumsy in his hand, but Robert calculated speed and distance to the nearest oncoming guard, side-stepped him on his approach, and swung his weapon backwards along the man's sword arm and down his calf, severing tendons. A second, surer slice cut the guard's pig squeal short as Robert gained the measure of the sword.

Cautious murmurs of encouragement rippled through the cage and some of the prisoners edged onto one knee as if ready to spring, but none as yet joined them. "Stay close," Robert said to Dodzi, "I will do what I can, but if attacked, drop to the ground, for they will think you weary and defeated. Then strike." He gave an upward thrust of his blade to illustrate, wiped sweat from his palm and readied himself as another two guards neared. But Dodzi sprang forwards as he launched a nimble assault on the guards, narrowly avoiding the defensive blow, and bringing a man down despite his opponent's greater height. Dodzi rammed his calloused heel onto the man's spine and the dagger into the base of his skull to unbridled cheers.

"*Trader?*" Robert muttered, incredulous. "In what?"

Seizing their chance, several unbound captives ran towards the nearest alleys where they disappeared like rabbits into narrow slits between buildings. Robert and Dodzi cut through advancing guards, but more were joining the fight, emerging down the steps of the largest building and closing in on the open space until both men were surrounded on all sides except the rear where the gaping cage awaited them. Bare armed and with legs protected by nothing but leather boots to the ankle, these new, black-robed guards brought a raw resolve to the fight.

Robert rotated his sword wrist to loosen it at the same time adjusting his balance and grounding himself in the market's gritty surface, legs both immovable as a mountain, yet as fleet as a deer, grim tension hardening his jaw as the guards began to encircle them.

Dodzi let out a yell and ran at the phalanx while Robert, eyes aching from intense focus, advanced, feinted and parried with neat, swift movements taking down each challenger with precision before facing the next. Sharp stones lacerated as he rotated on the ball of his foot, but it was irrelevant to the dance. Nothing but a dance — the music of death — stab, cut, thrust, flesh pared, blood flowing unconstrained, life curbed.

A barked order brought the guards to an abrupt halt in a close circle around the two men. Breathing heavily, Dodzi and Robert maintained their offensive positions as, from the top of the raised terrace of steps overlooking the square, a man — as opulent in form as his garb was rich — watched impassively from beneath an awning held aloft by four slaves. How long he had been there Robert could not guess, but that he was a man of standing was evident. Brushing sweat from his eyes and from the hilt of the sword, Robert revised his target.

The man's lips moved, and a guard standing beside him ran down the steps to where the slave master watched, and a woman was dragged from a cage by her hair and forced to the ground, her piercing cries ripping the air. Intent on his objective, Robert quickened his advance towards the steps, but the guard stepped behind the woman and with a violent sideways slice of his blade, silenced her.

The abrupt absence of sound sent shockwaves around the market, but almost immediately another woman was made to kneel by the headless corpse. The guard's sword drew back, readied. No longer blinded by the sun, Robert saw her clearly: not a stranger, but the woman from the oasis. From his position on the terrace, the corpulent man wagged a finger from side to side in slow sweeps and looked meaningfully at the kneeling woman.

Robert's blood pulsed thick and hot. He was so close now, only a matter of the few paces it would take to cover the distance to stop all this, to kill the man. He caught the eye of the young woman. She would not have him save her; he saw in her silent acceptance of her fate, her acknowledgement of his right to sacrifice her. Robert faltered, stopped. She looked at him, surprised; but the moment in which to strike had passed and he lowered his arm. Behind him, Dodzi followed suit. He had failed. Robert felt it in his bones, in the heart wrung out of him leaving him empty and without purpose; he saw it in the plea of the woman's eyes.

On the terrace above them, the man turned and walked back into the building, leaving the guards to close in. Their legs kicked from under them, Robert and Dodzi were thrown back into the cage and, at the base of the steps, the woman silently wept.

Retribution came swiftly and without mercy. First the men, captured while trying to escape, were lugged into the square where they were stripped of what clothes they wore and beaten with spiked clubs. Bleeding and almost senseless, they were tied to long reins and dragged behind horses in circles over the stony ground until their cries died with them.

Robert observed all this with growing horror. He had witnessed death so many times he thought himself prepared for whatever he might see. He had dealt it out enough as well, made its delivery something of an art form, but never to women and always, *always* to those able to defend themselves. He knew that among his peers there were men who enjoyed seeing others suffer, but they were not the norm, nor were they sanctioned by Holy Church even if it had been known to turn a blind eye. What Robert beheld now was a display of such flagrant cruelty that his hardened stomach quelled. Dodzi squatted next to him repeating incantations over and over again as he watched the scene, his twitching hands draped over his knees and his eyes red-rimmed. Not a sound came from the captives in the other cages, as if by remaining silent they might somehow escape notice and fade away.

The sun had long passed its zenith when merchants began filtering from alleyways into the square. They ignored the blood in the sand, more intent on the living captives than the dead. They strolled from cage to cage sizing up the merchandise, talking between themselves and gesticulating their interest or writhing their lips in dismissal. The cages were emptied, the livestock driven to the poles and shackled there in front of the platform. Children whimpered as they were separated from their mothers, and men and women laid bare before probing eyes, stripped of dignity, if any now remained. The man had returned to his terrace and now occupied a golden seat — a fat man, but in more ways than the doughy body he occupied. He surveyed the scene before him like a hungry cat observing prey. Replete in his isolated splendour, a canopy shaded him from the fierce sun and his feet rested on a padded stool. Either side of him slaves bathed him in air cooled with giant feather fans. He watched the proceedings with the same lack of emotion he had displayed earlier.

The slave master of Robert's own caravan accompanied the merchants, assessing his wares, encouraging them to stop and inspect any captive who caught their attention. Subjected to humiliating examination, the women tried to cover their breasts and genitals, only to have their hands beaten away and the prodding continue. Some were made to sing, their parched voices breaking on sad songs from faraway lands. Others couldn't raise a note and stood there confused and crying. Men suffered no less. One — a brawny lad Robert learned had been captured from his coastal village in Ireland — took exception to having his privy parts scrutinized only to have them removed without a moment's hesitation. He was left, kneeling, one hand clutching his excoriated flesh, the other holding the limp remains of his manhood while the men around him flinched away.

Robert braced himself. Like so much horse meat his mouth was wrenched open, his teeth inspected, the loosened tooth commented upon and the tender socket poked. He extended his forearms, displaying the battle scars, had his feet and strong legs felt. He endured the degrading review of his manhood with fortitude; but when the slave master repeatedly tapped the end of his whip against Robert's chest, accentuating the finer qualities of his musculature, Robert's temper frayed. He glared back at the merchants, fists clenching and unclenching in an attempt to control his anger. They took this as a display of strength, nodding approval and demanding to see his sword-calloused hands. Nearby, Dodzi was running on the spot with a fixed expression on his usually animated face.

The women and children were sold first, the highest prices for the boys on the verge of maturity, the girls showing the first signs of the women they would become. The maid with hair the colour of sand and voice of larks set up a bidding frenzy like mackerel among whitebait. Bruises from repeated pinching covered the soft, sunburned skin of her arms and legs and her eyes looked swollen and puffy. Robert couldn't bear to see her anguish as she was led away, but it stayed with him when he closed his eyes. When he opened them, she was gone, leaving him with a feeling that, somehow, he had betrayed her, and he found himself wondering whether the quickest way out of this nightmare was death. He didn't have long to contemplate it.

Hands bound in front of him, he was led onto the stone block made scalding by the sun. Bidding started in a crescendo, voices rising in volatile eddies as each vied with the other. One by one bidders dropped out, leaving three to continue the furious bartering. It was immaterial who won, for each looked as dire a prospect as the other. It fell to a man bedecked in so much gold that he rattled when he moved. Some accord was being reached when a slave ran up to the master and deposited a heavy bag in his hand. Head on one side, the slave master weighed it, looked up to where the fat man still sat on the terrace. He gave a genuflection, announced something loudly, and scuttled off with his winnings as the merchant erupted in jangling fists and outrage.

"What happened?" Robert asked Dodzi as they were taken from the platform.

"You, friend, have new master." Dodzi pointed to where a now empty chair sat on the terrace. "He will expect much; he pay many gold for you. He pay more gold than he even give for me. You win, O'bert, *you* win."

Win what? Robert thought. Whatever it might be, it certainly wouldn't be his freedom. And, somewhere, far, far from here, Isobel and his children waited.

CHAPTER TWENTY

The looking glass reflected a woman of indeterminate age, her fair hair coifed as a widow, green eyes, encircled with blue, dulled with grief. The lustre had gone from Isobel's skin through weeks of incarceration imposed by circumstance and the declining season; but she was still young, well, young enough, and she bore children readily. She was used to running a great household and had connections at Court and beyond that might serve any prospective husband's ambition. At the thought, Isobel felt the writhing, nagging sensation in her womb again. This child she carried — Robert's babe — would be born without him and, perhaps, grow to call another man father. She recoiled at the thought and of this *other* touching her where Robert had once laid claim. he would mix his blood with hers and she wasn't certain she could go through with her plan. But she must, she had to if she were to escape this injustice done to her and her children and reclaim the governance of their birth right. That would be something to negotiate with any future husband; but her first duty was to protect her children and the earldom and, whatever she might be willing to cede in her own body, they — and her dower lands — remained unnegotiable. Being willing to wed was one thing; but finding a suitable match while caged and confined was entirely another.

Clarence showed no sign of relenting. If anything, he appeared more determined than ever to bend her to his will. She waited outside his preferred audience chamber, having been summoned for one of his drubbings like a mulish esquire. She had once felt like that — young and uncertain as she waited on the Earl's pleasure — but not now. Now she proved as resolute as her lower rank and sex allowed.

She could hear his raised voice from beyond the door. He sounded displeased but then, when didn't he? She edged closer, now catching the lower, moderated tones of an older man. He seemed to be reasoning with Clarence and Isobel made out snatches of the conversation — marriage, contract, lands. Her heart caught in her throat. She leant back against the wall, head spinning. How could he know her plans? She had spoken to no one and Buena would never betray her, not even if her life depended on it. After all, how many people would be prepared to cut out their own tongue to protect a secret? And what a secret Buena protected. If a whisper of Isobel's own bastardy came out no man of any worth would seek a match with her and then where would she be? She needed a man willing to face down the king's brother and who would be willing — and able — to do *that*?

She could hear Clarence's terse footsteps as he paced the room, his voice fading and growing as he went back and forth. Close to the door he stopped and his sharp tones became clear as a crow's caw. Isobel couldn't help herself, but the thought of all the possible outcomes made it nigh on impossible to resist the urge to eavesdrop and, checking first that no one could see her do so, pressed her ear to the door.

"...I shall not be denied this, not by him nor any other who believes it their place to do so. Have I not made myself plain?"

The man's muted reply was too soft to be made out, but Clarence's was not.

"I have the will and I have the right. She will acquiesce, I have been assured of it." Another murmured response, then, "And so be it. Go forth as instructed and see what intelligence is to be had. I will deal with the lady directly."

Isobel barely had time to back away from the door when it opened abruptly and Clarence came out. He cast her a scant glance and strode off in a haze of ill-humour and musk-scented silk. The older man appeared with several parchment rolls under one arm and a leather document bag under the other. He bore the look of a clerk but the demeanour of a wise man and one well-used to mollifying a great prince. He bowed his grey head when he saw Isobel.

"My lady, His Grace regrets he is called away on matters of import. He expresses his sorrow and deems it his loss to be denied such fair company." He bowed again, more deeply this time, and Isobel was reminded of her father's courteous sincerity which, in gilding a lie, nonetheless made it the more palatable. As he straightened, a document dropped to the floor and rolled to her feet. Without thinking, she bent to pick it up. As she returned it to him she caught sight of the broken seal. It reminded her of something that, in the moment, eluded her. The man took it, quickly placed it in the document bag and, closing the door to the chamber, bid her good day.

She was still musing on what she had overheard as she returned to her room. Buena questioned her with a gesture, then frowned when Isobel did not respond immediately. "I need time to think," Isobel said and called for her mantle and pattens to take with her thoughts into the castle gardens. Buena gathered her own cloak. "No, I will go alone. Stay with the children; I will not be long."

These short winter days allowed little time for the weak sun to dry the cobbles and Isobel's patten-shod feet slipped precariously on the greasy stone. The garden was as empty as she expected and she found the nook she had spied before. In its dark shade the air felt cold against her skin, but it gave her the privacy she sought and, pulling her mantle to her ears, she gave consideration to her current situation and the niggling seed that sight of the broken seal had sown.

She did not have as long as she wished. Light footsteps sounded on the hard path, paused, and set off again. A figure appeared. Heavily cloaked and with a hood pulled over her face, at first Isobel did not recognise her. And then the figure turned. "Maud," Isobel called. "What do you do here?"

The girl started, mouth opening, then closed it with a snap. She swallowed. "Juliana is asking for you, my lady."

Tetchy, her concentration broken, there was no point staying any longer. "Come, we will return," Isobel said, rather more sharply than she intended. "Help me over these cobbles. I swear, I have less balance the more this child grows. He will have me over in a trice."

Buena helped her mistress from her garb, making a snort of disapproval when she felt Isobel's cold hands.

"Do not fuss," Isobel said, withdrawing them. "Where is Liana? Ah, there you are, my bee." Isobel went to her daughter who was playing pat-a-hand with Alice by the fire. She knelt beside her. "What is it, my love? Why did you want your Ama?"

Juliana stopped her play, fixing large eyes on her mother; but she didn't say anything.

"Liana?" Isobel asked again, "why did you call for me?"

"I didn't, Ama," she said, and held out her hands in an invitation to play. On the other side of the room, Maud watched.

Isobel kept her thoughts to herself but remained vigilant. She suspected — was certain — she was being observed and at any moment would receive a summons from Clarence; but the call did not come. Indeed, whenever she saw him — and that not often — he appeared preoccupied. Occasionally he entered his wife's chamber when Isobel was there, passed some remark, and left again as soon as he could, as if being there placed some burden of expectation upon him. Lady Isabel seemed relieved by his absence. She had good days and bad but, overall, the decline in her mood and her health reflected the dour sense of foreboding that hung around the place. Even her children visited less often, which she seemed to accept; but what alarmed Isobel most was the duchess's growing ambivalence to her baby. It was as if the light had gone from her and even this small spark of life was not enough to ignite it again.

She bade Isobel sit with her and watched with lacklustre eyes as her friend cradled her son and sang to him. And, when Isobel encouraged the duchess to hold him, she did so for the shortest of time before she handed him back, citing her lethargy as the reason. "It is as if the tide has gone out," Lady Isabel tried to explain one day. "I feel so weakened, Is'bel. I know not how long it will be before I am called from this life."

In the past, Isobel would have tutted and chivvied the duchess into a sunnier mien; now she knew she would fail before she tried.

No one could fathom the cause. Lady Isabel had fully healed from the birth, held no fever, her blood flowed clean and bright into the letting bowl. All food was personally prepared by trusted servants and the drink tasted for contamination. That left the physic. On most days the physician himself oversaw its administration, nodding his approval when his patient took the draught in one go. Sometimes he left the powders to be given as instructed by her women and it was on these days Isobel was especially heedful.

*

Expressionless, Mistress Twynyho received the twist of paper from the physician's apprentice. She placed it on the makings table in the little pallet room where the other ingredients lay gathered. Hand hovering over the mortar, she glanced over her shoulder. The apprentice watched from the door. "You may go," she told him.

"I am to make certain of its correct assembly, mistress."

Mistress Twynyho drew to her full height. "Impudent knave! Do you intend overseeing my duties like a girl new from her mother's skirts?" Quick as a flash she boxed his ears. "Be gone with you!" Face flushed and eyes bright with anger, she watched the youth leave the room with head bent and rubbing his ears. She turned back to the table and, picking up the physic, slipped it into her purse. Her head whipped around at the sound of movement behind her.

Isobel looked from Mistress Twynyho's hand concealing the purse to her startled face.

"I... Lady Langton...I did not see you there..." She bobbed awkwardly, fumbling the purse out of sight.

Isobel followed the movements without comment, turned away, and re-entered the duchess's chamber.

Mistress Twynyho hurried after her. "Lady Langton! *Please!*" She touched the edge of the Isobel's gown. "Might I speak with you, my lady?"

Once in the mural passage and out of earshot, Mistress Twynyho cut to the chase. "My lady, do not think ill of me; it is not what it may seem."

"*What*, is not as it seems?"

Mistress Twynyho hesitated, then fished the twist of paper from her purse. "This, my lady. The physic I am meant to give Her Grace."

"Then why have you not done so?"

"I think … nay, believe, my duchess ails on taking it. You must have seen so yourself, my lady?" she added, anxiously.

Isobel failed to confirm or deny what she might be thinking. Instead, she said, "How long have you been secreting the physic?"

"On my honour I mean no harm to Her Grace! I would do nothing —"

"That is not what I asked," Isobel said calmly. "Answer me."

"These past two months — when I may. But oft times the physician gives Her Grace the physic himself."

"And then?"

"And then Her Grace ails. But she recovers strength when I do not give her the dose. My lady, you must have seen it? I *know* you have seen it!"

"You believe there is malintent towards Her Grace?"

"I am certain of it," Mistress Twynyho rushed. She looked up and down the mural passage to check they were still alone. "Someone close to Her Grace. Someone who might benefit from her death." She crossed herself. "May God preserve her."

"Amen," Isobel replied automatically, mulling over Mistress Twynyho's admission. "Whom do you suspect — the duke's enemy? No? Who then?"

"Someone not far from where we stand now, my lady, and with whom you have also had dealings. He is one who plays all the cards and rolls the dice to his own satisfaction."

Isobel felt her colour rise and flee in quick succession. "What evidence do you have other than your own suspicions?"

"I … have none, my lady."

"I see," Isobel said evenly. "However, without evidence none will treat our complaint with any gravity."

It took a moment, then, "My lady, you *do* believe me?"

"I, too, have perceived such things as give me cause to doubt good intentions, but without testimony, none will take our report. And even if I could persuade someone, I am as much a hostage here as if I were bound in chains and cannot bring word to any outside these walls without being observed." Tilting her head, she fixed Mistress Twynyho with clear eyes. "But you might."

Mistress Twynyho's face reflected the welter of anxiety that had dogged her for weeks. "You wish me to convey a message, my lady? But I cannot abandon my duties; Her Grace needs me, and the babe —"

"I am being watched," Isobel cut in. "Unless you know of another, whom else but you can be entrusted with such an errand?"

"I have kin," Mistress Twynyho said slowly, her brow wrinkling as she worked through her thoughts. "I oft send a small feast day gift and receive one in return."

"And the feast of St. Andrew is almost upon us. It is proper to mark such an occasion, is it not, mistress?"

The two women — the one older and with time-worn eyes and loosened skin around her jaw, the other young and determined and not yet cowed by the years — exchanged looks instead of words and understood everything.

"Yes, my lady. These matters must not pass."

CHAPTER TWENTY-ONE

Shouting and truncated thuds woke Robert from blessed oblivion. For a moment he was an esquire again, waking to the mists of the north and the youthful exuberance of his peers in the practice yard. A stinging swipe across his legs brought him hurtling to his senses and a harsh order to his feet. Without pause to shake sleep from his head, he, Dodzi and the other men crammed into the airless slave pens, were driven with cudgels out into a high walled enclosure.

The sun had not yet risen and the remaining night was cold on his skin. Robert lifted his face to the square of lightening sky and inhaled air unbound by man and nature. For the beat of a bird's wing, he was free again. He curled his fingers around the petals of rock he kept hidden and thought of Isobel. Safe in the nursery, his children would be stirring with the dawn, but their dam — sleeping beside him in their own chamber — would roll against him in their deep-down bed. Warm and sleepy, he and she would greet the new day in gentle undulations, then lie, content, listening to the last call of the night birds and the first of the day. *Isobel*, he breathed her name, and imagined her faint reply.

"O'bert. Take." Dodzi thrust a slab of grey, rough bread into his hand bringing him back to reality with a jolt.

"My thanks," Robert murmured and, offering a short payer of gratitude, crossed himself. He did not see the cudgel until it slammed into his hand and the second blow that knocked his bread into the dust. Thick-thighed and muscle-bound, the man wielding the club yelled into Robert's face, spraying spittle in volleys as the other captives backed away as far as the walls allowed.

"Down, down!" Dodzi hissed, kneeling and patting the sand beside him.

Robert dropped to the ground, bending his head and hoping the next clout wouldn't kill him. A gob of glistening mucus landed next to him. Somewhat mollified by Robert's act of submission, the guard rattled off half a dozen more words and then wandered off to find someone else to flay.

Dodzi retrieved the bread and brushed it free of grit. "Eat," he said. "Eat now."

Thick welts were emerging across the back of Robert's hands and one of his fingers was dislocated. He yanked it straight, swallowing the pain. He took the bread viewing it with distaste.

Dodzi tore a chunk, chewed. "You say '*Great* father'."

Avoiding eating on the side with the sore tooth, Robert queried, "Great father?"

Dodzi pointed upwards. "Great father God. You Christian, you are in-fidel. Guard say you must convert. Or die."

Robert stopped eating and sat back on his heels. "I will never convert. I would rather lose my life than my soul."

Dodzi rocked his head from side to side until his mouth was empty and he could speak. He wiped his lips on the back of his long-fingered hand. "O'bert, you die," he stated. "Your wife, she sad. She…" He rubbed his knuckles into his eyes in imitation of crying. "She sad you die, I think," he said again just to make sure Robert understood.

Robert did. With his forefinger he drew a vertical line in the dust and then a short horizontal, dissecting it. Dodzi leaned over and scrubbed the image out. "No, no," he said firmly. He checked the guard hadn't seen. "You keep that — here…" he placed his hand over his heart, "…and here." He tapped his head. "No man here. You keep God here. Keep God safe, He keep *you* safe."

"You do not understand. I must maintain my faith —"

Dodzi's eyes flashed darkly. "I understand." He lowered his voice again. "In this land there many gods. All gods. Men say their god is master; I say *my* god master. Men fight, men die, but only god know who master is."

"In my land, there is but one God," Robert said quietly.

"I like see your land. I like to…" He screwed his face, trying to find the word but instead raised his hands to the heavens.

"Worship?" Robert suggested.

"Yes, wor-ship, not die. In your land men not fight, men not die. Your land is peace for God."

"Peace?" Robert scoured the sky, recalling the land of his birth. "All I have known is war. Even when we do not fight, we battle. Do you understand?" Dodzi shook his head and Robert grimaced. "No, well, nor I at times. There is little sense to any of it," he added almost to himself. "How is it that you fight like a soldier?"

"*So*-jer?"

Robert held out an imaginary dagger and proceeded to kill the dust. "You fight — very well — better than most men, yet you say you are a trader."

"In my land, my village, all boys must learn fight before they are men. Fight lion, fight beasts, fight men who come to village to take our women and goats."

"Is that how you came by those marks?" Robert indicated the three dark lines scored on the high point of Dodzi's cheek like the wounds from a three-clawed cat.

Dodzi shook his head in broad sweeps. "They are marks of being man. Dodzi fight good, Dodzi kill lion, Dodzi a man." He pretended to nick his skin. He searched around and found a small piece of charcoal. He held it out for Robert to see, crushed it between two stones and then rubbed the resulting black powder over the scars on his cheek. "Now you see," he said. "Now all man see." He pointed to his cheek. "In O'bert's land, boys fight?"

"They do," Robert said, "but not to become men."

"Then … why fight?"

Robert picked up a pebble and rotated it between his fingers. "Good question. I wish I knew the answer." He threw the stone at a scurrying beetle. It landed in front of it and the creature diverted course and continued on its way. In a flash of memory, Robert sensed Isobel's reprimand for his callous disregard for the creature's life, and felt chastised. "Boys fight because they do; it is their nature. But some boys are *trained* to fight because that is their life — that is what they *must* do."

Dodzi drew air through his teeth as he thought about that. "These boys only fight?" he asked. "They do not make, they not trade?"

"Certainly not! For knights it is the noblest way of life to fight for God, honour and our king."

"No trade?" Dodzi checked.

"No trade," Robert confirmed. "We have men trade for us. We fight; they trade." Then, "Do you know the nature of the man who has bought us?"

Dodzi wiped the soot from his cheek and lifted his shoulders in a non-committal way. "I have seen this man. He master of all Sijilmasa. He called Babu — father of his people."

"This is a good thing?" Robert asked without hope, but Dodzi declined to answer and Robert was unable to press him as guards started pushing men into a rough line. "What now?" Robert muttered.

As the sun rose above the rooftops and cast the first shadows, a man, whose glossy skin contrasted with the brilliant white of his fine djellaba and bearing a staff with a round, ornamented top, entered the enclosure.

"Master," Dodzi mouthed, "*Rayiys*."

The master stood, tapping the head of the staff against his palm while surveying the shabby group before him. He did not look impressed. Finally, he used the staff to point and nine or so men were separated from the others and led from the courtyard via a door in the wall. Another dozen were taken back inside the compound in which they had been kept overnight. That left four standing in the gathering heat of the rising sun: Robert, Dodzi, a man built like a bull, and a tall, well-made youth who had attracted much attention in the slave market. The master turned and went back the way he had come and, flanked by the two remaining guards, the four men were prompted at sword point to follow.

From bare-walled antechambers, squat and dark, they progressed through a series of courtyards, each separated by a guarded gate set in thick walls, and each more fair than the last. They entered an enclosed space made brilliant by walls of polished marble carved with intricate shapes. Trees scented the air with delicate blossom, and white doves rose from tiered fountains when they approached, rising into the blueness and settling on green glazed roofs to perch and preen. Not yet warmed by the day, the air was cooler here, the silky floor cold underfoot on which they left their tawny prints. Slaves scuttled after them with brush and cloth to wipe the surface clean.

"My wife would marvel at such beauty," Robert whispered to Dodzi, earning a particularly hard blow from the guard behind them.

"My wifes, also," Dodzi breathed.

They left the courtyard and passed through a doorway, the frame pierced all around with shapes through which a light breeze filtered the heat. Inside, charcoal smouldered in brass braziers releasing an aromatic, resinous scent which permeated the darkened interior. It took moments before Robert's eyes adjusted to the high-ceilinged room in which they had arrived. Patterned shutters tamed the light from the windows, casting lobed quatrefoils upon the floor and across a gem-studded gold chair as wide as a small bed and adorned with cushions of vivid patterned silks and the pelts of exotic animals. Another brazier next to it sent slow spirals of scented smoke into the decorated ceiling and, on the low table before the chair, ewers and platters of gold. Not even at his king's court had Robert seen such opulence as this. But this was not Court, and the man whom he was obliged to call *lord*, not his king, and he would serve no other.

Subtle movement in the deep shadow at the far end of the room caught his eye. He focused, then stifled a yell. An animal — low slung and svelte — padded on broad feet towards them. Short sandy brown fur covered a muscular body, smaller than the lions he had seen at the Tower menagerie, but much bigger than the cats that roamed the stables at home. Its wedge-shaped head was topped by outsized tufted ears. Most striking of all, the animal's large eyes were outlined in black, as if painted, and a stripe down the centre of its head made it look as if it were frowning. It opened its jaws in a silent hiss, revealing needle fangs.

Dodzi shouted in alarm and the other two prisoners would have run but for the guards coshing them to the ground where they cowered with arms held over their heads. At the click of a tongue, the animal stopped its progress and sat quite still, watching them, and from the doorway where he had been observing, the man known as Babu advanced.

Dressed all in white as before, the only points of colour were a yellow waist sash and a large green gem pinned to the extravagant coils of white silk on his head. A large knife, its sheath embellished with stones and distinct in form, lay tucked behind the sash. Not a knife for eating, but for killing. Babu's sloped forehead led to a long nose made more prominent by the oiled and pointed beard, all adding to the imperious look with which he surveyed his newest purchases. He came flanked by two huge men, dressed entirely in black, each carrying long, curved swords.

The slave-master prostrated himself in front of Babu, laying his staff in perfect alignment alongside him. Forced to the floor with the other men, Robert came face to face with the staff, blinked in case he mistook what he saw, and looked again. Carved out of a single piece of black timber, the long shaft was topped with a polished ball of wood into which many sharp, white shapes protruded the like of which he had just seen in the animal not far from him now — teeth — made for rending.

The slave-master rose and, one by one, had each captive stand and be subjected to his close inspection. It seemed that this man interpreted the will of his lord, taking his instructions in a look, a wave of a hand, or a word spoken so softly only he could divine it. The slave-master paid particular attention to Dodzi, making him shuffle in a circle on the spot and bend and flex. He waved a ringed finger and Dodzi was taken to one side where the other men waited.

He surveyed Robert last. With eyes narrowed, he had Robert hold out both hands palm up showing the calloused pads of his sword hand, then turned them over. He inspected the scars on his body, his stance. Finally, he tapped Robert's hand where the indentation of his great ring had left its pale mark. Robert raised his eyes beyond the slave-master to where Babu watched and found himself looking into unblinking orbs the colour of dark amber and similarly flecked. He held Babu's gaze with his own, his head held high.

The first jarring blow on his back made him nearly lose his footing, but he regained it and continued to stare without wavering. The next — to the back of his knees — caused his legs to buckle; but he rose again, tendons shouting in legs firmly planted in anticipation of another assault. From nearby, eyes wide and frightened, Dodzi shook his head in warning. Robert burned with defiance; he would not let go even if his life depended upon it. And not just for his own dignity, but that of his king and of his family and, above all, his God. Like a sudden fire flooding his veins, it became imperative that he uphold his honour — for his father and brothers, his wife and their children — even if it meant his flesh would shrivel and his bones turn to dust in this desolate place. A third strike brought him again to his knees, and the head of the staff swept down across the bridge of his nose in an audible *crack* as skin and bone fractured. Robert choked on blood as a foot on the back of his neck ensured he did not rise again. Through a veil of pain, he saw Babu's once pristine white slippers, now spotted with blood, turn and walk away.

Dragged back to the slave pens and left in a heap on the floor like so much dung, he propped himself in a corner and gingerly felt the damage to his nose. It had stopped bleeding but the swelling made it difficult to breathe and there seemed to be multiple lacerations. He attempted to straighten it, but the ensuing pain made him retch and his head swim, so he curled on his side and waited for the nausea to pass.

He was alone bar a few men, the others taken God only knew where. He understood his behaviour to have been reckless and here, awaiting his fate with a mashed face, he might have reason to regret it. But he didn't. His nose might be broken but he wasn't; his limbs bruised, but his spirit remained whole. The more they beat him the stronger he would become — at least so he resolved, because anything else was defeat. His whole life had been in service to his king, lord to his people, husband to his wife. Without it where would that leave him but devoid of purpose and, without purpose, dead? Whatever they wanted of him he would deny it, for in that he controlled his own destiny — even if it meant his death.

The only light in the pen came through the iron bars of the door separating the room from the rest of the complex, but it was enough to allow him the distraction of working away at a damaged mud brick with a shard of stone he found. The few men too ill to work and left in the pen to moulder were in no fit state to watch or care what he was doing. Only when Dodzi returned later to find him inching the brick from the wall, did Robert feel any need to explain. "It'll be safe in here," Robert said carefully through his swollen face, placing the rose-petal rock in the cavity he had made for it. "Whether I live or die, it will be safe here, for my dove, for my Isobel."

Days of hunger and uncertainty passed recorded in notches scratched on the wall. Above them, hidden in the dark, he incised a small cross and a rough paternoster to mark his prayers. Dodzi and the others had been taken, as they were each day at dawn, to the training grounds, when footsteps heralded guards. Two entered — one went to check the condition of the three sick and dying men, the other, dressed in the black djellaba of Babu's personal guard, stood over Robert.

"*Nahd*!"

Robert stood unsteadily, the man's command clear. Three days without food, without sight of the sun, and he was ready to eat the dust on the floor had his throat been less dry. He was taken down dark passages towards a soft mewling that became louder, until they emerged into brilliant sunshine. He squinted, one-eyed, at the courtyard surrounded on all sides by small arched openings in front of which were stakes and, on each stake — sitting on the crossbar under a canopy — a hawk. So many birds, some types of which he recognised, others new to him, but all beautiful and deadly.

A bird upon his leather-wrapped wrist, Babu had his back to Robert, close enough that Robert might cross the space between them and break the man's neck before he could turn around; but his blood beat sluggishly in his veins, and the hands he readied shook.

"My birds." Babu spoke Portuguese in clear, accented tones as if he had been halfway through a sentence. He held the bird aloft, inspecting it. "I have an appreciation of beauty, but each must serve its purpose or it has none. In my country, there is no place for something unless it is of use." He turned around, facing Robert. "I am certain this is something you understand." Still reeling from the man's command of Portuguese, Robert could do nothing but stare. "I see that you do. I am Abu Umar Salim Ahmad," he said in a way that suggested Robert should have heard of him. "What name do you go by?"

No, that would be too easy. His name was his own and he would keep it. Robert maintained his silence.

With the tip of his finger Babu — Ahmad — stroked the bird's domed head. "Perhaps a little refreshment will ease your conversation." He replaced the bird, removed his glove, and walked through a narrow door. The guard poked Robert to follow.

In the fair chamber of their first meeting, finely carved, translucent stone screens covered the windows across which filmy material waved in the light breeze. A large round tray, suspended on short legs and set before the throne-like chair, held intricate dishes of chased silver, piled with foods. Fragrant grains with mixed meats steeped in saffron; dates and dried fruits and bowls of a creamy concoction. Robert salivated.

"Sit, eat," Ahmad invited, directing Robert towards a squat cushion on the floor, while he himself dropped with surprising suppleness onto his chair, simultaneously crossing his legs and resting each hand on a knee. Suspecting a trap, Robert remained standing. His stomach growled.

"You hunger, no?" Ahmad said, dipping fingers into a silver bowl of scented water held by a slave. It would need to be if it were to disguise the smell of sweat and degradation that clung to Robert's clothes and followed him wherever he went. Even the brazier burning sweet resins was no match for the filth. If Robert felt offended by his own presence, he was certain this elegant man in his pristine garb must also; but if he was, Ahmad did not show it. It was not why Robert refused to sit: there were matters of conscience that far outweighed his hunger or any niceties he might hold.

"In my land," Ahmad said, "it is considered a matter of courtesy to be seated when invited and to dine on what is offered."

"In my land, free men are not held against their will, nor are they subject to such base treatment as I am now."

Ahmad paused in dabbing the moisture from his fingers. He let the cloth drop. "And yet I make offer of friendship. Sit, please you." He pointed to the cushion.

"Am I free to leave?"

"You are here as my guest. Let us make conversation. There is much I wish to know about your land."

"Do you intend to release me?" Robert insisted, standing his ground.

"That will depend."

"On what?"

"On our conversation."

Remembering Isobel's careful observances, Robert studied Ahmad's face, the way the smooth brow all-too readily creased along ill-tempered folds, the lines at the corners of his eyes the result not of laughter but of squinting against the sun. But there was intelligence there also, and where there was wit might also be reason.

Conscious of how innocuous he must appear with his blood-smeared face and broken nose, his jaw covered in an unruly beard, his torn nails ragged and unkempt, Robert sat with as much dignity as he could muster. He washed his hands with care in the bowl held for him by a fair-skinned slave, dabbing them dry as if he sat at the lord's table in his own court, and aware at all times that he came under the scrutiny of the other man.

Ahmad waited until Robert finished his ablutions, then with his own hand, lifted pieces of meat, adorned with flowers and roasted spice, onto a small dish and offered it to him. "You will find the delicacies here as fine as any at your own table." When Robert made no move to take it, Ahmad shrugged his brows and placed it before him. "Eat," he said, raising a fragment of meat to his own lips.

Robert's stomach ached, it smouldered as if devouring itself, but still he refused to assuage it. Instead, he made the sign of the cross and, placing his hands together, closed his eyes as he bowed his head. He heard a sharp rasp of breath. When he opened them again, his captor observed him coldly.

"A man of faith," he stated, with unnerving calm, and continued to eat.

Unable to resist any longer, Robert lifted a piece of meat to his mouth and tentatively tasted it. Fragrance enveloped him, the delicate flavours almost overwhelming senses blunted by the coarse fare on which he had existed. He felt the roof of his mouth tingle with unfamiliar spice, scorch with salt, sear with astringent lemon. Indifferent to those around him, he devoured the meat, and another, and yet a third while Ahmad looked on. Only when Robert had scooped enough grains into his mouth with his fingers in the manner of the Moors, and feasted on fruits preserved in honey and saffron, did he manage to bring his appetite under control. If he should die now it would at least be with a full belly.

From somewhere not far away, but muffled by thick walls, a murmuring sing-song filtered through the stone screens.

"My scholars," Ahmad remarked. "Each day they learn the pillars of wisdom: numbers, arts, and the Qur'an and what it is to be a servant of the prophet Mohammet, may His name be praised. Male children must be taught these things if they wish to serve me, for I will allow only true believers the honour of such duty. This, you understand, no? I see that you do."

"In my country, as in all Christendom, we serve the one true God in Jesus Christ."

Ahmad shook his finger from side to side, much as he had done days earlier. "You have been misled by your priests. But we will come to that; we have time. First, I wish you to tell me of your country. It is a rich land, no?"

"Why do you ask, if you know this already?"

Ahmad took up a silken square and delicately patted his lips. "Why else but to send merchants to your country for trade? Without trade what are we but a barbarous people living each day merely to take what we can from the earth so that we might live long enough to see the next. But with trade," he expanded his hands to encompass the room, "we have that which our many lands have to offer and all shall grow fat on such riches. I know the land of your people; I know it to be a fat land."

"What do you want of me?"

"I wish you go to your king. I wish you to say that I, Abu Umar Salim Ahmad, Khalid of these lands, extend my hand to him in friendship that our peoples might trade freely and make our lands fat. This is what I want."

There was a *but*, Robert could sense it, and he doubted anything that came from the mouth of this man could be relied upon. Still, he kept his counsel. More than that, he kept close which king he served, for it seemed clear that Ahmad considered him to be of Portugal, and his true identity remained his own — his little bit of England. "Why do you believe my king would listen to me?"

Ahmad surprised Robert by letting out a laugh; he did not think the man capable of humour. "Because you are a great lord in your country, no? You think I cannot see it? You think me a fool!" He restrained his mirth and continued. "You are my slave yet you have the bearing of a lord. Your hands are hard from many years of battle but you fight with the ... what is the word ... elegance of one trained from youth to do so. And at sea you commanded your men... Ah, yes, do not be surprised by my knowledge for I have ears and eyes beyond these walls. I know your worth; your finger, here..." he tapped Robert's hand, "...wears a great ring. Am I not correct? I wonder, then, why it is you have not said who you are. Perhaps you would be ransomed and free?"

"Am I to be ransomed and released?"

Ahmad spread his hands. "Of course. Only a free man can undertake such a matter as I propose."

Robert stood abruptly. "Then I will leave now."

Ahmad sniffed and continued to sit. He adjusted the sash at his waist and made himself more comfortable on the cushioned chair. "The repast is not yet complete." He waited until Robert, with reluctance, sat down again. "Now, we will drink together and you will tell me about your king. I wish to know what sort of man he is."

Robert had no desire to satiate this man's curiosity as to do so played into his hands; but the thought of imminent release was more compelling, and the more they conversed the better he would understand Ahmad's real intentions. Whatever it might be, the man appeared in no rush. A small stone dish filled with ash-hot charcoal was placed before him, a silver ewer beside that, and an elaborate box, no bigger than a hand's span wide and as half deep, presented with a bow. From this box Ahmad poured earth-red beans into a chaffing dish placed with precision over the charcoal.

"They must be stirred or they will burn," he said, doing so with a simple wooden spoon. "There is art in the making of *qahwah* and it is one I have made perfect as you will see."

An aroma — overpoweringly intense like sweet roasted nuts but stronger — emanated from the dish. Now glossy and darkened, the small beans were tipped rattling into a stone mortar, the blackened interior evidence of many such makings.

"I have traded much gold for these," he said, taking one between his fingertips and examining it. He brought it to his nose, inhaled deeply, his eyes rolling alarmingly into his head.

He replaced it with its fellows whereupon he ground them into a coarse dust. Taking the pulverised remains of the beans, he poured them into the ewer of water having first tested the heat. He swirled the ewer's contents and set it aside. Two small, steep-sided bowls were presented to him, each with a cone of straining cloth inside. Into these he carefully poured the black liquid so pungent it made Robert's eyes water. He coughed and blinked.

"Qahwah. It is said that the Prophet himself, may He be praised, gifted it to Man so that he might drink and not be intoxicated as Christian men are, to their great shame."

Robert didn't rise to the jibe; instead, he accepted the small cup and sniffed the contents.

Ahmad looked affronted. "I do not offer you poison. Poison is for, how do you say? It is for the base man." He turned his head and spat into a bronze vessel. It was instantly whisked away by one of the slaves and replaced by another. "Now, you drink," he insisted.

Robert took a wary sip. Hot and as bitter as it was black, the astringent liquid scoured his mouth leaving a metallic taint behind. He tried to keep his face from reflecting his revulsion.

"More, more," Ahmad said, watching Robert's reaction as he ventured to test the liquid again. "It is good, is it not? It is better than riches." He downed his cup in one go, his eyelids fluttering in ecstasy.

"It is like nothing I have tasted before," Robert said truthfully, conscious now of an uneasy sensation in his guts. He wondered how he could avoid finishing the drink under Ahmad's hawk eyes and reluctantly concluded he could not. He screwed his courage and, holding his breath, drank the rest in one go.

"Your king," Ahmad said, helping himself to more *qahwah*, "tell me about him."

Robert's lips felt numb and his head thrummed and everything in the room became brighter. "My king," he said, his voice swelling with pride, "is a great man. His face is radiant like the sun and rules over our lands and all who know him bow down before him and call him lord." He heard the words tumble from his mouth and could hardly believe what he heard himself say. It was like being drunk, but wine never felt like *this*.

"Does he have much gold, numerous slaves, many wives?"

"Mush — much gold," Robert corrected himself. "But we take only one wife. The king has one wife and she is very beautiful, the most beautiful woman in all Christendom." He shook his head to clear it of this prattling nonsense, but the words kept coming. "And no slaves — all men in our kingdom are free."

"You say your king is great yet he has but one wife and no slaves. I say he is a poor man, this Christian king. Look at my riches — I have many wives, many sons, and *many* slaves, as Allah has willed it."

"Nor do we have camels," Robert muttered sarcastically before he could stop himself.

Ahmad chose to ignore the comment. "I wonder if your king is, hmm, how is it said in your tongue — without potent? Feeble? He lacks sons so has no need of more wives?"

Robert's skin blazed along with his temper. "My king is not impotent and has sired many children! It is not our custom and it is against God's law to take more than one wife. Only the infidel and those barbarous and without God take more wives and make slaves out of men!" He could have kicked himself.

This is exactly the sort of reaction Ahmad wanted, Robert could see it in the man's eyes which now gleamed darkly.

Without warning, Ahmad stood. "Come, I will show you how a *barbarous* people live."

Through a series of rooms and enclosed courtyards he walked with swift steps, each space different, each enriched with cool carved stone and tiles of green and blue and white. From inside one building Robert thought he could make out women's voices and singing, to be told, "My many wives and concubines, all beautiful, all fertile as the earth when planted with my seed." There, Robert thought, that arrogance that crept into Ahmad's conversation from time to time. A man who felt the need to boast of his riches often wore beggar's shoes.

At last they came to a small door leading out onto a parapet. In the shade of the tower, Ahmad surveyed his land, the oasis lushly visible beyond the myriad buildings making up Sijilmasa. He pointed to dozens of dots of humanity labouring on buildings, some carrying baskets filled with mounds of what looked like lime, others on wall heads and rooftops pouring water and ramming something between boards. "My slaves build a *new* Sijilmasa," he said with evident pride.

"What happened to the old one?" Robert asked caustically, the effects of whatever he had drunk waning now, leaving him feeling nauseous and irritable and lacking the caution he knew he should adopt.

"A man with slaves is a rich man for he can achieve anything. This city is the heart of the Tafilalt; it beats, here." Ahmad placed his fist over his heart. "I, Abu Umar Salim Ahmad — Babu to my people — am the heart of Sijilmasa. I, who am the true descendent of the Prophet, will make it rise from the desert. What was destroyed by the faithless I will rebuild. Now, can your king do this without slaves? No, he cannot!"

"My king does not need slaves. Free men build willingly." Well, perhaps not willingly; they grumbled a lot over their jugs of ale and complained they were never paid enough, but that had always been the way with labouring men and was as normal to them as commenting on the weather. But they were free to make their complaint, free to earn their wages and free, once they had paid their dues, to do with them as they wished. Their lives might be one of toil, but they were *free*. Looking at the men straining and sweating below under the watchful eye of the slave guards, Robert truly realised for the first time what it was to be a free man. And he was not.

As if he read his mind, Ahmad leaned close to Robert. "These men, they are nothing. They mean *nothing*. They will live and die and their bones will be made into the walls of my palace. You, lord, have a choice. You need not live and die like these men." He clicked his fingers and two of the guards jogged to the nearest group labouring under the intense sun, selected a man at random and dragged him to one side.

Robert looked on as the slave struggled with the guards, grunting and whining as he tried to free himself. They hoisted him between them so that his legs dangled and with a single movement, propelled him bodily into the air like the trunk of a tree. For a moment he rose, body twisting, and then he came crashing head-first onto the solid ground. He lay still and crumpled, his neck bent at an unnatural angle, while the other slaves continued to work as if they had seen it all before.

The tense nausea that had dogged Robert since taking the *qahwah* tightened into a ball that raced up his gullet without warning. He leaned over the wall just in time and decorated the flat sides with the contents of his stomach. He straightened, feeling drained and unaccountably exhausted, wiping the fresh sweat from his brow with the back of his hand.

Ahmad clapped his hands and spoke to a slave in a waspish tongue. He then addressed Robert. "You will go."

"Go where?"

"Go," Ahmad said, waving him away and turning his back on him so Robert had no other choice than to do as bidden.

Brief the sojourn on the wall head might have been, but Robert had scoured the defences from his vantage point and noted the points of egress. If he had the chance he might run. *Run where?* he thought sourly. Where, in this land of dust and infidels might he find refuge, and how would he know where to look? With that sobering thought lying in his brain like tidal sludge along the Thames, he trailed after the slave, aware that behind him a guard held a drawn sword to his back.

Instead of being led to the slave pens, he was shown to a chamber built into the outer wall, and there abandoned. A small window set high up let in a square of light. Furnishings of a low table and a bed on stunted legs, criss-crossed with rope and laid with simple cushions, afforded nothing that might lift him high enough to see outside and get his bearings. The door opened and a woman of small stature and robust build entered carrying folded clothes and a pair of shoes. She placed them on the bed without looking at him and backed out as two slaves came in carrying a substantial bronze basin between them, followed by others bearing great ewers of water.

Scoured, scraped and buffed until his skin was red raw, beard trimmed and hair tamed, Robert stood in clean clothes alien in texture and design contemplating this change in circumstance. It wasn't clear to him, other than Ahmad's stated intention to use him as an ambassador, what his true motivation might be, because Robert doubted that anything the man said reflected his inner thoughts. Nonetheless, cleansed of desert filth, fed and watered, he felt newly invigorated and able to think more clearly. His stomach still niggled which, he suspected, was the result of the strange drink Ahmad prized so highly, but he was mentally more alert and the fog that had dogged him had lifted to present a sharper world.

Left alone, he inspected the chamber thoroughly. The light from the window had shifted, the air from it cooler than before. Too small for a man of his shoulder breadth to squeeze through, it might yet allow him to see enough to gauge his whereabouts in relation to the one weak point in the defences he had spotted earlier. From the look of the light and the way it moved, he calculated that the room faced north or north-east, the direction he would be travelling when — if — he became free.

He hauled the low table to the wall and used it to give him additional height from which to leap up and grab the window edge. His arms were weak from lack of weapons training, but he managed to pull himself up for long enough to peer over the open sill. Buildings, stretching in an irregular curve, made up the inner face of the wall opposite. He made out piles of building materials — wood, baskets, basic tools — and men going back and forth. The body of the broken slave had been removed and there was nothing left to show he had ever been there, as insignificant as a pebble on a beach. The view was brief but enough to confirm what he had seen before. The question was whether he would ever get the opportunity to exploit it?

Muscles burning, Robert dropped back onto the floor.

Ahmad surveyed Robert with a sharp eye the following morning as the sun rose, neither declaring satisfaction nor condemning what he saw. Beside him, the wild cat sat unblinking in its broad collar of gold and rubies. "Come," Ahmad said tersely, and Robert didn't know whether it was he being summoned or the animal. As it turned out, both were obliged to follow.

The walled enclosure beyond the slave pens where Dodzi and Robert had first been taken reverberated to the harsh sound of metal against metal and the grunting of men, as Ahmad watched the training session from a balcony. Robert spotted Dodzi. Bent coiled and ready to spring, blood from a thigh wound mixed with disturbed dust as he leapt and turned. He spun on one foot and caught the other slave with a thrust of his sword from an unexpected quarter. The man yelped as his arm reddened, and he dropped his weapon and tried to stem the flow. Dodzi lowered his sword. A guard strode up to them shouting, and Dodzi shook his head, pointing to the wounded man. Without breaking step, the guard brought his raised blade down and the man's partially severed head flopped sideways as he fell. Dodzi stood staring at the body, shock written over his face and his weapon limp in his hand. The guard thrust him towards another slave and instructed them to fight.

"These men train as my personal guard; only the very best will be admitted to that high honour."

"And those who fail?"

Ahmad shrugged. "As you see. I must be able to rely on their skill and utmost loyalty. There are those among my kin who would have me killed. I am certain you understand?"

"I understand why some would want you dead," Robert said quietly. "Why do you show me this?"

"Why?" Ahmad said, stroking the ears of his wild cat to their very tips. "So that you may know the price of failure."

CHAPTER TWENTY-TWO

Sometimes, Queen Elizabeth thought to herself, knowledge could be considered a burden. It placed upon the beholder an imperative to act, whereas ignorance might be deemed a blessing to those who preferred to let life take its path to its inevitable conclusion like a slow river wending its way to the sea. She was not one of those people. Knowledge was power and, in the same way that a river might be diverted to provide a source of energy to drive a water wheel, so information could be used to deflect, redirect, and distract the natural course of events. For what was the use of God-gifted wit and position if not to use it in her especial role of supporting her sovereign lord and husband in the Divine workings on Earth?

Edward found the lesser matters of governance irksome, whereas she saw the value of it, and he was content to let her filter and deal with such things — especially when it concerned widows. So, now, here she was again with another little problem to solve. That it pertained to her brother-in-law Clarence, and therefore very much concerned her husband, made it ... both deliciously entertaining and potentially useful. The queen knew that her husband should probably be made aware of this message from the recently widowed Isobel Langton, conveyed through another widow, Ankarette Twynyho, but unless the intelligence constituted a threat to the security of the realm, she was more than capable of handing it.

What to do with it? Elizabeth had banished her ladies from the chamber while she considered the message in solitude. The weather had turned and the wind laid siege to the shutters; before long it would snow. It was clear that the Duchess of

Clarence ailed, and whether by another's hand or God's was almost irrelevant. The point was that, if she died, Clarence would be a widower with prospects. If she lived, however, although his dynastic aspirations might be thwarted, he was also less vulnerable to Elizabeth's own objectives. On balance, the queen considered the Duchess of Clarence's demise the better of the two options; it gave her room for manoeuvre and greater scope to handle her problematic brother-in-law.

There were further implications to consider: if she intervened and helped Isobel Langton, she might make the young woman obligated to her. Even better, she thought, her fingers tapping out the rapidly developing strategy, she could secure a husband for the girl, one upon whose loyalties she could rely.

There was also Isobel's youngest son. Clarence wanted wardship of the boy-earl, and there was nothing Elizabeth would like better than to disappoint him of *that* ambition. Of course, Felice Langton would have her nose put out of joint if her own son did not succeed to the title, but then that wasn't the end of the world. Felice would soon be wed to someone who owed his rising status to the queen's gift, and would be kept busy keeping the lusty-loined man between her own sheets and not someone else's.

The smile dropped from Elizabeth's face. She was acutely aware of her own fading youth and, although Edward still frequented her bed, he also kept company the warm-eyed women of Court. One day, she, too, might lose her allure and then where would that leave her? If her position had previously relied upon her beauty and the hot urgency of Edward's youth, it must now be based upon something much deeper and long-lasting and resilient. Hence the trouble she had taken all these years to attend to her own affinity. Under no circumstance would she find herself in the position of these two widows; hers would be unassailable.

When Edward's ardour finally waned, he must be obliged to look on her not merely as his wife, his queen and the mother of his children, but seek her as counsellor, advisor, the rock upon which any that opposed her — them — him — must break. There was no room for complacency; her position depended upon her vigilance.

And as to the current question of what to do with Isobel Langton's message, by controlling the information reaching the king both in content and timing, she might manipulate matters not only to his short-term benefit, but also, in the longer term, her own. To that end, there were things which Edward did not yet need know. On that sobering note, she slipped Isobel's message into the fire.

"Edward," Elizabeth said later, placing herself in front of him and using a voice he could not ignore. "I am come into some intelligence that concerns me greatly."

Quelled of all desire to venture out into the foul weather, her husband had been engrossed in the exquisite detail of his latest acquisition: a book of illuminations wrought with such finesse that it had taken his breath away when he first saw it. He dragged his eyes from the page he had been studying.

"Hmm, what is that? Have you seen this, Lizbet? Remarkable!" His eyes drifted back to the page.

"Edward," she said a little more sharply, "it concerns your brother, Clarence."

"What has he done now?" the king said with a barely audible sigh but without raising his gaze.

"It is not what he has done but what he plots ... plans to do," she said, injecting a note of indignation. "I cannot believe he would undertake such an action without first consulting with his liege lord and brother! It is almost as if he..." She shook her head. "No, no I cannot believe he would be so brazen. Disregard my words; they are but a voice to my concern for your weal and rule. Now," she said brightly, "Yule is almost upon us and I had thoughts of a wondrous guising to entertain you."

Edward exhaled noisily, both in recognition that his precious time alone was now over and in exasperation that it was his brother, yet again, who was the subject of the disruption. He closed the large book with care, realigned his chair at an angle so that he could face his wife, laced his fingers and in a resigned voice, said, "You have something to tell me?"

King Edward was in no mood to be conciliatory. That Clarence was similarly minded came as no surprise. What was a disappointment, however, was Clarence's lack of effort to conceal his recent dealings, as if either he didn't care whether the king knew, or that he thought his older brother too weak, feeble, *impotent*, to do anything about it.

Edward eyed him sitting opposite, his brother's shoulders hunched about his ears with the look of a recalcitrant page about him. If Clarence wasn't crowing about something he was sulking instead, his mood as variable as the weather and as quick-changing as the boots he chose to wear. The ones he wore now were yet another new pair — knee-high, exquisitely fashioned and still smelling of the expensive tan hide he favoured. His grousing about his pecuniary status obviously didn't extend to his lavish wardrobe.

"So," Edward said, shifting in his chair and wondering how quickly he could finish the conversation he had hardly started.

"Why do you shun my court, George? Thrice now you have failed to come to my invitation."

"Summons," Clarence threw in with a barely restrained snarl. "I would have thought that obvious."

"And why is it I need summon you at all? I expect you to be here, to be seen at Court, especially at this time. I thought I made that clear."

"So that we can be one family — united — the Sons of York?" Clarence said bitterly. "I am not made welcome here. Unlike others."

"Perhaps that is because you skulk around making your discontent known to anyone who has eyes to see or ears to hear. You hardly bring mirth to my Court unless it be at my expense. And what reason have you to be malcontent, eh?"

"You favour others above your own brother," Clarence began and the king grunted a laugh at the familiar gripe. "Shower them with land and offices, listen to their council when I, *I* am as much our father's son and you should cleave to me before your ... before any other. You entrust Richard and listen to his advice above mine — *mine*! Am I not older that he? Am I not to be trusted with matters of import? Do you not *trust* me, brother?"

"Trust, George? That is a good question. Can I trust you?" That brought Clarence up short. Edward continued, "I understand that you have Robert Langton's widow and children in your *care*."

Clarence took on a guarded look. "Where have you heard that? Do not tell me; your *espirionesse* has told you, hasn't she? I have long suspected she has informants in my household and now you confirm it."

Edward maintained his I-will-neither-confirm-or-deny-it expression. What did his brother expect? After all, Clarence no doubt had individuals at Court who gathered and sifted information on his behalf. What he didn't know, and Edward hoped to God he didn't suspect, was that Lady Isabel was only too willing to supply her cousin the king with what he needed to keep an eye on his brother. "Does it matter who tells me?" Edward said. "It is my place to know what sickness afflicts my realm, George. Is it true? Do you hold Langton's family?" Clarence shrugged in the dismissive way he had that never failed to irritate his older brother. "I trust you have no ambition in that quarter. The wardship is in my gift, and mine alone, and I have no desire to see it settled upon any other unless it is of my choosing."

"No? Who is that? Not our little brother, perchance?"

"Your resentment of Richard does you little honour. If I were to grant the wardship to him it will be because —"

"He is dutiful."

"Because he has never given me cause to doubt his loyalty; can the same be said of you?" Edward allowed his temper to cool before continuing. "Langton was Richard's sworn man; it is natural that he protects his widow and oversees the future settlement of his heirs."

"And has the benefit of it."

"And you seek the same out of the beneficence of your heart? No, I think not."

"So, you will grant the wardship to Richard?" Clarence pressed.

The king rose to his considerable height and stared down at his brother. "It is none of your concern. You will permit the lady to return to her estates — *with* her children, George — and I wish to hear no further report that might cause me disquiet. Do you understand?"

Clarence shot his brother a look coloured with anger and resentment. "I wonder how you might learn *that*," he spat.

"There's another thing," the king said, disregarding the comment. "I hear rumour that you intend to send your son, Edward, to Ireland. Tell me that there is no foundation of truth in this because I will be sorely grieved to hear it. What, do you suppose, will be made of such an action by those who would observe it, hmm? They might say that the Duke of Clarence believes his son is not safe in this realm, or that the child's father intends to establish a base of power across the sea. And why would the king's brother desire that, do you think?"

Clarence took a moment before replying. "And *do* I have reason to fear for my son's life? Do I need to seek protection from across the sea?"

"If you have nothing to hide you have nothing to fear, have you?" the king said with an undercurrent of menace, "from whichever quarter I might learn of it." He smiled suddenly. "But what is all this talk of threat and fear? You shall let Isobel Langton go back to her lands and you will return to your own. In time, I expect to see you here at Court, with young Edward and little Margaret and the infant, and with their loyal dam, and we will make merry as kin should and let the children play." The king didn't wait for an answer, nor for confirmation that Clarence would do as bidden, for his brother had said all in the quick, sideways look he had made when his duchess's loyalty had been mentioned. For she was faithful and could always be depended upon to furnish him with the information he needed. Was Clarence aware, did he know?

As Edward watched his brother take his less-than gracious leave, he could not help but wonder whether he had placed Isabel, Duchess of Clarence, in even greater jeopardy.

*

Clarence was not one to be thwarted. If life had taught him anything it was that nothing came to the man content with his lot. Ambition had to be fuelled by action, and planning followed by decisive action is what he did best. Edward might be king, but the she-witch he married wore the crown. If he ventured to look under Elizabeth's skirts, he swore he would see a pair of balls, and iron ones at that.

Once — so long ago he had almost forgotten those early days — he might have been tempted to test the woman's fidelity; now, any desire born of her unattainable beauty lay forgotten in years of bitter acrimony and mistrust. That she wanted him out of the way he did not doubt; that she might make a move against his children, he feared. The sudden and unexpected death of his Mowbray cousin and ally — the Duke of Norfolk — had left him wondering whether he was as safe as Mowbray had believed himself to be.

King's brother or not, he felt vulnerable, and vulnerable was not something Clarence did. He would make himself unassailable and secure the future for himself and his heirs and, if that meant denying his brother's direct command, so be it. Perhaps it would make the king take notice of what was so clearly going on beneath his nose. So, Isabel put her loyalty to her cousin above that of her husband, did she? He would deal with that. And if Edward lost one source of information, he was not about to gain another in the form of the Langton woman. No, Isobel Langton would remain exactly where she was, denying all except himself the benefits she might offer. As for his other plans — ones that went far beyond the petty scheming Edward's limited mind envisaged — Clarence must take matters forward before they were taken from him completely.

*

Isobel held out the book so that the duchess could see the page from which she had been reading. "This one," she said, pointing to the tiny group of flowers painted into the gaily decorated margins of the Book of Hours. "See? Next to the strawberry."

Rubbing her eyes with a knuckle, Lady Isabel peered at the illustration. "It is all bleary, Is'bel, I do not know how you make them out. My eyes are so weak."

Isobel abandoned her chair in favour of a stool next to the duchess. "Can you make it now?"

"Ah! So it is! I would never have known if you had not shown me." Lady Isabel called, "Margaret, Juliana, come and see what has been spied in my little book."

The girls clambered onto their respective mother's knees and companionably poured over the bright images, giggling at snails and pretending to pluck petals from miniature flowers and put them in each other's hair. Isobel began to count the tiny roses and paused to let the girls continue. When Juliana began to falter, she held up her hands. "Now measure the number with my fingers," she instructed, seeing the deep frown on her daughter's brow dissolve into understanding. "Lady Margaret, can you make twice the number again?"

"Six!" she piped up, clapping at her own cleverness and falling backwards over her mother's lap to kick her legs in the air. Her head upside down she stopped all of a sudden. "Papa!" she exclaimed and rolled off Lady Isabel's knees and ran to the door from which her father watched. "Papa! Papa! I counted six!" Margaret declared with all the bravado of the young.

Expressionless, Clarence looked down at her and then at his wife and finally at Isobel. He grunted as if he had come to a decision, turned on his heel, and left. The women exchanged glances and Lady Isabel rolled her eyes heavenwards and pulled a face, making Isobel laugh.

"On the morrow," the duchess asserted, "I will rise early and bedeck myself in my finery, for I feel Yule coming on and you know how I enjoy the festivities!" She beckoned Mistress Twynyho. "Pray you have my gown of murrey brought forth from the garderobe and," she tipped her head on one side, thinking, "my kirtle of crocus... No, no..." she rushed as Isobel gave a slight shake of her head, "make that the rose silk with the hem in gold-worked suns and little white roses. There, that should surely please him if nothing else does." She dimpled with laughter. "How else to raise his mood but remind him of his great nobility?" she intoned, puffing out her cheeks.

Isobel smiled but, to her eyes, thought Clarence even more afflicted with an excess of black bile than usual. She had seen that look before, when he turned his thoughts inwards, and then Heaven only knew what would come of it.

Andrew charged ahead along the paths yelling war cries and waving his short wooden sword at imaginary enemies the following morning, while Juliana scampered after him yipping like a dog as Margaret held her on a lead made of ribbon.

"I recall you doing the same, Cecily, when you were Liana's age," Isobel remarked, watching the children flit between the trees lining the alee and in and out of the clear, thin sunlight. "You were happy then."

She didn't expect an answer so was surprised when Cecily said, "Yes." The girl walking beside her was sombre and quiet as usual, and not at all the lively sprite Isobel used to call her little *imp*, but the expression she wore now was almost wistful.

Cecily saw Isobel looking and quickly reordered her features into the blank countenance Isobel had grown to expect.

"If we are permitted the use of the books, what history would you like to study today?" Isobel prompted. "A little Tacitus? I used to enjoy the histories over all the other texts except, perhaps, Cicero. He had such wit!"

"I care not what I study, madam," Cecily answered. "Let the choice be yours."

Isobel bit her lip. It was not the lack of affection that hurt but the indifference that had persisted since Cecily had re-joined the family. Despite the rebuffs, Isobel couldn't help but try to mend the fracture that divided them. But each attempt and failure reminded her of the wound she had inadvertently inflicted on the girl and her own need to make amends. "Perhaps you might help Drew with his declensions later, while I teach Liana her letters?"

"As you wish, my lady."

Isobel was relieved when she saw one of the duchess's servants holding her skirts free of her feet as she hurried towards them.

"I expect Her Grace wishes to discuss her choice of gown again." Isobel said to Lucie and Alice. "Stay with the children and ensure Liana does not find any puddles; her other shoes have yet to dry from the last one. I will not be long."

Isobel knew something was wrong the moment she turned the corner and saw the cluster of whispering women at Lady Isabel's door. They made way for her as she approached and she entered the room without knocking. The shutters remained closed and a smell of vomit pervaded the air. The physician and his apprentice stood at one side, their heads together, murmuring in that way doctors do when the news is not good.

Isobel went straight to her friend and took up the limp, dry hand lying on the embroidered coverlet, the other clasped to her breast. "Your Grace?"

Lady Isabel opened her eyes and Isobel was shocked to see such despair in their depths. "Is'bel," she said barely audibly. "They would not … let … me send…" She closed her eyes, a 'v' forming between them. She swallowed carefully. "I do not feel well, Is'bel. I —"

The physician angled between them. "Your Grace," he said, his shadow casting over her as he leaned forwards. "I have sent word to His Grace, but he is from the castle, madam. Hunting," he added as if it made any difference.

"But Her Grace was so well yestereve, master," Isobel said. "Why has she sickened so swiftly?"

The physician looked up at her over his shoulder. "Why indeed, my lady? I am most concerned, as will His Grace be when he hears of it."

Isobel saw it in his eyes; heard it in his tone. She stepped back her hands suddenly clammy and caught Mistress Twynyho looking at her with an alarmed *is-this-it?* expression.

"Is'bel?"

"I am here." Isobel went to the other side of the bed. Lady Isabel fumbled for Isobel's hand again and clasped it with surprising strength. Her blue-tinged lips were as unnatural as her sallowed skin, her eyes unnaturally dark and staring in their sockets. The strings of her neck stood out as she tried to sit up; but her strength left her and she sagged back on her pillows where she almost disappeared against their whiteness. "What is happening to me? Am I dying? Is'bel, do not let me die, I am not ready."

"Hush, my sweet, this is but a moment; it will pass and you will feel yourself again and be choosing your gown for Yuletide ere long." Silently, Isobel castigated herself for the lie, but the pain in Lady Isabel's face eased momentarily.

A huddle by the door and whispered instructions indicated that the priest had been sent for. Isobel shuddered internally as her hope for her friend died, but she mustered a smile. "Perhaps you might bid your Fool to wear the same gown, Your Grace, and then what a merry sight that would be!"

"My gown... I want the crocus kirtle. Little Edward likes the crocus kirtle..." Her eyes flashed wide and stark. "Where is Edward? Where is my Margaret?"

"Safe and well. They are playing in the sunlight and chasing squirrels. Shall they be sent for?" Lady Isabel looked blank for a moment. "Your Grace, would you like your children to attend?" Isobel asked gently and received the faintest nod in return.

Isobel began to give the instruction, but Lady Isabel clung to her and, with clumsy fingers, pressed something into the palm of Isobel's hand. Behind them, the spectre of the priest appeared.

"Pray for me, my Is'bel," the duchess whispered, her eyes reflecting panic. "Keep this and remember me. Do not let me be forgot."

Sometime later, as the bells began to toll their sombre message, Isobel looked at the jewelled amulet she still clutched in her hand. It had left its imprint as clearly as those last words Lady Isabel had spoken, and it occurred to Isobel that not once had her friend asked for her husband, Clarence, as she lay dying.

PART FIVE

CHAPTER TWENTY-THREE

The sudden death of the Duchess of Clarence brought the castle to a standstill. Preparations for Yule seemed aberrant in the circumstances and were abandoned in favour of solemn masses for the dead. It was as if the duchess's father had died again, and those who remembered the Earl of Warwick and cleaved to his memory mourned no less for his daughter. Clarence donned clothes of lamentation and could be seen in the chapel with hands clasped in prayer from which his gold beads swung.

Isobel attended the elaborate mass for the dead feeling as if hope had been sucked out of her. In some ways it reminded her of her own recent loss; in others it seemed more real, more immediate, for she still could not come to think of Robert as gone. Despite her distrust of Clarence, she could not believe that the misgivings she had harboured against him might have come to pass. And yet her friend was dead, suddenly and without apparent cause.

People died. Death was a frequent visitor and who knew when he might call? Isobel's own father had slipped away peacefully one night sitting in his chair, whereas her mother had wasted away over many months. But this was different, as if the pall of suspicion coloured the bereavement, and despite the constant vigil in which she kept her own soul prepared, Isobel felt the shock of Lady Isabel's death and the absence of her friend and confidant deeply.

"When is Papa coming home?" Juliana said some days later. Curled up on her mother's knees she snuggled against Isobel's furred collar and sucked her thumb. Isobel stroked her daughter's hair, starkly reminded that Margaret and Edward no longer had a mother to cling to, and that baby Richard would grow never knowing his dam. The pathetic waste of it all caught in her throat. A fatherless child was one thing, but to be without your mother? She recalled the months after her own mother's death and the void it had left at home.

Home. Mistress Twynyho said that the message had been safely taken to the queen and Isobel had no reason to disbelieve her; but still no word came, and she lingered in this shadow life far from home and liberty. Why had the king not acted against his brother? Had the evidence Isobel provided been insufficient to persuade him of the truth of it? Perhaps, she thought miserably, when it came to it, the king favoured his own brother over his sister-in-law. Would it be so surprising? Blood, after all, cleaved to blood, and ties of consanguinity proved stronger than steel. But he was King and, above all, sworn to administer justice in his realm no matter who the felon. She laughed cynically to herself. What had the king done to protect her when the Earl had taken her bodily and held her against her will? But that was then and this was a matter of another order, and one he could not — should not — ignore.

Arrangements were being made for the removal of the duchess's body to Tewkesbury for burial at the abbey. Isobel kept her little family to their room as if, she acknowledged to herself, death might be catching. Nor did she want to run the risk of bumping into Clarence. By maintaining a low profile, she hoped he would forget about them and they might become invisible.

Robbie snuffled, dozing in Isobel's arms, and Andrew and Juliana squabbled over nothing. They had been pent up in the room for days. They could not stay there indefinitely and the longer they remained the greater the risk that Clarence would turn his fierce eye upon them. If the king wouldn't help them, Isobel would have to shift for herself. It was time to act.

"Bayna," Isobel said in a low voice, shaking her maid awake later that evening when the children and her servants had at last fallen asleep. Instantly alert, Buena's hand reached under her pillow where she kept a knife. Isobel shook her head and putting her finger to her lips, beckoned her to the window where they might not be overheard. Wrapping her mantle around the pair of them, she whispered, "We must prepare to leave while Clarence is distracted. He has more to consider than our small affairs and we must take our chance. The others must not know, only the two of us."

Buena's brows rose in a question.

"It is best that way; what they do not know they cannot tell." Isobel didn't answer Buena's sharp glance towards the sleeping servants. "We will take nothing but that which we can carry. With all the guising and amusements about the town, who will notice us? Remember that time in Beaumancote when Lord Robert and I passed unnoticed?" *Robert*. She felt her child move at the tide of grief his name conjured. "Bayna, what would he say if he saw his family now?" Isobel held her breath until the pain of loss passed.

Buena slipped her arm around Isobel and held her tight. Then she held a finger aloft, made it two that scurried away into the shadows, and nodded her approval. "Good," Isobel said, "then let it be so."

Clarence kept to himself over Yule. Isobel could not leave without visiting the nursery one more time. Cradling the infant, Mistress Twynyho looked around as Isobel entered the room.

All light had left her face, her normally busy mien subdued. Isobel intercepted the curtesy by embracing her. "How is the little one?" she asked, stroking his cheek with her finger. He turned his mouth and made sucking noises.

"Lord Richard is hungry, my lady, but well enough." Mistress Twynyho didn't sound very sure. She took a fleeting look at the other women in the room as if she suspected them of eavesdropping and turned her shoulder to them.

"I expect he misses his dam," Isobel said softly, "as do we all. May she find everlasting rest."

"Amen," Mistress Twynyho responded, her eyes welling.

"I know how you care for him," Isobel said gently.

"Like my own, my lady. I'll let no harm come to him, upon my life I will *not*." A flash of anger gave way to sudden fear. "Have you heard the rumours? His Grace suspects that my lady was poisoned. What if…?" She put a protective hand over the infant's head and murmured a prayer of guarding.

"Lord Richard is in no danger from anyone here. There is nothing to gain from his death. Be assured of it, mistress, he has his father's protection."

Mistress Twynyho gave the slightest nod and Isobel, after kissing the older woman's cheek, offered her a small smile. "Now, I must be about my day. The children have been pressing me to take them to an entertainment and so we shall. God rest you, Mistress Twynyho; you have been a loyal servant to Her Grace and a friend to me. May He keep you safe."

The sounds of tambours and pipes marked the rhythm of the dancers dressed in such fantastical costume that it was hard to tell what was man and what his guising. St George chased the fiery dragon, stealing kisses from unwary maids and earning the odd clout from their lover or dam. The scent of hot pies and warmed ale and pigs' trotters, sold from stalls pitched for the purpose, filled the cold, still air, and the overcast sky acted as a backdrop to the lively flames of the torches held aloft to light the way.

Holding Andrew's hand tightly, Isobel pressed into the crowd, despite her inclination to break away and breathe air free of the odour of ale and sweat and damp wool. There were times when being taller would have been useful; this was not one of them, and she used the massed humanity to conceal their progress.

Keeping a careful eye on the children and maids so not lose sight of them, Isobel made a show of pointing out the revellers while scanning the faces for anyone from the castle who might have followed them. If it was difficult for her to see because of her small stature, so would she be hard to spot in a crowd — if only she were not so obvious because of her fine dress. She ducked down and from the basket over one arm pulled a felted hood of leaden blue and another of Kendal green. "Let us join the guising," she said cheerfully to Andrew as she removed his hat and pulled the blue hood onto his head, arranging the fabric over his shoulders in a short cape to cover his mantle. She yanked the simple headdress from her own head and donned a green hood so deeply cut that it threw her face into shadow. "There, how does this look?"

"I cannot s-see your face, Ama," he laughed, trying to push the hood from her head, but she pulled it all the closer and adopted a wicked grin and a twinkling eye.

"All the better for the guising, young master," she said. She popped up and checked the whereabouts of the girls, taking a moment to spot them in their now simple attire. She signalled to Buena.

The premature dusk deepened as Isobel and Andrew slipped away from the crowds and down the alleys. Moments later Alice and Maud appeared, then Lucie with the girls, and finally Buena with Robbie.

Maud looked nervously over her shoulder the way they had come as a figure moved down the alley towards them. "Where are we going, my lady?"

"Ee, I'll 'ave non of tha', girl," Isobel said loudly, broadening her accent and standing with her hands planted on her hips. "I'll 'ave ee sent straight back if yer give me any of yer lip."

Maud blinked at the ferocity in Isobel's voice, but the man passed, bouncing off the walls of the narrow passage as he swayed.

"Quiet," Isobel warned and continued down the way.

"Lucie, why does Ama sound funny?" Juliana piped up.

"Shh, my poppet, it's a game," Lucie answered.

Running dark and swift and deep the Avon appeared an unpassable barrier. "How do we cross the river, my la— mistress?" Alice asked in a whisper. "I see no bridge."

"Nor do we need one," Isobel answered, looking up and down river until she spotted what she sought. "Follow me."

Moored against a stump of wood, the rowing boat bobbed and pulled against its tether like a restless horse. A single plank ran from shore to the mooring, the crumbling edges glistening wet.

"Where is the ferryman?" Alice asked.

"Merrymaking or abed," Isobel said, eyeing up the plank. "Or so I hope."

She lifted her skirts and, despite her additional burden, ran the short distance to the mooring post, then hopped down into the boat. She hauled the boat towards the bank by its tethering rope. "Quickly, jump in," she urged, taking the strain of the eager current and feeling her muscles stretch. "Drew, come on, I know you can do it."

Buena took his arm and helped steady him as he clambered in.

"Cecily, you next."

Cecily's foot slipped on the wet bulwark and Isobel caught her, easing her into the bottom of the boat. "Stay low," she cautioned.

Juliana began to whimper as Lucie swung her out over the edge. "Flying angel!" Isobel sang out quietly as Cecily caught the little girl. "There, that's my bee. Maud, you next." Maud dithered. "Come on, we have no time to waste."

Maud hung back. "I am afeared of water, my lady. Let me stay. I will say I lost you in the crowds and returned of my own accord if any ask."

"We all go or none," Isobel said, beginning to pant with the exertion of keeping the boat close to the bank and feeling the weight of her distended stomach.

Grabbing Maud by the arm, Buena propelled her towards the boat and Lucie and Alice pulled her in. The boat rocked wildly for a moment and then Buena stepped nimbly in with Robbie. The vessel lay perilously low in the water with their combined weight. Moving with care to the central thwart beside Buena, Isobel directed the young women to best balance the boat adding, "I need you for ballast."

"But ... the ferryman?" Alice asked again. "We cannot take his boat."

In answer, Isobel took up one oar and Buena the other and, side by side, the two women let the river take them, dipping the long oars into the current and steadying the boat in the stream.

Mouth gaping, Maud gripped the sides. "We'll be drowned!"

"Quiet girl!" Isobel warned. "Keep low and still or you'll upset the boat and I will drown you myself!"

"My lady, I did not know you could do such a thing!" Alice said, her soft voice squeaking.

"There is much you do not know about me," Isobel said. "Hush now, we are about to pass under the castle walls. Pull your hoods and mantles over you and lay low."

Shipping the oars, Buena and Isobel bent down, covering their own heads and tucking their hands from sight as the river bore them beneath the towering great walls of the castle and the ever-watchful eyes that guarded it.

London could be a dreary place in the depths of winter. The flowing tide barely covered the mud flats as the laden barge approached the wharf where outbound vessels idled empty of cargo until the Christmastide celebrations ended at Epiphany. A sharp wind from the east penetrated their salt-laden clothes as they disembarked, stiff-limbed and exhausted after days huddled together among the bales of hay. To Isobel's relief, no one waited for them and, having paid the barge master for their passage, they stole from the river unnoticed and unseen.

Rising above the buildings nearby, Langton Place sat sturdy, silent and unlit. Sleet began to fall in the encroaching darkness as Isobel watched for any signs that the house might be under surveillance. Sleet became snow and Juliana started to cry.

"Ama, my pingies biting," she whimpered, reaching out and shoving her mittenless fingers against Isobel's face. She was cold — they all were — and the child shivered despite being held close to Alice, whose own nose dripped as sleet slid down it in melting drops.

"Come," Isobel said, and led them down the side paths to the rear of the house where the welcome aroma of warm horses emanated from the stables. "Stay here." She left them bunched in a crook of the building where the overhanging jetty offered some shelter from the wind, and tried the handle of the hefty gate. It was locked. She traced the walls until she came to the rear of the separate kitchen block. Smoke sifted from the great chimney and she could make out faint voices and laughter. She knocked on the passage door. No answer. She knocked again and then, frustrated, put her shoulder to it.

"My lady, we did not expect your return!" The chief steward of her London residence mopped sweat from his flushed neck where his shirt lay open. He had been fetched from bed when a harried servant ran to find him, although whose bed that might be Isobel did not ask. That would wait. Now there were more urgent matters to attend.

Seated at the table in her husband's chamber where he conducted estate business, she laid her hands palm down on its surface. "I return, Master Debden, to find this house run amok and its security lax."

Debden coloured. "My lady, we did not know of your arrival."

"Clearly."

He swallowed. "And it is the eve of —"

"I care not if it is the Second Coming," she growled. "Assemble the household."

Once they appeared, Isobel surveyed the faces gathered in front of her — many young and new to the household; others well-worn by service and years — all in their cups to some degree and each eyeing her with caution. She looked for signs of hostility or guilt in their faces, anything that might question their loyalty to her and her son. She reminded them to whom they owed their duty, that the honour of the Langton family was their own and that they reflected it, and said that, although Earl Robert might be gone from this world, his son was not. She reprimanded their inattention to security and urged them to guard against such an omission in future. To ram home her message, she put all on an hourly watch. To the steward, however, she had more to say.

"Master Debden, you will leave my service."

The man gaped. "I ... my lady —"

"You failed in your duty to protect this house, its honour, and its people. You cannot be relied upon to perform your duties without direct supervision. There is no place here for any person upon whom I cannot rely, and I cannot rely on you."

He began to bluster and puff. "But, my lady, my father served the Old Earl right well and Earl William never made complaint about my service." He sputtered to a halt at her set expression and adopted the air of one wronged. "You'll not find another who'll serve a woman, not one like yourself."

Isobel inhaled through teeth set so close they ached from her attempt to maintain her temper and her dignity. "And, Master Debden, you will return the silver ewer that is missing before you go."

Isobel laid her head against the back rail of her husband's favourite chair, turning it until her cheek rested on the worn surface where his shoulders had rubbed the paint revealing sleek wood. She allowed herself a stolen moment in which to recall the touch of him, his smell, the sound of his breath close to her ear. But it hurt too much to remember and she sat up again.

His table was as he left it, a quill upon its stand with the little knife with which he sharpened the tip; the curious stone in the shape of a curled snail with which he fiddled when at rest; the glossy blue-steel feather of a pie Andrew found discarded in the garden last spring. Precious things, Robert's things. His absence pressed in from all sides filling the void with his loss, every inch of this place part of him, every part of him gone. She would find no comfort here. More pressing still was their security. The stout walls that surrounded them afforded a mere illusion of safety and she must act swiftly to secure it. She needed to speak with the queen.

CHAPTER TWENTY-FOUR

Despite the late hour, the Palace of Westminster glowed as if it drew all the light and life from around it and poured it into the heart of Court. Thin, icy snow broke crisply under Isobel's feet and her breath stood in streams upon the air. Revellers spilled from an open door, skidding on ice and tumbling in a heap before her. She stepped around them as they laughed and flailed and walked towards the door.

Queen Elizabeth's hand flew to her mouth and, standing next to her, King Edward's colour came and went as he absorbed Isobel's news. "And you say you have evidence of this?" He sat heavily in his oversized chair making the joints creak, and indicated a padded stool. "Sit, before you fall, my lady. By Jesu, you are pale."

"Your Grace, for many months now I have been frequently in the Duchess of Clarence's company, and had the opportunity to see her when in health and as she ailed."

"And when she died?"

Isobel looked down at her folded hands. "Yes ... no, Your Grace, but shortly before. She gave me this." Isobel opened her hand, revealing the amulet in her palm, "as a token of our friendship and her trust."

"Trust?" the queen said.

"That I would bear this truth to those in a position to hear it, Your Grace."

Hard little lines appeared around the queen's mouth as it pursed. "It is a wonder that you did not convey your concerns sooner, madam. This might never have come to pass and the duchess be yet alive." She crossed herself and pressed her lips to her beads like a nun. "One might question why —"

King Edward interjected. "Let Lady Langton have her say."

Isobel raised her eyes to meet his. "Forgive me, but I sent a message to Your Grace when I thought I had proof of ill intent. I believed it safely delivered and Mistress Twynyho was certain of it. Had I known it was not, I would have attempted to send another by different means."

King Edward drew his fair brows into a sharp crease. "Who is this woman of whom you speak — Twyn—?"

"Ankarette Twynyho, Sire — a good and honest widow who served Her Grace of Clarence faithfully. It was she who first suspected something was amiss. She did all in her power to preserve her lady's health."

King Edward exhaled. "But to no avail."

"No, Sire."

"I had no knowledge of such a message, merely that you and your children were kept at my brother Clarence's pleasure. I am aggrieved that you found it necessary to make shift yourself to repair to your own property. It was not what I had intended and my displeasure will be made known. This question of the message, however, is grievous indeed, and will be investigated."

Isobel must have flicked a look at the queen because the king caught her glance.

"Her Grace is not to be concerned with this. Henceforward, any and *all* intelligence relating to my brother will be conveyed directly to me and none other. Is that understood?" He continued to address Isobel but she had the distinct impression that it was not for her ears.

"As Your Highness wishes," Isobel said, dipping her head.

The king fell silent, his top lip curling up to his nose as he was wont to do when deep in thought. At least he had not ignored her message but had, for whatever reason, been ignorant of it. She kept her eyes lowered appropriately, but from under her lashes watched the queen's stony expression and wondered what was going on behind those blue eyes of hers. King Edward might not have received the letter, but the queen must have had sight of it for how else was it known that she and her children had been kept virtual prisoners? And if the queen had received the note as intended, why had she not told the king about Isobel's fears for the duchess? But he knew now. It might be too late, but perhaps some justice for Lady Isabel might prevail after all.

The queen beckoned to Isobel to follow her to the side of the chamber where a table bore the remains of an intimate supper which Isobel seemingly had interrupted. She settled into a chair and bid Isobel sit beside her.

"We are sorely vexed by the news you bring us this night. Had we been aware of the missive you sent us, we might have saved our dear sister. Rest assured, we will find it, and the culprit who secreted it shall be severely punished."

Isobel doubted very much that the message still existed to be found. She noted, also, the use of 'we' and 'us' as if that somehow removed the queen one step from the lie.

"I understand," the queen continued seamlessly, "that the last few months must have been taxing for you. I was sorely grieved to hear of Lord Langton's death, may he attain repose in Heaven." She crossed herself. "And now that you find yourself alone and without protection and so great with child… Lady Langton — Isobel, if I might be permitted to call you by your given name — you must refer to me should you ever need help. Look upon me as your friend, for I, too, have suffered the grief of widowhood and what it is to have fatherless sons." She smiled sadly, imparting a sincerity Isobel questioned whether she felt. "I know that we have not been such intimates as I once hoped, but do not bear this burden alone, and let me aid you in any way I can." She squeezed Isobel's hand. "You need not thank me," she said, leaning closer, "I am certain you will repay me in time. Now," she said brightly, rising, "you must eat a little before you return home. Take a cup of wine and some dainties to strengthen you."

"Before you leave, Lady Langton," the king said, taking her slim hand in his as she rose from her curtsy. "Although it might not be a consolation to you now, believe me when I say that the loss of your husband is mine also, for I counted him the best of men, and a true friend. I will ensure the succession of your son to the earldom, and your freedom to oversee his inheritance. You have nothing to fear from my brother, my lady, of that I can reassure you. You have my word and my protection." He lifted her hand to his lip and, to Isobel's surprise, kissed it. He stopped suddenly. "What is this?" he said, turning her hand over and examining the torn and blistered palm. "How did you come by these?"

Isobel blushed. "I ... rowed, Your Grace, from Warwick," and when he looked astonished, clarified, "I took a ferryman's boat. Not so very far, just enough that I could make certain our escape," she said, as if that somehow lessened the crime. "I will make reparation, Sire," she finished solemnly.

"And thence by sea to London, you say. In a barge. You — and your children."

"And my servants, Your Grace; I could not have done so without my servants."

He regarded her with undisguised admiration. "Thank God for your servants," he murmured, "and for stout-hearted English women."

*

374

Isobel watched the lively fires dance on the muddy shoreline on the return river journey from the Palace of Westminster, accompanied this time by the king's own men. The question, she thought to herself as she retreated further from the cold into her mantle, was now that the king had this information, what, if anything, would he do with it? For, if there was one thing she had learned about the Duke of Clarence these last months, once bitten by a plan, he never, ever gave up.

As much as Isobel was grateful for the king's assurances, she was even more so for the level of defensive measures Robert and William Langton had taken to ensure the security of their London home. That is, as long as someone didn't leave the front door wide open in a fit of absent-minded laxity. Nonetheless, she upped the levels of security, mounting a watch day and night and making random inspections when her household least expected. When she caught one in a moue of discontent, she lectured him on the necessity of preparedness. "After all," she reminded him, "we know not when an attack might be made, nor the hour of Christ's coming, and we must be prepared for both." Her servant looked nonplussed and she left him to work it out.

She also sent messages north to Tickhill, warning them to be vigilant and requesting a body of armed men to reinforce the small garrison in London. *'To ensure our comfort,'* she had written to Hyde and the constable, although they would know how to interpret her words.

As to her own solace, she found little. Sleep evaded her. She found her temper short and everything irritated: the starlings chattering in the chimneys, the shouts from children playing in the streets, calls of hawkers peddling their wares. When a door banged or steel sounded upon the stone floors, she jumped —

skin tautening over her jaw already tensioned and aching from clenching her teeth, her pulse thudding — until she had identified the source.

Her appetite waned. She found herself pacing the building when all others were abed, checking doors and shutters, the metal guards set before the fires, the sentries on watch. And then, having done so once, restlessly doing it again. Only warmed wine with ginger seemed to take the raw edge off her nervous energy and calm the rattling claws in her stomach. On more than one occasion she caught Buena looking in her direction, only for Isobel to snap at her for doing so. The children read her mood and kept away. She suffered remorse at the dejection in their faces, and then anger at herself for feeling it.

She felt besieged, as trapped as she once had done at Beaumancote; but the enemy remained invisible, as much part of her mind as reality. Yet she would not leave the house, fearful of being followed and of what she might find when she returned. Nor would she allow the children from her sight, not even into the garden, though their whining annoyed. She tried to tackle estate affairs, knew that without the experienced services of the steward much of the administration fell to her; but she was unable to focus for more than a few moments before she lost patience and stalked away from the table, inflicting her irritation on any and all in her way.

Isobel rejected visitors as a matter of course, even those she suspected were sniffing out the potential for a swift and prosperous marriage. Some tried a number of times and were left standing on the doorstep looking uncomfortable or frustrated. After a while they stopped coming. All, except one.

Lord Richard Raseby had been a persistent caller ever since he discovered the family had returned to London, but she had not yet met with him.

"For all the saints!" Isobel snarled. "What does he want *this* time? Say I am not at home."

"Madam, Lord Raseby insists you will wish to see him when you hear his news," her steward said.

"News? What news?" She scowled. "Is he alone? Does he come with many men? Are they armed?"

"He has but a servant with him, my lady." With his thick, fair hair and big-eyed lack of sophistication, the young man whom she had promoted within the household to take on some of the duties of the steward had been overawed at first, but now dealt with her rages with a calm, detached demeanour. In quieter, more reflective moments, Isobel admitted he appeared to be competent and would grow well into the position. Now, however, she considered her options with barely restrained testiness.

"Very well, Baxter, let him in, but have all here on alert and guards posted at each entry way. Just in case." *Just in case of what?* A small voice whispered in her ear. She flapped it away with her hand. Baxter looked at her with concerned hazel eyes. "Go to!" Isobel barked. "Before I change my mind."

Changeable. That is what she was, yet she couldn't help it. She felt entombed in the house but more so in her body and worse in her mind. She had ventured into the garden now and again but found no comfort nor freedom from her thoughts. She would rather be there now, despite the dour weather, than here, receiving Lord Raseby.

Isobel rose heavily as Richard Raseby came into the chamber bearing an ivory cane under his arm and an impossibly broad beam on his jowly features. "My dear Lady Langton!" he exclaimed, walking straight up to her, clasping her shoulders in his big hands and kissing her on both cheeks. He stood back and his smile dropped. "Such tragic news about the earl, may he find eternal peace. My deepest regrets, dear lady, and in your present state, too." He shook his head in big, slow swings. "Such a loss, and to those poxed Barbary curs, may they know the flames of Hell and the edge of my sword!" He harrumphed. "I beg pardon for my outburst. Were I a younger man, I would make crusade and seek vengeance on the infidel."

"Thank you, my lord," she responded without emotion.

"Now, now, enough of that. You are looking a little drawn. Ho, there!" He hailed Buena, standing at a watchful but respectable distance to one side. "Fetch Lady Langton whatever fancies might ease her. What a brute I am, my lady, to come without a thought to your comfort."

Isobel recalled seeing Lord Raseby the Yule before last at Court with a pretty dumpling of a wife, remembering sharply, that, had she not died, Robert's niece would have been his wife now. As if he read her mind, Raseby said, "Perhaps things might have been different if Lady Margaret had not been taken from us too soon." His jowls sagged. "Such a sweet girl."

Isobel gathered her manners and fought to direct her thoughts. "And Lady Raseby — I trust she is in health, my lord?"

"Ah. Alas, Lady Raseby is at the mercy of our Lord. She was visiting her sister in Norwich when she contracted the pestilence — as did all her family. All dead now." He genuflected then scratched at a place on his scalp, lifting his extravagant chaperon and revealing short, grey hair standing in thick tufts like bleached bog sedge. "Yes, all dead. I wonder, sometimes, whether the Lord has seen fit to take my wives as punishment for my sins."

Did God visit death upon the innocent in retribution for the iniquities of another? Is that why Robert was taken from her — as punishment for her many offences with his brother? But was the offence hers when she neither sought nor found pleasure in it?

Raseby was still talking. "You must be wondering why I am here," he was saying. "As you are not at Court, I thought you might not have heard the news and, as you were an intimate of the duchess —"

"What news?" she broke in.

"I have no desire to be the cause of distress, dear lady, especially in your delicate state of *maternité*, but the little babe, may Heaven have mercy upon him, died not long after his dam." Raseby seemed genuinely downcast by the thought. "I see you were not aware of this information, but I believed — as you were close to the duchess — that you would wish to know. Being a grandsire thrice over, I feel the loss of such a young soul myself."

"Yes," she said, numbly. "Thank you."

"His Grace of Clarence, as you can imagine, is beside himself with grief. He has even implied— although no one considers it likely — that both the child and his noble mother died of *unnatural* causes." Raseby raised his brows meaningfully as Isobel shot him a look. "Indeed," he continued, "I, too, was outraged at the suggestion. But these things do happen, indeed they do, and the Duke of Clarence has his enemies. It is rumoured he seeks those culpable." He leant forward, looking concerned. "There, there, do not alarm yourself, my lady; you have no cause to be afeared for none will wish *you* harm."

He chatted on blithely unaware of the turmoil he had initiated. Eventually, he took note of her short responses and made ready to leave. "One last thing, dear lady," he said, arranging the folds of vivid blue velvet brocade evenly around his substantial body and settling his ornamented belt. "I would rest easier if I knew you had protection —"

"From what?" Isobel said, coming sharply into focus.

He looked surprised. "My dear Lady Langton, from any that might take advantage of your current situation." The silver ferrule of the cane ticked when it struck the floor as he put his weight upon it. "Honour your humble servant by letting me visit again that I may be assured of your welfare?"

Where had she heard that one before? She sighed, preparing a stout rebuttal, but the concern she saw on his face was such that she could not question his honesty. This was hardly Thomas Lacey and certainly not the Duke of Clarence. Something in her must have softened because Raseby beamed again. "My dear Lady Langton," he said, bowing deeply, "until next time."

Lord Raseby must have read more into the conversation than Isobel intended because rumour of their forthcoming marriage reached her through servants' gossip. She balked at the thought and raged to herself as she braved the January snow, storming about the garden, using the thick falling flakes as camouflage from would-be assassins. Once she had worn herself out and calmed down, she took herself — frozen to the bone — back to her solar where she confronted Buena.

"I am surprised he considers me a suitable match, given my association with Earl William. I would think he'd deem me tainted goods."

Buena did what she always did when Isobel let fly: remained a pool of calm in her mistress's storm. Using the language of her hands, she spoke as eloquently as if she had a tongue to voice her thoughts.

Isobel watched and sighed. "You are right, I suppose. My lands are worth a dainty piece and the boys bring him ready-made sons as he has none of his own." She grimaced. "Do you think he expects to sire more children by me?"

Buena's gesticulations made her views clear on *that* subject.

"Ugh, you're right; he's a man who enjoys the trying. How many wives is it now — three? Four? — and I to be the next? I might make it a condition of our contract: separate beds and *I* keep the key to the door. No," she relented, "he deserves better than that. He is not unkind and seems passing fond of the children. And he is mighty prosperous. There have been rich benefits to his many marriages; he has chosen his wives with care." She thought back to his tales of bloody valour upon the battlefield. "He is also well-versed in warfare; we would be protected if nothing else. Will the king allow it? Lord Raseby has always been loyal, even when the tide turned against the House of York. It is one of the reasons why William held him in esteem, even if he did find him brutish in his manner sometimes." She smiled despite herself, remembering the Earl's wittily caustic, but apposite, comments when they were alone together, and then felt a stab of guilt because she had thought of him and not his brother.

"How can I remarry when I hold only Rob in my heart? It feels like betrayal. And so soon. But what choice do I have if we are to be protected from every knave and jack who seek advantage over us? Yes," she scowled at Buena's silent comment, "I most certainly include the most noble prince, the Duke of Clarence in that. When has he shown us due honour as befits his station and ours? He is no worthier than all the other dogs. Nay, he is worse; he should know better. No, I will not be quiet. I care not who knows it!"

Buena whipped her hand over Isobel's mouth and stared fiercely into her eyes until her mistress gained a modicum of control over her temper.

"I am so tired, Bayna," Isobel confessed as the fight drained from her. "It seems I am always running from something or someone or have to fend against this or that. Look at it all." She swept her hand over the piles of documents waiting to be reviewed: the pleas and demands, contracts and fines; dues, invoices, reports on goods sold and those awaiting payment. "Does it ever stop? I mean, just look at this one, I have not even read it yet."

Glumly, she picked up a folded letter with a large red seal, broken and dangling on its ribbon, probably seen by Robert, but left unanswered until his return. She pieced the unequal halves together and tilted it towards the flame, trying to make out the imprint in the slumbering light. It looked familiar. She screwed her eyes. "Fetch more light." An elegant horse tripped across the seal bearing the figure of a woman carrying a hawk. "I have seen this image before," Isobel said and, curiosity getting the better of her, she opened the letter.

Skipping the usual pleasantries until she came to the meat and purpose of the contents, she read with a deeply ingrained frown, pinching her top lip between forefinger and thumb as she concentrated. Then she read the signature, checked the salutation, and made doubly sure of the signatory. She sat back, the letter open and forgotten as she took in its significance.

"Buena," she said, looking up, "I must hasten to Westminster."

*

Felice reviewed the contract with a cold eye. "This is not what was agreed."

The tonsured clerk inclined his head but not his manner. "It is as Lord Newton instructed, madam."

Felice held out the contract as if tainted and dropped it on the table. Antony Newton might have recently risen within the ranks at Court, but he was hardly an earl even if he desired to be one. And therein lay the nub of the problem: his ambition outstripped his rank. Felice suspected he was having second thoughts, at least, that was what she supposed lurked behind this sudden change in their contract of marriage.

"I made it perfectly clear that I am to retain my dower lands and those acquired since the death of my most noble husband." She emphasised that last point, resenting to her very core debating personal matters with a mere clerk whose naturally fringed pate made him look ridiculous and tested any authority he thought he might have. She pushed the unsigned contract back across the table.

"If Lord Newton wishes to discuss the substance of this agreement, he knows where I am to be found." She dismissed the clerk with a turn of her head.

Although her lands were the one thing she would not concede, she realised that she had little room for manoeuvre. Newton sought to marry above his rank and she was the best on offer in a fluid market. An outbreak of fever or war might, at any time, make more widows and she had little doubt he would be off sniffing their tails if he thought the deal was a better one than she afforded. She must pin him down while she could — but not at any price.

Felice learned a long time ago that a promise was the more alluring for being withheld, something she was quite certain the queen had exercised *par excellence*. She would play a waiting game and bring the pup to heel. But not for too long lest he find another skirt. Besides, there was an additional card she could use, and one at which he would be unwise to baulk, unless, that is, he wished to risk offending the queen.

Leaving the security of her home, Isobel sensed the windows of the buildings she passed watching each step she took away from it. By the time she made the palace by boat and horse her skin was clammy, her head hurt and she felt dizzy. Now she waited in the hope the king would grant her a few minutes of his time, for this was something she believed he would wish to know.

She was not alone and the hubbub from those gathered in the antechamber bounced off the walls and drilled into her skull. There was nowhere to sit so she squashed herself against a window as far from the others as possible and waited, hoping to remain inconspicuous, but imagining probing eyes and wagging tongues. Even here, in the heart of Court, the Duke of Clarence lined the purses of those willing to be bought. That woman there, with the hem of fur worn bald in patches, who kept giving her glances, or the thick-lipped man, talking incessantly, whose restless eyes inspected the faces of everyone in the room. Did Clarence see through their eyes? Was he watching? Isobel wanted to melt into the walls and disappear.

The door opened again and expectant people surged in a tide only to pull back in disappointment when they were not called, whereupon the incautious clamour resumed. Isobel pinched the skin of her hands, willing her heart to calm. She concentrated upon the faces of those around her — their stance, their gestures — and the noise abated, and she began to piece together the conversations they made without words. She imagined the lies behind the smiles, the envy, the boredom.

She noted the men whose faces showed the real direction of their thoughts, the twist of a lip indicating derision, the puckered mouth, disagreement. Some wore masks, others projected quite a different image to the one their body told. Was she as transparent?

Three young men of about her own age caught her particular attention as they stood vying with one another in loud voices. Their ridiculously flamboyant dress and long-toed shoes made them courtiers on their way up. Had they already made it into the king's inner circle they would not be kept waiting out here, nor would they deem it necessary to demonstrate their position so flagrantly. As it was, their ambition was writ large on buttocks and cods paraded with all the arrogance of youth, whose assumption seemed to be that somehow their manly display impressed everyone and themselves. They reminded Isobel of cockerels flaunting bright feathers to indifferent hens. She laughed.

One of the men turned around at the unexpected sound, his ill-tempered scowl dissolving when he saw her. He abandoned his fellows and sauntered over and gave an unnecessarily elaborate bow.

"Lady…?" he queried.

"Langton," Isobel said, silently castigating her stupidity in drawing attention to herself and seeing his unguarded look of surprise become speculative. "Sir…?"

"*Lord* Newton," he said with a flourish. "Lord Anthony Newton," he said again in case she didn't catch it the first time. "You await the king's pleasure, my lady?"

She was tempted to point out that she wasn't there for her health then thought better of it. After all, this pottage of people was as much about seeing and being seen as it was about being granted an audience with the king. Most would leave without having that singular honour but might, nonetheless, have come away with a morsel of information here, or a new connection there. There were more ways than one of climbing the greased pole. Her eyes skipped involuntarily to his thighs for signs of oil and regretted it as he misinterpreted her interest. His loose-lipped smile broadened and he pulled back his short cloak revealing more than he needed.

"Well, my lady," he breathed with easy charm, "for my part I believe my time here has not been wasted." He narrowed the gap between them until his muscled hose-bound thigh pressed against her. "It is hot in here; perhaps you will do me the honour of accompanying me somewhere less, mmm, populous?"

Smoothing the corrugations of her gown and emphasising her heavily expectant state, Isobel took a step away. "I regret, my lord, I am in mourning." But then he knew that, didn't he; it was her estates he wished to woo. "Ooo, this child I bear pains me. Oh!" She winced convincingly as she pressed her hand to her stomach. "Sweet Mary, I feel the child move!"

Newton's grin fell away as easily as it had come; but he didn't need to find excuses to abandon her because a rush of silks and a hush had him turning to see what new opportunity presented itself as the queen crossed the room looking neither left or right but purposefully forward. Newton hurried forwards and made a gushing bow, obliging her to stop or collide with his bent head. "Most gracious madam," he said, addressing her feet.

The queen's mouth twitched. "Anthony, what do you do here? Ah," she said, spotting Isobel close by and raising her brow perceptibly. "I see. Lady Langton, wait on me. Ladies," she addressed the women behind her, "remain here."

Isobel followed the queen, sensing the curiosity of the others as she passed, the odd low-voiced comment, a question. And then, at the entrance to the room, a word, whispered audibly: "*Whore!*" Isobel spun around to find the iron eyes of Felice Langton boring into her and the woman's furious glance towards the young man with whom she had just been talking.

CHAPTER TWENTY-FIVE

Robert had lost count of the weeks since his arrival at Sijilmasa and the time spent in transit from the coast. The images of his wife and children faded in daylight only to be recalled in vivid detail in his dreams beside the faces of his dead brothers and father.

He would wake in a sweat in the obscurity of the night and piece together the truth of his existence until his racing pulse slowed and he could grip reality. He feared those dreams, but most of all, he dreaded the dead, dark hours in which he lay awake besieged by the past and stalked by fears for the future. It was in that time that he thought most about William, and then about Isobel, and his love for the two became confused and angry and sometimes he imagined they were together again. And then Robert would surface from the shallow sleep into which he had fallen and curse the night demons that would lie in wait for his unguarded mind. But most of all he feared for his wife and their fatherless children and the trials they would face without his protection. For his own welfare he cared little, for he was losing hope each day that passed.

Day brought another sort of gilded hell and one just as confusing. He was woken at dawn, bathed and dressed after the custom of the Moors, and escorted to the church they called a mosque, whereupon he waited outside until Ahmad had finished prayers and joined him. Robert caught glimpses of the interior, the carved marble and stucco, dazzling tiles, the rugs laid in rows across the floor. Their strange script danced across the walls, but there were no statues, nor paintings, and bells did not fill the air with their resonant song. When the guard assigned to him knelt in prayer, Robert stole the moment for his own devotions, quickly crossing himself and offering silent supplication to God. If caught in the act, retribution came swift and hard, and his back bled for days after the beating.

After prayers Ahmad would bid Robert join him to break his fast as if he had a choice in the matter. If Robert was broken and bleeding, Ahmad showed no curiosity nor any sign that he noticed, his conversation far-reaching and becoming noticeably more animated after his *qahwah*. Then Ahmad would have Robert accompany him on his daily inspection of his city kingdom, extolling the qualities of all that was laid out before him — the library filled with scrolls and manuscripts, tablets and books from ancient times and far-away places. Even a little Book of Hours from Flanders lay among the collection, an exhibit which Ahmad delighted in showing Robert and commanding him to read from it, even though he did not understand Latin.

On one occasion, Ahmad led Robert towards the women's quarters, loudly praising the virtues of his wives and concubines, and boasting that they were the best of all women that walked upon the earth. Only men of faith might take such a wife in this life, for any other would sully the loins of the chosen. That night, a slim-thighed woman slipped into Robert's bed, arousing desire and shame in equal measure, and a hunger for soft-fleshed comfort that remained unsatisfied. The following morning he saw the triumph in Ahmad's eyes, and turned his own away lest his humiliation could be read.

"Convert," Ahmad urged him, "and know that such amusements will be yours at your bidding, for under the laws of my people, a man may take many wives and be blessed."

"I have a wife," Robert answered. "I need no other, for she is the best of wives."

"Ah, but she is just one wife. Women are gifted by God for the pleasure of men." Ahmad selected a sweetmeat of green-coloured crushed nuts in one hand and honeyed rose petals in the other and held them up. "Women are like delicacies — each different, each to be savoured." He placed a sweetmeat on his tongue and drew it into his mouth, sucking the flavour from it before chewing and swallowing. He licked his fingers. "Convert and know such delights for they are yours for the asking. *Any* pleasure," he emphasised, "any *desire.*"

As frequent as the temptations Ahmad laid before him, Robert was also shown the alternatives should he continue to deny the daily exhortation to deny his faith and convert. Each day he was taken to the slave pens, to the building sites, to the punishment yard, to the training courts. And every day Robert witnessed the arbitrary cruelty, the disregard for life, that had a slave plucked from the ranks at random and subjected to a beating or to execution because Ahmad willed it. When Ahmad realised that Robert refused to be intimidated by the daily bloodletting of others, he changed tactics.

The thin baton came from nowhere, tearing the skin on his back and knocking the breath from him. Robert lay, momentarily dazed, dust lining his nose and mouth, grit in his eyes. He pushed himself up on his elbows and looked around. The guard stood over him, motionless. Everything about him was black — from his beard and eyes to the clothes that he wore. It marked him out as one of Ahmad's personal guards, his elite. Robert started to rise, but the guard swung the baton down onto the arm he brought up to protect his head. *Crack.* Robert grunted as pain rocked up his arm and into his shoulder. The guard stood back and Robert struggled to his feet, cradling his forearm. A small crowd gathered outside the mosque where Robert had been obliged to wait for Ahmad as usual. They shuffled aside as Ahmad appeared and walked past Robert as if he were invisible.

At breakfast, Ahmad fed the spotted cat with slivers of raw meat while Robert looked on, nauseated by the spectacle and the searing throb that now consumed his arm. He could not eat. With his skin torn, his robe stuck in patches to his back, which bled anew as the fabric ripped the binding blood. The cat gazed with indifferent eyes.

"What do you want of me?" Robert asked through teeth clenched against pain. "What do you think will be gained by beating me?"

Ahmad raised an eyebrow as if surprised that Robert didn't know the answer to his question. "*Tahul*," he said. "Convert."

"You know I can — *will* — not forsake my faith." *Thwak*, a swingeing blow knocked him sideways.

"Convert," Ahmad said impassively.

Robert lay against the wall, making no effort this time to move. "Why?" he rasped. "Why is it so important to you that I convert? If it is a matter of bearing your messages to my king…" The cat left its master's side and soft-pawed across the marble floor towards Robert. It sniffed Robert's leg and he flinched as a rough tongue licked his ankle. "Upon my honour, if you release me, I will do so."

Ahmad inspected his fingers and obviously found them wanting. A bowl of perfumed water was placed before him into which he dipped them with delicacy. "No *kafir* will serve me as my ambassador; only those of the True Faith may have that honour that I might be proved a worthy believer, Allah be praised. All who serve me must convert."

"I am *not* your servant. I will *not* convert."

Ahmad raised a wet finger and both the guard and Ahmad's slave stepped towards Robert, bent down and grabbed him by the ankles. A quick jerk had him on his back before he could twist around and defend himself, and the guard smashed the baton onto the soles of Robert's exposed feet. Excruciating pain surged up his legs, exploding in a yell of agony. Each stroke intensified the pain, a fire radiating from the tender arch of his feet in burning sinews. The beating continued until, almost senseless, Robert was dragged from the room and taken back to the slave pens and there left to rot.

By the third day he could no longer walk and they beat him where he lay. When they finished and left him alone with the dying, he scraped away the dust and stone and retrieved the little rock rose he had secreted, and held it to his chest mumbling feverish prayers and nonsense as his mind drifted. That night, as the slaves piled back into the pens, ignoring him, Robert wondered whether he had drowned out there in the vast seas after all and this was Hell. He began to laugh, a hard, harsh sound that turned into grief because why did he endure this torment for his faith if already damned?

By the time the guard came the following morning, Robert hunched in the farthest corner of the pen, waiting. If there was one thing he could control, it would be the fate of the rock rose from which he would not be parted again. Wrapped in cloth, he had bound it to his inner thigh beneath the bagged breeches. If discovered, he would probably be beyond caring; until then, it would remain safe. He twitched at the sound of footsteps on the hard floor outside the pen. What part of him would they break that was not already broken?

Ahmad's face appeared above Robert where he lay slumped on the marble floor. "Am I not merciful?" He clicked his fingers and a slave appeared at his side with a silver cup from which Ahmad proceeded to drip liquid into Robert's parched mouth. "I say again, am I not merciful for I give you the choice to accept the one true faith. I could give the command and you will die."

Robert muttered something and Ahmad bent down to catch the flimsy words.

"No, no, my friend, *I* will be the one to choose whether you live or die; that is not for you to decide. I can give life and freedom or I can make you suffer, but I will not let you die. It is your choice *how* you live. Deny your false beliefs and live a free man."

Robert heard Ahmad's voice from far away in the painted beams of the ceiling as he rocked on waves of pain and fever. "Let me die," he mouthed. "Sweet Jesu, let me die."

The guard came into view and Robert moaned and struggled to get away. But his limbs did not obey him and, exhausted, he lapsed, gratefully, into the comfort of the dark.

When he woke, something had changed. He lay with his eyes closed, listening to the sounds around him. He made out birdsong, the ticking of crickets, noisy rasps which he came to realise were his own breaths, and a soft exhalation that was not. He opened his eyes cautiously. He was back in the room he had previously occupied, but he was not alone. A woman of indeterminate age waited immobile in front of him. On seeing him awake and trying to sit up, she started to talk in her strange language and pushed him down again. To his shame, he had no strength to resist.

The woman wrung cloths in a brass bowl and placed them across his brow. He became aware of his body limb by aching limb. His left arm had been bound, his feet also. A green stench emanated from poultices applied to his bruised skin and he had been bathed while in his unconscious state. In panic, his free hand sought the bundle strapped to his thigh, but the woman was rattling words again and pulling his hand away. She shook her head at him, put a finger to his lips; then, casting a quick glance at the closed door, from the low table picked something up and pressed it into his hand. He felt the irregular waves of stone petals and clasped it tight to his heart.

"Thank you," he croaked, finding it impossible to conquer the sudden emotion such a small act of kindness evoked. "Thank you. Bless you."

He never learned her name. As soon as he was able to support himself, he was trawled back to Ahmad's banqueting chamber and into his former routine. When he returned to his room, the woman was gone. The guard accompanied him everywhere. He stood outside the chamber when Robert went to bed and was still there in the morning. He never spoke, did not smile; but nor did he raise the thin baton to Robert again. Robert did not trust him, or rather, he did not trust Ahmad not to change on a whim.

On inspecting the long, dark armoury one morning, Ahmad pointed to a young boy among the many polishing the blades of weapons with ash. "This," he said, "does my bidding because it knows I own its life. If it disobeys, I will take it; if it fails to work hard, I will take it; if it observes me with insolence, I will have it killed."

Robert looked at the boy with his dark face whitened and hair prematurely greyed with ash. "Why do you tell me this?" he asked.

"This, I gift to you." He poked the child on the shoulder with his stick. "It is your slave."

"I do not want a slave — neither man, women, nor child. In my country it is abhorrent to own another being."

Ahmad's eyes hardened. "So you have said. But this is not your land, it is mine, and I own this," he tapped the boy on the head, "and I own you, and you will do as I please in my land. And it pleases me to give you this. It will do as *you* please."

"Then I refuse the gift."

"Ah, my friend, it is not for you to refuse. You will take it and if you do not, I will have it beaten. If you displease me, I will take off its hand. If you refuse me my will, I will strike off its head with my own sword. And it will be by your doing. I am a patient man, but even a patient man must know when to plant new palms and uproot the old, for old palms bear little fruit. Yet he must wait for the young trees to grow. He nurtures them, feeds and waters them, protects them. They bear him fruit and he rewards them with his care. But when all care renders nothing but barren branches, then he cuts them down and replaces them with new wood. Yes, I see you understand my meaning."

Robert perched on the side of his bed, resting his elbows on his knees. The boy hunkered in the manner of all street children, blank-faced and silent, awaiting instruction or a beating. Tight curls grew over his eyes and his nose dribbled. Every now and again, he rubbed his nose along the back of his hand, leaving a glistening trail on his ash-covered skin. The boy kept his eyes fixed on the floor. Robert did not want this boy; he did not want the responsibility of him. He did not want to form an attachment to a child he would be forced to leave behind when he escaped. And escape he would.

His own wounds had healed enough to enable him to traverse the desert, and the regular inspections of the building works confirmed the weakness in the defences of the town. Robert wanted out of this place, away from the confines and cruelty. But most of all, he wanted to see his family and walk with them on green grass down to the stony rivers where the trout swam and his children splashed bare-footed in the shallows. There they would try to catch the slim brown-spotted fish lurking beneath the flat stones. Juliana once managed to capture one in her small shoe and cried when she had to return it to its watery home. He could hear her now, snorting soft sniffs of disappointment. Robert opened his eyes half-expecting to see her but, there before him, the boy cried almost silently as a pool of yellow spread around his feet.

"Sweet Jesu," Robert said softly, "what have we become that a child is so frightened he pisses himself?"

Robert called out and the old woman came scuttling through the door. On seeing the boy, she shrieked and began hitting him about the head with sharp fists. "No!" Robert bellowed, taking the woman by the wrist before she could hit the child again. He made motions of washing. The woman looked at the boy and then at Robert, clearly confounded. "Wash the child," Robert said again, pointing to the boy who now cowered with his arms over his head. "Clothes," he said, fingering the cloth of his own tunic.

Muttering darkly, the woman took hold of the child's hand and all but dragged him from the room.

When the boy returned, bathed and clothed in clean rags, Robert reviewed the wisp of humanity before him. "What do I call you?" he asked.

"It has no name." Abu Umar Salim Ahmad stood by the open door, disregarding the woman who prostrated herself at his feet.

"Even my dogs have names and are better treated than this child."

Ahmad surveyed Robert with his strange hawkish eyes. "How it is treated depends upon you. Do *you* bow towards me? Do *you* obey my commands? Subjugate yourself and you will benefit from the munificence I offer. Refuse, and I will make my wrath known." He held out a long, braided leather strap off which dangled a collar.

Robert looked at it and then at the boy. "No."

Ahmad clicked his tongue and his guard stepped forward and hit the boy with his fist, sending him sprawling. Just as quickly, the boy regained his feet, head bowed and motionless. Ahmad continued holding the leash as Robert glared at him.

"It is not right…" Robert began and the guard raised his arm again. "Wait!" Robert said, coming between the boy and the guard. He took the lead from Ahmad's outstretched hand. Ahmad twitched his fingers in the direction of the boy and, terse-lipped, Robert bent down. "Jesu, forgive me," he whispered as he encased the child's neck in the collar. On rising, he noted the satisfied spark in Ahmad's eyes and swore to himself that, one day, he would be the one to put out the flame.

CHAPTER TWENTY-SIX

With sinking heart Isobel traced the progress of Antony Newton from the gate to the porter's lodge. She had given strict instructions that none should ride into the great courtyard, but that they should leave their horse, weapons, armed escort and any accompanying servants beyond the protective walls of her home. What they did or where they went after that she did not care, as long as they weren't near her or her children. By obliging any visitor to walk up the path she ensured they were entirely visible to the guard who kept perpetual watch. It also gave her enough time to consider her options. In this case, Newton had already spotted her at the window, so she could hardly claim she was not at home. Behind her, Lord Raseby was on all fours like a portly horse as Andrew and Juliana galloped around him, neighing.

Isobel felt more and more like a brood mare herself as she contemplated her next steps to safeguard her family's future as well as her own. Raseby took great delight in complimenting her on her advanced state of pregnancy and even confessed, with a shamefaced laugh, to having laid a wager on the outcome of the birth. The sex of the child, he said, mattered not a whit to him because little Robbie was hale enough. Although, he had added, another boy-child was always to be welcomed, as nobody knew God's will in these matters, and all too often it was the second or even third son who inherited, as indeed, her dear, late husband had proved. He himself had only daughters, a blessing though they were.

Isobel had clamped her mouth to avoid a pithy riposte but was all too aware of Drew listening to the conversation nearby.

Within the voided space where once her heart had been, she found it hard to warm to Richard Raseby, but could not deny that, for all his bluff and bluster, he showed genuine concern for her children's welfare, so she tolerated his visits, but did not encourage them.

Nor did she wish to see Antony Newton. She could hear his approach now, unnecessary spurs chinking against the floors. She might as well see two as one and part of her was curious to see the outcome of the men meeting. Anyway, whatever they thought they might achieve she would disappoint them, as she had determined to leave London and return to Tickhill before she was too great with child to travel.

"Are you certain?" the queen had asked in her most solicitous manner when Isobel told her of her plans a few days before. "I know of at least two lords who will be bereft in your absence." She had tittered like a girl.

Isobel remained straight-faced. "I am certain my lords will find greater amusement elsewhere, Your Grace. I am poor company and will remain so."

"Oh, no! I am told you are the subject of *much* distraction. Even yestereve, a certain lord made enquiry after you and let it be known to the king that he is in suit for a wife."

Isobel averted her head to disguise the look of disgust she felt sure must be mirrored in her features.

"After all," the queen had continued, "there is only so much my liege-lord can do to ensure your continued safety." Her glance slid towards Isobel, gauging her reaction.

Isobel had measured her words with care. "Such has been His Highness's protection that I no longer feel the need to pursue any other. I will return with my children to the north where I am certain the king's rule of law will continue to offer us security."

"My lords will be greatly disappointed," the queen said. "And I had hoped to see you settled on a match before long."

"Alas, madam, I fear I am a burden to any but my own company. I must see out my period of mourning in honour of my noble husband before I countenance any other."

"Can you afford to wait that long?" the queen said, crisply. Then softening her tone like a comforting arm designed to appease, "You will be missed by more than my lords, Isobel."

Why did she go on? Isobel's head throbbed, the soft words bludgeoning. "Madam, I think not; I offer little in the way of diversion."

"And *I* say that I will," the queen flashed. She had smiled although her eyes did not. "Promise me that you will send word. Often. And remember, I am *always* your friend should you have need of me, especially if my royal brother, Clarence…" She hesitated, pointedly. "Ah, no, that outcome is not to be countenanced. I am certain you will be safe enough."

That had been but a few days before and now here were two lords plying her with compliments and badly disguised ambition. Lord Raseby's saddle, fashioned from a cushion, tipped from his back as Antony Newton swaggered into the room and came to an abrupt halt when he spotted the older man. "Raseby," he said, giving the shallowest of bows.

Raseby shoved his bonnet back from where it had slipped lopsidedly over one eye. "Newton," he growled, without returning the pleasantry. "What do you do here?"

"Ensuring my lady is not troubled by unwanted company, and to offer this little gift." With an elaborate bow, he presented Isobel with a small painted box, opening it when she failed to and revealing a bright gilt ring, fashioned as clasped hands.

"A dainty bauble for my lady to assure her of my *fidélité*," Newton said, swinging his cloak away from his hip and exposing his fulsome manliness. Isobel pressed her lips together and replaced the lid. "Will you not wear it? As a token of our … friendship?" In moving a little closer his hip knocked against the pricket table with a metallic *tink*. Isobel frowned. "Ah, yes," he said, with a guilty smirk, drawing a shiny new dagger around to the front where it sat, emphatically, near his groin.

Raseby could hardly mask his contempt. "You bring a weapon into the presence of Lady Langton and her children?"

Newton gave a cursory look at the older man. "What of it?"

"It is brazen! The lady has expressly forbidden the bearing of arms within her dwelling. Such discourtesy cannot go unremarked."

"And who will mark it? You, old man?"

Raseby squared his broad shoulders, his short, thick neck tensing, and Isobel could imagine the fearsome spectacle he must have made on the battlefield that had earned him his reputation. William had valued his loyalty; now she could see why. Age did not matter to this man one bit. He would not stand down. There would be blood.

"My lords, I beg of you, let this pass," she said.

Raseby's dense eyebrows gathered as he took a step forward. "Ask my lady's pardon for your insolence, Newton, and I will be content."

Newton fingered the pommel of his dagger wearing a supercilious smile that was especially irritating. "For wearing this little thing?" He slid it out of its decorated sheath, holding it to the light and admiring its lines. "Surely my lady will forgive me for bringing my eating knife?" He tested the point with his finger. It broke the skin. "A necessary accoutrement for paring, mmm, fruit." He licked the bead of blood from his finger and, winking at Isobel, placed the tip between his moist lips and slowly sucked it clean.

Raseby's face developed the hue of a ripe pomegranate. "Knave!" he spluttered, his beefy hand going to his belt and, remembering his dagger's absence, bunched it instead.

Newton swaggered a step toward him. "Take heed to repeat that, or are you so in your dotage you have forgot the insult already?"

"*Contumely* knave," Raseby rumbled. "Base-born and made up so quick you forget such courtesy as befits the company of this lady."

Newton thrust his face into Raseby's. "*This* lady?" He threw a sly glance in Isobel's direction, making her coil inside. "And tell me, *who* is it that made me? Will you test yourself against the queen, my lord? To whom do you think Her Grace will give her preferment? You, bloated with age and tales of battle no one wishes to hear?"

"Battles I have fought and won in long service of my king. You, lordling, have yet to be tried."

"Tried?" Newton ran his eyes down Raseby's body to where his loins lay hidden by pleated cloth. "I have been tried and tested, and never found wanting in any respect that benefits a lady. What do you have to offer, you old cockerel? The only swell you make is with your belly."

"My lords, enough!" Isobel gathered the children to her. "Lucie, take them to Buena and stay there." She looked around and saw Andrew looking cross. "Drew, go to Lucie." He shook his head and placed himself firmly between his mother and the men, hands on hips and looking very fierce. "Andrew, go. Now!"

Cecily grabbed Andrew's hand and Isobel turned back in time to see the glint of Newton's blade as he thrust it under-hand towards the older man's heart. Moving surprisingly quickly, Raseby dodged the blade and it ripped through the thick fabric instead, wrong-footing the youth. Raseby brought his fist down hard on Newton's skull, and the young man crumpled, his knife clattering beside him. Raseby kicked it away where it slid impotently under a chair.

Isobel looked at Raseby, then at the barely conscious youth, and her simmering blood boiled. "Enough!" She threw the ring box to the floor. "That is e-*nough*! Take your anger and your gaudy playthings and leave me and my family in peace."

Raseby's face fell. "My dear Lady Langton, your pardon —"

"Do not *dear lady* me! I did not ask for such urgent attention, nor do I seek the company of any but my children, and certainly not a husband. And you," she directed at a dazed Newton who now staggered to his feet, his hand pressed to his head. "You come here flapping your cods and making your boast, but you have nothing to offer but vacant promises and empty words. You think me so dull-witted that I do not know you are contracted with another? Does the lady know you present me with spangles, or do you also gift her with lies?"

"Upon my honour —"

"Honour? I think not. Out! Both of you. Leave my house!"

Buena bent to retrieve the box from the floor. The corner had splintered to reveal plain, brown wood beneath the showy exterior. Isobel held out her hand. "Give that to me." She opened the lid and Buena grunted from beside her. "Yes, a pretty thing," Isobel conceded, "but the giver asks too much and I have nothing to tender in return. Besides," she said, rising with some difficulty from the chair. "He belongs to someone else. And she is welcome to him," she added with a grimace. "What Anthony Newton offers is nothing but baubles and padding; there is no substance of feeling behind it."

Her hem caught something under the chair. The polished pommel of the dagger glinted up at her. "Have it returned to Newton. No, wait," she said as Buena picked it up. "Let him fret upon it awhile; it is the least he deserves. He can find something else to pare his fruit or anything else he chooses."

Buena left to supervise the younger children and Cecily slipped into the chamber now that the men had left, and was scowling from the window at Lord Raseby's retreating back.

"Cecily, come away," Isobel said, aware that Raseby's visits brought more to the surface than her own tension. She had tolerated him because it seemed easier than constantly finding excuses not to see him. Also, he carried news of the world outside so that she didn't have to go out and seek it. And if it meant pretending to listen while he rambled on about his military escapades or his daughters — whom he still referred to as 'his little chicks' — and his grandchildren, so be it. Besides, her own children liked him and he seemed genuinely fond of them, and that went a long way to ameliorate him in her eyes. But she had no feelings for him other than that.

When she looked at him, which she did as little as possible, she felt nothing: no repulsion, no affection and certainly no desire. That side of her had died along with her husband leaving her withered inside. But Raseby was benign enough and his company undemanding, which was why she could not permit Cecily's open hostility towards him. "Come away," she said more sharply. "He will think you ill-mannered." Cecily continued to watch Raseby as he walked down the path between frosted bushes of lavender towards the gate. "Do you heed me?"

"I do not like him."

"Whether you like him or not, his age and station demand your respect, Cecily. It is not for you to elect to disregard him; it is not a matter of choice but of dignity."

Cecily turned her solid blue eyes on Isobel seeming, in that instance, so like her father that for a moment Isobel felt like the uncertain girl standing before him interrogated by his look. She regained her composure.

"You risk bringing dishonour to your family. Take a care to remember that in future," Isobel cautioned.

"My *family*?" Cecily's face became bitter. "*My* family is *dead*. Meg is *dead*, and you … let that man come here and…" She ran out of words. "He killed her!" she almost screamed, becoming the little girl full of rage that Isobel had once tamed.

"Lord Raseby? Of course he did not!" Isobel said, taken aback. "Why would you think such a thing? He was betrothed to Meg, but she took a fever. It was God's will that she be taken from us."

"She did not sicken until that … man came… She died because of him!" She pointed an accusing finger through the window to where she had last seen him.

"Cecily," Isobel said gravely, "Meg had the French ague, as did your uncle, but she was not as strong as he. It was by God's design that she be taken."

"Was it? Meg was better until *you* visited her."

The unborn child rolled in Isobel's womb and she gasped out. "Meg was dying, Cecily. Nothing could be done —"

"I remember, I was there. You left me."

"You were a child." Isobel reached out to her. "Cecily, you were a frightened little girl. You could not know the truth of it."

Cecily stepped back, her mouth curling downwards. "You left me there."

Isobel's skin chilled. "I did not wish to. I had no choice. You were not mine to take."

"Yet you call me *daughter* now, but I am not. Liana is your daughter."

"Cecily! I love you as my own child! How can you doubt it? Have I ever shown you less affection than my own children?"

"I thought you loved me, but you left. You took Drew and … and Moth and Bayna, but you left *me*!" She poked at her own chest in little, harsh stabs timed with each word and bruising Isobel with every sharp thrust of rejection and loneliness.

"Cecily, I could not take you with me. You have to understand; your fader was dead and your mother —"

"What right have you to make mention of my mother?" Cecil shot back. It was Isobel's turn to look puzzled. "You first abandon me and then you take me from my mother."

The unborn child tumbled again, its head grating inside. Isobel held her breath until the pain passed and let it out in a whoosh. "Cecily…" Another roll and this time Isobel bent double. "Your dam… I could not leave you with her; she has no natural feeling for you. She —"

"She is my lady mother. My brother is the rightful earl. *You* have no *right*!"

Tension ran in tremors down Isobel's legs and she felt sick. What was Cecily saying? But the words faded as the floor suddenly turned dark brown from the fluid flooding beneath the hem of her gown. Isobel creased in agony. "Fetch Buena," she gasped out. "For the love of Almighty God, get help!"

*

The little bundle lay swaddled in the cradle near the bed. "Let me see," Isobel said, her bloodless lips moving of their own accord. Her attendants exchanged glances, neither woman making a move towards the child. "Bring her to me," Isobel demanded.

Buena dropped the bloodied cloths with which she had been cleaning Isobel's legs and, bending down, carefully picked up the baby. She laid her in her mother's arms and Isobel parted the linen from over the infant's face. Her eyes were closed, her tiny button lips blue-tinged.

Parting the swaddling clothes, Isobel inspected the baby's fingers in all their perfection and, kissing them with infinite tenderness, tucked them away where they would be forever warm. Isobel's eyes filled and first one tear and then another anointed her daughter's face.

The baby did not stir. Robert was not here to see his child; he was not there to bury her.

CHAPTER TWENTY-SEVEN

Holding the canopy aloft on a tall pole, the child trotted behind Robert on a slackened leash. Under the escort of his guard, Robert had been permitted to leave the confines of the palace, perhaps as a test, but more likely to needle him with what he missed by refusing to comply. He now walked in the shadow of the canopy, along the narrow ways between buildings where the air was a little cooler, tracing his way back to the gate through which he had entered the town.

On the pretext of looking at the rugs piled high with exotic wares that flanked the main street, he counted the number of steps it took to cross the market square, noting the volume of traders that passed and the security placed upon them by the guardian at the far gate. Sentries paced the towers overlooking the wide spaces beyond the walls and a notable tension pervaded the air.

Hunger rendered the watchful guards red-eyed and even more short-tempered than usual. The atmosphere, Dodzi told Robert on one of their infrequent meetings, was only partly to do with the observance of the period of prayer and fasting the city had now entered that forbade the followers of Mohamet food between the hours of daylight. Ahmad's power within the walls of Sijilmasa was absolute; but outside, shoals of smaller fish with sharp teeth gathered. Ahmad had made enemies of his kin. They sought his destruction and he, in turn, looked to embolden his defences against them using the only effective means he did not possess: great guns. Ahmad had insinuated as much in their earliest conversation, probing Robert's knowledge of gunpowder and bombards. Dodzi confirmed it. "He want big gun, but he cannot get."

"Why? He is wealthy enough to purchase them."

"Now Portuguese king say no fire-gun must be sold to Infidel. Portuguese king very powerful — he control trade in fire-gun. No fire-gun here."

So Ahmad wanted great guns to defend Sijilmasa and possibly to extend his control over outlying territory. That explained the reinforced defences. Cannon and black powder would give him an advantage others did not possess. Ahmad wanted Robert to negotiate with King Afonso to secure weapons, but first Robert would have to convert. Robert would do neither.

On another visit, Robert explored the town to its farthest limits, pausing to rest in the shade of the gate through which he made out the tops of trees and the oasis beyond. The child Adil — from whom Robert had managed to coax his name — squatted in the dust next to him, humming a cradle song and tossing small stones in a game of his own devising. The way north and home lay on the other side of that oasis, but it was as busy as the streets of Tickhill on a market day, and he would not pass unnoticed. Robert knew no alternative way and Dodzi had made plain that any other would mean death. But death was preferable to a life spent here. Death assured resurrection, and what the alternative offered was beyond imagining. The most recent marks of his refusal to cooperate lay in reddened wheals across Adil's scrawny back, the skin broken and weeping where it stretched across his knobbly spine.

Closing his eyes, Robert leaned back against the wall. Christ forgive him for his failure to protect the boy. His chest itched but he resisted the urge to scratch and instead pressed his knuckles against the coarse fabric of his robe. Beneath, the crude cross he had incised into his skin using a splinter of stone and blackened with a ground up piece of charcoal, would heal. Whatever he said, whatever he was made to do, nobody could erase this declaration of intent. It would stay with him until the day he died; it was his cross to bear.

The guard grew restless. By the aspect of the sun, he would soon seek to kneel and bow his head to the earth in obligation to his god. For the purpose, he carried a small, thin rug tucked into the sash at his waist. At the given moment, this would be unrolled with a flick of his wrist and laid on the ground wherever they might be. A part of Robert admired such devotion. Would that all men showed the same dedication; would that *he* did so, Robert acknowledged grimly to himself. As it was, he knew that on his return, Ahmad's attempts to persuade would begin again; and Adil would once more bear the brunt of his refusal. It was only a matter of time before one or the other broke. He gave another glance at the walls, noting the increased security and the watchfulness, and called to Adil that it was time to return to the palace.

"Your dog is obedient?" Ahmad held a small switch with which he tapped at flies as they attempted to settle on the edge of the empty tray in front of him.

"The boy serves me well," Robert answered, ensuing he was between Adil and the switch.

"Does it? I say not, for you yet refuse to accept the true faith." Ahmad aimed the switch and neatly dissected a hapless fly.

"The boy is not responsible for my conscience. I alone must be held to account."

"Yes, so you have said," Ahmad said in a bored tone. "But still you defy the faith and I fail in my duty if I do not show you the path. You, therefore, are responsible for my soul as well as your own. It is for this that you must convert, for will you deny me my rightful place in paradise by your own selfish acts?"

In any other situation Robert might have laughed, but the convoluted reasoning from this twisted man left him cold despite the lingering heat of the day. "Your soul is a matter for you and you alone, as is mine."

In reply, Ahmad merely smiled without humour. He pointed the stick and one of the guards reached around Robert and lifted Adil bodily, suspending him by one arm and waiting for orders. Head cocked and mouth pinched, Ahmad reviewed the dangling child. With a twist of the stick he indicated, and the guard swapped arm for ankle, upending the boy. Adil began to make little whimpering noises in the back of his throat. Ahmad rose from his throne-like chair.

"For pity's sake!" Robert burst out, stepping towards the frightened boy; but Ahmad's slave blocked his way.

"Pity? What is this *pity*?"

"For the love of God, show mercy on the child!"

The switch tapped against Ahmad's palm as he inspected Adil from all angles before finally resting it against his exposed and grubby sole. Adil flinched and wriggled. "I see no child, I see only a dog that must be punished."

"Do you regard your wild beast as cruelly?" Robert asked, pointing at the cat now lounging on Ahmad's chair. "Would you treat your own son like this?"

"My son? This is not my son. This is nothing. It has no father. It is worse than a dog." Ahmad brought the switch down sharply on the boy's sole. Adil squealed and Robert lurched forwards; but the guards pinned his arms and held him back as Ahmad aimed another swipe and another. Adil writhed in pain, sobs becoming cries at each stroke.

"Enough!" Robert said, breaking free. He tore his own shoes from his feet. "Beat me if you will, but for all that is holy under the sun, let the child go."

"Will you convert?"

"I cannot."

"Cannot or will not?"

"I will not deny Christ."

The switch hissed and stung. Adil screamed.

"You can save your dog. You can stop its suffering if it means so much to you."

The switch flew, and Adil's screams became reed thin, his ankle bloodless where the guard gripped him. He tautened and recoiled as Ahmad struck again.

Robert broke free of the guards and lunged towards the child. "Stop!" he yelled and, breaking the guard's grip, released Adil, encasing him in a shield made of his own arms. "I yield," he said, protecting the boy's head. "If that's what you want — if that is what will satisfy you — I yield."

Ahmad's raised arm lowered slowly, an expression of curiosity replacing the calculated viciousness. He placed the switch neatly on the tray and arranged his garment about his shoulders with a precise shrug. He waved his fingers and the guards stood back. "You convert?"

The boy shook uncontrollably within the confines of Robert's arms. Robert gave a sharp nod of his head.

"Say it," Ahmad demanded. "Let Allah hear it."

"May God forgive me." Molten lead weighted his gullet, stifling words and making his head swim. Robert closed his eyes. *Forgive me.* He held Adil tightly, the child's terror reduced to whimpering. What price his conscience? Certainly not this child's life, deemed worthless because he had no father, no position, no place. Would God forgive his decision knowing, in His wisdom, that his conversion was forced upon him by compassion for this scrap? Or was his faith so weak that he took the smooth path and used the child as an excuse to make his own rocky way easier? Would the saints have given in so easily? No, he knew they would not. He should entrust God with himself and the child, knowing that death to this life was preferable to the death of the soul ever after. Yet this boy's existence was no more his, than Ahmad's to decide, for God had placed Adil upon the earth as surely as every other being. It was bad enough that Adil be enslaved — there was nothing Robert could do about that — but he had a duty to do what he could to protect the boy's soul.

The switch was back in Ahmad's hand. "Infidel — you decide — now!"

His hand protecting Adil's head, Robert said, "I will. On the morrow as the sun rises, I pledge that I will do what I must."

Even in the depths of night the oasis sang with a chorus of insects and the harsh call of frogs. Dark shapes darted past Robert's window, making clicking noises as they swooped at invisible prey. Robert had been marking the phases of the moon and now the stars stood brilliant against the inked sky; there would be no moon to lighten his way. He roused the sleeping child, whose feet he had bound in strips of cloth against the stinging sand, and warned him with a finger to his lips, not to make a sound.

The door proved of little consequence, the hinges giving way without much effort, and the inexperienced guard asleep at his post knew nothing as his own knife was used against him.

Robert eased the lifeless body to the floor and, taking Adil by the hand, moved swiftly across the first of the open courtyards.

A shrill alarm cut the air and Robert slid to a halt, heart beating hard — listening. No sound followed, only the settling of feathers as a startled bird returned to roost. Robert castigated himself for his carelessness: peacock and guinea fowl freely roamed the courtyards by day and acted as sentries at night. He would have to be more cautious.

He navigated the slave pens by their stink. From there it was only a short step to the training compounds where the slave guards slept. He left Adil in the shelter of a wall and made his way in the moonless night towards the farthest enclosure. He stopped under the high window, listening for the rumble of sleep from within. Bending, he searched with his fingers until he found a small stone no bigger than a pea and lobbed it through the window. He waited. Nothing, and was about to repeat the action when he felt a hand upon his shoulder. He jumped back, his arm already punching towards the unseen enemy.

"Shh," Dodzi warned, long and low and, without another word, the two men retraced Robert's steps to where the child still cowered.

"This way," Robert said in an undertone, counting each footfall until they reached the buildings under construction.

Even in the dark the uneven blocks of stone stood out as teeth against the night. They had grown since he had last been there and, from this aspect, they reached high above them. Stumbling amid the building debris, he searched for the breach in the defences he had noted on one of Ahmad's perambulations. His arm disappeared into the hole he sought where the doorway would one day be. Temporarily blocked with a thin layer of clunch, it would take a matter of minutes and brute strength to make a hole in it wide enough for them to squeeze through.

Between them, they picked quietly at the rubble, their movements becoming urgent, less cautious, as they detected the first whiffle of air cooled by the oasis. A soft moan issued from just beyond the wall and Robert held up his hand. A snort, a rumble. Dodzi put his eye to the aperture. "Camel," he confirmed, "and man," he whispered. "Many man."

"How far?"

"Not far — not near." He waved a loose-limbed hand indicating a short distance, but still too close for comfort.

"Asleep?" Robert placed his hands together in imitation of rest.

Dodzi nodded, then shook his head. "Some. O'bert, we not go that road. Too many. Too fierce." He drew his finger across his throat.

"We must," Robert mouthed. "There is no other way." He pressed his face against the wall and squinted as far as the hole would allow. He drew back and Adil took his place to look through the opening. "The camels are between us and the men; the men have fire and will be blind to what moves beyond." He mimicked the meaning. "We keep behind the camels close to the wall and go around the men and head north for Fez."

Adil jumped down and patted Robert's arm. "Not now, Adil."

"No, O'bert, this not work," Dodzi said, "I know better way where no man go. We go that way."

"Why do men not go that way?"

Dodzi shrugged. "Many man die. Many animal. No water. Fierce sun. Much sand. Much heat."

"And you fear the Berber?" Robert murmured.

"Berber worse," Dodzi confirmed.

"But still we must escape these walls or, north or west, there will no helping us."

Adil tugged at Robert's djellaba.

"Wait," Robert said as he would to his own son. "Then we must make this hole larger." He continued removing stone by stone as quickly and silently as he could. Dodzi joined in until the void stood big enough for them to squeeze through one at a time. "Adil, come," Robert said, but before either man could stop him, the boy nipped through the wall ahead of them and disappeared.

"Adil! Get back here!" Robert rammed himself through the hole, calling as loudly as he dared. Eyes adjusting to the indistinct shapes before them, he made out Adil darting towards the humps and mounds of the slumbering beasts.

Reaching the first camel, the boy whispered something to it at the same time removing the hobbling bands that prevented it from wandering off. He went to the second, the third, until all but the farthest animals were free. Scrambling onto the back of one camel, he dug his sharp heels into its sides. It climbed with a whoosh to its feet and Adil pounded its back with his small fists until it began to lumber and sway, disturbing the rest in a rumbling mass of scraggy-flanked animals. Adil urged his camel forwards, spreading alarm.

"He means to distract them," Robert said with a groan as the startled animals trampled tents and pots and fire as the Berbers scattered, yelling.

"We go this way — now!" Dodzi pulled at Robert's arm.

"We cannot leave the boy!"

"We go." He began to run, long-legged and low to the ground, hugging the wall. Robert took one last look at the little figure on the camel silhouetted by the rapidly spreading blaze before he, too, fled into the darkness.

They ran until the sound of men shouting and the high-pitched bleating of panicked camels was replaced by the melody of night insects. Robert stopped to catch his breath, bending double and searching the nightscape for any sign of the boy. What good was his own escape if he left the child behind to haunt him?

"Come, my friend," Dodzi said, as if he understood Robert's turmoil, and began to lope away at a steady pace. Robert waited for as long as he could, stretching his ears to every sound, before he turned in resignation and followed.

Sunrise brought no respite and they pressed on for as long as they could before walking in the burgeoning heat became unbearable and they sought the shade of scraps of vegetation marking the course of a dry riverbed. From the bank, Robert watched the spread wings of massive birds made minuscule by the great height to which they climbed on the rising air. He made monsters of them in his mind, following their wheeling progress across the sky until they became dots and vanished altogether.

"I could not save him," he said at one point, when the memory of boy and fire blended and he saw Adil engulfed in flame. "He was little older than my own son, and my responsibility, and all I did was lead him to death." His voice thickened and he would not speak again until he could control it. Protecting Adil was all he had to do and he had failed. Wearily, Robert passed his hand over his dust-creased face, tasting salt sweat and sand. "'*De die autem illa et hora nemo scit neque angeli caelorum nisi Pater solus*'," he recited. "'We know not the hour of Christ's coming. It is a mystery known only by God.' Do you understand?"

Dodzi continued to gaze across the riverbed and did not appear to have heard.

"No," Robert murmured more to himself, "nor do any of us. It is a Divine mystery." He was too tired to explain the point, too thirsty to care. Cradling the stone rose in his palm, he lay back against the mud bluff with his arm defending his eyes from the brilliance of the day. Without more than the food and water they were able to carry with them, he would be seeing Christ sooner rather than later. Perhaps Adil would be there. His father, brothers…

He lapsed into sleep, subdued by loss and lulled by the siren song of the whispering desert.

Robert woke with a start and made a grab for the dagger tucked into his sash. There it was again, a whistle, melodic and otherworldly. Dodzi slept next to him undisturbed. Robert scanned the drifting sands for any sign of life. The sun was still high enough to be hot, but its descent marked several hours after noon. They must be on their way.

He heard the sound again, this time a low sing-song voice, and he nudged Dodzi awake with his foot. Instantly alert, Dodzi crouched, watchful and wary. Then he broke into a grin. He pointed to the dunes and said something unintelligible. He tried again in broken Portuguese. "Sand…" He waved his hand in a loose motion as if conjuring air, "Spirits."

Robert frowned. "Ghosts — in the desert?"

"Much spirits, as many as this." Dodzi scooped a handful of grains and let it fall in a soft cascade. He stood up, laughing. "Come, we go now. We walk with ghosts." He chuckled again.

Robert made the sign of the cross, eyeing the rich, golden dunes stretching away to the south. He did not want to die here to add to the sighs of the desert. This was not where he belonged and, for the first time in months, in his minds-eye saw the verdant hills of home.

In the throes of death, the setting sun cast a lurid glow. Inch by inch the horizon to the east darkened with encroaching night and out there, somewhere, Ahmad's men searched for them. Dodzi had spotted movement shortly after they resumed their journey, too far to make out in detail, but close enough to be seen. Robert shivered as the sun took the last of the heat with it. "We cannot risk a fire. We burn by day and freeze by night; what a benighted place this is."

"This not hot," Dodzi said. "This…" He said something in his own tongue, tried to describe it in words Robert might understand. Failed. "It not hot time," he said.

Robert turned his back on the way they had come and shook the flask. "Whatever time it is there's little water left. We must find more and soon. How far to the next source?"

Dodzi shrugged, holding up fingers. "Three walks if we go this way; four if we go that." He pointed to the corrugated land rising up to the north, a maze of water-cut hills as red as the desert and as unforgiving. It was less direct but Ahmad would never find them among the gullies. More to the point, would Dodzi be able to navigate such inhospitable and unfamiliar land?

"There is not enough water to last us more than a day's march. Four days or three will make little difference."

"Then we go this way," Dodzi said. "This way great birds find our bones and carry our spirits to heaven."

"A thought to bring good cheer to accompany our blisters," Robert muttered. "Let us be off and see how far we can go before we are captured or the desert eats us."

They followed a gully snaking between weather-worn cliffs of ochre-coloured rock, conscious of the least sound that might indicate Ahmad's guards were close behind. At one point a scuttle of stones rattled down the steep bank behind them and they hid beneath the overhang in expectation of pursuit. But nothing came of it and, jangled nerves settling, continued.

The sky had swallowed the stars and no light now lit their way. Sometime before dawn, they could go no further without risking cracking bones on unseen obstacles. With water exhausted and empty stomachs grinding, there was little to do but huddle down until the sun rose and warmed them, and then move to the shadows to avoid the worst of the day's heat. The air seemed heavier here by the riverbed. It pressed against Robert's chest and made his ears ache. He tried to swallow the discomfort away but his mouth was as dry as the land. He coughed. Beside him, Dodzi rested his head on his folded arms, his breathing shallow and laboured.

With a tremendous roar the great guns released their lethal loads and the walls of Beaumancote came tumbling down amid smoke and fire. "*Isobel!*" Robert woke with a cry as another boom broke through his troubled sleep. He sat upright, blinking himself into consciousness.

In the dreary light of the desert dawn, Dodzi slept on. A low rumble spread across the sky. "Wake up!" Robert shook Dodzi. "Listen!" Nothing and then, "There — it sounds like … thunder."

An eye-splitting dash of light shattered the dark and a mild wind cooled Robert's nape. Moments later the first drops of rain fell. Dodzi let out a triumphant yodel and Robert, lifting his face to heaven, welcomed the warm, fat drops against his parched skin. Already the ground beneath their feet was darkening and the scent of damp earth rose in heady waves.

Robert licked the rain from his forearms, caught drops upon his tongue; no wealth could be greater than this in all the world and he the richest man of all. He grabbed the flask and held the rim against a rock from which a steady trickle now ran. "Rain!" he shouted, triumphant. "Rain, Dodzi, rain!" But Dodzi was washing his face free of grit and sweat, breaking into a song for which no translation was required because the joy in his voice said it all.

The storm passed all too soon, leaving water in pools, flasks filled, and the men's thirst satiated until their bellies swelled. Gathering sword and knife and staff, they set off west again with the emerging sun on their backs and banks of shining clouds marching away in great towers above the cliffs. The desert would bloom, Dodzi told Robert, and all men rejoice, for in some years not a drop of rain would fall.

"In my land," Robert said, "it rains so much that men pray for sun. It is ever green." He meant to make a jest of it, but Dodzi thought about this for a few moments.

"Your land is a rich land. I wish to see your rain and your green.."

"And I will show you one day, if God wills it." *If* God willed it. England seemed impossibly remote, something akin to a dream. Robert caught snatches in his memory, a face, Isobel's voice, but could not hold them in his mind's eye for longer than the beat of a wing. It was as if everything that happened in the last months had scraped clean the page on which his life was written and a new book begun. Only sleep brought her image sharp and clear, but with it, pain. This truth invaded the little joy the sudden rain had brought, and he found himself sinking into a despondency that was becoming all-too familiar.

The remaining clouds cleared, leaving the predictable blue filling the cleft sky above them and the damp earth steaming. The faintest rumble came from distant mountains and that, too, would soon pass. They trudged on in silence, each consumed by their own thoughts.

The thunder grew. Robert stopped and Dodzi cocked his head to listen. The rumble became louder, turning into a roar. Dodzi shrieked something and began to pull Robert towards the mud banks, and Robert turned in time to see a brown mass emerge from one of the ravines and swallow the riverbed. They scrambled up the cloven banks, clawing their way until high enough to escape the torrent of tawny water laden with broken branches and tumbling rock.

Panting, Dodzi beat his chest with a closed fist, speaking his own language and shaking his head. "*Wadi*," he said, pointing at the length of the now swollen river.

"*Wadi?*"

"*Wadi*. Rain make many water. Dodzi know this. Dodzi is…" He smacked his brow with his open palm, looking disgusted with himself.

"We need to get out of here." Robert scoured the sheer walls rising on one side and the tumbling waters on the other and, on the far bank, a raised beach of dry stones leading to safety.

"I go there," Dodzi said, pointing to the ragged ridge above them. "See land, see way."

"It is impossible to climb," Robert objected, but Dodzi was already finding small handholds and was ascending into the blue like a lizard. He crested the ridge.

A moment later he reappeared. "Not possible, not even for Dodzi."

"Then we must find another way, for I do not like our chances should Ahmad's men find us in so neat a spot. I doubt they will want to discuss terms." Robert scanned the riverbank, noting where the water was fiercest, chewing at the friable edges, and where the ground seemed solid and less liable to fracture. Edging sideways, he slithered to an outcrop.

"O'bert!"

"We can cross here when the water abates — goes down," Robert clarified, throwing a handful of dust into the spate and watch it be carried away.

"O'bert!" Something in Dodzi's voice made Robert look up. "See!"

Robert clambered onto a higher rock and followed Dodzi's pointing finger back the way they had come. He froze. Silhouetted against the morning sun the distinct shape of a camel headed straight for them. He couldn't make out the figure riding high on the animal's back, but it wouldn't be alone. To stay on this ledge where the sun made a beacon of them was courting death, to attempt to cross the river, madness. Of the two options, madness carried the lesser penalty, for God was merciful to those suffering *amentia*.

Dodzi half climbed, partially slid back onto the rocky ledge beside him. "We swim," Robert said, making movements with his arms and pointing to the river.

Dodzi's eyes flared wide. "No water!"

"It's our only way. I will help you."

Dodzi backed against the rock wall. "O'bert go. Dodzi stay; Dodzi fight."

Robert weighed up their chances against a fully armed group of men, highly trained and without mercy, and the odds of surviving the leaping waters. On balance they looked about even. As much as he was up for a fight, the likelihood was that Ahmad wanted them alive and that was beyond Robert's limits of endurance. He preferred the hazards of the river to the certainty of slavery. But he could not abandon his friend.

The camel had been goaded into a trot and over the exuberance of the churning water Robert imagined the ringing harness and the short *shoofs* of the animal's breaths. "There's no time; we must go. It is death if we stay."

"Water is death."

Robert smiled grimly, "Perhaps, but it is certain and it is quick."

Dodzi pulled a face, checked the distance between them and the fast-approaching camel, and gave a short nod.

"See there," Robert said, indicating a bend of the river where stones and earth jutted into the water, "the water is not so fast nor as deep. We let the river carry us to that bank. I will help you; I will not let you drown." He sat on the overhanging rock and thrust his foot into the water and felt the turbulence drag and the suspended grains of grit abrade his skin like a cat's tongue. It would be a miracle indeed if they survived, but the camel and its rider would be upon them any moment. "We jump together."

Side by side they stood on the edge. Across the water a yell went up. They had been spotted. "Ready?" Robert said. "One…" Another shout, and this time the rider waved his arms. "Two."

They plunged into the water, finding it deeper than expected, the tumbling current pulling and shoving, pummelling air out of their lungs. Robert felt for the riverbed, found some sort of foothold, lost it; regained it again, and grasping Dodzi's tunic, prevented him from slipping under.

Dodzi flailed neck-high, water churning and leaping, filling his mouth and nose. Wild-eyed, he lashed out, catching Robert on the side of the head. Shaking his eyes free of water, Robert let the current take him, tugging Dodzi off his feet so the man was forced to be guided by him or drown.

Kicking hard against the surging water, Robert managed to steer them towards the rapidly approaching shingled beach. Overshoot it and they would be cast downstream and Heaven only knew whether another landing place might be found before the writhing river consumed them completely.

He saw the torn and tumbling branch too late before it struck. Dazed, the wheeling sky and waters became one, his limbs limp. Then he became aware of stones grazing his feet and, with a last effort, kicked out for the shore. Something slapped into the water by his head only to be whisked away by the fast-flowing water. It reappeared — a camel's lead — and this time Robert caught the end and let the animal take their weight.

Winded, Robert lay face down until the world stopped gyrating and he regained his breath. Pebbles skittered as reed-thin ankles appeared in front of him. Rolling over and shielding his eyes, Robert squinted at a figure outlined by the sun. The figure moved, and a tousled-headed boy grinned back at him.

"Adil? *Adil* Praise God you are safe!" Robert exclaimed, forgetting all lordliness; but Adil said something in a rattle of words, pointing.

Feet still caught by the water, Dodzi lay without moving. Robert crawled over and shook him. He tried again. Still nothing and, filled with a sudden rage, Robert curled his fist. "I do not give you permission to die!" he roared and smashed his knuckles into Dodzi's chest.

The man jerked, began to stir, then, as his eyes flickered, he coughed, ejecting the contents of the river onto the coarse stones. Regaining his breath, he leaned on one elbow and rubbed his chest. "That, my friend, is *only* time you beat Dodzi."

Clasping Dodzi's shoulder, Robert leaned his forehead against the other man's. "That, my friend, is the last time you give me reason to." He grinned. "Come, I said I would not let you drown, and I am a man of my word. And look who is here," he said, indicating behind him.

After a thorough inspection, Robert concluded Adil had escaped serious injury back at the Berber camp, although how was anybody's guess. He laid his hand on Adil's curls much as he would his own son. "You have done well," he said softly. "Your father would be proud of you. *I* am proud of you."

Adil beamed up at him. He took Robert's hand and led him to the camel and, reaching up, patted the brightly coloured camel bag. Robert peered inside.

"Hah! You bring us a camel, water *and* food!" he exclaimed. "We have Paradise right here; we need look no further. Will this animal carry all of us?" he asked, peeling off his soaked shirt and djellaba and standing in nothing but his saggy breeches.

Dodzi checked the contents of another bag without looking up. "Camel carry Dodzi and Adil — not O'bert." He stuck his head in the bag, rummaging deeper. "O'bert too big, too…" He bulged his stomach out. His shoulders began to shake.

"Do you say I am fat?" Robert said, indignantly, looking down at the undulating muscle of his hard stomach, and the rest of him, lean-legged and without flesh to spare. "Remind me not to rescue you from the flood next time."

Dodzi raised his head and roared, startling the camel. He wiped his eyes and stifled his laughter. "O'bert, there be no *next time.*"

Adil had been watching the empty lands. Now he came sliding down the rocky outcrop, talking excitedly. Dodzi listened and his face straightened.

"He say men not far, O'bert. We make haste."

CHAPTER TWENTY-EIGHT

"…and as such, cannot hope to gain the Kingdom of Heaven."

So small, so helpless — how could Isobel's daughter be denied eternal bliss when her only fault was to die at the moment of her birth, the cord wrapped so tight about her neck that she had not even taken breath before being deprived of it?

"My lady, do you understand?"

Isobel understood well enough. The priest was not an unkind man, but her daughter had been born so swiftly that there was no time to execute prayers for a safe delivery or tie the protective amulet around her thigh. None had attended the birth who could stand in the priest's stead, nor had he made it to her bedside to absolve the infant in her final distress and, for that, her baby stood condemned by the sin into which she had been delivered.

The heaviness around Isobel's bruised heart intensified, choking her, and she gasped back a sob. So much sin — her own, her mother's — too much. The priest was uttering prayers of absolution to which she was expected to respond, but there was nothing she could offer except her tears, and they were not for her own salvation.

She stood abruptly, feeling her ruptured flesh tear anew, and the priest stammered to a halt. "I thank you for your ministrations," Isobel said frozen-faced, "but I seek solace in rest and prayer. You may go."

He was a young man and inexperienced, what did he know of the world? Although, no doubt it was a sin to think in those terms. He had done his best in the circumstances, and it was not his fault that inside she wanted to berate him and reject the wisdom of the Church. Yet more sins to heap upon all the others she harboured in her leaden soul, neither shared at confession nor shed in repentance. She wanted to scream and rend her clothes, but years of learning responsibility and tact forbade such an excessive display that questioned her piety and her faith. She could mourn the loss of her baby, but only within the confines and dictates of Holy Church, for aught else smacked of uncertainty.

"Repent," the young man advised solemnly, "and seek absolution for your sins that your child's burden may be made light by the Grace of God and intercession of all the saints." He made the sign of the cross rapidly before she had a chance to respond and Isobel wondered what he saw in her that made him question her reverence. Did she care?

The priest left her feeling burdened with guilt. Was it her own recklessness that led to her baby's death or punishment for her doubt? Was it something she did, or something she didn't do? In her mind she recognised the fact that, of all the babies born into this world, many were taken from life at birth or soon after, but in her heart could not align reality with her own situation; this was her baby, *their* baby, and their babies didn't die.

A sudden thought swept ice through her veins: if this baby died, what protection could she expect for her other children?

The thought dogged her waking moments, and in sleep she dreamt of death even though she kept the precious amulet, gifted to her by her dead friend, beneath her pillow with her dagger. Her baby lay in a tiny lead casket awaiting the monument Isobel insisted on having erected to her memory. The thought of having nothing with which to mark her short life was unbearable, even if the mason she instructed with its creation tried hard — and failed — to disguise his reservations.

Her stone image would rest next her father's, and the judgement of the world be damned.

In the week that followed the birth Isobel had seen nothing of Cecily. The aftermath of the baby's death compounded their argument and magnified her grief. While Andrew and Juliana clung to her all the more, Isobel was acutely aware that the distance between herself and Cecily had become a chasm. She had doubly failed in her duty as a mother to her newborn and to her husband's niece, a girl she regarded as her own. And when, finally, Cecily requested that she return to Felice, Isobel relented with little more than a murmur of regret, for how could she deny the girl when she had so abjectly failed her?

The birth and Cecily's departure had all but obscured the nagging anxiety that the flight from Warwick had engendered, but now it resurfaced with a vengeance. Isobel saw shadows at every window, whispers behind closed doors. The children slept in her chamber and she ordered a watch placed at her door, only for her to dismiss the man in case he be the assassin she feared. Isobel took to guarding them herself, taking it in turns with Buena, and her threadbare mind knew only turmoil. But the sentient part of herself understood it could not continue.

The maids stood gawping as Isobel cast clothing into the mouths of trunks.

"But … my lady, so soon after your confinement?" Alice ventured. "What about your churching? Should you not wait—"

"And stay to be reminded every day of my loss? I have no peace here; I cannot breathe." Isobel exhaled slowly and said more measuredly. "Instead of standing there like gate posts, go to it and see our goods assembled. We leave at dawn."

The thought of her churching rubbed salt into an open wound. Was she to give thanks for her own life when her daughter lay rotting in the ground? Or was she to be cleansed until deemed fit to be among the living? As it was, she felt in limbo — widow of a dead husband, mother to a dead child. Would churching change any of that? She might as well defile the walls of Tickhill as sully the streets of London.

Truth was that the thought of the Duke of Clarence taking up residence again nearby sent shudders of alarm through her that only distance might allay. And the men seen skulking in the shifting dusk beyond the walls of Langton Place had done much to hasten her decision.

"Maintain the watch," she instructed the sergeant, and for the umpteenth time she wished Philip Taylor back from the dead. "And alert me should you see anyone loitering."

"Aye, m'lady, he were there right enough, he and another fellow, but they took heel when we approached and they be gone for now. There's nowt to say who's their master."

Their master? Wasn't that obvious? It hadn't occurred to her that anyone other than Clarence might post a watcher. Why would they?

They left in the soulless dawn of a frozen day, grey streets giving way to frosted wheel ruts and rimed imprints of shod horses that sparkled under the early sun. Even the wretches that normally begged for alms around the city gates had retreated to what warmth they could find. Limed catkins adorned hazel boughs along the way and, as the day warmed, the ground beneath the horses and carriage softened, releasing the scent of churned mud and excrement, from which Juliana screwed her nose in distaste and hid her face in Isobel's mantle.

Days later, Hyde's bent form hurried across the bailey at Tickhill to greet them. "My lady!" he exclaimed, bowing, as soon as the carriage door opened. "Forgive me for not preparing a suitable welcome, nor sending an escort to ease your way."

Isobel gathered her travelling cloak about her and took his proffered hand. "I did not wish to make my travel arrangements known."

"The household is not prepared. Madam, I fear your just displeasure."

She doubted that very much. Hyde's meticulous organisation meant the household would spring to life at his word and had probably already done so if the scurrying activity evident beyond him was anything to go by. As for her displeasure, she had neither the energy nor inclination to spend on it. "Have the constable wait on me," she said, flat voiced. She turned to look up at the great tower, luminous in the clear light, and heard Hyde's intake of breath. She wondered what he saw in her that caused him to show surprise. She didn't really care.

"My lady," he said, "pray allow me to send to the kitchens and have repast prepared for your comfort after such a long journey."

Ah, so she looked that bad, did she? So be it. He offered her his arm and she found herself grateful for it. The children had escaped Buena and the maids and now chased each other yelling and whooping and relieved to be free. They, at least, were glad to be back.

"My lady?" Hyde said again gently, looking concerned, and Isobel realised that her cheek was wet. She wiped it dry.

"A meal — thank you."

Bathed and in a change of clothes Isobel felt more able to govern herself. She had welcomed the hot sops, warmed ale, and dainty meats Hyde must have thought she needed to nourish her spirit as well as her body, and now he and the constable stood in front of her awaiting instruction.

"Place an extra watch on the gatehouse, keep the drawbridge raised and let no one in or out of the castle without first knowing their business. And if you suspect the intent of any, have them detained and question them yourself."

"We expect trouble, my lady? From what quarter?"

"From the Duke of Clarence and any associated with him."

Isobel caught the men's exchanged glances. They could think what they liked, but she knew better.

"Madam, I thought His Grace a friend to us —"

"He might be *your* friend, lord steward, but he is not mine," Isobel whipped. "His Grace has proved himself unworthy of such confidence. He betrayed my husband's trust; he betrayed me, and he…" She bit back the words and finished the sentence in her head, *betrayed his wife*. "Under no circumstance is the Duke of Clarence, members of his affinity, or any of his men allowed to enter this castle. Is that clear?" Then to Hyde specifically, "I wish to speak to Master Secretary."

Hyde hesitated. "Master Sawcliffe is not here, my lady."

"Well, where is he? Send for him."

"He sought employment elsewhere, having obtained Divine guidance at the abbey at Roche, or so I understand. He believed that my lady no longer needs, nor desires, his service."

Isobel's temper flared. "Now that Earl Robert is dead? *I* am the new earl's dam and *I* say who is to go and who is to stay and I did *not* give Master Sawcliffe leave to abandon his position here. With whom did he seek service?"

"Lord Howes, my lady, but the contract is not yet made as I hear it. Master Secretary was most insistent he enacted God's will."

The constable grunted and rolled his eyes and Isobel was inclined to agree with his cynicism. Hyde was a sensible man in most respects, but his plain and devout nature made him somewhat blind when it came to matters of faith and he had a tendency to accept, at face value, the devotion of others. Expedient or not, Nicolas Sawcliffe would answer to her and soon.

"I expected you to be here when I returned, Master Secretary," Isobel said without recourse to pleasantries one dismal afternoon when bare branches wept in the incessant rain.

Smelling of wet wool and cloves, and still damp from his journey, Sawcliffe bowed his head. "Madam, I feared you would not return."

"Why?"

"You were absent for so long and when I heard you were lodging with His Grace of Clarence, believed you had no further use for me."

"That was not your decision to make. You owe your allegiance to this family and this family alone. You have a new lord to serve in my son and I expect you to do so without question."

His eyes glimmered in the candlelight as he raised them to meet hers. "My lady, your pardon, but which one?"

Isobel governed her anger, but only just. "Let me make myself clear, Lord Andrew is the new earl —"

"Ah, forgive me once again for my presumption, madam, but that is not the case, is it?"

Had she heard correctly? Sawcliffe bore the irritatingly servile smile as always, but his eyes spoke of something different — cunning, knowing.

"After all," he continued, "in the absence of Lord Robert's will, may God grant him peace, we must assume Lord Robbie to be the rightful earl, must we not? As the late earl's firstborn son."

Irritated by his assumption of 'we', and rattled by his brazen reference to Andrew's bastardy, Isobel cautioned her growing impatience. She had to remember that, in the eyes of the world, Andrew was indeed a bastard. She needed time to think. She turned her back on the man and walked with measured step to the lord's chair, folded her skirts to one side, and sat bolt upright in what she hoped looked like a posture of authority. She stuck her chin out and peered down her nose for good measure.

"I, and I alone know my noble husband's will in this. It is a privy matter for the family and not for discussion by its servants." Nails rattled her impatience on the chair's wooden arms where once Robert had sat.

Sawcliffe spread his hands. "Madam, assuredly, but the law speaks differently and in the absence of a written, *witnessed* will... Well, I need not tell *you* how confused things become when lines of succession become ... blurred."

Stunned, Isobel stared at him. Was he *threatening* her? She had to find out or she would tear herself apart with worry. "Remind me, Master," she said as evenly as she could and meeting his gaze directly, "of what *confusion* do you speak?" She detected a change behind his eyes: he knew something all right, but was he certain of it?

"My lady, I merely refer to the recent disturbance this realm faced."

No, he didn't, and he knew she suspected to what he alluded. But he wouldn't say it; instead, he would leave it hanging as an indistinct threat, a noose to be wrapped around her neck upon which he could occasionally tug to remind her who was in control. What would Robert do in this circumstance? What would William have done?

Robert would put this man decidedly in his place, while William... Sawcliffe would never have dared step so out of line and it would not have occurred to William that he would do so. What did Sawcliffe want from her, to release him from service? Wasn't she once told — by William or Robert, she couldn't now remember — that they kept Sawcliffe close because of what he knew about the family, and that his lines of information proved too useful to lose? She would like to have the constable arrest him and see him hang in the bailey as a warning to others.

The image of Sawcliffe gently swinging came to mind and something must have shown on her face because he gave her a sharp look.

"My lady?" he queried. But the law was not on her side and she would abide by it as her father would have done. When it suited him. But nor would she be bullied by a subordinate as she once had been.

"Master Sawcliffe, return to your duties."

His smile slipped. He hadn't expected that. "But, madam, the earldom, the succession —"

"Is a matter for the king." Reducing her mouth to an immovable line, she averted her face, dismissing him. Inside she writhed in uncertainty. Could she trust him with whatever secrets he held? He could not be allowed to leave her household, that was for certain. An enemy identified is so much easier to deal with than an unknown. But who would watch the watcher? Whom could she trust?

Why did she think she could find peace here in the castle when she carried her demons with her in the shape of fear and memories? The garden offered some distraction, but even here thoughts plagued her. Kneeling on sacking and thrusting the small spade in and out of the softened earth, notions circulated, going around and around, unable to escape her mind like swirling water confined in a bowl. Shrill birdsong shattered the peace, worms writhed in the soil and her frantic thoughts stalked her waking moments. Some part of her knew them to be irrational, but her feelings overrode her mind.

At night she struggled to sleep, kept wakeful by her booming heartbeat. In the morning it was an effort to rouse and she often lay bound up in her bedclothes after a night of tossing and turning, finding some comfort in their tight restraint, then tearing them from her because they choked.

Day or night, so devoid of rest had she become that one morning Isobel stumbled and would have fallen had she not put out her hand to save herself. Buena dropped the linen she folded and ran to help Isobel where she had crashed to her knees at the foot of the painted screen in her chamber. Isobel rubbed the bruised side of her hand. "Perhaps," she said, looking at the fragile dusting of pigment left upon her skin, "it is better my baby girl was not born alive into this world. She is safer with God and He will be merciful, won't He?" She looked up at the great painted tree climbing the panels of the room, finding her own image, her husband's. Gently she touched her fingers to his face and then those of her children, finally resting them on the blank spot where her daughter would have been. "My babe," she whispered. "My sweet Isabella."

Buena placed her arms around Isobel, much as she did when Isobel was no more than a girl and innocent of the world.

"What would I do without you, Bayna?"

Buena kissed Isobel's hand and then observed her with shrewd eyes. She tucked a strand of hair from Isobel's face then with a wide movement, encompassed creation. Isobel followed the woman's gaze, seeing what she saw: the land beyond the uneven glass of the window all soft shades of green and brown, sky the colour of a dunnock's egg, and the grey-white of the cloud. A ribbon of black water marked the course of the river, the hard-edged rooftops in buff stone and new yellow thatch. Isobel saw, but she felt nothing. She shrugged.

Once again Buena indicated the world outside the walls, brought her clasped hands to her own bony chest as if holding something precious, then tapped Isobel's breastbone.

"Yes, all this, Bayna; but it is not mine, but my son's, *if* he is allowed to inherit it."

Drained, she sat on the low footstool by the fire. Moth sidled up to her expectantly and put her muzzle on Isobel's knees. "Bayna, I'm so tired. Clarence held us against my will once before, but I fear he might take what action he deems necessary to secure his revenge and my silence, and then what shall become of my children? I should have encouraged Lord Raseby, not sent him away."

Buena grunted and wobbled her cheeks and Isobel broke into a bleak smile.

"Yes, but Anthony Newton?"

Buena strutted a few steps and thrust her hips in a suggestive manner.

Isobel shook her head. "He reminded me of Thomas Lacey, so never *him*." She stroked Moth's head absentmindedly. "What now? Do we wait as we did when Thomas attacked us at Beaumancote?" But there would be no Robert to come to her aid this time, nor was her adversary a lordling flexing his muscles. "What choice do I have but to find another champion?"

Her new-made gown lay stretched across the bed to avoid crumpling the delicate fabric until it had been worn for its intended purpose. Felice leant forward and picked a stray silver hair from the garnet cloth and inspected it against the light. It was one of her own. She flicked it away. What did it matter now? She went to the nightstand and retrieved the beaker of wine she had been drinking when she received the news of Anthony Newton's death, and, with deliberate care, tipped it sideways. Expressionless, she watched the steady stream of liquid stain the gown the colour of dried blood. Removing the coif from her hair, she dug her fingers into its thickness and in short, vicious movements, tore chunks from her head.

"When?" Queen Elizabeth asked when she heard the news. Her groom bent close so that only she would be privy to the intelligence. "How?" she said. Her fair eyebrows shot into neat arches. "Well, well," she murmured to herself. In fleeing the wrath of a father whose daughter he had sought to corrupt, Newton's overly long and extravagant rowel spurs had become entangled. The resulting fall broke his neck and accomplished what the father had not. Lady Fortune had been busy again. What a pity; the young man had been a willing — and pliable — agent of her own design. Not the brightest, perhaps, but definitely ambitious and she could have fed that ambition to her own advantage. She tutted suddenly, frowning. Newton had been a tidy answer to the irksome question of what to do with Felice Langton. His unexpected and, quite frankly, careless death, revived that problem and she had expended enough of her time on the solution as it was. She doubted whether another such opportunity would present itself again to the aging widow and young son. Which brought her to another issue.

Robert Langton's widow was still unmatched. The queen had enjoyed the jousting between young Newton and Richard Raseby, but Newton had never been a serious candidate for Isobel Langton's hand. She knew the king favoured Raseby — the man had been loyal throughout the dark years after all and his generous hand kept Edward's purse full — but a marriage between the young widow and the old bull would arguably place her beyond the reach of Clarence.

Ah, brother Clarence, what mischief did he brew now? The Langton girl had proved useful in that respect. The loss of her child was regrettable, any mother would feel the same, but she could still breed other children with another husband. Wrinkling her nose as she thought, the queen weighed up the benefits against the potential disadvantages. Perhaps not immediately, but Isobel Langton might yet, however unwittingly, play her part.

Isobel woke in a sweat. Something had intruded upon her dream. She heard it again: shouting from the bailey below. She had thrust one arm into her over gown and stuffed her feet into her slippers when the door flew open and sudden light blinded her. Moth leapt from the bed barking wildly and Isobel made a grab under her pillow.

"My lady, the duke is come!"

"How many?" Lucie blinked stupidly at her question. "How many men with the duke? How are they armed?"

Lucie helped secure Isobel's gown around her, avoiding the dagger she now clutched in one hand. "Perhaps three score, my lady. Their arms... I do not know how they are armed." She looked helpless.

"Are our men arrayed, our walls defended? Where is the constable?" Isobel gritted her teeth. "For all the saints, girl! Do you know anything?" The dog was bouncing around the maid adding to the mayhem. "Moth, down!" Isobel snapped. Then, "Have Master Hyde fetched and then ensure the children are secured here in the tower. Do you understand?" she demanded when Lucie looked more confused than ever. "Have the steward brought here *now*!"

"But ...my lady, he is in the baily ... greeting the duke."

"I beg pardon for the early hour and regret being the cause of such alarm." Gloucester cast about the bailey and along the walls where soldiers were beginning to disperse from their posts. Keen-eyed, he looked again at Isobel, summing up her anxiety. "I was upon the road south when I thought to pay my respects. I lament not doing so sooner." Again, that enquiring glance.

"Your Grace is welcome to what poor comforts we may offer," Isobel said formally, adding in a rush, "I am much relieved it is Your Grace. I feared it was ... another."

"Whom were you expecting?" Gloucester asked as they entered the privacy of the council chamber. Removing his gloves, he refused the chair offered him but accepted the warmed, spiced ale. "I have been on the back of a horse for too many miles; I'll not sit awhile. Pray, lady, be seated; do not stand upon ceremony. So, whom did you expect?" he asked again. "Not a friend, it appears."

How much should she tell him, if anything at all? Did he really decide to visit on the spur of the moment or had he planned to all along? And why? What if he was in league with his older brother? What if, what if... She wanted to shake her head free of this fog that lay about it stopping her from thinking clearly. And she needed all her wits about her to keep up with the duke's questions. The less she said, the more he pressed, until her head felt fit to rupture.

"I thought Your Grace the Duke of Clarence," she blurted out.

"My brother?" Gloucester frowned. "Why need you to defend yourself against my brother?"

"Did Your Grace not receive my message? I sent it from Warwick before Christmastide."

"I did not."

She felt overwhelming relief that he was not part of all this, and found herself telling him things she had kept so long to herself, and other matters that perhaps would have been wiser not to reveal. As she spoke, he grew quieter, his demeanour more intense. His level gaze fixed on her face as she described the past months, her suspicion about Isabel of Clarence's death, the threat made to herself and her children, and the fear she still harboured. When she told him about being kept at Clarence's leisure in expectation she would sign away her rights to raise her own children, he narrowed his eyes. But as she outlined the facts surrounding Lady Isabel's death as she had witnessed them, his disquiet grew into disbelief, then clouded into outrage.

"Why did you not seek my help? I would have given you counsel and my protection."

"I did send a message — in a ball as a gift for Your Grace's son. I knew no other way to contact you that would escape detection. It seems I was wrong."

"A ball? I thank you for the notion of the gift for Edward, but it did not arrive as you intended."

"I am glad," she said, feeling it acutely. "I feared that Your Grace might ... I mean, that you..." She stumbled to a halt caught in her own confusion. She wanted to trust someone, trust *him*, but she had spent so many months in edgy watchfulness that she questioned her own judgement.

He came to sit beside her, looking earnest. "You have no reason to doubt my good lordship, nor will I give you one. I was deeply grieved to learn of Lord Robert's death. He was a true man and someone I trusted. I would not have allowed his widow and children to be so abused. I will not now."

Unable to respond, Isobel pinched the pad of her finger between her nails, squeezing and pushing at the welcome discomfort it caused.

Gloucester put his hand over hers, stilling the restless motion. "The moors and fells are very fine at this time of year when snow lies thickly upon them, but they are remote as you may remember — sometimes impassable — and few risk the journey. Perhaps you will do us the honour of residing a while at Middleham? My duchess would welcome your company and be grateful for any intelligence you might have of her sister. She mourns her loss; they were close as children."

The fells. Isobel recalled their wild beauty unfettered by convention. She remembered riding alone with Robert to the reeded banks of the stony river and there making love in the shelter of crabbed hawthorns. They had felt as unbound and reckless as the dragonflies darting about on rattling wings. Precious moments all but lost to her burdened memory. Now

Gloucester offered her safe haven, protected by his oath and the wild, wide land. She looked at him then, wandering if this was a velvet trap, but saw nothing but sincerity in his eyes.

As if he read her doubt, he said, "You will be free to come and go as you wish. Do you trust your people to maintain your estates in your absence?" She nodded. "Then my home is yours for as long as you care to stay."

PART SIX

CHAPTER TWENTY-NINE

Tamed by time, the torrents turned into rivulets then into pools in which tiny black creatures writhed and squirmed. The air became a frenzied mass of buzzing insects, biting and nipping the muzzle of the camel, swarming around the heads of Robert, Dodzi and Adil, catching in their hair.

Walking beside the camel, for the umpteenth time Robert swatted the creatures away only to have them return with vengeance. Every bare part of his skin was besieged, smattered with the blood of the slaughtered and the rising lumps where their enfilade had succeeded. Adil covered his head and crouched as low as he could against the camel's back, while Dodzi, riding with him, slapped the whining swarms, cursing them in his own tongue.

"This is intolerable," Robert said. "We must leave the river or be driven mad — if we're not eaten alive first." He spat an insect into the drying mud. Dodzi craned around behind them and into the distance as far as the twisting walls of the wadi allowed. Robert followed the line of his gaze. "It is a risk worth the taking. If they are still in pursuit they will also be hounded by these scavengers of Hell. You know these lands; can we traverse the higher ground?"

"I know only the river, O'bert." Dodzi probed the landscape before them. "We go there." He pointed to where a seasonal stream intersected the river, the sloped areas either side rising in broad, shallow steps towards higher ground.

Full of treachery, the pitted land forced them to stop as soon as the last light left the sky. They camped beneath an overhang of rock which afforded them some protection; but, without the warming effects of movement, nor the benefit of a fire, they shivered in the cloudless night. Sharing the remaining dry bread and dates, exhausted, they snatched sleep between incessant scratching.

"O'bert!"

Robert woke to the imperative in Dodzi's voice and shook sleep from his head. Dodzi canted his ear as if listening. Away from the dying riverbed, the air was free of the moaning insects. Instead, a steady breeze wove sighing among the rocks, carrying the sounds of shifting sand, the tumble of stones and chatter of invisible birds.

"What is it?"

"There!" Dodzi mouthed, and this time Robert caught the exhaled *whoosh* of an animal. Beside them, their camel chewed the air, seemingly unperturbed.

They crawled to the ledge and peered over the sheer drop. In single file, the swaying rumps of a handful of camels and their riders made their way along the skinny riverbed. The sun had not yet risen high and the ravine cast deep shadows, but here on the side of the sharp gradient, the light picked Robert and Dodzi out as clearly as a fire at night.

Robert pulled back from the precipice. "We cannot stay here."

They waited just long enough for the last of the camels to pass from view and then, gathering their few possessions, led their animal to the edge of the plateau. Dodzi gained his bearings. "We go that way," he said, his back to the sun as Robert mounted the camel and lifted Adil behind him. "Once there is village but no caravan pass now. No men. We go that way and come to the sea in three, four nights."

No longer shades of brown and gold, the landscape blazed in a haze of bright green spotted with points of vivid colour. It occurred to Robert that Isobel would want to know the name of every flower and the detail of their growth. He pushed the distraction aside. "We must risk travelling in daylight. There is little enough cover, but what we lose in concealment we gain in speed. Our water will last no more than two days if we ration it, but if we stay by the river, we will be either bitten to death or caught by Ahmad's guards. We can make the best speed in the open and hope to outrun them."

Dodzi might not comprehend everything Robert said, but he understood the urgency of it. With a click of his tongue, he pressed the animal into a rapid trot.

In the heat of the afternoon, the remains of the mud brick village looked to be nothing more than a tumble of rocks sitting in a wide dip in the uneven terrain. Shimmering air made all indistinct and they approached with caution. Dodzi slipped from the camel's back to scout the area while Robert used the additional height the animal afforded to spot any signs of danger.

The place seemed deserted, the remains of date palms and broad shrubby trees a hint of what might once have been. Collapsed roofs left the interiors open to the ravages of the desert and it had climbed inside the empty carcases. Narrow alleys, no more than a camel's width, led to the interior, where several buildings were still partially roofed. Dodzi joined Robert and Adil as they reconnoitred the most promising. Tufts of grey-green, low-growing plants invaded crevices in the walls, releasing an aromatic scent like thyme when crushed. Once inside, and finding the heat less intense, they dropped exhausted to the ground.

"Did you find a well?" Robert asked, arm flopped over his eyes.

"Yes, but little water. Perhaps … this much." Dodzi indicated a hand's depth.

Robert opened one eye. "Better than nowt," he said in a broad Yorkshire accent. The gnat bites itched and burned and he wanted to tear at them with his nails; but he had shunned his djellaba and hours under the fierce sun had left the skin of his neck and chest raw and he dared not scratch at it. "Damnable things. God alone knows why He created them for I do not." Restless, he climbed to his feet. "I'll fetch water and check our best defence should we be spied here." He turned around. "Adil, go… Where is he?"

"Adil bring…" Dodzi screwed his face, trying to find the word, gave up, and motioned instead.

"Wood — for fire?"

Dodzi nodded. "Yes, for fire."

Fire. The absence of one was made more profound by the promise of it. Despite the dying heat of the day, Robert shivered. He gathered the flasks and went back outside into the gathering cold of a desert dusk.

When he returned, pungent smoke filled the space, almost making him gag. "Sweet Heaven, what is that smell!" Holding his breath, he leant close to the new flames that tested the makeshift hearth in the middle of the floor. Dry, dun-brown nodes the size of goose eggs smouldered among blazing twigs, making his eyes water. "It smells like … gunpowder. Adil," he said to the boy, "is that what I think it is?"

Dodzi grinned. "Camel." He patted his behind. "Make good fire, no?"

Adil picked a camel turd from the pile he had ready to one side and offered it for Robert's inspection. Robert pulled a face and declined and the boy burst into peals of laughter.

"I thought we might chance a fire within the confines of this dwelling but, by all the saints, we'll be discovered by this reek!" Robert held his nose between finger and thumb and made such comical faces that Adil rolled from side to side, clutching his stomach. "Well, I am glad that someone is happy," Robert glowered, winking at Dodzi. He chucked him a flask and sat back to drink his own, allowing the water to drip onto his chest, splashing some over his arms to relieve the itching. "This village — do you know why it was abandoned?"

Dodzi wiped drops of water from his lips and shook his head. "In time of my father's father, caravans come from Sijilmasa, but the wells dry up; there no water for the palms."

"Yes, but there is water here now."

"Water, yes, but how long? Not long, not many time."

Robert considered the amount of rain that had fallen from the one storm and that the well was already almost dry. The villagers must have despaired as, year on year, they saw their crops struggle and their animals die. Water was life, worth more than gold. "I came across bones in some of the huts and near the well," he said. "People died here."

"Died, yes," Dodzi said, suddenly grim. "I think nômade — wandering men — come; they kill for water, for slaves. Nômade have no land, all land. They are *diabo*." He turned his head and spat.

"They come here now?" Robert asked.

"No water, no well, no nômade," Dodzi said simply.

"Still, it is a chance we better not take for any longer than necessary. We leave at first light."

*

Camel dung and palm leaves festered in the hearth, producing a thick smoke that coiled through the gaping hole in the roof. Humming to himself and rocking back and forth on his heels, Adil fanned the fresh flames. A shaft of sunlight illuminated the boy, reminding Robert of Andrew drawing words in thin snow. The sun would soon melt the snow and with it, his memory. The sun. He shot upright. The sun must be far above the horizon to make its way in here, and that smoke as certain a signal as a pennant to any close enough to see it. "Get up!" He nudged Dodzi's leg and started kicking dust to douse the fire as Adil scrambled out of the way. "We have slept over long."

Regarding them with doe-eyed disdain, the camel unfolded its long legs and reluctantly followed them into the walled enclosure set before the house where centuries of open hearths to one side had burned the stone pink. Pieces of charred wood were all that remained of the last fire. Robert bent down and ran his fingers through the ash and sand. "This was lit not long ago." He stood, looking around the rippled blown sands drifted against the walls. "And there," he said, pointing to the disturbed surface where indentations made their own little dunes. "Hoof marks?"

Dodzi inspected the area. "Camels and mens," he confirmed. "Many camels, many mens."

"Idiot! How did I miss the signs?" In admonishing himself for his lack of attention to their security, Robert then remembered their fatigue and the low light of the previous evening. "Perhaps they were part of a caravan," he suggested without conviction.

Dodzi's expression said it all. "We go now," he said, taking the camel's lead and checking their direction by the aspect of the sun.

At the edge of the village, they paused while Adil clambered to the top of a ruined wall to scan the surrounding land for signs of life other than the lizards he sent scurrying into the crevices. He called down.

"No men. We go," Dodzi translated.

Adil began to climb down but suddenly his body stiffened as he stared at something the men couldn't see, then he jumped the rest of the way, landing on the ground in a heap. He scrambled to his feet waving towards the north and, grabbing Robert's hand, began tugging him to the camel.

"Boy say men coming," Dodzi said.

"Ahmad's guards?"

"He say not, he say nômade."

"We go south," Robert said, hoisting Adil onto the animal's back, "and use the cover of the village to mask our retreat."

The village's rubbled remains had barely been lost to view when Dodzi spotted another group of camels and riders racing across the sands at an angle to them. At the same moment, a cry went up and the camels curved towards them. "Guards!" he cried in alarm. "Guards find us. We too heavy; not make speed to escape."

"They must have seen the smoke." Robert measured the distance between the rising clouds of orange dust as the guards thundered towards them. "We cannot hope to survive out here without protection; we must return to the village and fight."

"The nômade come to village," Dodzi said. "They come, O'bert, they find us!"

"I'm counting on it," Robert said, and urged their animal into a run back the way they had come.

Among the ruins, Dodzi backed the camel into a roofless building and gave Adil the reins with strict instructions and a warning to hide and not to leave the animal at all costs. He then joined Robert who had scouted the area and found a place that gave them a view of the way leading north and south while offering them cover. Disarmed by the river, all they had now to defend themselves was a knife and staff, and mercy was out of the question. Robert didn't rate their odds in an open fight, but here among the mud brick walls they had a chance.

A thin spiral of smoke from their night fire still rose from the centre of the village. "Look," Robert said in a low voice, nodding in its direction. A heavily garbed man, sword drawn, appeared briefly as he circumnavigated the building, then another and yet a third. "They expect to surprise us there. The others must be surrounding the house."

Loud voices declared the nômades had discovered the place to be empty, and they now spread out and began to search the area.

Dodzi pulled at Robert's sleeve. "They find us!" But Robert made no move to leave.

"Wait," he cautioned, craning to see above the broken parapet. "There!"

With their hooves raising a storm of dust, the camels with Ahmad's guards thundered into the village without slowing, hollering their strange-tongued cry.

"They think to flush us out." Clutching the knife and with a wild glint to his eyes, Robert grinned. "Stay here and be not afraid, my friend, for this is what I was born to do." He jumped, landing in the soft sand and haring towards the middle of the village shouting, "*Aloo, aloo, a York! A York!*"

He saw one of the nômade first, dodged sideways and came across one of Ahmad's guards still mounted on his camel. Robert darted into a narrow alley, through a tumbled wall, and out behind the animal. He whacked it on its rump with the flat of his hand and it leapt forward into the path of the nômade.

The desert-robed man yelled a warning to his companions and stabbed up at the guard who had just about regained his balance. The fracas spread like fire, igniting the tribesmen vastly outnumbering the guards.

Using the cover of the buildings, Robert legged it back to Dodzi. "Time to go," he said without halting to see if he was followed. They left at a run, leaving a confusion of harsh cries and steel rising through the dust cloud behind them.

It occurred to Robert as they rode north and west, that if they had not overslept and Adil not made smoke, the three of them would have been caught in the desert without shelter or the means to evade death or capture. "A miracle," he said, so softly that only the wind could hear, and then, "Amen," out loud, to which Adil chirped "A'min," and burst into laughter.

CHAPTER THIRTY

Isobel journeyed north in a waking dream accompanied by Gloucester's men. They took another route from the one she had travelled before with Robert and the air smelled different here. Light took on a thinner hue, and the remains of sparse plants growing among coarse weather-beaten grasses were unfamiliar. As the first flakes of snow began to fall she observed them with lacklustre eyes and wondered that she had ever been entranced by such things before. Here on the high moor, stunted trees grew warped by the wind, and in the lessening light of the gloaming, their twisted features looked like the fell mountain folk who stalked the villages at night to steal away stray children. Isobel hugged hers closer. Not long after, as snow began to gather in loose drifts, a dozen horsemen rode out to accompany them as they made the final leg of their journey to Middleham.

In the uneven light of the cressets illuminating the stair, Anne, Duchess of Gloucester braved the biting chill to greet them. "Come in and thaw yourselves," she urged as Isobel rose from her stiff curtsey. "There will be time enough for pleasantries. This cold will eat our bones."

Isobel followed her into a chamber heated by a lively fire and numerous stands in which candles glowed, dispelling the dark.

"It is warmest by the hearth," Anne continued, "but anything will be so after your journey, I think." She swivelled around and broke into a smile as she spotted the children hanging back. "Now, who do we have here?"

Isobel bent down to Andrew and whispered, "Remember what I taught you: do courtesy to Her Grace and be..." But

Andrew, needing no prompting, took a step forward and bowed. He straightened, chin up and proud, and Anne clapped her delight.

"Oh, what gallantry! Such a handsome boy. I believe he will win the hearts of many ladies one day. And who is this?" she asked, turning to his sister, who had somehow managed to envelop herself in Isobel's travelling cloak from where she peeked out.

"'Liana," she lisped, sucking her finger, her eyes still round and dark with recent sleep.

"This is Juliana," Isobel said. "Please forgive her lack of manners, Your Grace, she is a little quiet on first meeting."

"She is yet very young and the journey long." Lady Anne brought forth an embroidered purse and bent down to the girl. "Lady Juliana, I have confits in my purse, would you like one?"

The child nodded vigorously and Anne smiled at her enthusiasm. Isobel nudged her daughter.

"'T'ank you," Juliana said in a small voice.

"Children, now we are friends," Anne said, "I wish you to call me *tante*. Can you say that?"

"M-Madam la Grande Duchesse *Tante*," Andrew said with such gravity that Lady Anne laughed delightedly. He grinned up at her.

"It means *aunty*, my sweet," Isobel murmured to her daughter, and emboldened by the confit, Juliana said, "Tanty! Tanty! Tanty!"

"Juliana, no!" But Anne declared *tanty* be the most perfect word and from now on that is what she would be called.

"Come now, you must be weary. My noble husband sent word that you shall receive whatever you need for your comfort. The fires are lit in your chambers and the kitchens have prepared hot dishes to warm your stomachs. I know that

I am *always* hungry when I have been travelling." She stopped, looking suddenly concerned. "Lady Isobel, what is it, do you ail?"

Unable to speak, Isobel covered her face with her hands and Anne called out to an attendant, "Quick, quick, fetch the physician!"

Isobel shook her head and, wiping her face, managed, "I am quite well. Forgive me, Your Grace, I ... I..." She couldn't continue; she could not find the words to say how Anne's kindness touched her, how the normality of this situation was so far removed from the last months spent in anticipation of peril. Perhaps Anne understood, because she placed her arm around Isobel's shoulders and, beckoning to the attendants to follow, led her away from the curious eyes of the household.

Once in the privacy of the chamber set aside for her, Isobel allowed her cloak to be taken, her furred hood removed, and to be shown a chair beside a thriving fire. Finger by finger she removed her gloves, but it took an age and she tore them from her hands in weary exasperation. Anne sat opposite, looking concerned. Isobel felt she owed her an explanation; but how to express something that encompassed so much in so few words?

She didn't need to. Anne leaned forward and placed her small hand lightly on Isobel's. "You are quite safe here."

Isobel gave her a quick look, assessing her words but seeing only the warmth and candour in the younger woman's face.

"My noble lord forewarned me that you have endured much recently. I felt such loss for you when I learned that Lord Robert had been taken from this life." She crossed herself with her free hand. "I can imagine your grief; I remember when the Prince of Wales was killed at Tewkesbury," she flashed a glance, and Isobel gave a brief nod to show she recalled Anne's first husband and his violent end. "I thought my life over, that it could not be worse, but then when I went to live with my sister and her husband…" Her lips tightened. "George wanted me in a *nunnery*," she said, indignation bubbling through. "I was the widow of the Prince of Wales and he wanted rid of me!"

Her voice quietened. "My sister tried to protect me from his wrath, but George, well, you know what he is like, do you not? That is why you are here, to keep from him. My sister…" Anne's voice wavered as she looked directly at her, and Isobel read in the young woman's glistening eyes so many unanswered questions. Here, sitting in front of her, was the one person who had been closest to her sister at the time of her death. Did she want confirmation that what she had heard rumoured was true? If she did, Anne didn't ask directly but instead continued, "It was my noble lord who found me and you who helped him, do you remember?"

Isobel thought back to those early days of her own marriage, dim now and overlaid with layers of life.

"His Grace wishes you to feel safe — you and your children, as do I. You do feel safe here, do you not?" Anne asked anxiously.

Did she? Could she? "My Lady, I … do not know." Isobel sensed her eyes burning again and silently chastised her weakness. But she was so tired, bone-tired of always being on guard, of seeing greyness but never the sun, of this sorrow that weighed down her every day from the moment she woke to when her exhausted mind lost its grip on consciousness. She saw no future — not here, not at Tickhill, nowhere, and part of her wondered whether, if she slipped from this life, anybody would notice or even care. Everyone wanted something from her — Raseby and Newton, Clarence, the queen, perhaps this young duchess, even her own children — and she had nothing left to give. What they saw was a widow, land, information, a mother, but what was she other than a shell, empty and devoid of hope?

Anne drew back and whispered something to one of her ladies. "Lady Langton," she then said, firmly, "I have given instruction that the lords Andrew and Robert and Lady Juliana join my little Edward in the nursery. You, my lady, need rest." She stood up.

"No!" Isobel clasped Anne's arm in rising panic. "Please, no, do not take my children away from me!"

"*Away* from you?" Anne's voice softened. "My dear Isobel, of *course* they will not be removed from you. No more I would have my own sweet boy taken from me." She looked at Isobel's stark face. "Perhaps it is best they sleep with you tonight," she conceded, patting Isobel's arm. "Do not let your concerns burden you; the children will stay and I will ensure that you are not disturbed."

True to her word, Anne made certain that Isobel and the children were left alone. They kept that first night, with doors locked and shutters firmly closed, together in the canopied bed keeping each other warm. Isobel slept without dreaming, waking occasionally to see her children were safe and to check the whereabouts of the knife beneath her pillow.

After a week of watchfulness, when nothing untoward happened other than Robbie getting a splinter in his finger, Isobel relented and allowed the children to the visit the nursery with Buena to meet Lord Edward. Juliana was delighted. She bounced onto the bed where Isobel rested that afternoon, bubbling with excitement.

"He's *my* friend," she announced grandly, pointing at her own chest. "We played and he chased me and I chased him and I was a bear and I went growl, and he was a boar and he had tusks like this." She wiggled her fingers in front of her mouth. "Ama, can I play again? Please, Ama, please."

"I expect so," Isobel said. She knew that, despite everything, Juliana and Andrew had missed the company of Clarence's children. "Drew, did you play with Lord Edward?"

He sat next to his sister on the bed. "He is too little and I am too b-.big," he said with an earnestness that made Isobel's heart ache. "But the mistress of the nursery allowed me to look at Lord Edward's books, and I l-liked those. But," he said, pulling a face, "Robbie made me ashamed." He looked to where Robbie was trying to escape being changed into fresh linen by Lucie.

"Why?"

"He made a smell."

Juliana held her nose. "*Poff, poff, poff,*" she sang, upside down, kicking her legs. "Robbie made a smell. Didn't you, Robbie?" She twizzled over and pulled faces at her baby brother.

"It was *not* amusing, Liana," Andrew said.

"I am certain Lord Edward did not mind, Drew. It is in the nature of bairns to make smells. You used to not so long ago."

"I did not!" he exclaimed with all the indignation he could muster.

Juliana began to chant, "Drew did a smell, Drew did a sme—"

"Liana, I did not. Ama, I didn't!"

"Shh, all right, Drew, all right." Isobel placed her hands over her ears and squeezed her eyes shut against the rising tide of children's voices. Irritation surfaced with a snap. "Enough, Juliana. I said *enough!*"

The little girl rolled upright, pouting, and crossed her arms. Isobel regarded her warring offspring. It wasn't fair to expect them to be anything other than children. "I think," Isobel said, swinging her legs over the hard edge of the bed, "that I have spent long enough in this chamber. It is time we visited the garden."

Bundled against the cold they ventured outside. Her legs lead and her head empty — except for the mess of pottage that made simple thought impossible — Isobel pulled her hood over her face and kept a wary eye on the entrances to the pleasance as they passed each one. Finding a patch of sun, she took up position on a broad seat with the stone wall to her back and a clear view of the garden, while Juliana and Andrew ran off to explore under the watchful eye of the maids.

Carrying Robbie, Buena sat next to Isobel. She had refused to let her mistress from her sight since they had arrived at the castle and she, too, looked sallow beneath her ever-hued skin.

"Am I doing right by my children by being here?" Isobel asked, adjusting the dagger she kept hidden in the loose sleeve of her gown. "We are so far from home."

Buena grunted and deposited Robbie in Isobel's arms. Surprised, Isobel looked at her son and saw that, without her knowledge, he was no longer an infant. He pressed wet fingers against her mouth and chirruped. She felt her heart stir. "M'ama," he gurgled. "M'ama." She pressed her face into his wispy hair and he wound his chubby fingers into her veil, tugging with enthusiasm and, when thwarted, climbed down off her knees and toddled off across the thin snow after his brother and sister.

"Buena, go with them, I will tarry here. No, go, I will be right enough." She watched Robbie gather speed and confidence and then dared lean her head back against the wall, close her eyes, and imagined the weak sun warming her skin for the first time for many months. From somewhere nearby, a titmouse's *tsee-tsee-tsee* became a scolding *churr-churr*.

"There you are!"

Isobel looked up and saw Anne approaching with a small boy in tow.

"No, no, do not rise; let me sit with you awhile." Anne sat down next to her, all cheerfulness and smiles. "Look who is here, Tedward. Come and greet Lady Isobel."

The little boy of no more than perhaps three winters, his fine, fair hair curling around a sweet-natured face, dimpled as he smiled back at his mother.

"Tedward, say 'Greetings, Lady Langton'." Edward buried his face in his dam's skirt. "Oh dear, his noble father desires him to be well-mannered and I do try to encourage him, but he is rather timid."

"Lord Edward," Isobel said, dipping her head to see him, "what splendid boots you have." One eye peeped out and Isobel could see the beginnings of a smile and then he stamped his feet and stood up. "Yes, indeed, my lord, very fine boots."

He laughed, exposing a neat curve of tiny teeth.

Juliana came tearing up the path towards them, her own fangs bared, hands curled as talons. "Raaaaaaaaa!" she roared, making Edward jump.

"Liana, no!" Isobel said, but the boy was off after her, making his own animal noises and leaving his mother laughing and clapping her approval.

"Such a sweet girl!" she exclaimed, watching the children pounce and play in the snow, Juliana, now throwing handfuls into the air for Edward to catch, and then running off, neighing like a horse. "There," she turned to Isobel, "I knew they would be friends. Now, how do you fare?" she asked, taking on a more serious mien. "My noble husband will be returning soon and will want to hear of your progress."

"Is His Grace still from home?" Isobel said, surprised. She had spent so long in self-imposed exile that time itself appeared distant, everything remote, even her hands, held tightly in front of her, seemed to belong to someone else. "Your Grace, I must ask your forgiveness."

Robbie had returned and Anne was making faces to make him laugh. "Why? What is there to forgive?"

"Two things, Your Grace: my discourtesy, for I have not thanked you for your kindness, nor shown diligence as your guest. I have hidden away —"

"Fey-di-fey, what do I care about that! Although," Anne added, "I fain would hear what intelligence you have."

"About the Duchess of Clarence? Yes, that is where I have also failed." Isobel unhooked the bulky purse from her girdle that she had kept at her waist since leaving Tickhill. She slipped the gold toggle from its silken loop and turned the purse upside down, and the green stone beads slid into her open palm. She gave it to Anne who took it and held it in both hands. "And this, Your Grace." Isobel found the carefully harboured letter and gave it to the young duchess. "I should have given these to you when I arrived, for your noble sister entrusted me with them and I know that you were much on her mind in her last days."

Anne gave a small nod and swallowed. Isobel rose and, locating her children's voices, left the duchess to read her letter in the little patch of sunlight.

It had been late when Gloucester finally arrived home. Now bathed and supped and dressed in clean linen, he rested by the fire listening to the wind testing the shuttered windows. He imagined the fingers of air slipping through the cracks in the painted wood, bringing with it the scent of fell and river. He remembered being a boy at the castle, hearing the voices of the dales at night whispering and moaning when silence had at last fallen on the hushed halls. And later, when he first came to this place as its lord, those same voices had become the ghost of Warwick mocking and challenging his right to his daughter and his lands. Warwick no longer haunted his dreams nor stalked his waking hours, for he had been told exactly where he belonged and it was not here, it was not now. With wine cup resting on his chest, Gloucester reflected that much had changed since those early days as a young esquire, no more so than he had become lord of the Neville lands in the north.

He heard a soft sound behind him, breaking his reverie. From the relative darkness by the door, Anne tiptoed in slippered feet into the light of the fire. She perched on the edge of a cushioned chair before it, gathering her night gown away from the spiteful hearth.

"Wine for Her Grace," he said as the groom of the chamber hurried across.

"Did you find your journey comfortable, my lord?"

"Comfortable? No, but it passed and I am grateful to be home."

"Was your sojourn at Court … advantageous?" She appeared pleased with her choice of words because she gave a swift nod to herself making her look like a small mouse.

"If you mean will the acquisition of five new manors be of benefit to us, then yes, it was indeed *advantageous*."

"That is well," she said. "And is there any news from Court? How does the king?"

"My brother is in good health — as is the queen and all the princesses and the princes. I believe the lords and ladies who attend them also to be hale, as with the Lords Spiritual, clerks, the clergy, and their servants. What is it that you really wish to ask, Anne?" She blushed and wriggled her feet under her skirts, and he yielded a little. "Do you fare well? How is our son?"

Her face brightened, eyes shining. "Very well, my noble lord. Tedward — Edward — has grown so much since last you saw him and now talks away. You will be pleased. Oh! And he has new friends. Juliana and Andrew Langton," she clarified. "They are such poppets, especially little Liana — for that is what she is known by — and they play so well together. But you have met the Langton children before, have you not? I quite disremembered. Anyway, only today, when Lady Isobel and I were —"

"How does Lady Langton?"

Anne's face fell. "The melancholia has gripped her and she has oft been in her chamber and would only allow her servants to enter. But she has been better of late." Anne didn't seem very certain of that. "Lady Langton is very grateful to you, noble husband."

His finger stroking the side of the cup, he asked, "Has she said aught?" Anne looked puzzled. "With regard to your sister, may she find peace. I believe they were close friends."

"Only what Lady Langton told you. If you desire it, I can enquire further? If there's anything else I can do —"

"No, Anne, I thank you, but that will not be necessary." He let the back rail of his favourite chair take the weight of his head and closed his eyes. "You have done well to comfort her. Let the lady rest and find what succour she can." An image of Isobel Langton, distressed, beleaguered, imposed itself on his memory. "Yes, indeed, she has been ill-used by my brother and we will make amends."

CHAPTER THIRTY-ONE

The warming sun brought Isobel out into the garden again like an insect detecting pollen. The walls surrounding it made her feel more secure and, now that she had become familiar with its configuration, she could spend time here knowing she could flee to safety in only a matter of steps. She became aware of her shallow, tight breaths and consciously let her shoulders drop to allow more clean, clear air fill her lungs. It made her dizzy.

She found the stone bench and sat on the cold, roughened surface with her fingers gripping the edge — a new-born sensation of which she had not been aware before. Where had she been these last weeks? Wrapped up in her world of fear and misery, she concluded. Yet this had been here all along, and her children, had they been here too, growing and living despite everything, despite her neglect?

The first signs of a change in season lay in the naked vines clambering overhead and new buds beginning to swell. Allees and arbours, paths and beds provided the structure within which nature had been captured and laid out for all to admire. Isobel could see it, but the cobwebs in her mind prevented her from thinking and feeling. Reaching within, she battled the fine silk strands, tearing herself free of the sticky threads. But on liberating herself, she awoke to find herself facing a thicket of thorns that was pain and despair.

"It will take time."

Isobel jumped to her feet. Startled, she didn't answer as Gloucester sat down and bid her sit beside him.

"I did not mean to frighten you. I thought you had seen me."

She shook her head and stumbled an apology. "Time, Your Grace?"

"The garden — it will take time to grow into itself, or so I am assured. It has changed since you saw it last; what do you say?"

She looked at it blankly then saw the raw edges of new-planted beds, immature shoots, unblemished urns. "Yes, Your Grace; time will allow it to flourish."

"And soften, I think. The pair of urns are from Florence — the finest marble, exquisite workmanship — but they lack something. I could not make it out at first, but then I thought that perhaps it is because they are new-made and, like so much that is recent, they are too harsh." He examined them thoughtfully. "Time will blunt their sharp lines and diminish their bleak facades, as it does with us all." He shifted his gaze to meet hers.

"I wish it were so."

"It will be," he said quietly. He stood again, stretching his arms in front of him. "I was in the saddle too long the other day and need to move. My lady, will you keep me company?"

They walked down the paths, Gloucester occasionally stopping to ask her the name of a plant she thought he probably already knew. At an intersection where the paths met at a raised pool shaped as a quatrefoil, he came to a standstill once again. Water fell into the pool from a lipped fountain fed by a water course. Gloucester let the water run glistening through his fingers, the ripples catching the light.

"Water never ceases to amuse me; it is always changing. Brr, but this is cold!"

Isobel touched the current, felt it weave around her fingers.

Gloucester shook the water from his hand and offered her his clean kerchief to dry hers. "I have been at Court of late. His

Grace the King made mention of you." She stiffened, waiting. "His Highness is grateful for the intelligence you furnished, my lady, and the spirit in which it was gathered. He is also cognisant of the unjust manner in which you were held, the lawfulness of which is … questionable. The rule of law is of grave concern to the king no matter whom it involves." He paused and Isobel thought it was probably so that she could take in what he had said; but she didn't need time — she understood precisely.

"His Grace also believes it is in your best interests to make a marriage that will furnish you with the guidance and protection of a husband. While there is wisdom in such counsel, I advised that I thought you unwilling to make such a match at this time, given your recent bereavement and the treatment you received at the hands of our brother."

"I thank Your Grace for your agency," Isobel breathed, her jittery pulse settling.

"But I am minded to recommend that you consider a match, forasmuch as I understand your delicacy over this matter, while Robbie is a minor and you without the surety of a husband, your state is precarious, Isobel. There is no guarantee of your safety and that no move will be made against you when you return to your own estates."

"The Duke of Clarence?" she asked, bleakly.

"He has lodged a petition based upon a letter of testament he claims bears Earl Robert's signature. You are aware of such a document?" he asked when Isobel bowed her head, biting her lip. She nodded. "I do not wish to cause alarm, but believe me, my brother will pursue what he deems is his by right and I cannot protect you should the law be judged in his favour."

"But the king vouchsafed his protection, Your Grace!"

"The king was not aware of your husband's wishes, nor that any such bond of friendship existed between them. Nor was I," he added.

"It didn't. Robert felt gratitude towards His Grace of Clarence, but it was no more than that. He left in haste, and had he time to consider, I am certain would have acted differently. Robert did not expect to die," she said softly. "He thought he would return."

"And he left no will?" Gloucester asked.

"No."

"Then I say again, consider your options, because if you remarry, my brother will have no claim upon you or your children."

"But my ... husband would," Isobel said, hating the disloyalty of the word as she said it. "My children — Robert's children — will be subject to another man's will."

"Marriage is a contract between two people; as such you can, within reason, come to an agreement with your spouse that, while your son is in his minority, the person most fit to oversee his education until he enters a noble household to continue it, is the one who knows and cares for him best. You."

"An agreement bound and protected by law, Your Grace?"

"I admit, it would be difficult to make such a settlement binding, and hence the nature of the man must be such that he honours your wishes."

An acrid laugh escaped before Isobel could stop it. "Does such exist?"

Gloucester took a moment in which Isobel wondered whether she had overstepped her right to such honest opinion; but his expression eased. "Indeed, for Earl Robert was one such man, was he not? And where there is one, there may be others. I do not say it is easy, for how can you replace someone

469

so beloved? Nor are you doing so, but are looking instead to secure your safety and that of your children in such a way as to ensure the *potential* for happiness."

A compromise? She regarded the ring Robert had given to her on their marriage, the blue stone catching the light, and wondered whether she could ever forgive herself for betraying his memory by marrying another man. Then she thought of the Duke of Clarence's festering anger and veiled eyes. "A compromise," she conceded.

"Attacop, attacop, spin me a web!" Anne sang, holding little Edward by one hand and Juliana by another, as together they danced in a circle while Andrew did his best to clap time. Spotting his father, Edward broke away and ran towards him. He tripped over, landing with a bump, and Gloucester swung his son high into the air, kissing him as he brought him securely into his arms. "How fare you, my son?" he asked and Edward threw his arms around his father's neck.

Anne rushed up to them. "Oh! Are you hurt, my poppet? Let me look at you."

"You have not taken injury, have you?" Gloucester asked the boy. "There, no harm done. Edward, are these your friends?"

Finger in his mouth, the child looked at Andrew and Juliana with large eyes and nodded. "'Liana," he said, pointing a wet finger at the girl and wriggling.

Gloucester raised an eyebrow at Isobel and she offered a smile in reply. She gave a slight frown at Andrew. He took the hint.

"Your Grace, I am at your s-service." He bowed in his most courtly way.

Gloucester's eyes laughed, but he kept a straight face. "And willingly I accept it, Lord Andrew. What nature of service might this be?"

Pulling his brows together, Andrew thought. "I, um, I can ... fight, Your Grace."

"Can you now? Well, that is of great service indeed! And what is your weapon of choice, my lord?"

This required more consideration, then, "I can fight with a s-sword like my papa." He swished his arms about in imitation of swordplay, nearly hitting his sister in the process. She punched him on the arm. "Ow! Liana!" he protested, pushing her back. "That hurt." She stuck her tongue out at him. Edward gave a squeal of laughter and she giggled.

Gloucester regarded the pair, his eyes slightly narrowed. "My lord Andrew, a knight must fight with skill and valour, but he must temper his warlike nature with faith, honesty, humility, and chivalry — especially towards those who look to him for protection. Only then can he be called a great knight and worthy of the praise and admiration of men. Being the superior, you are bound to your sister to keep her from harm, which includes refraining from pushing her, when, no doubt, she deserves it."

There, that humour Isobel had detected before.

Andrew looked suitably thoughtful, and Gloucester turned his attention to Juliana, who was making faces at her brother's back. "And this must be the Lady Juliana. How now, my lady? You were but a child when last we met. Anne tells me that you are a good friend to our son, Edward."

Juliana stopped gurning and instead twirled on the spot and flapped her skirts. "Yes." She did a little jump. *Your Grace*, Isobel mouthed from behind Gloucester. "Your *Face*," Juliana pipped. There was a sharp intake of breath from Anne as Isobel died a little inside. She reddened.

"Your Grace, your pardon, Juliana will be rebuked for her discourtesy —"

"It seems, Lady Langton," Gloucester interjected, "that just punishment is required." He bent down, picked Juliana up and tucked her under his arm.

Isobel reached out for her. "Please, Your Grace!"

"My noble lord!" Anne cried, "Surely…"

"Nay, ladies, some slights cannot be overlooked." With his son under one arm and Juliana under the other, he marched away with the children kicking and writhing, their dams hurrying after.

Andrew followed at a trot. "Your Grace," he called, "Juliana is but a g-girl and she has childish ways. Please forgive her and punish m-me instead. I am her superior and must take the rebuke."

Gloucester stopped by the fountain and turned to face him, astonished. "Well, my Lord Langton, what chivalry is this? Here, I have a child who needs be taught her manners and yet, before me stands her brother, who has learned his and is gallantry personified. What am I to do?"

Isobel swore he winked at her as he turned and plopped Juliana in the water. The girl sat there, stock-still, her mouth rounded in an 'o'. Then she let out a squeal, tried to stand, gave up, and sat in the pool pouting with her clothes and hair sticking to her limply.

"Now, my lady, who am I?" Gloucester asked, and Isobel saw the naughty glint return to her daughter's eyes.

"Juliana," she warned.

The girl wrinkled her nose. "Your. GRACE," she said, and brought both arms down on the water, sending droplets shimmering in an arc towards him.

"I see," he said slowly, brushing the fragments of water from his clothes with his spare hand while Edward giggled and attempted to escape. "And you, my son, had better learn the lesson ere it is needed." He dunked Edward into the water next to her.

Edward looked at his father, deliberating whether it was worth crying or not, decided it probably wasn't, and began hitting the water instead.

"Have a care! Tedward, do not do that! Oh, you will take cold!" Anne tried to lift her son from the pool but succeeded only in becoming soaked as he escaped her arms and crawled to the other side through the fall of water to continue the game. "Edward! Juliana! Come here!" She looked to her husband to instil some discipline, but he was watching the children, arms folded and grinning broadly, so she turned to Isobel for help.

But Isobel was standing, both hands over her face and with her shoulders shaking, making strange whooping noises as she fought for air. Anne forgot the mayhem behind her. "What is it? Isobel, what is the matter?" she said, putting an arm around Isobel's shoulders.

Isobel shook her head, removed her hands and, with tears streaming down her face, managed to control her laughter.

"You will *not* do that again," Isobel cautioned her daughter as she and Edward were dried and dressed by the nursery fire. "Juliana, I do not jest; you cannot say things like that to anybody, but especially not to His Grace."

Juliana began to shake her head and Andrew bent down to look her in the eyes.

"Liana, Ama is right, His Grace is very important. He is the king's brother." Juliana looked as if she neither knew nor cared. Andrew tried again. "Liana, do you remember when we were in the garden with Lady Margaret? Do you remember what happened when the pot fell over?"

Juliana's impish smile vanished and a shadow enveloped her eyes. Her fingers went to her mouth and she nodded. "He was angry," she said in a little voice.

"Yes, he was, and His Grace of Clarence is also the king's brother. You do not want to make His Grace of Gloucester angry like that, d-do you?" She shook her head gravely. "Then promise me you will be good and obedient and do courtesy to His Grace and to Her Grace as well. Promise?"

"Yes," she whispered.

"Ama, Juliana has given her word that she will be good and I know that she will be."

Isobel looked at her son and saw the man in him, so like his father. She parted his hair from his eyes. "When did my little Drew grow up?" she said.

"I am not a boy anymore, Ama. And I wish to be called Andrew."

One morning Isobel awoke to the caw of crows and a rattling of claws upon stone. She opened the shutter and birds rose arguing into the air. The hour was early, the sun not yet warm, but the air from the fells was fragrant and the castle went purposefully about its day as witnessed by the crowns of heads that passed to and fro far beneath her window. This morning was a bright morning. Today, she realised with a jolt, began with hope.

She went, as she always did, to the nursery to collect her children to make their private devotions as a family. Juliana and Edward were playing pat-a-cake, Robbie ran in circles as fast as he could to escape Lucie's ministrations, but of Andrew there was no sight.

"He left with one of His Grace's pages, my lady," Alice told her, taking Juliana's comb from its case. "But not long since."

The sense of peace evaporated as Isobel negotiated the stairs, the nagging anxiety returning with every step. Andrew should not have left the nursery without her permission. He might be anywhere, with anyone, doing anything. He thought he was grown, but he wasn't; he was still a child and the sooner he accepted that the better, before anything happened beyond her control. She picked out the *tang ting* of metal against metal, the grunt of effort, the shouted commands, and all but ran outside feeling the months of inactivity weighing her legs.

The practice yard took up most of the area. Bizarre structures of wood and canvas dotted the space at which youths of varying ages took turns to compete for skills at arms. On one side, two young men wielding swords circled each other, trying to find an advantage, and there, watching alongside Gloucester, was her son. Isobel stopped short. Gloucester was explaining something and Andrew listened, then, taking a step back, imitated the movement he was shown. Gloucester made a comment and Andrew's face expanded into a broad beam. Isobel hadn't seen a reaction like that for, oh, so long: unfettered joy — no, not joy so much as *achievement*.

She hung back as Gloucester demonstrated another move then watched intently as Andrew attempted the same. Gloucester adjusted the boy's stance and Andrew tried again, this time earning a nod of approval. Before her eyes, Andrew grew with the praise. She left them to it and walked back the way she had come with a mixed sense of pride and purposelessness, as if that part of her son had moved on, moved away.

Later, Gloucester bid her join him. He was not there when she entered the room he used as his privy chamber for matters of estate. She hovered near a table neatly laden with scrolls and unfolded documents, several feather pens, ink in a pot, fine sand in a glass. A book lay open on a shaped cushion to one side, the pages weighted with silk ribbon from which onyx stones hung.

Directly in front of Gloucester's empty chair, parchment lay ready for his use. Books were everywhere: on shelves and stands, on a small table by the lit fire under its canopied hood, on the side of a reading table across which a large map lay. Light from the window illuminated brightly coloured rugs on the floor, and picked out the gilded ball flowers of the blue and red panelled ceiling on which white roses displayed. She waited and, when no one appeared, arched her neck to see what Gloucester had been reading. *A Mirror For Princes*. A small carved piece of wood sat next to the book, and a single-bladed knife.

Curiosity getting the better of her, she picked up the object and examined it. A partially formed bear emerged from the wood, its mouth agape, one paw raised and ready to strike. She smiled.

"It is for my son," Gloucester said, joining her. "A plaything — with a purpose." He didn't say what that purpose might be. He took the bear and measured it by eye. "It requires more work and a better hand than mine." He replaced it on the table. "I thank you for attending me; forgive me for keeping you waiting." He indicated a chair and sat in his own. "I understand from your son that he has not yet been placed in a household. Have you given consideration to his future?"

Isobel gave a single shake of her head, curious where this was leading.

"Andrew is a fine boy — diligent, intelligent, and with the potential to make a good soldier. He is of an age where he will learn quickly. This is important. I have seen too many who, without guidance, become wayward and difficult, learning faults both of character and practice that are hard to undo."

"I will guide him as I have always done, Your Grace. I teach and direct him in matters of learning and conduct."

"Yes, and it is to your credit that he has knowledge beyond his years and conduct befitting his station. But he will not be a child for much longer. If God wills it, Andrew will grow into a young man and will require the direction offered by those trained in the art of war and leadership. In such a place, he will also have the influence of his peers and the advantage of being raised in a great household."

He was right, she knew it; Drew needed the guidance of a man in a man's world, but whom could she trust when she sometimes couldn't trust herself?

Gloucester continued. "You told me once that my brother Clarence was prepared to offer Andrew a place in his household, is that correct? And you rejected it because of all the reasons you gave when last we spoke." He leaned forwards, his arms resting on the table, his hands open towards her as if he wanted her to accept what he had to say. "I am not my brother, my lady, and Andrew will need a preferment when he is older. A young man in his position —"

Her head snapped up. "His *position*?"

"Yes." He leaned back, frowning now. "He will have to make his way in life as any young man in his situation."

"Your Grace, Drew has his position, he…"

"He…?" Gloucester prompted, but when she didn't respond, said, "I wish to offer Andrew a place in my household with a view to becoming an esquire. My own son — John — has such a placement, and he is no less beloved for his bastardy. There is no shame in it."

Heat rushed in a wave up her neck. "I am *not* ashamed of my son! Bastard or no, he is every bit my son, *our* son, and he will have his inheritance."

Gloucester kept his voice level. "I cast no judgement on his parentage, the circumstances of which I am privy to as much as any man; but Lord Robert would wish to see the earldom passed to a child of his own loins as the law directs." He paused. "I understand if, through your natural feelings for your son and his father, you would see Andrew raised to the peerage, for Earl William was esteemed the best of men; but if feelings were all that determined our actions, misrule would hold sway and where would it end? The law is there to protect good governance, and the law of inheritance resolves such issues as arise here. Robbie is as much your son; would you see him disinherited in favour of Andrew?"

She saw how this must seem to Gloucester, as it did to everyone who cared to comment on it, and it made her all the more protective. She wanted to say 'yes' but then that might lead to a whole other problem. And if she told Gloucester her secret — something she had never done before — would that change anything? After all, whatever his parentage, Andrew had been born out of wedlock and that would reflect on not only her own virtue, but Robert's honour as well, and that was something she could never do now that he was no longer alive to defend it.

Gloucester was waiting with that intense look he always adopted when something of great importance needed to be understood — his head set slightly forward, his observant eyes focused and unblinking. She wanted to share the burden of truth she carried and this might be the very man she could trust; but not now, not yet, not when so much was at stake.

She gathered her words and ushered them into line. "Your Grace, I thank you for the charity you have shown us and for your good lordship, but Drew is not yet ready to leave his family."

Gloucester sat back in his chair, fingers interlinked on his chest, regarding her with an expression she found hard to interpret. "So be it," he said, rising and obliging her to do so. "In the meantime, while you are my guests here, it would please me to have Andrew join my pages and attend their lessons. Will you allow it?"

Isobel evoked her son's eager face as he learned a new move. She would not deny him the opportunity to experience that again, so she bowed her head in acquiescence. "If it please Your Grace, I will."

"One other thing," he said, as if reluctant. "This arrived yestereve. I would have given it to you then, but did not want to disturb your rest."

Isobel took the letter with its prominent seal begging her attention.

"The messenger was instructed to wait upon an answer," he said, and when she merely nodded, prompted, "will you not open it? Here." He fetched a thin blade, heated it for a moment in the hearth, and gave it to her, handle first. "Whatever it contains, news is best confronted lest it fester."

She turned the letter over, slipped the warmed blade beneath the seal, and began to read the eager message it conveyed.

CHAPTER THIRTY-TWO

With the changing season came a return of the heat. Between the canyons of rock, the temperature became so intense that Robert and Dodzi abandoned the gully floor and sought what relief they might in the breeze that flowed along the higher land. The seasonal waters had long since dried and with it the determined insects. They returned to walking through the night until dawn, except where the terrain became so unreliable that they resorted to the stifling heat and shadows of the valley once again. Food had run out, the tepid water in their flasks low, and Dodzi ventured to the sparsely populated villages in search of supplies. He returned one evening laden with food and news.

"They think I make *haj* to Sijilmasa so make gift of food." He grinned, squatting next to Robert and doling out his treasure of flat bread and dates, wilted green leaves and small lidded baskets of spiced, coarse-grained wheat. "I did not tell them truth." He scooped up a handful of sand and rubbed his hands clean.

His head throbbing, Robert gratefully accepted the flask. "I am thankful and would that I were able to repay their generosity when they have so little to spare. Did you learn how far it is to the coast?" Adil was eying the food with a hunger usually reserved for adolescent boys. "Eat," Robert said to him, then, "How far?"

"We come to the sea at full moon."

Robert lay back against the rock. "So long?"

Dodzi shrugged. "We come south," he said, indicating the first stars as they appeared in the evening sky. "It make longer walk."

"It cannot be helped." Robert stretched aching limbs. "It was either go south or risk running into tribesmen again. It was a miracle we escaped last time; I would not test God's forbearance the next." He rubbed his wrist where the joint twinged and with resignation stood up. His head swam momentarily and he put out a hand to steady himself until it cleared. "Too much sun," he murmured.

"You not eat?" Dodzi said, offering him one of the woven baskets.

"I am not hungry and we must make what distance we can while the heat is from the land." His face felt puffy and scorched and he welcomed the thought of cool air on his skin.

Wrapped against the cold desert night and navigating by the stars, they travelled along the smoother ground left by the floods. Robert tried to calculate the number of days before they had sight of the coast, but the numbers kept shifting, and he gave up. They took turns in walking to save the camel. Robert's limbs grew heavier by the mile and he longed for the touch of the sea. He threw his make-shift cloak from his shoulders.

Dodzi called down to him. "O'bert, what you do?"

"The walking makes me hot."

"You ride now?"

It was tempting. Niggling aches lodged in his lower back and his head pounded with each step. But the camel was hot; he could feel the heat emanating from its tatty coat and its stinking breath turned his stomach. "My thanks," he said, "but I'll walk."

By the time the sun rose enough to become unbearable, Robert walked half asleep, his shoddy steps uncertain so that, now and again, he stumbled. Dodzi reined the camel in under the shadow of a bluff. "O'bert, we stop now." The animal knelt and he slid from its back and, extending his arms above his head, shook his shoulders free of fatigue. Whorls of dust materialised across the sun-baked surface. "O'bert!" Dodzi called out as Robert continued towards the ocean lying far over the horizon. "We rest."

Adil bounced off the camel and ran after him.

Heat shimmered in waves and the light hurt Robert's eyes. Features in the landscape blurred and he couldn't tell whether it was his sight that dimmed or the fabric of the desert. And the pain in his head was expanding, filling the cavity until it threatened to burst. His arm shook loosely in its socket, and a child's voice was saying something that rattled between his ears, jabbing and jarring as he pulled at Robert's hand.

"Drew, let go," Robert murmured. He heard footsteps behind him. "Isobel?" He tried to turn but one foot remained stubbornly rooted, catching on the other as he twisted to see. He lost balance, toppling sideways, and landed with a heavy thud on the ground. It was too much effort to move and he stretched out his hand towards her. "Is'bel, the sea." But she vanished in the wisp of dancing dust and he grasped nothing but sand.

The sand rocked, swayed, jolted, and Robert with it. The chaotic motion seemed to last forever until it was replaced by a wallowing, a sinking sensation, then stillness. Something touched his cheek. Robert tried to lift his arm but couldn't find it and let out a moan of frustration. The tickling set up again, moving towards his mouth. The air shifted in a sudden waft and the tickling stopped to be replaced by a low *zzzzz* that rose and faded along with Robert's momentary consciousness.

Ice seeped into his bones and he ached with it. He attempted to wrap his arms around himself, but his limbs wouldn't obey, instead shaking uncontrollably and making his teeth rattle like loose stones in his skull. Incessant cold radiated from inside until his whole existence became pain, and he slipped again into oblivion.

He wished he remained there for as he rose from that place of nothingness, he entered a state of flame. Fire crept, licking and exploring his searing skin, filling his lungs. He fought for breath, to free himself from the heat, to rise from this hell and seek free air; but his body remained pinned and demonic voices jabbered around him. In attempting to open his eyes, he met nothing but darkness, and the darkness wept.

At some point of clarity, Robert moved his fingers, feeling cloth, becoming aware of pressure under his back and beneath his heels. Far-away voices filtered into his consciousness, becoming louder, insistent, and then, abruptly, a solid shape appeared, blocking the light. Robert tried to cry out but succeeded only in releasing a croak as he scrabbled to escape the fiendish figure bearing down on him. It towered, an unwieldy monster of great proportion, shrouded in shadow and head enveloped so only its eyes gleamed from the depths. In his terror, Robert found his voice, thrusting out his arm in a feeble attempt to save himself. "Sweet Jesu! Be gone, foul creature!"

The figure loomed closer. "Eh, I don't know about that, my lord, but I'm here right 'nough." The demon unwound the mass of cloth covering its face, revealing unmistakable fissured features and shrewd blue eyes. "Your pardon if I gave fright, my lord," Philip Taylor said, "but these here winding sheets do nowt for my aspect." He shook the cloth, releasing clouds of fine red dust from the folds. "Though you'll excuse my bluntness if I say that your own'll give cause for alarm among maids, mark my words." Taylor bent closer with his meaty hands spread on his knees and peered at Robert.

"You drowned." Robert closed his eyes and, shaking his head, attempted to free it of the apparition. On opening them again the image remained, swimming unsteadily before him. "You are not corporeal… You're dead."

"Not when I last looked." Taylor slapped the side of his face and pinched his cheek. "Aye, still here and breathing, my lord, though some'll say that's more the pity. Here." He held out his hand, concern clouding his face when Robert shied from it. He placed his big paw gently on Robert's shoulder. He turned his head as someone entered the room. "I reckon my lord's still gripped by ague." He stood up and was replaced by Dodzi carrying a bowl. He put it to Robert's lips.

"Drink, O'bert, it help you."

Robert stayed Dodzi's hand. "Am I dead? Is this Hell?"

"No, O'bert," Dodzi said. "This is Agadir. God is good, my friend." Dodzi beamed. "You live."

Over days Robert's limbs became his own again, heavy at first, but increasingly responding to his commands. Water need no longer be dripped into his mouth and he could sip without spilling much. Some people he recognised — Dodzi, Taylor, Adil — others were strangers, but mostly he was left alone to sleep or to listen to the world taking shape outside the room with its beaten mud floor in which he found himself. Shrieking demons had dissolved into the cries of seabirds; clattering bones became wind-blown stems tumbling across nearby open ground; braying no longer mocked him, but grew into the eager declaration of donkeys awaiting food. He regained his other senses, too, his stomach turning at the oily reek of fish and pungent dung, the sweat on his own body, and the fresh, light fragrance of the sea.

The sea. He could make out its steady suck and surge upon the shore, and he longed for sight of it.

Small waves, as white as fresh snow, broke the surface of the restless sea. From where Robert sat on the outcrop overlooking the crook of the bay, he could make out fishing craft from which men cast nets into the ink-dark ocean. Mews darted and dived around the vessels or bobbed in the choppy water. Larger ships nodded at anchor — Portuguese carracks making port in the bay. Occasionally he heard a shouted order or the crack of canvas.

As he watched, a bedraggled group of bewildered people were herded over the disturbed sand towards a boat waiting in the shallows. Already he had seen other such human merchandise loaded onto ships bound for the northern countries. Robert recognised them for what he had been: he smelled their fear, divined their despair, but cast his eyes south, away from their misery in case it infected what little sense of peace he had found here. It remained wafer thin and he ever vigilant. Where the strand ran into the sea, the shallow water reflected the sky in colours of azure and nettle green, a great shore curving into the distance as far as his sore eyes could see. He would not be caught again. From here he would see them coming.

"If you sit out here under the sun, my lord, you'll be taking a fever again, and I'll not be scraping you up and sailing you home to have my lady flail my arse for letting ye get that way."

Taylor put both arms under Robert's and helped him stand. "You sit in the shade under the canopy and behave yoursen."

"Tell that to the sun," Robert said dryly, nonetheless welcoming the intervention, "it keeps shifting."

"Aye, well, my lord, you'll just have to shift yourself with it, won't ye? Can't be having the sun doing its worst, or next time you might not be looking at my fair visage when you wakes."

"It was your countenance that near killed me, Taylor."

The man grunted a laugh because they both knew that Robert's life had hung so close that the mere beat of a wing might have pushed him over the edge, and neither man wanted to see him enter Purgatory just yet.

Taylor indicated the carracks with a jab of his head. "If we have success with them Portugan folk, we'll be taking one of them afore long, I reckon. Get my Earl home to good English fare and a cup o' warm ale; that'll set you up like nowt else." He fingered his chin, scratching through the rusty beard growing there. "I could do with ale, come to that. Nigh on a better part of a year without is a sin in my reckoning, and you know how I feel about sinning, eh, my lord?" Robert could barely hear him, as his head slumped and his eyes closed. "Aye, my lord," Taylor said softly, "it's time we went home."

CHAPTER THIRTY-THREE

"*I am not my brother*," Richard of Gloucester had said and, watching him now as he played games with the children, Isobel saw the truth of it. In the shelter of high stone walls that embraced the early spring sun, protected from the damp ground on pallets spread with hides and softened with velvets and fur, Isobel sat with Anne and Robbie while the older children stalked Gloucester. He would let them get so far before turning around and roaring with bared teeth and hands extended. Then the children scattered, screaming, and he would catch one or other and it was their turn to be hunter of the prey.

After following the antics for a while, Anne chatted away happily about this and that, engaging Robbie with peek-boo and tickles before he grew tired and slept stretched out on the cover. Picking at the sour-sweet suckets and the pastries drenched in honey, Anne talked, sometimes about nothing, but often about Gloucester. She demonstrated a deference Isobel had never shown her own husband. It irritated at first, but gradually Isobel became accustomed to hearing Gloucester referred to in such terms as 'my noble husband' or 'noble lord', and she then accepted that Anne did so from genuine fondness, not fear. She could see why. Isobel found him difficult to say no to, not because she was anxious about how he might respond, but because the force of his argument was such that she felt inclined to agree on most issues to which he turned his sharp mind. Occasionally she found his intellect intimidating, but she held her own, and responded as robustly as the extent of her knowledge and experience allowed.

It was Andrew's turn to be the bear and he put the extra height he had grown over the winter to his advantage. Gloucester added a layer of complexity to the game and Andrew now ran after his smaller quarry with one arm behind his back. It all ended with Edward falling over Juliana and bursting into tears, with Andrew looking frightfully apologetic and Gloucester assuring him it had been a fair game. Anne ran to comfort her wailing son, smothering him in kisses from which he fought to escape.

"Let him be," Gloucester said. "He has to learn to govern himself."

"But he weeps!" Anne remonstrated. "Have pity, my lord."

"I will have pity when it is due. He is not hurt, but seeks your attention with lamentations he does not feel and which you duly afford him. He will learn to cry for the wrong reasons."

Anne tutted, wetting her kerchief and wiping away the boy's tears. "No harm comes from a mother's love."

"Unless it be misplaced. There, Anne, look, you have rendered him more clean than when he entered the garden."

Isobel became distracted by a furious buzzing nearby. A newly emerged bee had become entangled in the remnants of a web strung between severed stalks of lavender. Isobel broke off an aromatic stem and pulled the sticky strands away until the creature was free of its bonds, then she dipped the tip of her forefinger into honey. Sensing food, the bee stopped fretting. "Good morrow, master," she addressed it. "Will you take your fill?" She held out her finger and the insect made tentative investigation before finally crawling onto it.

"I have sent Andrew to his lessons; I rather think he wished to escape to the safety of sword practice." Gloucester threw himself down on the rug. "What do you have there?"

"How do you magic it?" Anne asked.

"Nay, it is not magic, Your Grace, but a little piece of their own creation on which they might sup." Isobel brought her finger closer so they could see the small drop of honey glistening on her fingertip and the creature sipping.

Anne laughed. "Look, noble lord, see how Isobel enchants bees! Tedward, look!"

"I merely talk their language, Your Grace; it is such sweet conversation."

Anne looked momentarily confused. "You can talk their tongue?"

"And do they listen, my lady?" Gloucester asked with a sideways smile.

Isobel considered the creature on her finger. "When it is their mind to do so, Your Grace. If I speak softly and sit still, they might come to me."

"And the purpose of this endeavour?" he asked.

"It proves most fruitful, for bees make our orchards fertile and our bellies full. Also," she mused, "it is good to be kind to creatures, for are we not all of our Lord's Creation?"

"Certainly, but we are given dominion over the beasts."

"Then are we not even so beholden to show kindness to those over whom God gave us rule?"

"Stricture — guidance, perhaps. There must be order for good rule. Without order there is chaos; with chaos comes ferment, war, disease and want."

"Does that preclude kindness?"

"No, but kindness in itself does not bring peace. If we are kind to a dog does it obey? Does a child listen to his father if there is no structure?"

"Harmony, then. We seek harmony with creatures, with our kin, with God — is it harmony that provides peace?"

"Law, good rule, strength — in these, peace prospers and harmony falls upon a land."

"And kindness," Isobel insisted.

"And kindness," he agreed, "might flourish where it is borne out of respect for those that bestow it."

"And thus it is with beasts," Isobel said with a note of triumph, "for in a well-ordered garden, harmony is created where thought is given to the comfort of creatures, who, in return, bless us with their bounty."

"And conversing with them is part of that process?" Gloucester looked at her with teasing eyes, inviting a response.

"No, Your Grace, I merely like talking to them," she said simply. "I doubt they listen." She pressed her lips together to prevent laughter escaping, her nose wrinkling instead. "There, it has had its fill. My lord Edward," she leaned towards the little boy, "shall we return it to a bough where it might continue its work?"

Edward extended a tentative finger, but his mother moved him onto her lap where he couldn't reach. Gloucester looked away, suppressing a sigh.

Isobel rose and, finding a suitable place nearby, encouraged the bee onto it. She observed it for a moment. On her return she spotted a red-stemmed intruder in the border. Reaching, she pinched it out, releasing its pungent scent.

"Where is the compassion in that?" Gloucester called. "Would a little kindness not have brought forth a fine plant?"

Isobel detected the quiver of humour in his lips and was sorely tempted to throw the red-robert at him; but that sort of reaction was reserved for husbands and brothers and he was neither. "Your Grace, sometimes we must be stern in order to be kind," she intoned with false sincerity and a little wag of her finger, to which he raised a chuckle.

Anne twisted around to face him. "Isobel is quite correct for are we not told that, 'He that spareth the rod hateth his son'?"

Edward yawned and rubbed his eyes. Gloucester regarded the small boy. "I had better fashion a rod, then, for I love my son dearly and would not see him spoiled. From what wood should it be made, Lady Isobel, for surely you know the best?"

"Hazel, I believe, makes the worthiest switch," Isobel said promptly. "As Your Grace can tell, I use it frequently on my children." She grabbed Juliana — who was riding perilously close on Edward's hobby horse — and made little snapping movements with her fingers making her daughter squeal and giggle before putting her back on her feet.

Gloucester stood up and, with great solemnity, retrieved the horse by its bridle and holding it aloft declared, "Then, I too, at the exhortation of my duchess, shall take pains to lead my son with a whip and rein in his childish excesses. We shall saddle him with duty and hobble him with guilt, lest he startles and flees his stable of probity."

Isobel creased with laughter and Gloucester swept down close to her and said in an undertone, "I am glad I amuse," before planting himself on the rug again and ruffling his son's hair.

"You will not beat Tedward unduly, will you, noble lord?" Anne asked anxiously. "He is yet so young and has not reached the age of reason whereby he might know right from wrong. I am certain he is a dutiful boy. Are you not, my bear? Say you will always be dutiful to your noble sire?"

"Peace, my wife. While we are instructed to rebuke, we must also 'correct and encourage with great patience and teaching,' which, I believe, I have proven oft times — especially *great patience*."

Isobel tried not to laugh, but it came out as a snort instead. Anne dimpled and shaking her head in mock chagrin, climbed to her feet. "I know not who is the most merciless: my noble husband or my gracious friend, for both are incorrigible in their amusement. I will return. Lady Isobel, will you mind Edward? Juliana, will you come with me?" She held out her hand.

Isobel whispered in her daughter's ear, "Tanty Grace will take you to the privy; do you need to go?" Juliana nodded and trotted to Lady Anne.

"Her Grace is most thoughtful," Isobel remarked, watching them chatter as they went. "She always knows when something is needed or what makes someone comfortable. It is a rare aptitude and one not easily acquired."

"Mmm." Gloucester was lying on his back with one arm behind his head, chewing a stem of grass. He chucked it aside. "Yes, Anne is most considerate." He rolled onto his side, facing her. "I am told another messenger arrived from the south. You have had a response?"

"I have, Your Grace." Isobel continued stacking one wooden brick upon the other and encouraging Robbie, who was beginning to fidget, to do the same, aware of Gloucester's burning curiosity.

"And?"

"And he insists on coming himself forthwith to escort me — us — to London. He assures me of his protection until our marriage, and his intention to be my devoted lord in all wise." She broke off before her voice betrayed her; but Gloucester had been watching her closely.

"Richard Raseby is an honourable man, Isobel; he will abide by his good intention. You will be safe in his care."

"I should not be so afeared in my state of widowhood that I *need* such protection," she said fiercely. Her mouth tightened and she drew breath and, with great effort, drove the sourness into a stone-walled compound somewhere in the nether regions of her heart, and locked the door.

"I am sorry," Gloucester said quietly, and meant it.

"So am I," Isobel said, tempering. "I thank Your Grace; it is what I must do to ensure my children's security." He enfolded her hand lightly and she responded with a small smile.

"Your Grace." Gloucester looked around and sat up as his steward stepped forward and bent down to whisper to him. Gloucester's face went still and then he shot a glance at Isobel. He gave swift nod, rose, and to Isobel said, "Pray, bide here a while longer, if you will."

He reappeared moments later, his former good humour replaced by grim resolve. "Edward, take Robbie and go to your nurse. Lady Langton, if it please you, accompany me."

Alarmed, Isobel held back. "What is it?"

"It is best we speak privily," he said, his voice laced with urgency. "Please, come."

She could not move, her feet fastened to the grass as dread threaded her veins, her worst fears realised despite all the assurances that had finally lulled her into some semblance of security. All gone. All dead.

"Th-the Duke of Clarence is here, isn't he? Do not let him take us!"

Gloucester's frown deepened. "It will be better if you just come with me. Without delay."

Compared to the sparrows' noisy chatter and the brilliant sunshine of the garden, Gloucester's privy chamber was quiet and dark. It took Isobel a moment to adjust to the light.

"Be seated," he said, but sitting made her feel vulnerable, so she remained standing as if that somehow gave her immunity from whatever might happen next. He moved towards her. "Please," he said.

She didn't sit, her knees wouldn't bend. He didn't insist but looked at her in a way that made her shiver because he wanted to tell her something and whatever it was required the privacy of his own room and his undivided attention. That sort of news was always bad.

"Word has come from London."

Her mind raced, tripping over itself in haste to make sense of the unknown. "Is Lord Raseby come? So soon? I ... I am not ready... I cannot go..."

"Isobel," he said firmly, "I want you to listen. Ships from Portugal made harbour a week ago."

Ah, was that it? Dowager Countess Juliana must have died. Isobel's hand went to her chest as she exhaled in sudden relief. She knew she should feel something, for with her sons dead, who would mourn the old woman now? Isobel began to make the sign of the cross, but Gloucester stayed her hand and, taking both in his said, "Isobel, the Earl — he is alive."

Outside in the sharp light of the day, life continued. She could hear children running and shouting at play, the cry of birds from the mews, the rattling wheels of carts. Normal things. Life. She blinked. Gloucester still held her hands and he looked at her as if he expected a reaction. Isobel felt the urge to laugh, cut herself short and shook her head to clear it of nonsense.

"But he is dead," she insisted. "The Earl is dead. I know, I was there, I watched him die."

"You misunderstand," he said, articulating slowly and clearly. "Isobel, I do not speak of Earl William but of Earl Robert. Your husband, my lady, lives."

There must be some mistake. Here in Langton Place the man in Isobel's bed cocooned under layers of covers could not be her husband. His sickly yellow pallor lay beneath skin the colour of tanned hide, dishevelled patches flaking on his cheekbones and brow and over a nose bent and misshapen. Who was this imposter? She turned to leave.

"Isobel?" His distorted voice called her back.

"Rob?" She went to his side, examining him closer. He looked back at her, pleading with *his* eyes. "Robert?"

He fought free of the coverlets, his hand shaking but determinedly finding hers, his skin hot and dry as he clasped it. "Do you not know me?"

She looked again, looked past the damaged veneer. "Robert!" she cried in relief. "I dared not hope when I heard … I thought it a mistake, a trick of the mind. I thought…" And all the months of grief and loss and fear, of running and hiding, of being strong and failing, erupted in a volley of unanswered questions. "Where have you been? Why did you not come back? Why did you leave us?" She beat her hand against his chest, and then both together — furious and grief-bound and guilty all at once for all he had left her to face alone and everything she imagined he had suffered in his last hours of life without absolution, and how that had haunted her every moment since she learned of his death. And now he was here, broken, but alive. It was too much.

He lay there and took it all as she hammered against him, his face creasing in misery. "Forgive me," he croaked.

She stopped, breathless, shocked to see tears form in his eyes, and horrified by her own reaction. "Where have you been?" she whispered, her fury spent. She laid her head on his chest, felt its slow rise and fall beneath her cheek. "Where have you been?" she repeated, not angry now, but bewildered. She felt the lightest touch on her head.

"With you, my dove, *always* with you."

Something in the way he said it had Isobel raise her face to study his. She was not the only one who had suffered, but what that might entail she could not tell. It would wait. She caressed his cheek with gentle fingers. "You are home now, my love," she said softly, "and all will be well."

He released a breath, a long, slow exhalation bound with memories. "Yes," he said, looking at Isobel as if seeing her for the first time, "all will be well."

HISTORICAL NOTES

And in the secunde weke of Marche, the xlix. yere of the regne of Kynge Herry the vj, and in the x. yere of the regne of Kynge Edwarde the iiij, the same Kynge Edwarde toke his schippynge in Flaunders

The Chronicles of John Warkworth, d 1500

1471 proved to be a year of two kings. Edward IV returned from exile and defeated the last hope of the Lancastrian faction at the battle of Tewksbury. The subsequent capture of the ailing Henry VI, and his death in the Tower of London shortly after, eliminated any remaining legitimate claim to the throne that could match Edward's own. Yet the country remained unsettled. Unreconciled loyalties still remained both in England and abroad. At the courts of the French King, Louis XI and James III of Scotland, exiled Englishmen waited for a turn in fortune that both countries were only too willing to aid and abet.

Closer to home, King Edward's middle brother, George, Duke of Clarence, had survived by deserting his father-in-law Richard, Earl of Warwick, and returning to the family fold; but he was far from satisfied. If Clarence had learned from his past mistakes it wasn't apparent in his subsequent behaviour, and if Edward thought he had won peace at last, he was sorely tested by his brother's simmering malcontent.

Meanwhile, at almost 20 years old, Richard, Duke of Gloucester was coming into his own and seeking to build his nascent affinity. It was perhaps inevitable that the king's two brothers would clash when they married Warwick's heiress daughters and sought to divide the huge Neville estates.

If anything had become startlingly clear from the civil war that had engulfed the country from the mid 1450's, power lay in establishing relationships, and survival depended upon the ability to call on those who had sworn fealty. Nothing was more important than developing networks of formal bonds of lordship, friendships between peers, and less tangible associations with burghers and merchants, guildsmen, gentlemen, and yeomen. Unlike Clarence, Edward had learned from his past errors. He cracked down on incipient insurrection and established his authority with an uncharacteristic finality that left little room for doubt. No longer watching his back at home, Edward looked to secure his borders against foreign interests intent on causing trouble.

The Hundred Years War had left unfinished business which now Edward sought to conclude.

Louis XI of France — that arch meddler in foreign affairs and the thorn in the sides of England, Burgundy, Portugal and the Spanish kingdoms alike, had taken full advantage of England's internal conflicts to further his interests. But in 1475, with the almost wholehearted support of his nobility, Edward launched a massive invasion of France, if not to take back the kingdom for the English, then to impose such a defeat that he might dictate terms.

As it was, fate intervened when Louis made a treaty between Edward's ally and brother-in-law, Charles, Duke of Burgundy, depriving Edward of the Burgundian support he needed to crush the French. Louis swiftly capitalised on the situation, agreeing terms with Edward that brought the English king — among other things — a vast annual pension without having to strike a blow, and bought Louis valuable time in which he could strengthen his position. Edward left France with his army intact and with the promise of full coffers, but the gains lacked lasting substance. Those Englishmen who had looked for foreign land and connections with which to consolidate their own positions at home acquired money, but little else.

Of particular concern to Edward in mounting his invasion had been the security of his borders and the safe crossing between England and the continent, or rather, the lack of it. The Hanse merchants posed a major threat in the incessant tit-for-tat attacks on English vessels. Edward paid dearly, buying off the Hanseatic League with a highly favourable treaty, and secured his northern borders with a truce with Scotland, sweetened with the betrothal of his daughter, Cecily, to the young son of James III.

Attacks on merchant shipping endangered trade, and trade was key to a stable economy and content Englishmen. Like kings before him, Edward tried to control home-grown piracy, not least because it threatened hard-won treaties with potential foreign allies whose ships fell prey as much to English opportunism as enemy vessels. Even lords such as the Earl of Warwick and John de Vere, Earl of Oxford, were not averse to picking off a merchant ship when the need arose.

There was no national policy against piratical behaviours. Edward suffered both the complaints of his nobles and merchants as well as those of foreign powers, whose own shipping fell foul of English privateers and sought recompense for their loss. But other than entreating captains to form convoys in the hope they might dissuade attacks through strength in numbers, there was little Edward could — or would — do while he had other more pressing matters to occupy his attention. As a result, raids on English vessels continued — and not just on ships, as the ports and villages along the English coast knew to their loss — and not only from alien lands, but from English-born pirates, too.

A growing threat came from North African ports along the infamous Barbary Coast. Salé was yet to become the pirate capital of the Mediterranean it did in the sixteenth and seventeenth centuries, but the groundwork was actively laid in the decades before. The swift galleys of the Barbary pirates operating out of the Moorish ports of the Iberian peninsula and North Africa haunted the more sluggish, heavily laden and coast-hugging European cogs, hulks and carracks that ran the gauntlet from northern Europe to the Mediterranean. Laden with furs, wax, timber, and hides, these vessels returned with cargoes of silk and salt, spice and gold. If such merchandise was not tempting enough, the ships carried a bonus in their crew. Thus the miserable trade in humanity, with raids as far north as Iceland south to the shores of Scotland, England, France, Spain, Portugal and the Baltic states, joined the long-established commerce in people taken from the African continent and beyond.

Attitudes to slavery in England were mixed, but to be enslaved and subject to the authority of a non-Christian was viewed with horror by most, and considered anathema by some. What lay at the heart of the issue was the risk of conversion — either enforced or willingly — for there could be no greater loss than the death of the soul and an eternity divorced from the hope of salvation. This was no idle threat promulgated by the Church to control the Christian population, but a very real, visceral fear of damnation that dominated life for many individuals. To renounce one's faith was to reject not only the God of their forefathers, but the community and culture into which they had been born. Given this, it is less surprising that some of the few European slaves who regained their freedom sought anonymity on their return. Some chose not to return at all, but made new lives in foreign lands instead.

There is nothing new in this trade in people, nor in the subjugation of one person by another howsoever achieved; it is a singularly human problem, inflicted upon itself, for which only Humanity can find the solution.

GLOSSARY

Arras — a woven hanging (tapestry) of very great value associated with Arras, a town in the Duchy of Burgundy, now northern France.

Aumbry (ambry) — a recessed wall cupboard.

Ave — the (often) smaller beads used in groups of ten — a decade — or five, when repeating the Ave Maria or similar prayers using a chaplet or paternoster. See *beads*.

Beads — a set of beads of varying number used for 'bidding' prayers and personal devotions. Beads could be made from anything and everything, be simple or extravagant, have markers dividing them, be many or few, terminate in a tassel or cross, be in a single line or circular. Beads might be worn as a necklace, around the wrist or waist, or carried in a purse or pouch. They were an essential part of everyday devotional life as a Christian.

Bulwark — the upstand of the ship's side from the upper (weather) deck.

Caravel — a smaller, faster ship than the carrack, by the mid-15th century the Portuguese development of fore and sterncastles, and the adoption of a square-rigged sail in addition to lateen sails, made this manoeuvrable ship capable of longer ocean voyages.

Carrack — larger, sea-worthy sailing ship developed in the 14th century from the cog, and popular particularly with Portuguese and Spanish trade.

Chaperon — elaborate headgear worn by men, often with long 'tails' that could be draped around the neck and shoulders. Gradually lost favour towards the end of the century.

Chaplet — a short set of beads of varying number for saying personal devotional prayers (chaplets).

Chewit/chewette — little sweet, savoury, or mixed pies filled with meat, cheese, peas, or fruits and probably similar to the mince pies we know today.

Cog — a broad-bottomed ship used extensively for transport and cargo.

Coif — a close-fitting cap, used by men and women, made of linen (or similar) and worn by itself or under other headgear.

Constable — in terms of a castle, the constable was responsible for the maintenance of order and the soldiery retained for its protection.

Cott (cot) — a small house for agricultural workers (cotter/cottager) with an enclosed area for livestock and possibly a barn.

Crenel — the low sections on castle battlements.

Cresset — a metal basket or container, filled with flammable material, suspended from a ceiling or mounted on a pole to provide light.

Dagged — a toothed decorative edge used with hangings.

Daub — air-dried mud bricks; mud applied to outer surface of a building to make it weatherproof.

Doublet — worn over a shirt by men, a sleeved or sleeveless garment of varying quality, decoration, and fabric, belted at the waist to give the appearance of a short skirt of fabric. Doublets became increasingly short throughout the period, especially for young men.

Dun brown — sandy light brown.

Dwale — a medieval medicinal drink for pain relief and for inducing deep sleep. Made to recipes handed down from mother to daughter, master physician to apprentice, it might contain (among other things) lettuce, henbane, opium, belladonna, bile (gall), and various other herbs. It was understood that dwale-induced sleep might result in death if the patient could not be roused.

Forecastle (fo'c'sle) — in a 15th century ship, a raised structure in the bow akin to the sterncastle.

Gambeson — a quilted, padded jack(et) used as an additional (or the only) defensive layer in combat and for warmth. It could be made of fabric, boiled leather, or a combination of materials.

Gaud — a marker bead in sets of beads making up a chaplet or paternoster. Often larger, decorated (as in "gaudy"), or a different colour or texture from the groups of aves.

Gonne/gonners — a gun/gunners.

Guising — dressing up in masks and/or costumes.

Gunnel (gunwale) — a band of wood to reinforce the top rail of a ship or boat.

Hennin — women's headgear in a short and blunt or long cone shape. Worn over a fabric under-cap and covered in a rich material. It hid the hair entirely and might be worn with or without a veil. Later versions might be split into horns and known as a butterfly hennin. These might be heavily jewelled or decorated.

Hood — worn by all classes and both sexes depending on the weather and the situation.

Hose — single leg or joined with a gusset, men and women's stockings/tights. Some were footed, that is, had a shaped foot, whereas some were more like leggings.

Jetty — the upper floor/s of a building built out over, and overhanging, the lower.

Kendal — a coarse woollen cloth, often dyed green, associated with Kendal, Cumbria.

Kirtle — worn over a smock and under a formal gown, a kirtle was usually made of a contrasting colour and fabric and was meant to be seen beneath the outer gown.

Lateen sail — a triangular sail mounted at an angle, mostly used in the Mediterranean region.

Majesté — (French) majesty.

Mark — a unit of account (not a coin) common throughout Europe. 1 mark equals about 160 pence.

Mew — seagull.

Michaelmas — feast of St Michael celebrated on 29 September. It was common practice to mark important events such as marriages or the exchange of contracts, tenancies, etc., on, or with reference to, feast days in the Christian calendar.

Mullion — the vertical stone, brick, or wood element between panes of a window or lancets.

Mural hall/passage — a passage built within the wall of a castle or fortified building.

Murrey — a burgundy colour. Murrey and blue were the colours adopted by the House of York.

Nômade — (Portuguese) wandering, nomadic (men)

Palfrey — a lighter-weight horse, smooth of gait, used for riding by high-status women and children as well as men.

Paternoster — from the Lord's Prayer (Pater Noster), using a set of beads of varying number but often 10, 50, or 150 beads, with dividing markers for saying prayers.

Pattens — an overshoe of wood or leather to raise feet out of the mud. Clogs are an example of this.

Peter's Pence — the plant we now call honesty.

Pleasance — a formal, fair garden.

Points (point) — the (often) metal pointed end of a tie or lace used to make the threading or the lacing of a garment easier. We use them now on the end of shoelaces.

Posset — a nourishing, warming, comforting drink made by combining cream or milk with ale or wine, adding sugar or honey, often egg, and flavouring with spices (think of eggnog). Now made as a thicker version and served as a dessert.

Pricket — a stemmed candle holder, more often with a spike with which to secure the candle.

Quarrel — a crossbow bolt (a short, thick arrow).

Reeve — a manorial office. A reeve oversaw the work undertaken on manorial land.

Rondel dagger — a well-balanced weapon commonly carried by soldiers of middling status, knights, and merchants.

Rosary — prayers of a number of forms said using a string of beads of varying number.

Rowel spur — highly decorated spurs featuring long shanks and large rotating rowels, became very fashionable during the 15th century.

Sel or **sal** — a salt cellar — high status, decorative and functional piece for the lord's table.

Serpentine — light cannon. Could be used as an anti-personnel weapon when mounted on ships.

Shift/smock — a linen, silk, or later cotton undergarment worn next to the skin to protect the kirtle and outer gown from sweat.

Smatter/jangle — gossip.

Solar — a private (bed) chamber for the lord and his family.

Splinders – splinters.

St Andrew, feast of — 30 November.

Sterncastle — (aft or aftercastle) — raised structure at the stern (rear) of a larger sailing ship, often with a cabin or stowage area, and giving the advantage of height in a sea battle.

Steward — a manorial office; the senior officer retained to manage the manor and estates and to represent the lord in his absence. Often drawn from gentry, the position required a good degree of education and management skills and was endowed with a great deal of trust by the lord.

Suckets — candied fruit peel.

Sweetmeats — delicacies made with honey or sugar such as small cakes, wafers, or preserved and embellished fruits.

Tawny — an orange colour; think of tawny marmalade.

Tiller – mode of steering employed by many ships and boats before the development of the ship's wheel.

Weld — bright yellow from the plant *reseda luteola*.

Whitelime – whitewash made with lime as a paint for walls

Xebec — similar to a galley — a ship of the Mediterranean and North Coast of Africa (the Barbary Coast) used for trading and piracy as oars and sails made xebecs fast.

A NOTE TO THE READER

I'm often struck by how some events or periods in a country's history are viewed in isolation, as if they exist as an island while the world around them continues oblivious to their internal turmoil. This view is challenged through archaeological survey as well as documentary evidence lodged in the archives of other realms. What they show is a more connected world than perhaps once was thought, and this is just as much the case for the generations living through the Wars of the Roses as others before and since.

One aspect of internationality and connectivity is the dark world of piracy and slavery and the effect it had on king and country, merchant and noble and, of course, Isobel's little family in *Degrees of Affinity*. It is not the whole story by any means, nor is it meant to be a treatise upon the subject, for that is beyond the scope of this book and its tale. How can we begin to comprehend the countless lives affected by the trade in human suffering that stretched across the globe and down the millennia to the present day? Most victims were names known only to their kin and friends, and now forgotten. We might still find inklings of the terror that piracy inflicted in the recesses of coastal village psyche which suffered from raids; but more often than not, the subject is glamourised and commercialised by local museums, books, film and TV, as if piracy is a thing the past and, as such, has the benefit of distance to ameliorate the horror of its reality.

For background research, I drew on the experiences of those affected first-hand, largely in the two centuries following the period in which I am writing. Bizarrely named 'The Golden

Age of Piracy', there are a few, rare and fascinating accounts from survivors of slavery. Archival material from ambassadors, priests, and merchants lend an additional perspective into the trade.

As with research for the two previous books in this series — *Wheel of Fortune* and *Sun Ascendant* — pictorial information and artefacts play a vital role in understanding the past. Early maps, paintings and illustrations, ordinary everyday items and precious objects, the remains of a medieval ship or a cart, all render substance to the overall picture of life in other times and places. Written accounts of trade and exploration, whether sponsored by foreign governments such as those of Portugal or the Spanish kingdoms, or undertaken by individuals of any nation, provide a fascinating view into the late Medieval mindset as attitudes towards the slave trade changed. Collating information from different countries can provide alternative narratives to received history by contrasting observations, and corroborate yet others through common experiences.

What is less known, and goes largely unremarked in the historical record, is the mental and emotional toll upon individuals and the impact upon their families. Using modern psychological analysis and an awareness of mental health issues, we are better equipped to understand the inevitable trauma of such acts of violence.

For information on North Africa in the fifteenth century and the region we refer to as Morocco, original records provide an invaluable narration. Most well-known are those of El Hasan ben Muhammed el-Wazzan-ez-Zayyati, often referred to by his simplified name of Leo Africanus. Born in the Moorish city of Granada, he travelled widely in the latter part of the fifteenth century to North Africa and further afield with his diplomat uncle, subsequently providing detailed descriptions of some of the places he visited. That he was captured and enslaved by Christian pirates, and on his conversion, freed by Pope Leo X only to return to North Africa and recant, is one of the intriguing twists of fate.

Nothing compares with feet-on-the-ground experiences, but in beginning research on medieval Sijilmasa, COVID intervened before I could visit the ruins. Instead I have gleaned as much as I can from topographical and archaeological information, satellite imagery, and travel blogs, as well as references taken from historical accounts by traders and travellers to this enigmatic desert city. From its pivotal role as entrepôt for North African and sub-Saharan trade and culture, the skeletal remains now lie amid the engulfing sands of the Sahara. To gain an idea of its former splendour, I studied descriptions of the vast city built by Sultan Moulay Ismail in Meknes two centuries later. For an impression of the notorious slave pens, the accounts of European captives taken by Barbary Corsairs to Salé and Tangier or Cairo offer a chilling insight into the conditions they endured.

By the late fifteenth century, Sijilmasa was succumbing to changing trade routes and political upheaval. For the purpose of this story, the once great city — now beleaguered by competing tribal conflicts — is controlled by an ambitious petty lord attempting to rekindle its former fortunes through European connections. Ahmad might be a fictional character, but he is a composite of many such rulers who came and went with the sands.

And throughout *Degrees of Affinity* there is Isobel's story. She endures her own form of physical and mental incarceration. For her, like many other women before and since, it must have seemed frighteningly easy to slip into a state of entrapment, disempowered by her gender and marital status as well as her position in society. In this she was as much at the command of others as those bound by bonds of service. If only such things were the stuff of fiction and a matter of the past.

If you enjoyed *Degrees of Affinity* and would feel comfortable leaving a review on **Amazon** or **Goodreads** that would be greatly appreciated. If you would like to know about other books in the series and forthcoming releases, why not drop by my website at: **www.cfdunn.co.uk** or connect on with me on **Facebook** or **Instagram**.

C. F. Dunn

Sapere Books is an exciting new publisher of brilliant fiction and popular history.

To find out more about our latest releases and our monthly bargain books visit our website: **saperebooks.com**

www.ingramcontent.com/pod-product-compliance
Lightning Source LLC
Chambersburg PA
CBHW031024030726
47497CB00004B/995